# How to Lose a Duke in Ten Days

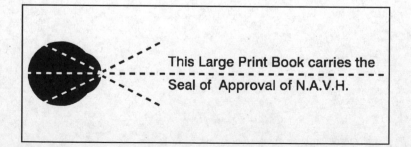

This Large Print Book carries the Seal of Approval of N.A.V.H.

# How to Lose a Duke in Ten Days

## AN AMERICAN HEIRESS IN LONDON

# Laura Lee Guhrke

**THORNDIKE PRESS**

*A part of Gale, Cengage Learning*

GALE
CENGAGE Learning®

Farmington Hills, Mich • San Francisco • New York • Waterville, Maine
Meriden, Conn • Mason, Ohio • Chicago

GALE
CENGAGE Learning

LIBRARY OF CONGRESS CATALOGING-IN-PUBLICATION DATA

Guhrke, Laura Lee.
    How to lose a duke in ten days : an American heiress in London / Laura Lee Guhrke. — Large print edition.
        pages cm. — (Thorndike Press large print romance.)
    ISBN 978-1-4104-6822-2 (hardback) — ISBN 1-4104-6822-4 (hardcover)
    1. Nobility—Fiction. 2. Heiresses—Fiction. 3. London (England)—Fiction. I. Title.
PS3557.U3564H69 2014
813'.54—dc23                                    2014009848

Published in 2014 by arrangement with Avon, an imprint of HarperCollins Publishers

Printed in the United States of America
1 2 3 4 5 6 7 18 17 16 15 14

*In loving memory of*
*Michel Loosli*
*March 15, 1949 — March 10, 2013*
*Rest in peace, my friend.*

# PROLOGUE

*Kenya, East Africa*

The chanting woke him, a primitive, repetitive melody that brought him slowly to consciousness. As he awakened, his first sensation was pain, and he tried to draw back, to return to oblivion, but it was too late for that.

The chanting was the reason. It went on and on, and the more he tried to ignore it, the more deeply it seemed to grind into his brain. He wanted to cover his ears and obtain some blessed silence so he could sleep, but he could not seem to lift his hands. How strange.

His head was aching fit to split. His skin prickled as if he were being pierced by thousands of white-hot needles, yet, inside his body, there was a deep, bruising cold, as if his skeleton were made of icicles. And his leg — something was wrong with his leg. The pain he felt seemed centered there, in his right thigh, and radiated outward to every other part of his body.

He wanted to open his eyes and look, see what was wrong with his leg, but once again, he could not seem to make his muscles obey his will. His mind felt dazed, unfocused. What was wrong with him?

He strove to think, but thinking seemed to take far too much effort, and when the chant quieted to a low murmur, he began sinking back into sleep.

Visions and sounds danced across his mind, so quick that he wasn't sure if they were a dream or an explanation. A tawny blur, searing pain, and the sharp rapport of rifle shots echoing across the Ngong Hills.

The picture in his mind shifted, and he saw a girl in a blue silk frock, a tall, slim girl with a freckled face, titian hair, and green eyes. She was looking at him, but there was no flirtation in her glance, no come-hither smile on her pale pink lips. She stood so still, she might have been a statue, and yet, she seemed the most alive, intense creature he'd ever seen. He caught his breath.

She couldn't possibly be here, not in the wilds of Kenya. She was in England. Her image faded, receding into a mist, and though he tried to bring her back, he couldn't, for his brain felt thick, his wits like tar.

Something cold and wet touched his face, a compress that brushed across his forehead, then over his mouth and nose. He shook his head from side to side in violent protest. He hated having anything over his face; it always made him feel as if he were smothering. Jones knew that. What was the fellow doing?

The wet cloth brushed against his face again, and he managed to shove it away. His body was shaking. He could feel it, involuntary shudders deep inside. He was so cold.

That perplexed him. This was Africa; he was never cold here. England, now, England was cold, with its constant dampness and drizzle, its standoffishness and class-conscious snobbery, its frozen traditions.

Even as those disparaging thoughts went through his mind, another rose up right behind them.

*It's time to go home.*

He tried at once to dismiss the notion. He still had work to do here in Africa. He was in Africa, wasn't he? That pang of uncertainty impelled him to open his eyes and lift his head. The moment he did, everything spun violently, and he thought he might be sick. He squeezed his eyes shut until the nausea passed, and when he opened them again, he saw things that were blessedly familiar — a canvas roof and walls, his battered ebony trunk desk, piles of skins, his rolled maps shoved in a basket, his black leather traveling trunk — things that had comprised the elements of his home for half a decade. Inhaling deeply, he caught the scents of sweat and the savannah, and he felt a rush of relief that reason had not utterly deserted him.

Two men with skin of coffee black stood by the entrance to his tent. Two others knelt on either side of his cot, still mumbling that infernal chant, but there was no sign of Jones. Where the hell was Jones?

One of the men kneeling beside him reached out to press a hand against his chest, urging him to lie down. Too weak to resist, he sank back onto the cot and closed his eyes, but when he did, he saw the girl again. Her green eyes glittered like peridot jewels as they looked into his, and her bright hair seemed to glow with incandescent fire beneath the gaslights of the ballroom.

Ballroom? He must be dreaming, for it had been years since he'd last been in a ballroom. And yet, he knew the girl. Her face again receded, and checkerboards took her place in his mind, checkerboards of pale

10

green fields and golden meadows, their squares framed by darker green hedgerows. These were Margrave lands, and they spread out before him as far as his eyes could see. He tried to turn his back on them, but when he did, he saw the Wash, and beyond it, the sea. The scent of the savannah was gone now, replaced by one of green turf and meadowsweet, of peaty fires and roast goose.

*It's time to go home.*

That thought came again, bringing with it an inevitability that overrode the chanting in his ears.

The fields, the hedgerows, the ocean, the eyes of that girl — all the images in his mind melted together into a brilliant viridian carpet, then faded, not receding into a mist but falling away beneath him like a fissure opening in the earth, and then he saw . . . nothing. All around him was the blankness of a void, and he felt a throb of fear, the same sensation that raised the hairs on his neck sometimes when he was in the bush. Danger, he knew, was very close at hand.

Suddenly, the chanting stopped. Voices flowed over him in rapid bursts, anxious and fretful voices, speaking Kikuyu. But though he was fluent in most Bantu dialects, including this one, he could not seem to comprehend what they were saying.

The voices rose to a higher, almost frantic pitch, and suddenly, he felt his body being lifted from the cot. The movement sent a fresh wave of pain through his already-aching bones. He cried out, yet no sound came from his ravaged throat.

They were moving him now, carrying him somewhere. The pain was excruciating, particularly in his thigh, and he felt as if his bones would snap like sticks at any moment. It seemed an eternity before they stopped.

Dry grass rustled beneath him as he was laid down, and then he heard the rasp of metal cutting through turf and dirt. What the bloody hell was going on?

He forced his eyes open again and found that directly above him was the outline of a silvery crescent moon, but its lines were blurry against the night sky. He blinked, shook his head, and blinked again. Suddenly, the moon came into focus.

It was the African new moon, lying on her back, surrounded by all the glittering diamonds and black velvet of the night sky, a familiar sight to him. Every night, when everyone else was asleep and the fire was low, he would lean back in his canvas chair, his legs stretched out and his muscles still aching from the day's safari, and he would stare up at these constellations as he drank his evening coffee. In Kenya, nights like this were commonplace.

It was far more rare to have such a clear, beautiful night sky back in England. There, day or night, the sky was usually misty, the air damp and chilling. But in summer, on a clear day, England had its moments. Punting, and croquet, and picnics on the lawn at Highclyffe. Good champagne. Strawberries.

The sharp sting of saliva hit his mouth at the thought of strawberries. He couldn't remember when he'd last had strawberries. It seemed like a lifetime ago.

*It's time to go home.*

The girl's face came to him again. Thin and resolute, with a square jaw and a pointed chin, pale with translucent, luminous skin under a dusting of freckles. With its sharply angled auburn brows and high cheekbones, it wasn't a soft face, nor was it beautiful. Instead, it was arresting, riveting, the sort of face you saw across a ballroom and never quite forgot.

But she wasn't just a girl, he realized with sudden clarity. She was his wife.

*Edie,* he thought, and something hard and tight squeezed his chest, something painful, like a hand around his heart. How strange, he thought, to become sentimental about a woman he barely knew and a place he

13

hadn't seen for years. Even stranger that they should be beckoning him from thousands of miles away, pulling him with forces too strong to deny, and he knew he couldn't stay here any longer. It was time to go home.

The voices came again but still too low for him to make out words, and thoughts of home were forgotten. He turned his head, and, between blades of savannah grass, he was able to discern the same four men he'd seen in his tent, but he was still unable to see Jones anywhere. The men were a short distance away, but though their dark skin made them barely visible in the dim light, he was able to recognize them. They were his men. He knew them, knew them so well that even in the dark, their movements told him their identity.

They were digging with English shovels, another curious thing, for the Kikuyu had no use for most English implements. As he watched them, awareness came slowly, like dawn breaking, and everything that had seemed incomprehensible until now suddenly made perfect, terrible sense. These were his men, his best, most loyal men, and they were according him an honor usually reserved only for tribal chiefs, the highest honor the Kikuyu could bestow.

They were digging his grave.

# CHAPTER 1

Tea and scandal, as writer William Congreve so shrewdly pointed out, have always had a natural affinity, and every season, the matrons of British society developed very decided preferences as to which scandals would be served with an afternoon cup of Earl Grey.

The Prince of Wales was a perennial favorite, for obvious reasons. A prince, the ladies felt, ought to be scandalous, particularly one whose parent was so deadly dull. Bertie could always be counted upon to provide many delightful tidbits.

The Marquess of Trubridge had been another reliable source of gossip until he'd settled down to domestic married life and become disappointingly lax in that regard. His wife, however, still held a bit of interest for the ladies of the ton, for though the initial shock of her marriage to Trubridge had worn off, many still found it fascinating that the former Lady Featherstone would wed another rake. Hadn't she learned *anything* from her first marriage? Assurances that she was quite happy with Trubridge a full year after their wedding were usually greeted with a disbelieving sniff and a cautionary tale or two about fortune hunters in general and why any girl with sense ought to stay away from them.

At which point, discussion invariably turned to the Duchess of Margrave.

Everybody knew the duke had married her for her money.

After all, what other reason could there be?

Not her beauty, the more attractive ladies were quick to point out. With that tall, thin figure and that unruly ginger hair? And my dears, those freckles!

And it certainly wasn't her social position that had caught the duke's eye. Before coming to England, Edie Ann Jewell had been Little Miss Nobody from Nowhere. Her grandfather had made his money in trade, selling flour, beans, and bacon to hungry gold miners on California's Barbary Coast, and though her father quadrupled the family fortune by shrewd investing on Wall Street, that fact had made little impression on the New York society, and when a scandal compromised her reputation, any chance of social acceptance had seemed lost. But a move to London and a single season sponsored by Lady Featherstone, and Little Miss Nobody had snared the most eligible — and most indebted — bachelor in town with all her Yankee millions.

The press on both sides of the pond had touted it as a love match, and it had certainly seemed to be so, but less than a month after the wedding, it was publicly demonstrated that love, if it had ever existed at all, had gone awry. Having cleared his family's many debts with his new wife's dowry, the Duke of Margrave had departed for the wilds of Africa, and he'd been there ever since, with no apparent intent of coming home again.

Abandoned and alone, the duchess had turned her attention to managing all the Margrave estates *herself.* Granted, she had competent stewards and plenty of money, but still . . . many ladies shook their heads with heavy sighs . . . what a burden for a mere woman to have to bear.

And was it really *comme il faut* for a duchess to manage estates on her own? Matrons of the ton debated the point over endless plates of cucumber sandwiches and seed cake. The younger ladies tended to defend the duchess and put the blame on Margrave, pointing out that he was the one who went away. If the duke were at home and not exploring his way across Africa, his wife would not be forced to act in his stead. Those of the older generation usually inserted a withering reminder at this point of the existence of the duke's younger brother, Cecil. He was the one who ought to be managing Margrave affairs in the duke's absence, and the fact that he wasn't being given his rightful opportunity to do so only served to demonstrate the duchess's ignorance of the way things ought to be. But, then, what else could one expect from an American?

Breeding tells in the end, one of the ladies was wont to say at this point in the discussion. Gadding about the estates, digging up gardens, tearing down follies, moving fountains that had been in place for over a century . . . this was no way for a duchess to behave. And what about the interior changes she was forever making? Gaslights, bathrooms, and heaven only knew what else — such modern devices could only serve to tarnish a house's beauty, intrude upon its harmony, and play havoc with its domestic routine. Think of the poor servants, the ladies told each other. What would a chambermaid *do* all day if there were no chamber pots to be cleaned?

And what did the family think of it all? The Dowager Duchess put on a brave show, of course, though she couldn't possibly approve. Lady Nadine, on the other hand, told everyone she liked the changes made to the ducal residences, but of course, she would say so. The duke's sister was one of those amiable, empty-headed girls who never seemed offended by what anyone did. Cecil, though, surely he must resent the situation. No wonder he spent so much time in Scotland.

Some said the duchess enjoyed wielding the powers that were the special privilege of the sterner sex. Others did not see how that could be so, for what woman could enjoy the coarse and burdensome duties of men?

The one thing most of the ladies did agree on was that the duchess was to be pitied, not judged. There she was, poor thing, the ladies said, their unmistakable relish thinly veiled by a pretense of concern. She filling her empty days with masculine responsibilities, with her husband off in Kenya, and without even children to comfort her. Yes, poor, poor thing.

The duchess's reaction to these discussions, whenever she chanced to hear of them, was to laugh. If only they knew the truth!

Her marriage was perfect. It wasn't the sort of marriage the British approved, for there was no heir. And it wasn't the sort Americans approved, because it wasn't based on love. And it certainly wasn't the sort of marriage she'd envisioned as a young, romantic girl. But Saratoga had succeeded in stripping her of any romantic notions she'd ever had.

Just the thought of that place and what had happened there still made Edie slightly sick. She turned her face away so Joanna wouldn't see her expression as she struggled to blot out the dark day that had changed her life forever.

She concentrated on the warm sun that washed over her in the open landau and breathed deeply of the fresh English air, working to shove away the smell of a musty Saratoga summerhouse and Frederick Van Hausen's hot, panting breath on her face. She listened to the clatter of carriage wheels so she wouldn't hear the sound of her own sobs or the whispered titters of New York society about that hussy Edie Jewell.

Like a phoenix rising from ashes, she had created a new life for herself out of the wreckage of the old one, and it suited her down to the ground. She was a duchess with no duke, a mistress with no master, and much to the bafflement of society, she liked it that way. Her life was comfortable, safe, and as predictable as a finely tuned machine, every aspect within her control.

Well, perhaps not every aspect, she amended ruefully as she looked at the fifteen-year-old girl seated across from her. Much like herself, her sister Joanna was not amenable to being controlled.

"I don't see why I have to go away to school," the girl said for the fifth time since the carriage had left Highclyffe, and for perhaps the hundred and fifth time since the decision had been made. "I don't see why I can't continue to live at home with you, and have Mrs. Simmons, like I've always had."

More than anything, Edie wished that were possible. Already, she was missing her sister, and the girl hadn't even boarded the train yet. Still, she knew it wouldn't be good for either of them if she showed how she felt. Instead, Edie pretended a staunch indifference to Joanna's arguments. "I couldn't possibly subject dear Mrs. Simmons here to another year of you," she said with a cheer she was far from feeling. "You'll be the death of her if I do."

"That's not the reason." Joanna's brown eyes looked back at her in an accusatory fashion. "It's that silly business with the cigarettes. If I'd known you'd send me away because of it, I'd never have done it."

"Ah, so it's not your conscience that's bothering you. It's what you see as your punishment."

At once, Joanna's face took on a stricken expression. "That's not true," she cried. "I do feel badly about it, Edie. I do."

"As you should, Joanna," Mrs. Simmons interjected from her place beside the girl. "Cigarettes are a nasty, most unladylike habit."

Joanna paid no heed to that comment, for she knew from long experience that working on the formidable Mrs. Simmons was futile. She kept her gaze fixed on Edie, and beneath her straw boater hat, her big, doe eyes glimmered with tears. "I can't believe you're sending me away."

Edie's heart twisted at those words even though she knew quite well she was being manipulated. In every other aspect of her life, she was confident of her decisions, sure of her ground, and not easily governed. But Joanna was her weak spot.

Mrs. Simmons, thankfully, had the resolve Edie lacked where Joanna was concerned.

But during the past year, the girl had become too ungovernable even for that good lady to manage. Numerous times, she had recommended finishing school, and after the incident with the cigarettes, Edie had capitulated at last, much to her sister's dismay. The four weeks since then had seen Joanna bent on a relentless barrage to wear down her resolve. Fortunately, Willowbank Finishing School for Girls had been willing to accept the Duchess of Margrave's sister for the very next term. If Joanna's campaign had lasted much longer, Edie knew she probably would have given in.

Joanna needed school. She was at an age where she needed the discipline and the stimulation that would come from it. She needed the polish and the chance to make friends. Edie knew all that, but she also knew she would miss her sister terribly. Already, she could feel loneliness closing in.

"Edie?" Her sister's voice intruded, tentative, penitent.

"Hmm?" Edie turned her head, relieved by the distraction, and looked at the girl across from her in the open landau. "Yes, darling?"

"If I promise never to do anything bad ever again, can I stay?"

"Joanna, this must stop," Mrs. Simmons

said before Edie could answer. "Your sister has made her decision, I have been engaged for another post, and you have been accepted at Willowbank. That, by the way, is a high compliment to you since Willowbank is a school of great distinction. Mrs. Calloway accepts very few of the girls who apply."

Edie forced herself to speak with a lightness she didn't feel in the least. "And at Willowbank, you'll be able to paint and study art, which you love more than anything. You'll make friends and learn all sorts of new things. Why, that clever brain of yours shall be occupied from morning 'til night."

"I probably won't ever know if it's morning or night," Joanna grumbled. "The windows there are so tiny, one can hardly see out. And it's dark and dreary, and when winter comes, it's sure to be freezing cold. Ugh."

"Well, it is a castle," Edie pointed out. "But don't you think it'll be rather fun living in a castle?"

Joanna was not impressed. She made a face and fell back against her seat with a heavy sigh. "It'll be like living in the Tower of London. It's a prison."

"Joanna!" Mrs. Simmons's voice was

sharp with rebuke, but Joanna, irrepressible, opened her big eyes wide as she transferred her gaze from Edie to the indomitable, elderly woman seated beside her.

"What?" she asked with a pretense of injured innocence. "The Tower was a prison, wasn't it?"

"It was." Mrs. Simmons gave a sniff. "And if you keep vexing your sister, she might send you there instead of Willowbank."

"If she did, could I enter through Queen Anne's Gate in a boat?" Joanna's face brightened at the notion. "That might be good fun."

"Until they cut your head off," Edie put in. "Behave at Willowbank the way you've been behaving at home, and I daresay Mrs. Calloway will be tempted to do that very thing."

Joanna's expression turned sulky, but she couldn't seem to think of a clever reply to that, so she lapsed into silence — plotting, Edie had no doubt, yet another argument for why boarding school was a bad idea.

The girl was understandably apprehensive about going. Their mother had died when Joanna was only eight. Daddy, occupied with business affairs in New York, had found leaving Joanna in Edie's care upon her marriage the best thing for everyone, and the sisters had seldom been separated. But Edie knew she couldn't keep Joanna tethered to her side forever, as much as she wished she could.

She studied her beloved sister across the carriage, noting the girl's beautiful face with mixed feelings. On the one hand, she was thankful the physical flaws that had so plagued her own youth would never torment her sister. Joanna's nose was aquiline rather than pug, with nary a freckle in sight. Her hair was auburn without a hint of carrot. And her figure, though slim, was already much more rounded than Edie's would ever be. She was also, thankfully, not quite so tall as her elder sister.

But though Edie was happy to see Joanna blossoming into the beauty she had never been, it also made Edie more determined than ever to guard and protect the girl, to make sure that what had happened to her at Saratoga never, ever happened to her baby sister.

She knew that at Willowbank, Joanna would be safe and protected and fully chaperoned, but nonetheless, she desperately wanted to turn the carriage around, and when the vehicle slowed, it almost seemed as if Fate were granting her that wish.

"Whoa," her driver said from the box above, pulling hard on the reins and bringing the carriage to a snail's pace.

"What is it, Roberts?" Edie asked, straightening in her seat. "Why did you slow down?"

"Sheep ahead of us, Your Grace. Quite a lot of them."

"Sheep?" Curling her gloved fingers over the top of the carriage door, she half rose from her seat and eyed the mass of sheep in the road ahead with both relief and dismay. Guided by a pair of men on horseback and a group of dogs, they were headed in the same direction as the carriage, moving at an excruciatingly slow pace. "Will it make much of a delay?" she asked, sinking back in her seat.

The young man twisted his head, looking over his shoulder at her. "I'm afraid so, Your Grace. At least twenty minutes, I'd say. Perhaps longer."

"Goody!" Joanna bounded gleefully in her seat. "We shall miss the train."

Edie glanced at the watch pinned to the lapel of her blue serge tailor-made, and confirmed that was a definite possibility. She leaned sideways, craning her neck to see past the horses, then she glanced up at her driver again. "Couldn't you just nudge the carriage forward?" she asked, feeling a bit desperate. "Surely the sheep will move out of the way rather than be run over by the horses?"

Roberts gave her a wry look. "That would be supposing the sheep had room to move over, Your Grace. They're massed together pretty tight, and with the hill on the right and the ha-ha on the left, they've nowhere to go but straight down the lane."

"So until we reach the road that turns to Clyffeton, we'll be moving as slowly as this?"

Roberts's confirming nod was apologetic. "I'm afraid so. I'm sorry."

"Ha!" Joanna cried, triumphant. "And there won't be another train until tomorrow."

Another day of being worked on by her sister? Edie leaned back against the leather seat with a groan. She was doomed.

The carriage moved forward at a crawl while Mrs. Simmons sat in impeccably lady-like silence, Joanna smiled with barely restrained triumph, and Edie tried to brace herself for another twenty-four hours of her sister's attempting to weaken her resolve.

Half an hour went by before they were able to turn from the lane and leave the sheep behind, and though Roberts made up some of the lost time by speeding up the pace of the carriage, the train coming from Norwich was already huffing clouds of steam as it readied itself to pull out of Clyffeton's tiny station.

Roberts had barely brought the carriage to a halt before Edie was out of the vehicle and racing toward the station. "Bring the luggage, Roberts, would you?" she called over her shoulder as she ran up the steps and opened the door. Without waiting for an answer, she went inside, passed through the small, empty station building, and emerged out the opposite side onto the platform. It, too, was empty, save one man who leaned back against the pillar behind him in a careless pose, hat pulled low. Surrounded by stacks of luggage, he seemed to have no inclination to board the train, and Edie could only presume he had just disembarked and was now waiting for a carrage to be procured for him.

Foreign, she thought at once, but she passed him by without a second glance or another thought as a man she recognized as the stationmaster stepped down from the train. "Mr Wetherby?"

"Your Grace." He straightened to respectful attention at once. "How may I be of service?"

"My sister and her governess are to take

29

this train, but we are terribly late. Could you perhaps persuade the conductor to delay departure another minute or two so that they have time to board?"

"I will try, Your Grace, but it can be dangerous to delay a train. I will see what I can do." The stationmaster bowed with a tug of his cap and bustled off to once again board the train and find the conductor. Edie glanced back over her shoulder, but the others had not yet followed her to the platform, and because she did not want to think about her sister's impending departure, she occupied her mind by giving the stranger nearby a more thorough study.

Definitely foreign, she decided, although she didn't know quite why he gave her that impression. He was dressed for the country in well-cut, typical English tweeds, but nonetheless, there was something un-English about him. Perhaps it was his negligent pose, or the way his brown felt hat was pulled sleepily over his eyes. Or perhaps it was the mahogany-and-ivory walking stick in his hand, or the worn portmanteau of crocodile leather by his feet, or the brass-studded black trunks stacked nearby. Or perhaps it was merely the steam from the train that swirled around him like mist. But something about the man spoke of exotic places far away from this sleepy little corner of England.

Clyffeton was a picturesque village on the Norfolk coast at the top of the Wash, and a place of strategic importance when Vikings were plundering England's coastline, but nowadays it was nothing more than a sleepy bywater. Even its boast of having a ducal seat couldn't save it from being quaint, insular, and hopelessly old-fashioned. Here, a stranger stuck out like a pair of red knickers on a vicar's washing line. Within an hour, the village would be buzzing like bees about this new arrival. Within two, his bona fides would be established, his background unearthed, his intentions known. By teatime, her maid would probably be able to tell her all about him.

"You stopped it from leaving."

Joanna's voice, dismayed and accusatory, interrupted her speculations, and Edie turned, the stranger again forgotten. "Of course," she answered, pasting on a smile for her sister's benefit. "It's a wonderful thing to be a duchess. They delay trains for me."

"Of course they do," Joanna muttered in disgust. "I should have known they would."

Mrs. Simmons came bustling up, gesturing to the two men behind her whose arms

31

were loaded with luggage. "I've secured a porter to assist Roberts with the trunks." She lifted the pair of tickets in her black-gloved hand. "Best we go aboard and not keep the train waiting any longer."

"All right, then." Joanna lifted her chin, trying to put on an indifferent air about it all. "I suppose I have to go since you're both so determined."

Beneath the nonchalance, there was fear. Edie sensed it, and though it tore at her heart, she could not give in to it. Desperate, she turned to the governess. "Watch over her. See that she's settled in and has everything she needs before . . ." She paused and took a deep breath. "Before you leave her."

The governess gave a nod. "Of course I will, Your Grace. Come, Joanna."

The girl's face twisted, broke up. Her defiance crumbled. "Edie, don't make me go!"

Mrs. Simmons's brisk voice intervened. "None of this, now, Joanna. You are the sister of a duchess, and a young lady of good society. Behave accordingly."

Joanna didn't seem inclined to behave like a lady. She wrapped her arms around Edie, clinging to her like a barnacle. "Don't send me away."

"Hush, now." She rubbed her sister's back, striving to keep her own emotions in control as Joanna gave a sob against her shoulder. "They'll take good care of you at Willowbank."

"Not as good as you."

Edie gently began to pull back, and though it was one of the hardest things she'd ever done, she extricated herself from her sister's embrace. "Go on, now. Be brave, my darling. And I shall see you at Christmas."

"That's forever away." Joanna wiped at her face and turned angrily away to follow the governess onto the train. She boarded without a backward glance, but it wasn't more than a moment later before she was sliding down the first window and sticking her head out. "Can't you come visit me before Christmas?" she asked, folding her arms atop the open window as Mrs. Simmons continued on toward their seats farther down the car.

"We'll see. I want you to settle in without any distraction from me, but we'll see. In the meantime, write to me and tell me everything. Who you meet and what your schoolmistresses are like, and all about your lessons."

"It would serve you right if I don't send you a single letter." Joanna scowled, her face still damp with tears. "I shan't write a word. I'll keep you in suspense all year long,

33

wondering what I'm doing. No, wait," she amended. "I'll do better than that. I'll misbehave. I'll smoke cigarettes again. I'll cause so much havoc, they'll expel me and send me home."

"And here I thought you'd want a season in London when you turn eighteen," Edie retorted, her voice shaking with the effort not to break into tears herself. "If you're expelled from Willowbank, the only season you'll get will be a place far more remote than Kent. I'll send you to some convent in Ireland."

"Empty threat," Joanna muttered, wiping at her face. "We're not Catholic. And besides, knowing you, I doubt I'll ever have a season. It'd be too much for your nerves."

"You'll have a season." Even as she gave the assurance, she found the idea of safeguarding her sister by putting her in a convent far more appealing. "If you manage to behave yourself."

Joanna sniffed. "I knew you weren't above blackmail."

The whistle blew, signaling that the train was about to pull out, and as her sister stretched out her hand, Edie reached up to give it a quick squeeze. "Be good, my darling, and please, for once in your life, do what you're told. I shall see you at Christmas. Maybe before."

She knew she ought to stay until the train was gone, but another moment, and she'd fall apart. So she smiled one last time, waved brightly to her sister, and turned to leave before she could start bawling like a baby.

Her escape, however, proved very short-lived. As she started back across the platform, the voice of the stranger calling her name stopped her in her tracks.

"Hullo, Edie."

Even her beloved sister was momentarily forgotten as she turned to the man on the platform. Strangers did not speak to duchesses, and Edie had been a duchess long enough to be astonished by the fact that this one had spoken to her. And when he pushed back his hat to reveal his eyes — beautiful, brilliant gray eyes that seemed to see straight into her, her astonishment deepened into shock. This man was no foreign stranger.

This man was her husband.

"Stuart?" His name was a startled cry torn from her throat, but he didn't seem to notice that in it was none of the joy a reunion between husband and wife ought to convey. He doffed the hat and inclined his head a bit though it was hardly a bow, for he didn't bother to straighten away from the pillar, and that almost impudent gesture only served to confirm the ghastly truth that her husband was here, a mere half dozen feet from her, and not the thousands of miles away he was supposed to be.

Good manners dictated a greeting of some sort beyond that mere cry of his name, but though she opened her mouth, no words came out. Unable to speak, Edie could only stare at the man she'd married five years ago and hadn't seen since.

Africa, she appreciated at once, was a hard land. That fact was evident in every aspect of his appearance. It was in his tanned skin, in the faint creases that edged his eyes and his mouth, and in the sun-torched glints of gold and amber in his dark brown hair. It was in the lean planes of his face and in the long, strong lines of his body. It was in the exotic walking stick in his hand and in his keen, watchful eyes.

During the years of his absence, she'd wondered on occasion what Africa was like. Now she knew, for in the man before her she could see many aspects of that particular continent — its harsh climate, its nomadic nature, its wild, adventurous spirit, and the uncompromising toll it took on those who were merely human.

Gone was the carefree, handsome young man who'd blithely married a girl he didn't even know, left that girl in charge of his entire retinue of estates, and gone off for parts unknown with happy insouciance. Returning in his place was someone completely different, someone so different that she'd passed right by him without so much as a glimmer of recognition. Never would she have thought five years could change a man so much.

But what was he doing here? She glanced past him to the black leather trunks stacked on the platform, to the suitcases and portmanteaus around his feet, and the implications of all that luggage hit her with sudden force. When she looked at him again and saw his mouth tighten, that tiny movement confirmed the awful suspicion forming in her mind more effectively than any words.

*Home is the hunter,* she thought wildly, and her dismay deepened into dread as she realized that her perfect, husbandless life might be crumbling into dust.

# CHAPTER 2

Only the most self-deluded fool would have thought she'd be glad to see him, and Stuart had never been a fool. Nonetheless, even he wasn't quite prepared for the look of horror on Edie's face.

He should have written first, giving her at least a hint of what was in the wind. He'd tried, but somehow, informing her of the situation in a letter had proved to be an impossible task. Each draft he'd attempted was more stilted and awkward than the one before, until he'd given up and just booked his passage home, with the rationale that something this important, this life-altering, ought to be communicated in person. Yet now, seeing her face, he wished he'd found a way to put it all in writing, for this moment was proving more awkward than any letter would have been.

It didn't help matters that of all the versions of their reunion he'd envisioned during the long journey from Mombasa, encountering her here on Clyffeton's train platform only a few minutes after stepping off the train had never been one of them.

His leg hurt like hell after the cramped train ride, reminding him — as if he needed reminding — that he wasn't quite the dashing young fellow he'd been five years ago. Standing before her now, he felt off-balance, askew, terribly vulnerable.

She hadn't recognized him, he knew, and if he hadn't spoken, she'd have walked right by. Had he changed so much? he wondered, or did her lack of recognition just prove how little they really knew each other?

She'd changed, too, but despite that, he would have recognized her anywhere. Her face had the same arresting quality that had first captivated his attention in a ballroom five years ago and had so insistently invaded his fevered dreams that fateful night in Kenya when he'd almost died. It was a softer face now than the one he remembered, not so sharp and fierce as it used to be, the face of a strong woman rather than a desperate girl.

He forced himself to speak. "It's been a long time."

She didn't reply. She simply stared at him, speechless, her light green eyes still wide with shock.

"I've —" He stopped, cleared his throat, and tried again. "I've come home."

Her head moved, an almost imperceptible movement of denial. Then, without any warning, she bolted like a startled gazelle, lowering her head and racing past him without a word.

He turned, watching as she vanished through the door into the station building. He didn't try to follow her. Even if he wanted to, there was no way he could catch her if she chose to keep running. Stuart's hand moved to his thigh, and even through the layers of his clothing, he could trace the dent along the side of his leg where muscle and tissue had been ripped apart by a very angry lioness. How he'd survived he still didn't know, but his days of running any-where were over. Even walking hurt, even after six months.

"So you're Margrave."

Stuart turned and found Edie's sister standing on the platform a few feet away, enveloped in a cloud of steam as the train behind her rumbled out of the station with what he could only assume was a very irate governess still on board.

He lifted a brow. "Aren't you supposed to be on that train?"

She glanced at it, then back at him, and on her lips was a triumphant little smile. "Oops."

Stuart did not smile back. He admired boldness and audacity, but he didn't think he ought to be encouraging those traits in Edie's little sister. Especially since he sensed she was already quite a handful without any encouragement. "And poor Mrs. Simmons?"

Her smile widened into an unrepentant grin. "Bound for Kent without me, it seems."

"And your luggage with her."

She made a face. "A trunk full of hideous school uniforms. I shan't mourn the loss. Besides," she added cheerfully, "if I'm here, I can help you."

"Help me?" He frowned, puzzled by the offer, for he couldn't imagine what assistance a fifteen-year-old schoolgirl thought she could provide him. "Help me to do what?"

"Win Edie back." She laughed in the face of his surprise. "Well, that is why you came home, isn't it?"

It couldn't be him. It simply couldn't.

Her heart pounding like the piston of a steam engine, Edie ran through the station and out the front doors, her only thought to get as far away from Stuart as possible. She paused on the steps to locate her carriage, and when she saw the open vehicle, she muttered a frustrated oath to see it standing empty by the corner. Roberts had, of course, followed them inside with the luggage, and she'd have to wait for him unless she wanted to drive the vehicle herself.

That would certainly cause the tongues of Clyffeton to start wagging, especially in light of the duke's return and the way she'd bolted from the station like a rabbit. Still, better that than to wait and have Stuart accompanying them back to Highclyffe. She needed time to pull her wits together, time to assimilate the impossible. Her husband was home.

"Your Grace?"

Roberts's voice behind her was like the answer to a prayer. She turned. "Take me home at once, please."

A frown of bewilderment crossed the driver's face. He hesitated, glanced back over his shoulder, and returned his gaze to hers. "Oughtn't we to wait for —"

"No." Waiting for Margrave was the last thing she wanted. Edie started toward the landau without another word, and after a moment, Roberts continued following her.

When they reached the vehicle, he rolled out the steps, she got in, and moments later, they were off. As he turned the landau around to take her back to Highclyffe, she glanced at the station, and when she saw no sign of her husband attempting to follow, she sank back against the seat with a sigh of relief.

Idiotic to dash out the way she had, but . . . bloody hell. She hadn't known what else to do. Stuart was home. That wasn't supposed to happen — ever. They'd agreed on that in the bargain they'd made five years ago, so what was he doing here?

The image of him on the train platform flashed through her mind, of him surrounded by trunks and crates, and she felt another jolt of the same panic that had sent her running out of the train station.

Edie took a deep breath and let it out slowly, trying to think, reminding herself that she didn't know for certain what had brought him home. He might have just returned for a holiday, to see old friends and family.

No, not family, she amended at once. His immediate family was all out of the country, and besides, family ties meant little to Stuart. Friends, yes . . . he might have come home to see friends. The vast amount of luggage might be gifts — ivory or skins or whatever it was he hunted on the African savannahs. She knew about his expeditions, of course, but beyond that, she wasn't quite clear how he occupied his time in Kenya, for they didn't correspond and never had. That had been part of the bargain, too.

Edie turned her head, staring out over sprawling green fields and hedgerows, but in her mind's eye, a different scene opened up before her — a dazzling London ball-room half a decade ago, and girls moving across the dance floor like color-washed rose petals floating on a breeze.

The years fell away.

Nineteen and nearing the end of her first season in London, Edie watched the girls on the ballroom floor with admiration and a hint of envy. She'd loved waltzing as a young girl, but even then, she'd never been much good at it. Impossible to be a floating rose petal when you were taller than your partner, and having shot up to a height of six feet by the age of fourteen, Edie always seemed to be taller than her partner. She also had the tendency to lead rather than be led, which generally resulted in smashed toes, embarrassing collisions, and frustrated partners. And even if she had managed to master the waltz, it would have done her little good, for ever since Saratoga, she could hardly bear to be touched. Not that any of that mattered much anyway, for no man ever asked her to dance. By now, every male from London to New York knew she was a giraffe, and at every ball, she spent most of her time lined up along one side of the room with all the other wallflowers.

Daddy had brought her to London in the hope things would be different for her here. Rich American girls not accepted by the New York Knickerbocker set could often find — or buy — a place in London society. He had even hired Lady Featherstone, England's most successful matchmaker, to assist in the effort to gain social acceptance for Edie. But much to Arthur Jewell's dismay, even an enormous dowry and the matchmaking Lady Featherstone hadn't been enough to sway any peer, however impecunious or desperate he might be, to marry his ruined eldest daughter. Of course, Edie knew her mop of curly, carrot-and-ginger hair, the splatter of freckles across her face, her towering height, and unprepossessing bosom hadn't done much to help her chances either. And though the outspokenness and independent spirit of American girls were characteristics that Englishmen seemed to find charming, in Edie's case, both traits had fallen rather flat. All in all, she was almost as great a social failure in London as she'd been in New York, even before whispers of her sullied reputation had started seeping over from the other side of the Atlantic.

Now, time was running out. In three days, it would be August 12, a date that marked the official end of the season and Edie's return to New York. Though Lady Featherstone had suggested they remain a bit longer, Daddy's business matters back home required his return, and given Edie's lack of social success so far, he couldn't see the point of prolonging their stay.

For Edie, going home meant disaster. It meant going back to the stifling atmosphere of Madison Avenue and the awful shunning at Newport, a return to the smothering shame and the horrid whispers behind her back. But far worse, going home meant seeing again the man who had caused it all.

Frederick Van Hausen was part of the Knickerbocker set, unquestioningly accepted by MacAllister's Patriarchs and happily invited by Mrs. Astor to her annual ball. Edie's family had never been part of the social circle in which the Van Hausens moved, but she would still see him. He lived only a few blocks from her home on Madison Avenue. His family's house in Newport was less than a mile from hers. Both fathers were members of the New York Yacht Club, and both owned racehorses that ran at Saratoga. Just the thought of seeing him ever again was enough to make her physically ill. To face him, even from a passing carriage or across a bookshop, to ever see again the contemptuous satisfaction in his eyes and the triumphant little smirk on his face would be unbearable. To look into his eyes and know that he was remembering what he'd done to her, that he was reliving the pleasure he'd gained by giving her pain, would be the pit of hell.

Marriage to an Englishman, she knew, was the only way to avoid what awaited her in New York. In addition, marriage would gain her a measure of control over her own life, and after Saratoga, control was something she desperately wanted. And yet, the idea of marriage was as unbearable as that of going back home, for marriage gave her husband the legal right to her body whenever he wanted it.

Edie's white-gloved hands curled into fists. The lilting music of a Strauss waltz and the hum of ballroom conversation faded as she once again strove to find a way out. But she feared there was no way out of hell.

"Ooh, look!" Beside her, Leonie Atherton's voice was an excited squeak that penetrated Edie's brooding thoughts. "The Duke of Margrave's just arrived."

Glad of the distraction, Edie drew a deep breath and followed her friend's gaze to the ballroom entrance nearby. When she spied the man standing there, she felt a flicker of surprise to discover there was at least one man in society taller than she was — a good two or three inches taller, by the look of him.

With thoughts of Frederick still at the forefront of her mind, she studied the man by the door, struck by the fact that he was as different from Frederick as chalk was from cheese. This man was no fair-haired Apollo with the face of a choirboy, the clothes of a dandy, and the air of the privileged. No, this man had a lean, tanned face and a devil-may-care demeanor, and he wore his impeccably cut clothes with a careless sort of elegance. His white tie was undone, his dark hair was unruly, and though he might be a duke, Edie wondered if he even gave a damn. Having been surrounded by ambitious social climbers all her life, Edie was rather amused by the notion of a man who didn't care how well-born he was.

"He's supposed to be one of the most charming men in London," Leonie said beside her. "And handsome, too. Even you, Edie, as fastidious as you are, must admit he's handsome."

She might be chary of men, thanks to Frederick, but that fact hadn't affected her eyesight. "I suppose he is," she conceded, "if you like that dark, reckless sort of good looks."

"And who doesn't?" Leonie laughed. "But you've got him pegged, that's for sure. He lived in Africa for two years," she went on with the knowing air of one who read the scandal rags every day. "He hunted things — elephants, lions, leopards, all that. Saved the life of some chieftain, I believe. Or maybe it was a British diplomat? Anyway, he's trekked through the jungles, navigated rivers, had all sorts of adventures. He's quite wild, so they say."

"He looks it."

"Doesn't he, though? It's said that half the girls in London were in love with him, and he left a trail of broken hearts behind him when he went away. He had to come back when his father died, but he desperately wants to return to Africa. He wants to live there forever. Can you imagine? But I doubt he'll be able to go."

"Why not?"

"He's the duke now, and I don't think a duke could live in Africa, do you? They have to manage their estates, and . . . and things." She paused, her knowledge of a duke's actual duties having apparently run out. "Not that being the duke does him much good, for he's in a difficult position. He's got heaps of debt. Everything's mortgaged to the hilt and the papers announced last week that his creditors have called his loans. They'll probably take everything that's not entailed."

"I see. Not only handsome, but a wrong 'un."

"Not him! It was his grandfather who gambled away most of the money, and whatever his grandfather didn't lose at the card table, his father sank into some very bad investments. Oh, if only he'd ask me to dance! He's said to dance divinely. But, of course, he can't do that, for we've never even been introduced. But it would be heavenly if he'd look in my direction and be so captivated that he'd march over to Lady Featherstone and request an introduction! She could tell him how rich I am," she added, laughing, "and he might marry me, and I could solve all his problems!"

Edie froze at her friend's laughing words,

staring at the tall man with the carelessly handsome face who stood a dozen feet away. Leonie might be joking, but for herself, did it have to be a joke? Mightn't it be just what she'd been hoping for?

For the first time since Saratoga, she felt a stirring of hope. Could this man be her salvation? she wondered. Could this Duke of Margrave be her way out of hell?

As if he sensed her scrutiny, he glanced her way, and when their eyes met, she sucked in a sharp breath. He had beautiful eyes — piercing, pale gray eyes that seemed to look straight into her soul. She wondered if perhaps she was also looking into his.

She was staring, she knew, and yet, she couldn't look away. *My escape from hell,* she thought, and the air between them seemed to stir, rippling over her skin like a cool breeze. She shivered and turned her head, forcing her gaze to the dance floor, but after a moment, she couldn't resist another glance at him. To her astonishment, he was still watching her.

He was smiling a little, head to one side, a quizzical little frown between his dark brows. She wondered what he could be thinking.

*A way out of hell.*

She was mad, she must be, she thought.

Mad with desperation and panic. She looked away again and tried to set aside the idea that was running through her mind. Handsome the Duke of Margrave might be, but the angled planes of his cheekbones, the strong line of his jaw, and the hawklike shrewdness of those beautiful eyes spoke plainly of a man who would not be easy to manage. Still, if he was leaving for Africa, that might not matter.

When he walked by where she stood, he didn't look her way, but she studied him from beneath her lashes as he passed, noting the easy, athletic grace with which he moved, grace that didn't come from navigating English ballrooms. When he melded into the crowd, she murmured something to her friend about needing a glass of water and followed him.

Making her way toward the refreshment table, she watched him as he paused to converse with a group of acquaintances, and she almost groaned in dismay as he led the beautiful and rich Susan Buckingham of Philadelphia out onto the dance floor. Though Edie had five times Susan's money, she couldn't hold a candle to her fellow American heiress in looks, and she feared the wild, crazy idea in her head might be doomed to failure before she could even try to implement it.

But she needn't have worried about Susan. Though they waltzed beautifully together, though she said things that made him smile and laugh, when the dance was over, the duke did not linger with her. Instead, he returned her to her place, bowed, and moved on, and Edie's hope flared up once more.

She knew she needed to get him alone, but she didn't see how she could manage it. And then, Providence, which had not been favoring Edie much of late, came to her aid. The duke paused at the other end of the refreshment table, lingering over the unopened bottles of champagne that were chilling on ice in an enormous silver bucket. She moved closer, watching as he pulled out, rejected, and returned several bottles. He finally selected one, but he didn't call for a footman to open it. Instead, bottle in one hand, he took up a glass from the table with the other and turned away, stepping out through the nearby opened French doors that led to the terrace.

He didn't seem to be slipping out for a rendezvous. A glance at the dance floor showed that Susan had been claimed by a new partner. He might be meeting someone else, of course, but Edie didn't think it likely since he'd only taken one glass with him. This was her chance if she had the nerve to take it. It might be the only chance she had left.

With that thought, she moved to the end of the refreshment table where he'd been standing, took up a champagne flute of her own, and after a quick glance around to be sure Lady Featherstone was nowhere in sight and no one else was watching her, she slipped outside to follow the duke. He was no longer on the terrace, but as her gaze swept over the moonlit gardens, she saw him striding away across the sweeping expanse of lawn. He seemed to be making for the tall boxwood hedges that formed a maze at the back of the grounds.

Moving as quickly as she dared, she followed, but by the time she reached the maze, he had already slipped into its labyrinthine depths.

She plunged in after him, but only a few minutes later, she found herself at a dead end, with Margrave nowhere in sight. She rose on her toes, elevating herself as much as she could in her flat slippers, but even as tall as she was, the hedge was too high for her to see over, and she sank back down with an exasperated sigh.

She assumed he was headed for the center

of the maze, but though she made several more attempts to follow, all of them proved useless, and she soon found herself hopelessly lost. Equally bad, she'd lost him. "Now what?" she muttered, staring into the dark green wall of yet another dead end.

"Looking for me?" a deep, lazy voice inquired behind her.

With a rush of relief, Edie whirled around to find her quarry less than ten feet away. But when she looked into those extraordinary gray eyes of his, her relief dissolved into something more like dread because her question to herself still remained unanswered. *Now what?*

# CHAPTER 3

"I usually don't care much for being followed, but in this case, I'm willing to make an exception." Margrave smiled at her, a flash of white, even teeth in the moonlight, and it struck Edie with sudden force that she'd just done something incredibly stupid.

Driven only by the single idea in her head, she hadn't realized until this moment that she was putting herself in a situation where history might repeat itself. Still, it was rather late in the day to be thinking about either danger or regret. What she needed to think of was what to do next. "What makes you think I was following you?" she asked to gain time and marshal her nerve.

"Wishful thinking?"

"Or conceit."

He laughed, and as he did, Edie realized the society gossip Leonie had heard was right. The man had charm. Even she, as immune to charm as she was to good looks, could feel the potency of both in this man.

"It could be that, I suppose," he conceded. "I do think rather well of myself. But now that you've put me in my place, may I offer a word of advice? If you do ever want to follow a man in future, I suggest you make less noise while you're about it, or he'll notice you're there."

Boldness, she decided, was her best bet at this point, and she took a step closer to him. "What makes you think I didn't want you to notice?"

His dark brows rose a notch. "And here I was, thinking this ball such a dull affair," he murmured. "So you admit you were following me?"

"Yes. I saw you, I heard a bit about you, and I decided I wanted to talk to you."

He began walking toward her. "Given this shameless conduct on your part, dare I hope something delightfully naughty is in the wind?"

Edie tensed, forcing down a jolt of panic, hoping this time she wasn't utterly wrong in her judgment of men. "I said I wanted to talk," she reminded.

"And that's all? How disappointing."

"That depends on the conversation."

He chuckled. "Fair enough," he acknowledged as he halted in front of her. "Talk it is, then, but the conversation had best be scintillating indeed, or I shall feel thoroughly let down."

He shifted his glass to the same hand that held the bottle of champagne, then he turned, offering her his arm. "Shall we?"

She hesitated, but a glance around reminded her that there was no escape except past him, and she doubted she could find her way out of this maze without him anyway. *In for a penny, in for a pound,* she thought. Putting her hand — lightly — on his arm, she allowed him to guide her out of her dead-end corridor and down a different path.

They took several more twists and turns before emerging at last into a clearing that appeared to be the center of the maze, where a gazebo of sorts had been erected. Roman in style, its limestone pillars were capped by a dome that glowed white in the moonlight, and steps all around the circular structure led up to a pair of curved stone benches.

"There, now," he said as he led her up the steps. "Here, we can converse in complete privacy. No one ever manages to find the center of this thing."

"You did."

"Earning your heartfelt admiration, I

hope? But in this case, it would be unde-
served. I stayed here at Hanford House
many times as a boy, so I found the center
of this maze long ago. Still, I am rather good
at navigation, if I do say it myself."

"Yes, I heard about some of your exploits
in Africa. People say you want to go back
and live there."

"More than anything in the world." He
set down his glass and began to open the
champagne. "But it may not be possible."

"Why not?"

"Let's just say I have responsibilities at
home."

"You mean debts?"

"All these questions." The cork popped,
and he let it fall from his hand. "I'm beginning to fear that's why you followed me.
Are you a journalist thinking to interview
me about my exploits? Like that woman —
what was her name? Nellie Bly?"

"I'm no journalist."

"Hmm, so you say. But can I believe you?"

"You'll just have to trust me." She held
out her glass and nodded to the bottle, feeling in desperate need of a drink. "Pour."

"Bossy as well as bold. What an intoxicat-
ing combination. If you are a journalist," he
added as he began filling her glass, "I must
warn you that I shall expect a great deal of

59

seductive persuasion on your part before I give away any of my scandalous secrets."

She didn't tell him her means of persuasion wasn't the sort he had in mind. "Rumor has it you are desperately in need of money," she said instead.

"Oh, rumor," he countered, his voice light. "Anyone with sense knows that's not rumor but fact. Still," he added as he poured champagne for himself, "I never discuss crude subjects like money while drinking good champagne. It's wrong, somehow."

She took a swallow from her glass. "Discussing money might be necessary."

"Why?" he asked casually as he set aside the bottle. "Are you proposing to become my mistress?"

Edie's heart gave a hard, panicked thump in her chest at the question, and she gave a nervous laugh. "More the other way around, actually."

The moment the words were out of her mouth, she wanted to bite her tongue off.

Even a man as worldly as this one couldn't take that sort of statement in stride. He blinked, giving her a dubious look as if fearing he might have misunderstood her meaning, and when he spoke, his voice still had a flippancy that told her he wasn't taking what she said seriously. "My hopes are rising with every moment we spend together," he murmured. "I've never been a gigolo before. What does it pay?"

She didn't know what a gigolo was, but she knew what he meant, and though paying him to be her lover wasn't at all what she had in mind, she didn't say so. "They've called your loans, I hear," she said instead, refusing to be diverted from the important topic. "If you can't raise the funds to pay your debts, what happens to your estates?"

"It'll be ghastly, I expect," he said, his voice filled with cheer, but in his dark, charming, reckless face, she could see a hint of desperation. "Everything that's not entailed will go on the auction block. I've heaps of relations, and they will wail and moan when the money dries up. They've no way of fending for themselves, you see, and I am their sole source of income. I'm only telling you this because the . . . ahem . . . fees for my services shall be quite steep. I'm not sure you can afford me."

"You'd be surprised what I can afford. But —" Edie paused, took a deep breath, and rolled the dice. "But I don't need a lover. I need a husband."

"Ah." He took a sip of champagne. "I was rather hoping for the other, for it would be quite a lark. I can't say I find the idea of being a husband nearly as exciting."

"If you marry me," she persevered, "I'll pay all your debts."

He tilted his head, studying her. "You really are an extraordinary girl. Do you make a habit of proposing marriage to random strangers?"

She flushed. "Of course not! I've never done this sort of thing in my life."

"Well, I've never been the recipient of such a proposal, so we're even there. Tell me, are all Americans as straightforward about these things as you?"

"I don't know. I only know that I haven't got time to pussyfoot around."

"Why?" His lashes lowered, and Edie's throat went dry as he cast a long, considering glance over her body. "Are you pregnant?"

She blushed hotly at the question, but she knew this was no time for girlish gaucheness. And given the circumstances, his question was a fair one. "No," she answered, shoving aside her embarrassment. "I'm not pregnant."

"Then I can't help but question your sanity for wanting to get married."

"Will you please stop making jokes?"

"You can't really blame me, can you? This isn't the sort of thing a chap expects when he attends a ball. Not that I'm complaining," he added, "for my evening has certainly become more interesting since you arrived on the scene. But it's leaving me a bit at sixes and sevens all the same."

He fell silent, considering, then he said, "Assuming for the moment that you mean what you say, can you deliver the goods?"

She frowned. "What do you mean?"

"How rich are you? Because you'd have to be enormously, obscenely rich to solve my problems, darling. Granted, you're an American — I can discern that by your accent. And it seems all Americans are rich nowadays, doesn't it? I can also see that you're wearing a smashing silk gown that probably cost more quid than I spend in a month, and you're draped in enough jewels to sink a ship. But still, I can't imagine even you have the blunt to pay off the debts of my reprobate ancestors, take care of my dukedom, and support me and all my endlessly sponging relations for the rest of our lives."

"That depends on how much money we're talking about," she answered, watching his face as he lifted his glass to his lips. "At the current rate of exchange, my dowry amounts to about one million pounds."

He choked. "Good God," he muttered

63

after a moment, staring at her in disbelief. "I'm not sure even the Queen has that much money."

"I will also receive an income of a hundred thousand pounds a year once I marry. I trust all that's enough to solve your family's financial difficulties?"

"Rather." He laughed a little, clearly confounded. "But my dear girl, you're mad. You must be to propose such a thing to a complete stranger. Marriage is a permanent thing — until death do us part, you know. If you had regrets later —"

"I won't have regrets." She could hear the hard resolve in her own voice. "As long as you mean what you say, and you really do go to Africa."

A hint of surprise showed in his face, surprise that told her he wasn't accustomed to a woman's disinterest. But it was gone almost at once, and he grinned at her. "By God, you don't spare a man's feelings, do you? What about my estates?"

"I'll manage them for you."

Thankfully, he didn't spout any horrid masculine doubts about a woman's ability to do so. "Why on earth would you want to take on such a thankless job? And make such a foolish investment? There's no money in land nowadays. You'd be sinking your entire fortune and future into what I assure you is a bottomless pit. You're willing to do that?"

Willing? She'd crawl to the devil and offer up her soul for it if it meant she didn't have to go back to New York. As long as the devil in question was willing to make the deal on her terms. She lifted her glass, and, over the rim, she met his incredulous gaze with a resolute one of her own. "I would, yes."

"Why?"

She sipped her champagne. "That is none of your business. I'm offering you an enormous amount of money. Be content with that."

"Money's all very well, but . . ." He paused, and she tensed as he looked her over. It was a thorough, thoughtful assessment, and she was afraid he was about to press further into her motives, but his next question belied that fear. "Have you got brains?" he asked. "Could you run things here in an efficient manner? I have five country estates to maintain, as well as a hunting lodge in Scotland and a house in London, and all of them need endless repairs and maintenance. Can you work with stewards and land agents? Can you order workmen about and supervise servants and see to the farms? Can you take charge and manage everything in my stead as well as I would do it myself?"

"Absolutely." She said it with complete assurance, which was such a crock, for she'd never been in charge of anything in her entire life. But she wanted to be. She wanted it so much, just thinking about it made her feel dizzy. Being a duchess meant a certain degree of freedom. It meant security. If the duke was absent, it could even mean paradise. "I can do anything that needs doing."

"You know," he murmured, still studying her, "I do believe you can."

"If you marry me, I will use my dowry to pay off your debts and those of your family. With whatever remains, along with my annual income, I will repair and maintain your estates and take care of your sponging relatives, as you call them. I will also provide you with a generous income. You can go off to Africa with no worries and a clear conscience and live the life you truly want to live. I have only one condition."

"What's that?"

"That you never, ever come back."

The fierceness of her voice caused him to raise an eyebrow. "Never is a long time."

"I don't want a husband in any sense but the legal one."

"Well, if I'm to be your husband in the legal sense, the marriage ought to be consummated. I presume you know what that means?"

She knew. Edie opened her mouth to reply, but even as she tried to speak, her throat closed up, and she couldn't form the words to answer him. Damn, this was no time for her nerves to go to pieces. She took a gulp of champagne, and the bubbles in the wine seemed to burn the back of her throat as she swallowed.

"I know what it means," she said at last, forcing the words out, her voice like the rasp of a saw in the quiet hush of evening. "But I don't see why it's necessary."

He studied her face in the moonlight for a moment without speaking. "If bedding me is as repugnant a notion to you as your countenance would suggest," he said at last, "I shall bow out now, for though I don't mind being a faithful husband, I've no desire to be a celibate one. Good evening."

He started past her to return to the ball, and Edie turned, clutching at his sleeve. "No, wait."

Margrave paused, and Edie forced herself to relax her grip. "It's not repugnance," she said, letting her hand fall. "It's nothing to do with you. It's just . . ." She stared into his face, helpless to explain. He had a countenance that would make any girl's heart race — any girl, that is, who wasn't broken inside.

Pain pinched her chest, and for one fleeting moment, she wondered what her world might be like now if it had been this man she'd met in that abandoned summer-house at Saratoga, instead of Frederick Van Hausen.

And if wishes were horses, beggars would ride.

Edie shoved aside pointless speculations of what might have been. "This is a business deal," she told him. "I don't want you getting any romantic notions about it or about me."

He seemed amused. "The conceit of the girl! What if our night together is so transcendent that you fall madly in love with me? What then?"

"Sorry to prick your vanity, but that won't happen. Look," she went on before he could answer, "I'm offering you everything you want from life. Don't allow your masculine pride to stand in your way. If consummating the marriage is truly necessary, I'll . . . I'll do it."

"You needn't act as if it's equivalent to torture, my dear. Most people consider lovemaking to be quite delightful."

"I don't expect torture. Nor delight. I don't . . ." She paused, battling back the fear that clogged her throat and twisted her stomach into knots. "I don't expect anything."

"I see. I'm a means to an end for you, and nothing more."

It sounded so terribly cold, put like that, and yet, she was cold. The desires that other women felt had been killed in her a year ago. "If we marry, I will . . ." She paused for another swallow of nerve-bolstering champagne. "I will sleep with you once to make it legal, but never again after that. Once we have satisfied the legal definition of matrimony, you are free to bed anyone else you wish. I shan't mind."

"You wouldn't be the first woman in the history of mankind to make that claim," he said wryly, "but you just might be the first one to mean it."

"I do mean it." She felt impelled to be as honest as possible about her point of view. "If you agree to my proposition, I don't want you doing so under the mistaken assumption that I desire you. I don't."

"I see. Dare I ask why not?" He took a sip of champagne. "Are you a lesbian?"

When she only stared at him in bafflement, he chuckled. "I'm asking," he said gently, "if you are attracted to women rather than men."

"God, no!" she burst out, shocked. Once again, she could feel heat flooding her face, and not for the first time, she cursed the fair complexion that enabled anyone to know when she was embarrassed. "Why would you ask me such a thing?"

"My masculine pride demands it. Somehow, it's a more palatable explanation than, 'Sorry, old chap, I just don't find *you* attractive.' Sadly, now that I know you're not that sort, I am all the more stung. And . . ." He paused, swirling champagne, watching her. "All the more intrigued."

She scowled. "Don't be. I'm not the least bit intriguing."

"I beg to differ." He downed his last swallow of wine and reached for the bottle to refill his glass. "You are, I can safely say, the most fascinating girl I've ever met. You have this cool, touch-me-not air about you that rather makes a chap want to try."

A cold wave of fear swept over her, but with an effort, she hid it beneath an air of amused disdain. "And what do you hope will be the result? That I'll fall into your arms?"

"I take it you won't? That's a shame,

then." He paused in refilling his glass, and again his gaze flicked downward, then back up. "For I suspect there's quite a fire under that cool, detached, practical exterior of yours."

"No, there isn't!" She flung her head back, meeting his quizzical gaze with a hard one of her own. "If you ever feel tempted during our marriage to prove otherwise, I'll cut off your income faster than you can say Jack Robinson."

"Prickly, aren't you?" he murmured as he set aside the bottle. "What happened to make you so? Some fellow break your heart and leave you vowing never to love again?"

"Something like that," she muttered, and looked away, but she could feel his inquiring gaze on her, and she sighed, knowing it was best to tell him her version of the gossip about her before he learned it elsewhere. "His name is Frederick Van Hausen. I've known him all my life, but his family and mine do not move in the same circle. I was so stupid . . ." She paused and swallowed painfully, trying to work up a palatable version of the events. "I was foolish enough to think . . ." She paused again, even in a heavily edited version, this was almost unbearable to explain. "We were . . . together, and word of it got out," she managed at last. "And now my reputation in New York is ruined."

"I see. And he didn't marry you? What a cad."

"Yes," she agreed with feeling. "The story is starting to spread here, too. I am damaged goods. It's only fair you know that."

"So you looked me over, made a few inquiries, then followed me out here to suggest I step in, do what he didn't have the intestinal fortitude to do, and save your reputation? If I refuse, am I to expect an outraged mama to appear and demand I do the honorable thing?"

"No. My mother died two years ago, and my offer stands on its own. If you refuse, you refuse, and that's the end of it."

"Becoming a duchess would be quite a sweet way to score off this Van Hausen chap for letting you down, I imagine. Still, it's deuced hard work being a duchess. It isn't the glamorous job you Americans think it is."

"I'm not doing this for the glamor, or even to save my reputation. I want to control and manage my own life. I want independence and autonomy. I want to be accountable to no one."

"But as my wife, you would be accountable to me."

"No, I won't, because I shall retain control of the money. You'll have to sign a prenuptial agreement to that effect."

"You do have brains. So what makes independence and autonomy so important to you?"

"That is none of your business, and if you ask me any more questions, the deal's off."

"Very well. If I'm to save my family from sponging off friends for the rest of their pathetic lives, I suppose I shall have to set aside my curiosity."

"So you accept my offer?"

"I'd be insane not to. And despite your heroic willingness to lie with me once for the sake of legalities, it won't be necessary. I prefer the women I bed to be willing."

Her heartfelt sigh of relief did not escape his notice, and he gave her a wry look in response. "Your ability to wound my vanity is boundless, it seems. Despite that, honor demands I tell you that nonconsummation isn't sufficient grounds for annulment under British law."

"You said it was!"

"Not precisely." He shrugged. "But I was curious to see how far you'd go to get what you want. Now I know."

Despite her relief, she couldn't help a flash of resentment. "I don't like being lied to."

"Best get used to it if you want to marry into the aristocracy. We lie to each other all the time. For the sake of honor, or to be polite, or even — sometimes — to deliberately deceive. But mostly, we lie to ourselves. I doubt," he added with bitterness in his voice, "we know how to be any other way."

She'd been in England long enough to know there was a grain of truth in what he said, but she did wonder at the bitter edge to his voice. Still, it wasn't her business. "I hope what you say is true," she said instead. "Because we will have to put on a convincing display of fondness during our engagement. If my father suspects otherwise, he'll never sign over the dowry."

"Then we shall have to convince your father of the depths of our mutual affection."

She ignored the hint of mockery in his voice. "It's not only Daddy we'll have to convince."

"Who else is there?"

"Lady Featherstone."

He nodded in understanding. "The matchmaking countess."

"She is a matchmaker, yes, but she doesn't arrange marriages of convenience. She expects her clients to have affection for each other. If she realizes that we're making a material marriage, she'll tell Daddy not to agree, and he'll take her counsel. And don't think deceiving her will be easy. She's a tougher proposition than even my father, and he's nobody's fool. Also, she knows everyone in society, and if there's any talk that our affection is not authentic, the fat will be in the fire."

"I can be very affectionate," he said, but when he moved a step closer, she flattened a hand against his chest.

"I believe you," she assured. "No need to demonstrate it when we're alone."

"Sorry," he apologized, but he didn't step back until she pushed. "Just practicing my part, you know."

"Well, don't overdo it. If we seem too madly in love, Lady Featherstone is sure to see through it. Or, she'll think we're being rash and insist on a long engagement. You'll have to play the part of devoted fiancé, responsible future husband, and affectionate friend. Can you do that?"

"Why not?" He looked away, staring at the house in the distance. "Playing a part is nothing new to me. I've been playing one for most of my life."

She inhaled sharply, the impact of his words like a punch in the stomach. "I know just what you mean," she whispered.

He looked at her again. "We'll have a long enough engagement to convince everyone we sincerely want to marry. Six weeks ought to be sufficient. After the wedding, we'll spend a couple of months at Highclyffe, my ducal seat in Norfolk, so I can show you how to run things and help secure your position."

"And then you'll leave for Africa and never return?"

He didn't answer at once. Instead, he gave her a thoughtful look. "Deserting you forever paints me rather a villain."

"And that bothers you?"

"Funnily enough, it does," he said dryly. "Still, it isn't as if I have many options. Saving my estates from collapse and returning to the place I love shall have to be my consolations."

"So we have a deal?" She lifted her glass.

He lifted his. "We do."

With the exchange of glances, the clink of glasses, and a final swallow of champagne, the agreement was made. As Edie lowered her glass, relief came over her in a flood, making her weak in the knees. She would never have to see Frederick's insufferable, smirking face again. She couldn't wipe out that awful day as if it had never happened, but perhaps she could at least put it behind her and build a new life.

Margrave gave a soft cough, interrupting her thoughts. "Now that we are to be married," he said, "there's something I need to ask you."

She felt a pang of alarm. "Don't think this arrangement will allow you to invade my privacy, asking intimate questions."

He gave her a look as if in apology. "This question is rather important. We simply can't proceed unless you answer it."

"Oh, very well. What do you want to know?"

He leaned closer, a faint smile tilting his mouth. "What the devil is your name?"

# CHAPTER 4

The carriage jerked to a halt, and Edie came out of the past with equal abruptness, realizing she had arrived at Highclyffe. Margrave, she suspected, wouldn't be far behind.

*I've come home.*

"Not for long," she muttered.

"I beg your pardon, Your Grace?" Roberts, standing by the carriage, gave her a puzzled look as he opened the door.

She waved a hand, shaking her head. "Never mind," she said, and stepped down from the vehicle.

The driver closed the door behind her and climbed back up on the box. Edie started for the house, but when she heard the carriage turning around in the drive instead of heading toward the stables, she turned as well, waving her arms to gain Roberts's attention.

He pulled the vehicle to a stop beside her.

"Your Grace?"

"Roberts, where on earth are you going?"

"To fetch His Grace from the station."

"You'll do no such thing!" The words came out sharper than she'd intended, and Roberts looked at her in abashed bewilderment. "I'm sorry," she said at once. "I didn't mean to snap at you. But . . ." She paused, inventing quickly. "But His Grace has no doubt hired a carriage to bring him from the station, so it would be a waste of your time to go back. Best to take the landau on down to the stables."

The driver eyed her dubiously for a moment. "If you're sure, Your Grace?" When she nodded, he shrugged in acquiescence and once again turned the carriage around.

"Be good to have a master at Highclyffe, won't it, Your Grace?" he called as he drove the carriage past her.

"This house has no master," she murmured as she watched the vehicle roll down the drive toward the stables. "Only a mistress."

Margrave might be home again, but Edie vowed he wouldn't be staying long. They'd made a deal, and she was living up to her part. She intended to make sure he lived up to his.

■ ■ ■ ■

*Well, that is why you came home, isn't it?*

The question of Edie's pert little sister hung in the air, still unanswered, even after a porter had secured him a hired carriage, and he and Joanna were on their way to Highclyffe. Not that his sister-in-law let the subject drop. No, they'd barely gotten under way before she broached it again.

"How are you going to set about this?" she asked, as the carriage started toward the road toward home. "Winning Edie back, I mean?"

He honestly didn't know. How did one win back what one never had in the first place? Five years ago, winning Edie hadn't been part of the plan. Oh, he'd had fleeting thoughts of what might have been, nights where he'd gazed up at the star-filled Kenyan sky and relived that moment in the ballroom at Hanford House when the sight of her had stopped him dead in his tracks. But then her words from that night would come back to him, and he'd force himself to put aside such pointless tortures. A man in the bush could go mad thinking that way about a woman.

Everything was different now, of course,

80

but only for him. For Edie, it was clear nothing had changed. One look at his wife's face in the train station had told him that. In fact, as things stood now, he probably had a better chance of making the quarter-finals at Wimbledon than he did winning Edie's heart. Truth be told, he wasn't sure she had a heart to win.

Still, one couldn't tell that to Edie's young sister, who appeared to have a rather romantic view of things. "You seem quite certain that's why I'm here," he said instead.

"Isn't it?" A hint of disappointment came into her face. "But what other reason could there be?"

He looked away, staring out over acres of land that had been in Margrave hands for nearly two centuries. By marrying Edie, he'd kept everything intact for the next generation, but at the time he hadn't thought much about the fact that the next generation wouldn't be his. And that was important now in a way it hadn't been before. Children meant part of a man lived on, even after his own death.

There was nothing like being on the verge of death, he thought, to make a man yearn for immortality.

He returned his attention to the girl. "Oh, I intend to win her over, trust me. I only meant that it's more complicated than you might think."

She nodded as if she understood. "Well, you have been gone a long time. You'll have your work cut out for you, that's certain. So . . ." She paused to settle back in her seat. "What's your strategy?"

He couldn't help a laugh at the blunt question. "You know," he said, regarding her thoughtfully, "you remind me a great deal of your sister."

"Edie?" Joanna seemed dubious about that. "Most people don't think we're in the least alike."

"Perhaps not in looks, no," he murmured, noting without emotion the perfection of the oval face beneath the schoolgirl straw boater. Joanna Jewell might only be fifteen, but she was already a beauty, and he suspected that when the time came for her debut, there would be quite a few broken-hearted young chaps in London as a result. Still, though Edie might not possess her sister's flawless features and freckle-free complexion, she had an attraction all her own, one he suspected she herself had never been able to see. "I wasn't referring to appearances, but cheek."

"You mean sass?" Joanna heaved a sigh. "You're right, and it's just not fair. I say sassy things, and I get into trouble, but Edie says whatever she likes, and because she's a duchess, no one ever thinks she's sassy."

"I did, when I first met her. Of course, she wasn't my duchess then. But I thought her very cheeky."

"You did?" Joanna leaned forward, eager to hear. "Why? What did she say to you?"

He thought back to that night in the maze at Hanford House for a moment before he answered, not sure what within that extraordinary conversation might be appropriate for the ears of a young girl. "She didn't find me the least bit attractive." He laughed a little at the memory. "And she made no bones about telling me so."

"But she married you. How did you change her mind? Whatever you did then, maybe you could do it again."

"I doubt it."

"Then what is your plan?" She sounded quite nettled with him for not having it all planned out.

"Assuming I have a plan, as you put it, what makes you think I'll share it with you?"

She shook her head, staring at him as if he had cotton wool for brains. "Because I can tell you whether or not it will work, of course! She's not going to just fall into your arms, you know."

That, he acknowledged with a grimace, was brutally true. Edie had never fallen into his arms. Not even once.

The image of her moonlit face, as luminous and smooth as alabaster, flashed across his mind, as vivid now as it had been that fateful night at Hanford House — so vivid, in fact, that despite his many efforts over the years not to think of her, he'd failed more often than he'd succeeded. It had been her image that had so persistently invaded his dreams during his delirium-filled fever, not the dangerous events that had almost killed him. Even now, he could hear her voice clearly, so resolute and un-compromising.

*That you never, ever come back.*

Well, as he'd told her then, never was a long time. Circumstances changed, and plans went awry. His certainly had.

He turned on the carriage seat, grimacing as he shifted his weight onto one hip and stretched out his leg. The sea voyage from Mombasa to Constantinople hadn't been too bad, even without Jones. He felt another grimace of pain that had nothing to do with his leg, and he put his valet out of his mind. Jones was gone, and there was nothing he could do about that. He focused on the pain in his leg instead. That was easier to bear.

On the ship, he'd been able to move about freely, but trains and carriages were a different matter. The muscles of his thigh had knotted up before he'd even reached Rome, and by now they were so constricted that he felt his right leg must surely be at least an inch shorter than his left.

"What happened to your leg?"

Stuart glanced at the girl seated opposite him. "Do you always ask impertinent questions?"

That made her grin. "All the time. It drives Mrs. Simmons mad."

"I don't doubt it. But to answer your question, I was mauled by a lioness."

Her brown eyes went wide. "Really? How exciting."

Stuart settled back in the corner of his seat, giving her a wry look. He unknotted his tie and removed his collar stud, something he'd been longing to do ever since he'd put them on. Nothing like a stiff, tight collar to remind a man of all that was wrong with civilization.

"It wasn't the least bit exciting, my dear girl," he assured Joanna as he dropped his stud into his pocket and pulled apart his collar. "I almost died."

"And now you have to use a cane," she said and frowned, looking thoughtful. "I

85

suppose you could do something with that," she said after a moment. "Edie's terribly tenderhearted."

He eyed her with doubt. "Are we talking about the same woman?"

"She'll melt like butter if you go about things the right way."

As agreeable as that sounded, Stuart's mind couldn't quite form the picture. Granted, he knew next to nothing about his wife, but the idea of Edie's melting like butter over anything, especially him, didn't seem the least bit likely.

"Oh, she tries to be hard and tough," Joanna went on as he continued to eye her askance. "But it's a sham. She's always finding homes for stray kittens and puppies, and she gets very upset when a bird flies into a window. She feels sorry for anything wounded."

"I suppose I do fall into that classification," he murmured. "So I'm to play on her sympathy?"

"Well, it wouldn't hurt to have her feeling sorry for you, would it? I can show you other ways to get on her good side, too. You see . . ." She paused to give him a confident smile. "I can wind Edie 'round my little finger when I want to."

That was probably true, for though there

might be some similarities in temperament between the Jewell sisters, there was one significant difference. It was clear that Joanna was hopelessly spoiled.

"That's very kind of you," he said, smiling back at her. "And you'll do this out of the goodness of your heart, I assume?"

She looked at him with injured innocence. "I want my sister to be happy."

"I'm sure you do," he agreed gravely. "Come, child, drop the other shoe."

She grinned, unrepentant. "I wouldn't mind staying out of finishing school."

"Ah. But what makes you think I can persuade your sister to change her mind about that?"

Her answer was simple, direct, and a damned sight too clever for a schoolgirl. "Tell her you want me to go so the two of you can be alone together. That's sure to make her keep me here."

Stuart began to feel for Edie. "I'm glad you're on my side," he murmured.

"So?" she prompted when he said nothing more. "Do we have a deal?"

He laughed, remembering those same words on Edie's lips five years ago. "You *do* remind me of your sister."

She leaned forward and stuck out her hand. "Is that a yes?"

He could see no disadvantage to the arrangement. The girl certainly seemed to know her sister well, far better than he. "Why not?" he said, and also leaned forward. "As you said, I shall need all the help I can muster."

As they clasped hands to seal their arrangement, he reflected that making bargains with impertinent American females seemed to be his lot in life.

So far, he couldn't complain about his luck in that regard, but now, he and Edie would have to negotiate a new, entirely different sort of marriage than the one they'd had in the past, and when Stuart thought of her appalled face at the train station, he knew that bargain was not going to be an easy one for her to make.

Stuart might not know much about the woman he had married, but he knew one thing. Patience was not one of her virtues. He and Joanna had barely stepped down from the hired carriage parked in the drive before the heavy oak front doors were thrown back and Edie came out to greet them, the butler and the housekeeper in her wake.

Not that greeting them could really describe her purpose, if her expression was

88

anything to go by. She was frowning like thunder. "What on earth are you doing here?" she demanded as she strode across the gravel toward the carriage.

Stuart opened his mouth, ready to restate the obvious, but he shut it again when he realized she wasn't talking to him. Her next words confirmed that realization.

"Why aren't you on your way to Kent, young lady?" she demanded as she passed him and halted in front of Joanna.

The girl gave a shrug. "I missed the train."

"Missed it?" Edie echoed. "How in heaven's name could you miss it? You were *on* it. And so was Mrs. Simmons. Where is she, by the way?"

"Still on board, bound for Kent," Joanna informed her with obvious relish. "Well, I couldn't wait for her," she added as Edie made a sound of dismay. "As it was, I barely had time to jump off the train myself since it was already moving."

"Oh, my Lord, you jumped off a moving train? Joanna Arlene Jewell, what were you thinking? You could have been badly hurt." She glanced down, her anger fading into concern. "Are you all right?"

"Edie, don't fuss. I'm all right. Didn't fall or twist an ankle or anything when I jumped."

"But you could have!" Her concern faded as quickly as it came. "And you did this . . . why?" she demanded.

"Because Margrave's come home, of course!" The girl waved a hand in Stuart's direction. "I knew who he was the second I heard you call his name, and I could see that things around here were about to get very interesting. I wasn't going to miss any of that!"

"You won't be missing anything," Edie assured her, "because Margrave isn't staying long. And," she added before either he or the girl could dispute that statement, "neither are you, little sister. There is another train tomorrow, and you'll be on it."

"But he's my brother-in-law, and I want to get to know him. I only met him once, you know, and I barely even remember it. And by the way," she added before Edie could speak, her tone indignant, "why didn't you tell me he was injured in Africa?"

"Injured?" Edie turned to him in surprise, and Stuart hastened into speech, for despite Joanna's assurance that it would help his cause, he had no intention of playing on Edie's sympathy. He didn't want pity, for God's sake.

"It's nothing," he said, hoping to dismiss any further discussion on the topic. "Noth-

90

ing at all," he added, giving Joanna a quelling look.

He ought to have known that wouldn't work. "It's not nothing," the girl cried and turned to Edie. "He got eaten by a lioness."

"Good heavens!" Edie burst out. "Stuart!"

"I wasn't eaten, only gnawed a bit. Then she decided she didn't like the taste of me."

Edie pressed a hand to her mouth and slowly lowered her gaze to his leg. "So that's why you've taken to carrying a walking stick," she murmured behind her hand. "I didn't realize . . ."

She paused, lowered her hand, and returned her gaze to his face. "Oh, Stuart," she said, and in her voice and her eyes was the pity he loathed and dreaded. "I'm sorry. How terrible."

"Not so terrible," he countered, keeping his voice light, ignoring the none-too-gentle elbow Joanna jammed into his side. "My tennis game's gone to hell, of course, and stairs take a bit more time than they used to, but other than that . . ." He paused and gave what he hoped was a careless shrug. "I'm quite all right."

"He's not all right," Joanna contradicted him. "He's lame. So —"

"I am not lame!" Desperate for a distraction, he glanced around, and when he saw the tall, portly fellow in black who stood by the front steps, he stepped around his wife and headed in that direction, displaying as great a show of vigor in his walk as he could manage. "Wellesley," he greeted in a hearty voice, "how delightful to see you."

"Your Grace." The butler bowed, and when he straightened, his impassive expression made Stuart grateful for the British custom of well-trained, impassive servants. "It is a great pleasure to have you back at Highclyffe."

"Thank you." He glanced around the butler, noting that the house's limestone façade, no longer cracked and crumbling, must have been replaced. "Everything running smoothly here, I trust?"

"Yes, indeed. Very smoothly." Wellesley glanced at his undone collar with a hint of disapproval and glanced past him. "Is Mr. Jones following you in another carriage? If so —"

"Jones isn't coming," he cut in, "but yes, a dog cart shall be arriving soon with the rest of my things." He turned to greet the spare, elderly housekeeper who stood beside the butler. "Mrs. Gates. Good to see you are still here."

"Oh, I'll always be here, Your Grace," she said, her lined face breaking into a wide smile. "As long as the good Lord allows."

"I'm glad to hear it. Have you enough housemaids under you to make my rooms ready even though I was terribly rude and didn't write ahead about my return?"

"Of course, Your Grace. I shall have your rooms prepared at once. And if Mr. Jones is not with you . . ." She paused to gesture to the lanky young man in livery to her left. "I'm sure Edward here would be up to the task. As first footman, he has served as valet upon occasion."

"His Grace won't need a footman for that," Wellesley put in. "I shall do for him myself until Mr. Jones arrives."

"Jones won't be coming." Stuart sighed, rubbing a hand over his face, reminding himself they had the right to know. "Mr. Jones is dead."

"What?"

Edie's shocked gasp didn't cause him to turn around. "It won't be necessary for you to valet, Wellesley. Thank you all for your solicitousness, but I shall do for myself."

"Yourself?"

The surprised word from both the servants was also echoed from behind him, and he turned as Edie came up beside him. "But surely you'll need help," she said, a frown of what might have been concern knitting her brows. "Without a valet, how will you manage?"

"I've grown accustomed to doing for myself, and I find I prefer it that way, at least for now. Wellesley, will you —" He broke off, his voice failing. He gave a cough and tried again. "Will you tell the other servants about Jones? I know some of them were quite fond of him."

"Of course, Your Grace."

"Thank you," he said with relief and gratitude. "Mrs. Gates, if you will have my rooms prepared and a bath drawn, I would appreciate it. I'll wait in the library."

Glad that particular room was on the ground floor, he gave a nod to the remaining servants and limped up the steps and into the house, hoping that everyone would now allow the subject of his injuries and his valet to drop.

Edie's demeanor indicated that she might actually have the heart he'd wondered if she possessed, but though her compassion for his condition might commend her character, he had no intention of using that to persuade her to make their marriage real. The day he needed pity to win a woman was the day he'd walk himself and his mangled leg straight off a cliff.

# CHAPTER 5

The library was so different from the room he remembered that Stuart stopped in the doorway, uncertain for a moment if he was in the right place.

Shelves of books still lined three walls of the long, rectangular room, but the fourth wall, the one that ran alongside the south terrace, had been stripped of bookshelves altogether. In their place were tall French doors that opened onto the terrace, framed by silk draperies of soft green. The room's walnut paneling had been removed and the walls painted a pale, buttery yellow. The once-gilded woodwork was now white, and the worn velvet upholstery of the furnishings had been replaced with a delicately patterned green-and-white chintz. The room was now airy and full of light, a vast improvement over the oppressiveness of the previous décor.

The library wasn't the only thing about

the house Edie had transformed. He'd already noticed that the north façade had been replaced, but a step outside verified that the south one had received the same treatment. The knot gardens were no longer a gnarled mass of overgrown boxwood, wild rose canes, and weed-infested turf. The Italianate potagers put in by the third duke during the reign of Queen Anne were now back to their original, intricate splendor, their roses blooming with controlled abandon and their low boxwood edges precisely trimmed. The once-rusty wrought-iron table and chairs on the terrace had been painted white, potted geraniums lined the balustrade, and beneath his feet, the cracked, crumbling flagstones of the past were gone. In the distance, the home farm looked tidy and the fields well tended. He hadn't had any doubt that Edie would capably manage Highclyffe and his other estates, not only because he trusted his instincts but also because annual reports from stewards and land agents over the years had confirmed it.

Despite that, he found it reassuring to see for himself that everything was in order. And yet, looking out over the immaculately groomed lands spread out before him, he wondered suddenly what there would be for him to do here. Edie had managed everything so well, what could he contribute?

*It's time to go home.*

The insistent need that had pounded through his head on that fateful night six months ago echoed back to him again, reminding him that he could have chosen to die. But instead, he'd chosen to live, to come home and accept at last the role he'd been born to. But then, he'd always known he would return one day. He just hadn't expected it to be this way. He'd rather fancied coming home to all the celebratory fanfare due to a famous traveler and explorer. He certainly hadn't envisioned himself limping in like a wounded animal.

Still, he was here, and he had responsibilities to assume. Patching things up with Edie was his first, his primary goal, for nothing else would matter without that. Not that there had ever really been anything to patch up. They hadn't been the happily married couple who had drifted apart, separated, and now had to reconcile. No, they'd been two strangers brought together by mutual need. They had certainly never been in love.

At least, he amended, she hadn't been. He thought of the first time he'd ever seen her in that ballroom and how it had felt. Like the hand of Fate grabbing hold of him, forcing him to stand still and look hard because in front of him was something worth noticing. He might have fallen, and fallen hard, if she hadn't so ruthlessly cut the ground from beneath his feet before he'd even known her name. Ah, well.

This was a new beginning, and a second chance. Not that the task ahead of him would be an easy one. He'd known then, and he knew now, that Edie had a wall around her it would not be easy to breach.

"You've changed."

The sound of her voice had him turning around to find her in the doorway to the corridor, watching him through the open French doors.

"A man's bound to change in five years, I suppose." He started back toward the library, but after only a few steps, he wished he'd remained where he was. With her watching, he felt acutely self-conscious as he came across the terrace and into the library, especially when he paused in the center of the room and noted that she had not come forward to meet him halfway. He hoped that was not a metaphor for their future.

"Stuart?" She hesitated a moment, then she said simply, "I'm sorry about Jones. Was that lions, too?"

"Yes. How do you think I've changed?" he

asked, rushing on, feeling a desperate need to veer off the subject of his valet. "Aside from the obvious, of course," he added with a forced laugh, shifting his weight to his good leg and holding up his walking stick.

She considered for a moment. "You're much graver than I remember. Not quite so glib and debonair as you used to be."

"Yes, my carefree youth has passed on, I daresay."

Her lips curved upward a bit. "Still undoing your ties at every opportunity, though, I see."

"It's not the tie, Edie," he said with a grin, hoping here was the beginning of a rapprochement. "It's the collar. One of the things Africa taught me was just how uncomfortable the damn things are. You've changed, too, by the way," he added.

"Have I?" She seemed surprised by that. "In what way?"

He studied her for a long moment, considering. It was the same face he remembered, with its angled auburn brows, spring green eyes, and dusting of freckles. It had the same stubborn, square jaw, pointed chin, and pale pink mouth, and he presumed her straight white teeth still had that slight overbite that showed when she smiled, though as he recalled, she'd never been one to smile much. Hers had never been a pretty face, he supposed, not by society's standards, but it was so vibrantly alive that its lack of symmetrical beauty didn't seem to matter. So what was it about her that was different? He tried to pin it down.

"You're not so thin now as you were then. And not so fierce. Not so driven. You seem . . . I don't know quite how to put it, Edie. You're softer, somehow."

She shifted her weight and looked away as if uncomfortable with his description. "Yes, well . . ." She gave a cough. "That's good."

Silence fell between them, a silence that banished any hope of immediate rapport and underscored the brutal fact that despite being married, they were two strangers alone in a room, grasping for something to say. Not that there was nothing for them to talk about — quite the contrary. Their future as husband and wife stretched before them, and if he'd survived for anything at all, it was for another chance with her, a chance to make with her a marriage that was real. He could hardly jump right into that topic, however, and he glanced around, striving for something neutral to say.

"I like what you've done with this room," he remarked at last. "The French doors to the terrace are a splendid idea."

"I did the same thing in the music room, the billiard room, and the ballroom. Since these rooms all flank the terrace, it was a simple improvement to make."

"Well, the ballroom would certainly benefit from the additional fresh air. That room was always beastly hot when it was full of people, even with all the windows open. And here in the library, the French doors bring in a lot more light. One can see well enough to read in here now. Before, I remember, one always had to light a lamp, even in the afternoon. Such a silly thing, I always thought, not to have adequate light in a library. But now, a lamp would only be necessary after dark."

"Not even then, really," she said, and pointed to one of several gold sconces that adorned the walls. "I installed gaslights in all the rooms ages ago."

He smiled. "How American of you. A most sensible thing to do."

Edie made a face. "Your mother wouldn't agree. She hates them. She breathes disapproval of them every time she visits."

He looked at her with sympathy. "Has she been very awful?"

Edie waved a hand. "Nothing I can't handle. Your mother's rather like a house cat. She wants to be pampered and catered to, and she's inclined to hiss a bit when she doesn't get her way."

"That sounds like an apt description of my entire family."

"It does, rather," she agreed. "Do they know you're here?"

"Mama and Nadine know. I came through Rome on my way home, and I called on them there. You knew they were in Rome, didn't you? Of course you did," he went on before she could answer. "Mama would never go anywhere without telling you where to send the quarterly allowance."

She did not dispute that rather cynical contention. "Will they be following you, then? Should I have more rooms prepared?"

He shook his head. "They're staying in Italy through the autumn as planned." He felt a twinge of stupid boyhood pain, but he shoved it aside, for he'd accepted long ago the indifference and utter lack of love in his family. "Nadine," he went on, "has an Italian prince on the hook at present, and if she came home now, why, he might slip free. Priorities, Edie. Priorities."

She nodded with understanding, for she knew by now just what his sister and mother were like. "Of course. What about Cecil?"

"Oh, I've plenty of time to inform him. The fly fishing's deuced good in Scotland just now, and the stalking begins next week. Even if I wrote today, I doubt my brother would be able to drag himself away from Stuart Lodge to come down and welcome me."

"If you really want to see him while you're here, I could cut off *his* allowance," she suggested with a touch of humor.

Stuart gave a shout of laughter and surprise. It wasn't like the Edie he remembered to make a joke. "He'd be down like a shot, wouldn't he? Still, it's not necessary to put him through that sort of shock yet a while."

She wrinkled up her freckled nose in a rueful way. "When you first told me what spongers they were, I didn't quite believe you."

"I did my best to warn you what they were like."

"True, but until I met them, I don't think I quite believed you."

"Yet, after you met them, you married me anyway," he murmured. "I have often wondered why."

"We both know why we married."

"Yes, yes, quite so. You came to me and proposed a very sensible arrangement, and I . . ." He paused long enough to take a deep breath. "I jumped at it. But what I meant was that I've often wondered why you chose me."

"Oh, I doubt you've thought about me enough to wonder about that," she said with a deprecating shrug and a laugh.

"And if you ever thought that, Edie, you were wrong."

Her humor faded at once. Her tongue darted out to lick her lips, as if they were dry or she was suddenly nervous. "Stuart, why are you here?" she asked in a low voice.

"I believe you already know the answer to that question."

She came into the library, crossing to where he stood. "I suppose . . ." She paused for a moment, halting in front of him. "I suppose your injuries are what brought you home?"

"Partly." At least, he amended to himself, they had provided the perfect excuse. "In a way."

His enigmatic reply caused a puzzled frown to crease her brow. "So you're home to consult a doctor?"

"I've already seen two doctors. One in Nairobi and one in Mombasa."

"I was referring to an English doctor."

"Both of them were English."

She shook her head. "No, I meant a specialist, someone who might have more experience treating injuries such as yours than a colonial doctor."

"It wouldn't matter."

"It might. Some of the doctors in Harley Street are quite clever," she added, and he could hear a hint of desperation creeping into her voice. "One of them might be able to offer a course of treatment, something that would put you right again. And then . . ." She paused again, and this time, it was a pause so palpably awkward, it made him grimace.

"Go on," he prompted. "And then?"

"And then you could go back."

He decided there was no point in sugarcoating the truth. "I'm not going back, Edie. I'm home for good."

She displayed no surprise. Instead, she nodded, but if he thought it was a nod of acceptance, he was mistaken. "You promised me you would never come back. Remember?"

He didn't tell her it was a promise he'd always known he might break. "My circumstances have changed, as you've no doubt observed. I can't lead the life I led before. No more hunting, no more safari work." He paused, for though all that was true, it wasn't what had brought him home. "Edie, I nearly died."

She bit her lip and looked away. "I'm

sorry, Stuart. Truly, I am."

"But?"

She looked at him again, and he saw the girl he knew, the girl who wanted no husband except in name. "Do you intend to break our agreement?"

If their marriage was to have a prayer of succeeding, he had to make her understand what had happened to him and why that mattered. "I saw men digging my grave, Edie. I watched them do it. I knew I was dying, and I can't begin to describe what that was like, except to say that that changes a man. It makes him instantly, keenly aware that everything he thought was important isn't important at all. It forces him to look at his life in a whole new light, reconsider his choices, perhaps make new ones —"

"And just which of your choices," she interrupted, "are you reconsidering?"

"I realized it was time for me to come home, take care of my estates, and you."

"I don't need taking care of."

He could see her expression hardening as she said it, but he persevered, for it had to be said. "I want to do my duty to my estates and my family and my marriage. I want to be a real husband." He paused, then added, "With a real wife."

Those words were scarcely out of his

mouth before she was shaking her head. "No. We agreed —"

"I know what we agreed, but that was five years ago. Things are different now."

"Not for me."

He ignored that painfully obvious fact, because his only hope for a future with her was in finding a way to overcome it. "But they are different for me, Edie. I don't just want what's over the next hill or across the next river. I want to be part of something that endures."

Her lips parted, but she said nothing. She stared at him, wordless, and he took advantage of the moment to finish what he needed to say. "Next time I look death in the face, I want to know that I'll have left something behind me that isn't just my bones and ashes. Edie . . ." He paused and took a deep breath. "I want children."

She staggered back a step, almost as if he'd slapped her. "You gave me your word," she choked out. "Damn you. You gave me your word."

She turned, and, for the second time in two hours, she began walking away faster than he could follow.

"We can't avoid each other forever," he called after her.

"I don't see why not," she shot back over

her shoulder. "We've been doing a splendid job of it for the past five years."

With that, she vanished into the corridor.

Stuart let out his breath in a slow sigh. This, he appreciated as he stared at the empty doorway, was going to be even harder than he thought.

"Of all the idiotic things to do!"

A disgusted feminine voice interrupted his thoughts, and he turned around to find Joanna standing in the frame of one of the open French doors, frowning at him. "Really, Margrave, if you're not going to take my advice, how am I going to help you?"

"I see that in addition to being impertinent and disobeying your sister, you also have no compunction about eavesdropping."

"Well, it's not my fault if you and Edie have a set-to where the doors are wide open! And anyway, I have a serious stake in this."

"If I find you eavesdropping on any more of my private conversations with your sister, or with anyone else, for that matter, I'll haul you off to Willowbank myself, tied and gagged if necessary. Is that understood?"

Her expression turned sulky, but she was forced to knuckle under. "Oh, very well," she mumbled, "I won't listen in anymore. But now that the damage is done," she added irrepressibly, "I have to ask what you were thinking. The part about children was all right, I suppose. Edie does like babies. But doing your duty to your marriage? And all that mush about being part of something that endures?" She made a sound of derision. "You think that's going to win her over?"

In hindsight, he supposed it did sound like an utter load of tosh, but it nettled him nonetheless that he was being given advice on romance by a schoolgirl. "And by playing on her sympathy, you think I'd have done better, do you?"

"Well, you couldn't have done any worse!" Having made that irrefutable point, Joanna turned away with a huff of aggravation and vanished from view, but her last muttered words floated back to him from across the terrace. "The way you're going, I'll never stay out of boarding school."

Stuart was in no position to dispute that prediction just now. And though he was no more inclined to play on Edie's sympathy now than he'd been before, he also knew that Joanna had a point. All the things he'd said to Edie were true, but they weren't what he'd need to say in order to win her. Unfortunately, he had no idea what were the right things to say. He'd always been rather adept at charming the fair sex, but his charms, as he was well aware, had never impressed Edie.

He knew a love affair gone wrong had broken her heart and ruined her reputation. He also knew she hadn't offered him marriage because she desired him, though discovering that had been rather a blow to his vanity at the time.

*I'm offering you everything you want from life. Don't allow masculine pride to get in your way.*

Well, he hadn't, and the result had been something akin to an Arabian Nights tale. Like a genie out of a bottle, she'd appeared and solved all his problems, absolved him of all his irksome duties, and handed him everything in life he could have asked for. Everything except her.

That night in the maze, he hadn't considered what effect their bargain would have on him, and during the frantic days before their wedding, surrounded by relatives and chaperones and an entourage of fawning journalists eager to report the details of the latest transatlantic marriage, he'd had little chance to ponder the topic. Beyond the understandable sting to his pride, her lack of attraction to him and her aversion to bedding him had taken second place to other considerations, like securing his estates. But afterward, alone together here at Highclyffe, it had begun to matter a great deal, and for reasons that had nothing to do with pride.

He'd begun to want her, more and more with each day that passed, and by a fortnight after the wedding, the bargain they'd made had begun to seem like Faust's deal.

He'd left early for Africa, a month earlier than they'd arranged, unable to tolerate the impossibility of wanting her and not having her. He even remembered the exact day he reached his limit.

He turned, staring through the open French door to the terrace, and his mind went back five years, to a warm July afternoon and tea laid out for them on that wrought-iron table.

They'd been touring the estate, a long day on horseback when he'd shown her some of the remotest acreage at Highclyffe. Gone all day, with no refreshment other than a few sandwiches at the home farm, they'd decided to have tea on the terrace before going upstairs to change, and Edie's voice, clear and filled with her American common sense came floating to him out of the past.

"Such a shame those acres to the south couldn't be made useful in some way," she said, handing off her black top hat and riding crop to a footman, then taking the chair Stuart had pulled out for her. "For crops, or pasture, or . . . or something. As it is, they're just a swamp."

"It is rather a bog," he agreed, moving to take his own seat across from her. "It's a problem with the slope of the land, you see."

"Can nothing be done about it?"

"We've done what we can." He explained the grading that had been done, the Henry French drains that had been dug, and various other attempts to deal with the problem as she poured tea for them.

"And yet, it's still a swamp," she pointed out as she handed him his cup.

"True," he agreed. "Any further measures would need to be taken by Lord Seaforth, and he won't make any improvements to his land that would also improve mine. He hates me, you see."

"Hates you? But why?"

He shrugged, took a swallow of tea, and leaned back in his chair. "Hating Margraves is a Seaforth family tradition. Back in 1788, the third Duke of Margrave, desperate for money, eloped with one of the Seaforth daughters to Gretna Green. The Seaforth version is that she was kidnapped, and it caused an enormous scandal. The relations between our families have been hostile ever since."

"But that's silly!"

"Possibly, but that's how things are. I tried several times to heal the breach while Seaforth and I were at Cambridge, but Seaforth wasn't having any. So, the feud, and the bog, remain."

"But that bog is a breeding ground for mosquitoes. Not to mention disease. Why, he has a pasture full of sheep just there! He's risking an outbreak of typhoid, or cholera, or any number of other contagions!"

"I agree, but what will you? As I said, it's how things are."

She made an exclamation of impatience at his repetition of that statement. "What if I just bought the useless land on his side? Then it could all be graded properly, couldn't it?"

He laughed, making her pause to look at him over her teacup, a frown of puzzlement crinkling between her browns. "Why are you laughing?"

" 'What if I just bought it,' she says with all the confidence of the wealthy American."

Her frown deepened slightly. "Are you making fun of me?"

"Perhaps a little." He smiled and set aside

his tea. Leaning forward, he went on, "Many Margraves have offered to buy that acreage — at least when our family's in funds. But no Seaforth will ever sell them to us."

"You could try."

"I already did. A week before we were married. Seaforth refused."

"Oh, for heaven's sake, this is absurd." She fell silent, and he could see her practical mind turning to find a solution. "What if someone else bought that land?" she asked after a moment.

"Seaforth might be persuaded to sell it to someone else, but who'd buy it? Land's a dismal investment these days, especially a sliver like that. Shoehorned between two estates, it's no use to anyone."

"Hmm . . . I believe Madison & Moore could be persuaded to buy it." Her lips curved in a tiny smile at his blank look. "Seaforth would never have to know that Madison & Moore, Incorporated, is one of my father's many companies."

"By God, that might actually work." He laughed. "You assured me you had brains, Edie, but you didn't tell me you were brilliant!"

She laughed, too, at the outrageous compliment, giving him a wide, radiant smile across the table, and all of a sudden, he couldn't move. It was every bit as riveting as the feeling he'd experienced the first time he'd ever seen her, but for a different reason. The first night, he'd been riveted by the sense that he was looking at something out of the common way. But this time, something else pinned him in place. When Edie smiled and laughed, it lit up her whole countenance, showed the gold sparks in her green eyes, and shattered the touch-me-not shield that usually enveloped her. Like a light illuminating the dark, a plain girl was suddenly beautiful.

His throat went dry, his pulses quickened, and, like a dam breaking, desire flooded through him. Until now, he'd been able to suppress it, ignore it, keep it at bay, but this time, it was so sudden and so overwhelming that it refused to be suppressed. He couldn't breathe, couldn't think, couldn't do anything but stare helplessly at the woman across the table as lust spread unchecked through every part of his body.

*This is my wife,* he thought, and at that moment, he'd have given anything to see her laughing like that, naked, amid a snowy pile of bedsheets.

"What a beautiful smile you've got," he said without thinking. "That's a sight I wouldn't mind waking up to first thing in the morning."

Her smile faded away slowly, and as he watched it go, he wondered if right now her heart was pounding as hard as his, if her body had the same burning ache as his and her mind the same torrid thoughts.

Her eyes, such a clear, pretty green, were wide with shock, but there was no jeweled hardness in their depths. Her hand lifted to touch the side of her neck, a hint of color washed into her pale cheeks, and he knew she felt, at least a little, what he was feeling. "Shall we, Edie?" he asked softly, rolling the dice. "We are married, after all."

She sucked in a sharp breath, her body stiffened, and he saw a wall come up between them like a physical barrier. "You gave me your word," she said, her voice low, cold, and withering, and any hope he'd persuade her to a tumble in the sheets went utterly out the window.

He'd left the next day without seeing her smile again. Sometimes, at night, sitting outside his tent in Kenya, he'd thought of her face across the tea table, soft with desire for that one fleeting moment, and he'd wondered what his life might have been like if he'd negotiated a different sort of deal, if he hadn't been so desperate to accept the

116

one she'd offered.

Now, as he stared at the wrought-iron table and remembered that day, he reminded himself that he had the chance now he hadn't taken then. He'd changed over the years, and so had she. However devastated she might have been as a girl of eighteen, six years was surely long enough to get over a broken heart.

There was passion inside his wife. He'd sensed it the night they met, and he'd seen it that day on the terrace. Brief glimpses, perhaps, but he knew enough about women to know he hadn't imagined it. He just had to figure out how to ignite that passion so that it burned for him.

Time was his ally. Despite her defiant declaration, it would be impossible for Edie to avoid him every hour of every day for the rest of their lives. They would be living in the same house, eating at the same table, reading in the same library, having tea at that same wrought-iron table. Bit by bit, if he was patient, he would capture her attention, break down her resistance, and light her fire.

It was just, he told himself, a matter of time.

"She's done what?" He looked up from the

plate of kidneys and bacon Wellesley had just placed before him, the butler's answer to his inquiry about Edie's whereabouts sufficiently astonishing that breakfast was forgotten. "She's gone to London?"

"She has, Your Grace. She departed on the early train at half past eight this morning."

He glanced at the clock, verifying that the train had gone nearly an hour ago. "Did she say anything? Offer a reason for going? Leave instructions what's to be done with Joanna? Where is Joanna, by the way? And what about the governess?"

"The duchess had a cable from Mrs. Simmons yesterday evening just before dinner. It seems that the governess disembarked the train at King's Lynn, but forwarded Miss Jewell's things on to Willowbank and will be returning by tomorrow's train. The duchess, however, chose to have Miss Jewell accompany her to town, and she left a letter for Mrs. Simmons with further instructions."

"I see." If avoiding him was Edie's strategy, she was doing a fine job of it so far. She'd had dinner in her room and remained there for the entire evening, and now, she was off to town. If she intended to make a habit of dealing with him by continually running away, his goal of a true marriage between them would be tedious business. "Did Her Grace give a reason for going or say how long she would be gone?"

"No, Your Grace. She simply said she fancied a trip to town. However, this may help to elucidate matters." Wellesley pulled a folded slip of writing paper from the breast pocket of his jacket and handed it to Stuart. "From Miss Jewell. She asked me to give it to you as she was leaving."

"Ah." The letter was not sealed, simply folded in thirds, leading Stuart to conclude it had been composed in a hurry. Unfolding it, he scanned the few lines and found his guess confirmed.

*We're off to London. She says she's seeing Mr. Keating on business, which doesn't usually take long, but this time, she's taking Snuffles, so it could be a while. Mrs. Simmons is to follow us in a day or two and take me from London down to Kent. You've got to come save me. I'll send word to your club where we're staying when I know. No time for more. Joanna.*

Stuart had a suspicion of just what business Edie intended to discuss with Keating, and if he was right, everything was about to get far more complicated. Grimly, he re-folded the letter, put it in his pocket, and picked up his knife and fork as he considered what his next move should be.

"Wellesley, who or what is Snuffles?" he asked as he resumed eating his breakfast.

"That would be Her Grace's dog, sir."

He didn't even know Edie had a pet. Another of the many things he didn't know about the woman he had married. "When did she acquire a dog?"

"Oh, it must be about four years ago now, Your Grace. She found it — by the side of the road, if memory serves. It had been injured. A puppy, it was, just a little bit of a thing."

"Ah." Joanna had assured him Edie had a soft spot for wounded creatures, and here was some evidence of the fact. "Mixed-breed stray, I imagine?"

"Oh, no, sir. It was one of the terrier pups from the home farm, but Mr. Mulvaney wanted to drown it, for it was badly injured, and he didn't think it would ever be a proper ratter. Well, Her Grace wouldn't hear of that, and took it upon herself to care for it."

He smiled. "The duchess has a soft heart, I've been told."

"She does, sir. Not that you'd know it sometimes. Raked Travis over the coals a month ago good and proper, then dismissed him with no letter of character."

"Travis?" He frowned, not recalling the name. "Who is Travis?"

"Second under-gardener. A new man, hired not long after you left."

Stuart noted in some amusement that to Wellesley, and to most English minds, having only five years of employment was considered being "new."

"What did Travis do that impelled the duchess to sack him?" he asked, curious.

"The second housemaid," he said in a low voice filled with significance. "It was rather a dustup. Mrs. Gates was inclined to dismiss her, and she consulted the Dowager Duchess, who was here at the time. The Dowager agreed that the housemaid needed to go, but the duchess got wind of it, and she wasn't having it." Wellesley leaned closer in a confidential manner and murmured, "She countermanded the Dowager Duchess."

"I'd have liked to see Mama's reaction to that," Stuart said, grinning around a forkful of eggs. "Go on."

"The duchess kept Ellen on, but dismissed Travis. The duchess," he added with a look of apology, "doesn't always understand the way things are."

"Quite so." Stuart suppressed his smile with an effort. "Things are different in

121

America, I imagine."

"I daresay." Those two words made short shrift of how things were done in America. "The Dowager Duchess attempted to explain to the duchess that dismissing the male servant whilst keeping the female servant wasn't quite the way things were done in an English household."

"And what did Her Grace say to that?"

Wellesley gave a dignified sniff. "She said, 'It might be an English household, but it is run by an American.' "

Again, Stuart had to suppress a smile. "Poor Mama. That ruffled her feathers, I'll wager."

"It would not be my place to say, sir. But the Dowager Duchess no longer stays long when she visits Highclyffe. The duchess, as I'm sure you know, has her own unique way of doing things. Still," he added, his face brightening a bit, "now that you are home, I'm sure things will soon be returning to the proper way."

"I doubt it," he said cheerfully. "I've never been one for the propers, Wellesley. You ought to know that by now." His breakfast finished, Stuart set down his knife and fork. "When is the next train to London, do you know?"

"Half past eleven, sir," the butler answered

at once. "But it doesn't go straight on, I'm afraid. You'll have to change at Cambridge."

"Your efficiency never ceases to amaze me, Wellesley." He pulled out his pocket watch and verified that he had plenty of time. "Have Edward pack a suitcase, will you? I'm taking that train."

"One suitcase? So you will not be staying in London long, then?"

"No, and neither will Her Grace." He returned his watch to his pocket, tossed aside his napkin, and stood up. "Not if I have my way about it."

# CHAPTER 6

Edie stared in dismay at the rotund, gray-haired little man on the other side of the large oak desk. "So I've no grounds? None at all? Not even . . ." She paused, her face growing hot. "Not even nonconsummation?"

"I'm afraid not. I know of no cases where a lawful marriage has been successfully set aside for that reason. Not in the past few centuries, anyway."

Edie reminded herself that she shouldn't be surprised by this information. Stuart himself had told her the very same thing before they married. But somehow, in coming here, she'd hoped Stuart had been mistaken. "You said to your knowledge there hasn't been a successful case. Could you have missed one?"

"Some court decisions do escape my notice," the lawyer admitted. "I would be happy to research the matter more deeply if you wish, though I am not at all optimistic about the chance of finding case law in support of an annulment."

"I understand. Do it anyway. What about . . ." She paused and swallowed hard. "What about divorce?"

Mr. Keating rubbed his nose and sat back with a sigh. "Even less likely to be granted, I'm afraid. As to grounds, you might make a case for adultery — if it's true, of course, and if you could provide names, dates, et cetera. But while adultery is sufficient grounds for a man, it is not the same for women. A wife needs two causes to divorce her husband. You would need something else along with adultery."

Her dismay deepened into desperation. "Desertion? Could that be considered a secondary cause?"

"But the duke has come back, so there has been no desertion. In the eyes of the law, he has simply returned from an extended trip abroad. And since he wishes to reconcile . . ." Mr. Keating shook his head. "You've no chance there, I'm afraid."

"Could he be persuaded to divorce me?"

"Your Grace . . ." The lawyer's voice trailed off into a sigh. He waited, but as she continued to look at him steadily, he went on, "If he chose to, yes, he could bring a suit, but there would still have to be grounds. Adultery, for example."

"Is there nothing I can do?" Her voice sounded terribly faint to her own ears, even within the hushed confines of Mr. Keating's paneled office walls. "Nothing at all?"

The lawyer gave her an unhappy look across the desk. "I realize the duke's reappearance in your life after so long must be a shock, but that shock will pass. Since he wishes to reconcile, I suggest you allow him to do so."

"You don't understand," she said, forcing the words out past the fear that felt like a stone in her chest.

"Many marriages are difficult, and often unhappy, but divorce is never a satisfactory solution. It is a messy, protracted, disgraceful business. Even if you had sufficient grounds, it would take you years to successfully break your marriage tie, and both your names would be dragged through the mud. And afterward, your position in society would be destroyed, your title stripped from you, and your reputation disgraced."

"So I would be ruined by a man, not once in my life, but twice," she muttered bitterly.

"I am afraid so."

"What about an American divorce?"

"You might be able to obtain a divorce in

126

several of the American states, but the resulting destruction of your reputation would be the same, and such a divorce would never be valid in any part of the British Empire."

She looked away from the compassion in the lawyer's face. "I see."

"Is there no way that you and His Grace could work things out?"

*I want children.*

Edie's hands clenched around the handbag in her lap so tightly her fingers began to ache. "There is no possibility of that, Mr. Keating. What if I leave him? Can he force me back? Can he force me to . . . to . . ." She paused, for she could not articulate her deepest fear. She simply could not. She could only stare helplessly at the lawyer, her face growing hot, her panic growing deeper.

Thankfully, Mr. Keating understood her question without further elucidation. "That's a nebulous area of law, I'm afraid. As your husband, he has certain rights." The lawyer gave a cough. "Rights of a conjugal nature."

A roar began in Edie's ears. The smooth leather back of her chair suddenly felt like the hard stone wall of a summerhouse. She heard the rending of delicate muslin drawers, and the sound of her own sobs. The scent of Frederick's bourbon-laced breath and eau de cologne hit her nostrils, and bile rose in her throat.

She lurched to her feet, and the room began to spin. Her handbag fell to the floor with a thud as she grasped for the edge of the desk to steady herself.

"Your Grace!" Mr. Keating jumped up. "Are you all right?" He circled the desk to come to her aid, but when he put a hand beneath her elbow, she pulled away.

"Of course," Edie lied, stepping out from the confined space between her chair and the lawyer's desk. "I just felt a bit light-headed for a moment," she said as she walked toward the window. "I'm perfectly well now, but I feel the need to move about a bit. It helps me think. Please, do sit down."

Mr. Keating picked up her handbag for her and put it on the desk, then he returned to his seat as Edie stood by the window. It was a hot August day in London, which meant the air wasn't at its most pleasant, but she didn't mind that, for the odors of the city smothered those of bourbon and cologne. She stood there for several moments, taking slow, deep breaths.

"I can't live with my husband," she said at last, and turned from the window. "How can I prevent it?"

"The only sure way is a legal separation of bed and board. Financial freedom is not a factor in your case, of course, but a legal separation would enable you to live apart without the censure of society."

In command of herself once again, but still restless, Edie walked to the opposite end of the room, where a wall of shelves was lined with legal volumes and deed boxes. "Would we need to have the court validate such a separation?"

"No. Private deeds of separation are fairly common."

"How quickly could you draw one up, Mr. Keating?"

"In a matter of days. But there are several things you must keep in mind, Your Grace. First, a private separation would probably be valid only as long as you remain chaste. If you were ever to take a lover, the duke could proclaim your adultery and invalidate the agreement."

"That will not be an issue."

"Quite so, quite so," he hastened to say. "But Your Grace, I'm not certain you appreciate the loneliness that comes to separated wives —"

"My husband was gone for five years," she interrupted. "I can assure you, I know what separation entails."

Mr. Keating opened his mouth, looking as if to say more on the subject, but something in her expression must have told him to let it go. "Very well, but one other problem still remains."

"What's that?"

"He would have to agree. Without his consent, no legal separation is possible without a court proceeding. As we've discussed, no court is likely to rule in your favor without sufficient grounds."

Edie sighed. "And just how am I to persuade him to consent?"

But even as she asked the question, Edie thought of the resolute gravity of Stuart's face, and she feared there was no answer. Still, she had to try, for he wanted what she could not give.

"Draw up that separation agreement, Mr. Keating," she said, striding to the desk to pick up her handbag. "I'll persuade him to sign it," she added as she turned away. "I don't know how, but I will find a way."

How she managed to speak with such surety, Edie didn't know, but, thankfully, it was not Mr. Keating's place to point out futilities. He nodded, and with that, she started for the door. Her stride was rapid, for she felt the need to move, to walk, to escape the chains she could feel tightening around her. Mr. Keating's voice stopped her before she could depart.

"Your Grace?"

She paused to look over her shoulder at the man who had been in charge of her private legal affairs since her engagement. "Yes?"

"Are you sure this is what you really want?"

"What I want is to be free, Mr. Keating. Free to control my own life. It's all I've ever wanted. This is as close as I shall be able to get, it seems."

With that, she left, closing the door behind her.

Upon leaving Mr. Keating's offices, Edie did not hail a hansom to return her to her hotel. She and Joanna were meeting her friend Lady Trubridge for tea, but that wasn't for an hour, and Edie was glad.

Just now, she felt like a panicked bird fluttering around a closed room, banging at the windows and yet never able to find a way out, no matter how she tried. She needed time for that panic to pass. She needed time to think.

She crossed Trafalgar Square, walked up Northumberland Avenue, and started up the Embankment along the river. It was a hot afternoon, but she walked at a rapid clip, scarcely noticing the sultry air, the dank smell of the river, or the lack of any breeze.

The only thing she noticed was the desperation that clawed at her insides. Thousands of miles apart and six years away, but the shadow of Frederick Van Hausen seemed to hover right beside her. She quickened her steps along the Embankment, faster and faster, until she was practically running, even though she knew one could not outrun a memory. One could not outrun fear. At least, she'd never been able to.

She stopped at last beside Cleopatra's Needle, panting, sweaty, her sides aching so badly in the tight confines of her corset that she simply could not go any farther without a rest. She glanced around, and when she spied a bench there overlooking the river, she sank onto it, wondering in despair what she was going to do.

She could not live with Stuart, or any man. Just the thought of it was almost more than she could bear. Other women felt arousal, welcomed lovemaking, wanted children. But inside of her, such desires were dead, killed by a brutal act and a brutish man, and though she'd scrubbed herself raw afterward, she'd been unable to wash it away. She'd told no one, but she'd been unable to prevent the gossip about her, though how it had started, she still didn't know. They'd been seen going in, or coming out, or Frederick had bragged, or — oh, hell, what did it matter now? The damage was done, and it could never be undone.

She'd thought Frederick wanted to be alone with her because he actually liked the tall, gawky girl with red hair and freckles who lived at the wrong end of Madison Avenue. Stupid, stupid, stupid.

Edie stared out at the Thames, and the sun glinting off the water must have been terribly bright, for it stung her eyes. She blinked, and everything blurred, and she realized it wasn't the sun's glittering reflection that burned her eyes — it was tears. Furious, she blinked again, forcing them back.

She shook her head, working to clear away any useless thoughts of desperation, self-pity, or despair. She could not think about the past, she had to deal with now and plan for the future.

Her reasoning mind told her that Stuart was not Frederick. He was a different sort of man altogether, but she knew that didn't matter. He was still a man, and he was her husband, and now, he wanted what she couldn't freely give him. He had the right to her body, and there would come a time, somewhere, somehow, when he would take it. She could not let that happen.

If a legal separation was the only way to prevent it, she would have to find a way to make him sign one. The question was how.

The first, and easiest, possibility was a threat to cut off his income. She held the purse strings, and if she shut them tight, he might knuckle under. If that failed, she could do the opposite. She could offer him more money, hundreds of thousands of pounds — all she had, if that would persuade him.

If those options failed, she would have to go abroad.

Her heart sank at the thought of leaving Highclyffe, and Almsley, and Dunlop, and all the other ducal estates. She'd refurbished those houses, redesigned their gardens, invigorated their villages, and improved their lands. The idea of leaving it all behind tore at her heart, but if Stuart wouldn't agree to a separation, she'd have to go away.

If going abroad became her only option, she would inform Stuart that she intended to return to New York and fight for a divorce from there, but that would only be to throw him off the scent, for she had no more intention of living near Frederick Van Hausen now than she had had five years ago.

No, she'd tell Stuart she was going home to New York. She'd buy the passage, just to make it convincing. But then, she'd take Joanna and slip away somewhere else — France, South America, Egypt, even Shanghai — it didn't matter where. Daddy wouldn't like it, but he wouldn't tell Stuart her whereabouts if she asked him not to.

She couldn't hide from her husband forever. She knew that. But maybe, once he understood that her refusal to live with him was final, he'd give up this whole crazy idea and let her go. Besides, with his income cut off, how long could he chase her around the world?

Her spirits revived a little at these plans, her sense of control over her life began to return, and she stood up, banishing any further inclination to feel sorry for herself. She would continue to be mistress of her own life. She would be no victim, not of her circumstances, not of Fate, and certainly not of any man. Not ever again.

When Edie reached the hotel, she did not go in. Instead, she walked several blocks beyond to the nearby Cooks office. There, upon inquiring about ocean liners to New York, she learned that the next one departed out of Liverpool eleven days hence. She reserved a stateroom suite, paid the deposit, and asked that the billets be forwarded to her at the Savoy.

Arriving back at the hotel, she paused in the Savoy's luxurious tearoom to inquire about Lady Trubridge, for it was nearly half past four. Upon learning the marchioness had not yet arrived, Edie continued on up to her rooms to freshen up and fetch Joanna.

When she entered her suite, she found her sister already dressed for tea and waiting for her. "At last," Joanna cried, jumping up from her chair and tossing aside the book she'd been reading. "I was growing worried. Where have you been?"

"I told you I had to meet with Mr. Keating."

"For three hours? Estate business never takes you this long."

Edie's gaze swerved away. She'd been vague about the reasons for their trip to town and her meeting with Keating. She knew Joanna would have to be told the situation and that it was likely they would soon be leaving for parts as yet unknown. Still, there was no point in bringing up the topic now, not when they were about to go down to tea. And she hadn't given up hope of convincing Stuart to abandon his intentions. "Yes, well, I went for a walk. It's a nice afternoon."

Joanna, understandably, looked at her as if she'd gone a bit wrong in the head. "It's London in the summer. It stinks."

No arguing with that. "Don't use the word 'stinks,' dearest," she corrected instead. "If you must refer to smell at all, use 'malodorous.' It's more ladylike. I'm going to change, and we'll go to tea."

She left the sitting room, only to find that her maid was not in her room, dressing room, or bath, and she stuck her head through the doorway into the sitting room. "Where is Reeves?"

Joanna looked up from her book, which she had resumed reading. "She took Snuffles down for a walk. She had to, since he was dancing in circles. They'll be right back."

"Well, you'll have to help me then. We've no time to wait for her, or we'll be late to tea."

Joanna followed her back into her bedroom and helped her out of her wrinkled green serge walking suit and limp undergarments. The Savoy, which had only opened a few weeks earlier, was the height of modernity, and the bath of her suite had both hot and cold running water laid on, enabling her to easily sponge away the sweat of her panicky race along the Victoria Embankment. Within ten minutes, she'd slipped into fresh undergarments and crisp frock of lavender silk. Joanna was just doing up the last button at her back when a knock sounded on the door of the suite.

"That's probably Reeves," Joanna said. "I'll bet she forgot her key. She's always doing that when we stay in hotels." She went to let the maid in, but a few minutes later, it was not Reeves who entered the bedroom. Instead, Joanna returned.

Edie caught sight of her sister in the cheval mirror and stopped fluffing the leg o' mutton sleeves of her dress in surprise. "Where are Reeves and Snuffles?"

But even as she spoke, she noted the strange expression on her sister's face and the sheaf of papers in her hand, and she knew it was not her maid who had come to the door. She cursed Cook's for being so efficient.

"Why are we going to New York?" Joanna asked, holding up the sheaf of papers. "These are steamship tickets."

Edie drew a deep breath. "We may go, or

138

we may not. It depends."

"Depends on what?"

"It's complicated, dearest."

"You're leaving him, aren't you?" The dismay in the girl's voice was unmistakable, and given that she did not want to go to boarding school, that dismay was rather surprising. "You're running away."

"We may not go," she reminded. "And even if we did, I wouldn't call it running away."

"What would you call it?"

A knock on the door saved her from having to answer. "Now, that's sure to be Reeves," she said, and brushed past her sister to head for the front door.

Joanna, of course, couldn't let the topic go. "It is running away," she said, following Edie into the sitting room. "And it won't solve anything."

"That's a fine argument from the girl who jumped off a train to avoid going to school," Edie countered, and reached for the door handle. "You should be agreeing with me," she added over her shoulder as she opened the door. "Running away is sometimes a perfectly acceptable strategy."

She turned, expecting to see Reeves, prepared to tease her maid about forgetting her key, but the words died on her lips, for

139

the person standing in the corridor was not Reeves. Instead, she found the man she was trying to avoid, the man who'd once been her salvation but who was rapidly becoming her nemesis.

"You!" she cried. "What are you doing here?"

"Is it me you're running away from, Edie? What?" he added at her groan of aggravation. "Did you really think going off to London would be enough to rid you of me?"

"Obviously not," she acknowledged with a sigh. "I should have bought tickets to Africa."

# CHAPTER 7

Stuart was not the least bit surprised by his wife's less-than-enthusiastic greeting, and he chose to let her dismay roll off him like water off a duck. Having armor plating was, he felt, going to prove useful in the coming days.

"Good afternoon, darling," he said with a smile. And though he hadn't a shred of hope she'd smile back, as he watched an answering frown etch its way between her brows, he couldn't help thinking wistfully of that day on the terrace.

"You have become the proverbial bad penny," she accused. "How did you know where to find me?"

"Wellesley, of course. It is one of the many duties of a British butler to keep his master informed about domestic matters. Being my wife, you are very much a domestic matter."

"There is no way Wellesley could have

known I was staying at the Savoy!"

"No, that's true, but even at this time of year, London is full of people who adore gossip. Shall we just say a little bird told me?"

"Little bird, my eye," she muttered, and turned to the girl standing by the bedroom door, who immediately pasted on an expression of wide-eyed innocence that Stuart suspected was quite familiar to Edie. "More like an interfering little sister."

Obviously realizing the jig was up, Joanna abandoned any pretense of innocence. "I thought Stuart should know where we were. In case . . . in case anything happened. What if you were run over by an omnibus or something? It could happen," she added, as Edie made a sound of derision.

"Of all the maddening, interfering, impossible sisters in the world," Edie muttered, "the good Lord just had to saddle me with you."

"And Daddy's in New York," the girl went on, dropping the sheaf of papers in her hand onto a nearby table, papers that to Stuart looked suspiciously like ocean-liner billets. "If anything happened to you, I'd be all alone in London, with no one to turn to."

"Your concern for my possible demise is overwhelming," Edie said dryly. "I ought to

142

tan your backside."

"Now, Edie," Stuart put in behind her, impelled to come to the aid of his ally. "Don't be so hard on Joanna. She was only trying to do a harmless spot of matchmaking."

Edie cast a wrathful glance at him over one shoulder, but before she could reply, a sound behind him caught his attention, and he turned to find Edie's maid standing in the corridor. In her hand was a dog lead, and at the other end, sniffing his shoe, was a small brown ball of fluff.

"Reeves," he greeted the pale, somber-faced woman in black with a nod, then he looked down. "This must be Snuffles."

At the sound of his name, the Norwich terrier looked up, planted his bum on the carpet of the corridor, and gave a bark of resounding agreement.

"Hullo, old man." Stuart bent down, sticking out his fist for further canine inspection.

Snuffles took a sniff, and his docked tail wiggled against the carpet in approval. Edie, however, didn't seem inclined to allow them to become further acquainted.

"Reeves, here you are at last," she said, and leaned through the doorway to grasp the maid's arm, but Stuart spoke before she could pull the servant inside the suite.

"Reeves, will you escort Miss Jewell down to the tearoom? I believe Lady Trubridge is waiting there," he added, ignoring Edie's sound of protest. "And then take Snuffles for a walk, if you please."

"He's just had a walk," Edie said. "He doesn't need another."

He turned, and through the doorway, he met his wife's aggravated gaze with a resolute one of his own. "Reeves, go," he said, without taking his eyes from Edie. "I'd like to speak with the duchess alone."

The maid hesitated, but only for a moment. The command of a duke outweighed that of a duchess, and she knew it. "Of course, Your Grace."

Joanna followed, and as she passed Stuart to go with the maid, she paused to give him an anxious look. He winked in response, and she must have found that reassuring, for the worry vanished from her face, and she followed the maid down the corridor without any further hesitation.

He waited until she and the maid had vanished around the corner with Snuffles in tow before returning his attention to the woman in the doorway, who was glaring at him, arms folded, apparently with no inclination to let him in.

"So Joanna is your spy within the gates?" she asked. "That explains how you knew where to find me. How did you manage to win her over?"

"Believe it or not, Joanna likes me."

She sniffed, unimpressed. "I suppose you told her you'll manage to keep her out of school if she helps you?"

He had no intention of betraying his ally. "I tell no tales," he said, and quickly changed the subject. Looking past her shoulder, he gave a whistle. "This place certainly lives up to its reputation. Even in Nairobi, everyone was buzzing about its being the height of luxury. Aubusson carpet, pink marble fireplace, crystal chandeliers. Those are probably genuine Ming vases on the mantel, so I should advise not throwing any of them at my head though I daresay you can stand the expense. The place is quite posh, isn't it?"

He waited, but when she didn't speak, he gestured to the room behind her. "Perhaps you should invite me in? Surely you don't wish to talk with me in the hotel corridor."

"I don't wish to talk with you at all."

"Edie, we have to discuss things. Although running away from me appears to be your strategy, it won't work forever. And if that isn't a good enough reason for you, remember that the more resistance you display toward my attempts to reconcile, the more dismal your chances are of winning any sort of legal battle with me later on. Courts hate intransigent wives."

She made a face. "I'm hoping my intransigence, as you put it, will impel you to realize the futility of your efforts."

He propped one shoulder against the doorjamb. "And what is your degree of success with that tactic?"

She sighed. After a moment, she stepped back and opened the door wide to let him in. "You have five minutes," she said as she turned away. "Then I have to join Lady Trubridge for tea. I won't keep her waiting longer than that because of you."

"Five minutes? Excellent," he said, with all the appearance of good cheer as he followed her into the suite. "Plenty of time for a drink."

"Perhaps." She turned to face him. "But that hardly matters since I'm not offering you a drink."

"More's the pity," he replied ruefully. "If your afternoon here in town was as enjoyable as my afternoon in a hot, stuffy train, we could both use a spot of whisky right now."

"I don't like whisky. I prefer tea." She

made an exaggerated show of looking at the clock on the mantel. "You have four and a half minutes."

"Don't worry, Edie. You have more time than you think. As I said earlier, I encountered Lady Trubridge in the tearoom already. I explained that I needed to speak with you, and that in consequence, you would be late. She quite understood."

"You did what? What gives you the right to be so high-handed?"

"Well . . ." He paused, giving her an apologetic look. "We are married. As your husband, I have the right to be high-handed. Speaking of Joanna," he added, cutting off her sound of outrage, "if you are running away, why are you taking her with you? Isn't she supposed to go off to school?"

"I suppose you shall try to persuade me against it with some British nonsense about how girls don't need to go away to school, or how it isn't wise to give them too much education." She held up one hand, palm toward him. "If so, don't. I've already had that particular lecture from your mother."

This, he decided, was the perfect opportunity to fulfill his promise to his young sister-in-law. "Regardless of what my mother's opinion may be, I think having Joanna go away to school is an excellent idea. I find higher education for girls quite commendable. Besides," he added, "with Joanna away, you and I shall have plenty of opportunity to be alone together."

She gave a laugh. "You and I will not be spending any time alone together."

"Of course we will. We are married."

"Stop saying that!"

"No sense ignoring the truth. As I told you five years ago, marriage is something that can't simply be undone. I'm sure Keating reiterated the point for you earlier today."

"How do you know I've met with Keating? Joanna again, I suppose. So is that why you're here? To find out what my attorney has advised and what I intend to do? I'm sure Keating didn't tell you anything, and I shan't either."

"I don't need to be told. I can guess. Keating advised you that there are no grounds whatsoever for annulment and insufficient grounds for divorce. I'll go out on a limb and add that he probably also strongly advised you against bringing either action, given the small chance of success and the certainty of scandal."

She stirred, looking uneasy, confirming that his enumeration of her attorney's opinion was accurate. "I intend to obtain a legal separation."

"Now I really do need a drink." He limped past her to the nearby liquor cabinet, set aside his walking stick, and poured himself a generous measure of liquor from the decanter. Fortified by a swallow of the excellent whisky, he turned around, glass in hand, to resume discussion of the subject at hand. "You're serious? You intend to pursue legal action?"

"Not if you stick to what we agreed."

"And as I've already told you, the life I had in Africa is over for me. I'm not going back, and I don't want to."

"You don't have to return to Africa if you don't wish to. You can live anywhere you choose, as long as it isn't with me. I'll still provide you an income. In fact, I'll double it. Hell, I'll triple it," she added, rubbing four fingers across her forehead, "if you'll just go away."

"I don't care about the money."

"You cared once." She lifted her head, defiance in her eyes. "You might care again if I cut you off."

"No, Edie, I wouldn't, because for me, money isn't the point. And besides, I've invested all the income you've already provided me and did rather a fine job of it, if I do say so myself. I managed to buy into some very profitable gold mines in Tanzania, as well as some diamond mines, shale fields, and railways. All are paying healthy dividends. I don't need your money."

Her slim shoulders sagged a bit, making it clear she'd hoped a financial threat would be enough to dissuade him. But she rallied almost at once. "Are those dividends enough to support your family?" she asked. "And what about Highclyffe and the other estates? I'll cut them off, too, Stuart. All of them."

"You'd do that? You'd really let it all go? Turn your back on everything you've built here? You'd stop providing an income to the villages and employment for the people who live there? You would really destroy everything in their lives?"

That hit a nerve, he could tell. Her face twisted. "I'm not the one destroying everything!" she cried. "You are!"

"No, I want to make sure all your efforts weren't a waste of time. Don't you see?"

She folded her arms, pressed her lips together, and didn't answer, making it clear she didn't see at all. Resistance was in every line of her, in her pose, in the stiff rigidity of her body, in the distance between them. They stood only fifteen feet apart, and yet, the gap between them seemed wider than the thousands of miles between England

and Kenya.

He swallowed the rest of his whisky, then set aside his empty glass, reached for his stick, and began walking toward her. It hurt after the cramped hours in the train, but he knew that if they were ever going to work through this, someone had to take the first steps. Hadn't he known all along that that person would have to be him?

"Edie," he said as he approached, "it's admirable what you've done with the estates, but what did you do it all for? I'm offering you — both of us — the chance to build something even greater than what you've already accomplished."

"And what is that?"

He stopped in front of her. "A family to leave it to. What good is Highclyffe, or any of the other estates we own, if we can't pass them on to our children?"

"I can't give you what you want!" Her voice wobbled on the last word, and she looked away. "I can't."

"Can't? Or won't?"

"Does it matter?" She walked around him and stalked to the liquor cabinet, obviously feeling that the conversation required a drink after all. "Mr. Keating said a legal separation is possible," she said as she poured whisky into a glass. She downed it all in one gulp, slammed down the glass, and turned to face him. "I intend to fight for one."

"You haven't a prayer of obtaining it without my consent."

"I don't need your consent if I offer sufficient grounds."

"Which you don't have."

"Don't I? How about adultery? Or shall you claim you've been celibate for the past five years?"

"Doesn't matter," he said, happy to sidestep that rather sticky wicket. "A legal separation is similar to divorce, and a woman needs two causes to have any chance at separation without her husband's consent. What's your other?"

"How about desertion?"

He felt compelled to point out the obvious. "But I'm right here, ready to reconcile and be a true husband to you —"

"With no regard at all for what I want!"

"That's not true, but even if it were, it doesn't signify. No court will accept desertion as grounds to separate unless I leave the country, you beg me to come back, and I refuse. That scenario is not going to happen." He once again started toward her. "And even if you were to succeed in obtaining a separation without my consent, think of the price you'll pay. You'll keep your title, but you'll lose everything else. Access to Highclyffe and all the other estates, of course, and your social position. A legal fight with me will cause you to be snubbed by many social acquaintances. And what of Joanna?" He halted in front of her. "Are you prepared to hurt her chances in society by forcing a separation?"

Her lips trembled, telling him he'd hit a tender spot. Her eyes shimmered, not with the hardness of resistance but with sudden, unshed tears. "My God, I'm trapped," she whispered, staring at him. "Trapped in a net of my own making."

"Is it such a bad net, Edie?" he asked gently and reached out to touch her face. "Being married to me?"

"You don't understand." She jerked at the contact, evading his touch. "You don't understand at all."

"No, I don't. Why are you fighting this so hard? Is it —" He paused, but it had to be said. "Is it this?" he asked, gesturing to his thigh with his walking stick. "I'm not the man I was when we met, I know, but —"

"It's not your leg," she cried. "Don't be a goose. It has nothing to do with you at all!"

He'd already suspected that, but he felt a

rush of relief just the same. "Then what is it?"

Her tears vanished. Her jaw set. "Let it go, Stuart."

"I don't think I will." He tossed aside his stick. "What's the real reason you're so opposed to a true marriage between us?"

She looked away. That stubborn jaw trembled, and her lips parted, but she didn't answer.

"I'm not such a bad chap, you know." He ducked his head to look into her eyes, smiling a little. "I'm intelligent, good at conversation, well-bred, easy to live with. Some women have even considered me quite charming and not half-bad to look at."

"Have they indeed?"

"You must think so, too. After all, one look, and you followed me out to the maze and blatantly proposed marriage to me."

"Not to take anything away from your charms, which I'm sure are considerable, but I chose you because you suited my purpose. That's all."

"You didn't find me attractive?" He leaned closer. "Not even a little?"

"You could have been five feet tall with a potbelly and bad teeth, and I'd have still done it."

"Then why didn't you?"

She frowned at the question, taken aback. "What do you mean?"

"You'd been in London for a full season, with Lady Featherstone introducing you to every peer in town, many of them in just as dire straits as I was."

"They weren't all going off to another continent."

"No, but I'll wager any number of them could have been persuaded to do so for the money you offered me. Yet, you admitted to me yourself, you'd never made any other man such an offer."

"I would have done if I'd thought of it sooner! But it wasn't until I saw you that I got the idea."

"Just so."

She made a sound of exasperation. "And you think the idea occurred to me because you were just so damned attractive?"

Granted, he'd had precious little feminine companionship the past five years, but not so little that he'd forgotten everything he'd learned in his life about women. She might not have desired him, but she damn well hadn't found him repulsive either. "If I'd been — how did you put it? — five feet tall with bad teeth and a potbelly, I don't think the proposition you made to me would have even occurred to you." Mentally, he crossed

155

his fingers, betting on his knowledge of women, and went on, "I think you were at least a little bit attracted to me the moment you first saw me. I know damned sure I was attracted to you."

"Oh you were not!"

"Indeed, I was. From the moment we met, I thought you were the most fascinating bit of skirt I'd ever seen. I even told you as much, if memory serves."

"Yes, but you didn't mean it."

"Of course I meant it." He gave a laugh at her astonished face. "For God's sake, do you think I'd have married you otherwise?"

"We both know you married me for the money!"

"Your money, as lovely and fortuitous as it was, my sweet, wouldn't have persuaded me to the altar. I knew what my family's financial situation was before I was fifteen, and if money was all I needed to tempt me to matrimony, I'd have married long before we met. No, I married you because although I've known plenty of women, I've never known one quite like you. I've never known one who could make me want her even while she's making it so painfully clear she doesn't want me. That intrigued me and attracted me, partly because — forgive me if I sound conceited — but it was rather a novelty. I wasn't used to it. But when the novelty wore off, the fascination didn't."

A hint of what might have been panic came into her face. "Yet, despite this fascination, you left after only one month, when we had agreed to live together for two."

"You kept talking about when I was leaving. By the end of a month, you were practically shoving me out the door, and a man can only tolerate that sort of situation for so long. Wanting you the way I did, I'd have lost my sanity if I'd lingered any longer. And it wasn't as if I was prepared at the time to give up Africa and stay in England permanently. I wasn't. But those last days at Highclyffe were rather a rough go for me."

"I . . ." She paused and licked her lips as if they were dry. "I didn't know that."

"Yes, well, it's not the sort of thing a man likes to admit. We like to think we're irresistible. Which brings me back to the material point. We're married, I'm home now, and you still haven't told me why you are so opposed to a real marriage between us. And don't tell me it's because of that chap from years ago, for I refuse to believe you're still pining for him."

"Pining?" she echoed, and for a moment, she stared at him, her face blank. But then she shook her head as if coming out of a

157

reverie and spoke. "Oh, but you're wrong. I am still pining for him."

Her words were so unconvincing, a child wouldn't have believed her, and he smiled, relieved to know at least he didn't have some other man's ghost to contend with anymore. "Still heartbroken, are you?"

"Devastated." She took a step back and grimaced as her bum hit the edge of the cabinet behind her, rattling the glasses and decanters. "Crushed. I'll never . . . I'll never love anyone else."

"Never?" He once again closed the distance between them. "Never, as I once told you, is a long time."

She lifted her chin. "Not long enough to want you."

"No?" He paused, studying her face, and oddly enough, what he saw there gave him more optimism about his chances than he'd felt yet. There was resentment in her face, and a hint of panic, but there was also something else: the challenge to prove her wrong, and just maybe, the faint hope he might succeed. "Uh-oh," he murmured. "Now you've done it. You've thrown down the gauntlet."

"What do you mean?"

"No man worth his salt could let such a declaration stand." He met her challenging gaze with one of his own. "I think I can make you want me."

Her eyes narrowed. "Many men think they can make women want them. Some are less than honorable in how they go about it."

"And you think I'm that sort of man?"

"I don't know."

"You damned well do know! Edie, we lived together for a month after we married, and I never once behaved dishonorably. Many a man would have chosen to exercise his conjugal rights after the wedding, promises be damned. But I didn't, did I?"

She didn't answer, but he had no intention of letting it go. "Did I?"

"No," she said at last.

"No, I was very much the gentleman. And as I said, it wasn't easy. Especially that last afternoon on the terrace. I wanted to ravish you over the cucumber sandwiches in the worst way."

She stared at him, and he thought perhaps she'd forgotten that day, but then, he watched the color wash into those pale cheeks, and he realized she knew precisely what he was talking about. His hopes rose another notch.

"You remember, don't you?" he murmured, leaning closer. "I made you smile, and I said I wouldn't mind waking up to that smile —"

"I don't know what you're talking about," she interrupted.

That was a lie, he knew it, and he couldn't stop the grin that spread across his face. "You know exactly what I'm talking about. I think you rather liked the idea of waking up with me."

"Really?" she countered. "As I recall, I shut you up quick."

"So you do remember?"

"Enough to know that I didn't welcome your suggestion in the least," she said, but even as she spoke, the color in her cheeks deepened, and she couldn't hold his gaze.

"Rot. You wanted to. You just weren't ready to admit it to me. Perhaps not even ready to admit it to yourself."

"You have a vivid imagination," she said, staring at his collar. "Have you ever thought of becoming a writer? Because you compose fiction beautifully."

"Is it fiction? Or am I simply recalling inconvenient facts?"

"The only inconvenient fact here is one you can't accept." She looked up, meeting his gaze. "I don't want you. I didn't then, I don't now, and I can't be made to in the future."

He shrugged. "If what you say is true, then

you won't mind putting it to the test. I think despite what you say, you do feel some attraction for me. What's more, I think I can prove it."

"And just how do you intend to do that?"

He considered, lowering his gaze to her pale pink mouth for a moment. "I think a kiss would prove it, don't you?"

Her eyes narrowed. "Try kissing me, Margrave, and I'll slap that conceited smile right off your face."

"No, no, Edie, you misunderstand me. I think I can persuade you to kiss me."

That made her laugh, a full, merry laugh that sounded — unfortunately — quite genuine. "And how long do you think it will take you to perform this miracle?" she asked.

He considered. She'd never agree to a year, or even half a year. "A month?"

"Ten days," she said abruptly. "You have ten days."

"Ten days?" Despite this unexpected capitulation, he felt compelled to voice an objection to the narrow time frame. "Really, Edie, that's hardly sporting."

"Ten days from tomorrow is when the next ocean liner sails out of Liverpool for New York, and I intend to be on it. I've already booked passage."

"New York?" He glanced over at the papers Joanna had dropped on the table, appreciating with some chagrin that they actually were steamship tickets. In all the scenarios he'd conjured of how their reconciliation might go, he'd never considered she would rather go back to America than try to make a life with him. "What about Joanna? Or are you now changing your mind about higher education for girls?"

"I know the British consider Americans terribly uncivilized, but we do have schools on the other side of the Atlantic."

"So running away is your solution? Is that how you handle every crisis in your life?"

She stiffened, showing that shot had gone home, but she refused to be drawn. "Ten days. Take it or leave it."

"I'll take it because I'm sure I'm right."

"Are you indeed?" She paused, studying him, her expression alert and thoughtful. "Sure enough to place a bet on it?"

"A wager? What, you mean money?"

"No, not money."

"What, then?"

She didn't even hesitate. "If I win, you agree to a legal and permanent separation of bed and board."

He straightened, staring at her in dismay. "But a legal separation means I'd never be able to have legitimate children."

"Which would make you no worse off than you are now since I have no intention of giving you legitimate children. And I'm leaving for America. Unless . . ." She paused, eyes narrowing. "Unless, despite your assurances about your honorable character, you intend to employ force and stop me?"

"Neatly done," he said, giving her a wry look. "Do you play chess, too?"

"Actually, I do, and I'm quite good."

"I can believe that."

"To spare my sister any scandal, and to make everything as simple as possible, your consent to a private and discreet legal separation would be the best solution."

"It's the most dismal thing I've ever heard." It meant he wouldn't be able to live with her, and without that sort of intimacy to draw her closer, his chance of ever winning her was reduced to almost nil. He knew that without his cooperation, she would never gain a legal separation, and he opened his mouth to reject her proposition utterly, but then, he paused to consider.

If he refused this bet, he had no doubt she'd be off to America like a shot. Once that happened, he'd have merry hell dragging her home again, even if the law was on his side. And if he did succeed in dragging her back by force, would it gain him anything but her enmity?

This wager, however, might give him exactly what he needed if he could turn it to his advantage. By agreeing, he knew he was taking an enormous risk, but hell, he'd never been a man for playing things safe. He could win a kiss in ten days, surely.

"All right," he said. "If you want a wager, I'm game, but I have conditions."

She looked at him warily, sensing the trap. "What conditions?"

"You have to come back with me to High-clyffe and spend the ten days with me there. And," he added before she could object, "during that time, you have to have dinner with me every night and spend at least four additional hours a day in my company. For two of those hours we'll do whatever you like, and for the other two . . ." He paused just a moment, slanting a hopeful gaze over her. ". . . we'll do whatever I like."

"None of which includes making advances on my person, or sleeping in my bed."

"I refuse to promise the former. Spurn my advances if you choose, but I will make them." He lifted his gaze to her face. "As to the latter, I won't come to your bed unless you invite me to, Edie."

164

Her jaw set. "That won't happen."

"The odds don't seem to be in my favor, that's true, but I live in hope."

She thought it over for a moment, then she nodded. "I agree. It is only ten days, after all." She started to step around him as if the discussion was over, but he blocked her.

"Aren't you forgetting something?" he asked. "We have to agree on what happens if I win."

"That's hardly necessary," she said. "Since you'll lose."

"A wager requires consideration on both sides. If I win, what do I receive?"

"What . . ." She paused and swallowed hard. "What do you want?"

He played his last card. "If I win, you agree to live with me permanently. No moving out, no running off to New York or anywhere else, no annulment or divorce attempts, no separation."

"Live with you for the rest of our lives? I can't make a promise like that."

The horrified tone of her voice reminded him that if he pushed too hard, she might withdraw and go bolting off to New York first chance she got, but he didn't care. If they were going to play this game, he intended to play for a win. "It's nonnegotiable, Edie."

"It's impossible!"

"You're the one who put the stakes this high. What's wrong?" he added, as she continued to shake her head in refusal. "Afraid you'll find me irresistible?"

Her sound of derision made short shrift of that. "Hardly."

He spread his arms wide. "Well, then?"

She bit her lip, head to one side, considering. "Oh, very well," she said at last. "I fear this is the only way I'll be rid of you without an exhausting legal battle. We'll begin tomorrow morning. Eleven o'clock."

"That's too late for breakfast and too early for luncheon, so I can only assume you have something else in mind?"

"Meet me at Victoria Station, Platform 9, and bring your things. The train back to Clyffeton shall be our first outing."

"The train?" He groaned. "Edie, you are so unromantic."

"You're the one who insists we spend these ten days at Highclyffe," she reminded. "So we have to take the train sometime. And you said I have my choice of activities."

"But on the train, we shall have no time alone."

"Exactly."

"So that's the way you intend to play it, keeping me at bay during every second we're together? You'll be dragging Joanna along as chaperone everywhere we go, I suppose?"

She didn't answer, but she didn't have to. There was a little smile on her lips that confirmed it.

"Have it your way and keep your secrets," he said, but he knew if she insisted upon using Joanna as a bulwark, he'd have to find a way to get around it. "I shall purchase the tickets and meet you on the platform at eleven tomorrow. But the things I'll plan for us to do will be far more enjoyable than hot, stuffy train journeys, I can promise you that."

A glimmer of something flared in her eyes — worry, perhaps even alarm — but it was gone before he could be sure. "Enjoy this game all you like, Stuart, but I've already instructed Mr. Keating to prepare a separation agreement, and ten days from now, you'll be signing it."

"Only if you haven't kissed me yet," he answered blithely. "And since we're sharing predictions, let me share mine. By the time that separation agreement arrives, you'll be having so much fun in my company, you won't want to leave me. In fact . . ." He

167

paused and pushed his luck by leaning even closer to her. "I intend to have you panting for far more than kisses by the time those ten days are up."

"Panting?" she echoed in disbelief. "You think I'll be panting over you?"

He answered her in all sincerity. "I hope so, Edie. Because if I can't make you want me, I don't deserve to have you." He paused, smiling a little. "Of course, you could just give in and kiss me now, so that we could move on to things even more pleasurable. I'll make it worth your while, I promise."

"And be deprived of all the glorious anticipation of panting over you? I wouldn't dream of it." Her hand came up between them, flattening against his chest, and she pushed him back with a smile that banished any scrap of hope on his part that she might be worried about the outcome.

She had every reason to be confident, he supposed, as he turned to watch her walk toward the door. Because right now, the notion of Edie's willingly kissing him seemed about as likely as a snowstorm in the Sahara.

# CHAPTER 8

Edie couldn't have imagined a better deal than the one she'd made. As a result, the dark cloud of dread that had been hovering over her since her husband's return began to lift, and relief took its place. To regain her freedom, all she had to do was refrain from kissing him for ten days. Since she had no desire to kiss him, how hard could that be?

That thought had barely crossed her mind before Stuart's words echoed back to her.

*I think I can make you want me.*

Her relief was displaced by a sudden glimmer of uneasiness. She tried to dismiss it. Stuart wouldn't employ force with her. As he'd reminded her, he never had before, he'd said he wouldn't now. One could never be absolutely sure with men, of course, but that wasn't the source of her uneasiness.

*For two hours we'll do whatever you like,*

*and for the other two . . . we'll do whatever I like.*

It was obvious his plan was to seduce her, but so what? She didn't know just how he intended to attempt it, but seduction only succeeded if a woman wanted to be seduced, and she most definitely did not. She was immune to all that.

Edie ought to have been reassured by that reminder, but instead, her uneasiness deepened. If she was immune, why did she need reminders?

The clock chimed, and she shoved aside that pesky little question. It was five o'clock, and she was supposed to be downstairs having tea. Stuart's five minutes had turned into half an hour, and she was still up here dithering.

She grabbed her handbag and left the suite to join Lady Trubridge and Joanna, and by the time she entered the tearoom, she had succeeded in pushing aside any feelings of worry. He could try all he liked to seduce her, but it would be like trying to coax a fish to fly.

Pausing by the door, she glanced around, peering between marble columns and potted palms, but the room was vast and every table filled with people, and she could not find her friend or sister amid the crowd.

"Your Grace?"

She turned to find the maître d'hotel at her elbow. "I'm here to meet Lady Trubridge and my sister."

"Of course." The man gave a bow. "Lady Trubridge is expecting you, and I believe Miss Jewell is with her. If you will follow me?"

He led her through the crowded tearoom and out to a beautiful terrace overlooking the Embankment Gardens and the river, where her friend and her sister were seated at a table by the balustrade. Belinda spied her approach, murmured something to Joanna, and both of them stood up to greet her as the maître d'hotel stepped aside with the announcement, "Her Grace, the Duchess of Margrave."

"Edie, dearest." Belinda moved out from behind the table to clasp her hands as the maître d'hotel departed. "It's been ages. How wonderful to see you."

"And you," she replied, pressing an affectionate kiss to her friend's cheek. "Sorry I'm late."

"Not at all," Belinda said, and gestured to her companion. "I've had Joanna to keep me company."

"Yes," Edie countered with a wry glance at her sister. "She's been telling you all about my unexpected visitor, no doubt."

"A bit," Belinda admitted. "But of course, I saw him before Joanna came down. He had just finished tea and paused by my table on his way out. When he learned I was waiting for you, he was kind enough to inform me you would be delayed."

"Yes," Edie answered with a sigh, wondering how much more interference from him she could expect in her social calendar during the coming ten days. "So he told me."

"It was a bit of a shock, seeing him, I must admit." Belinda added, "I knew he'd been injured, of course, but —"

"You knew?" Edie stared at her friend, astonished. "Belinda, why didn't you tell me?"

"He wrote to Nicholas, and one or two of his other close friends, but he didn't want to be the subject of gossip and asked them to keep mum. Nicholas did tell me about it, but he made me promise not to discuss it with anyone. I assumed Margrave would write to tell you himself."

"Well, he didn't. When I saw him, it was . . ." She paused, rubbing four fingers across her forehead. "It was rather a shock."

"I daresay," Belinda murmured, her perceptive blue eyes studying Edie's face.

"But what happened upstairs?" Joanna

asked, entering the conversation and cutting to the chase with her usual impatience. "Did you two make peace?"

"Joanna, really!" Belinda remonstrated. "Didn't you promise me not ten minutes ago that you would refrain from asking your sister any tactless questions?"

"You might as well ask the sun to set in the east," Edie told her friend, and when Belinda laughed at that, she was struck by the radiance in the other woman's face. With her black hair and blue eyes, Belinda had always been a striking beauty, but she looked especially lovely today. "Heavens, how well you're looking," she remarked, happy to change the subject. "What's your secret? A new face cream?"

Belinda laughed. "No, not a face cream. Something else entirely, but that can wait. Let's sit down."

She and Joanna resumed their seats, and Edie circled her sister's chair to take the seat opposite her friend. "Well?" she prompted, still studying her friend as she pulled off her gloves. "Tell me what on earth is giving you such a glow these days."

Belinda actually blushed. "I'm expecting a baby."

"A baby?"

She and Joanna said it at the same time,

making Belinda laugh. "You seem so surprised," she said. "But I have been married a year, after all."

"I think it's wonderful," Joanna said. "It almost makes me an auntie. I should love," she added with a mournful sigh, "to be an auntie."

Edie kicked her under the table. "A baby, Belinda? Truly?"

"You did say I was glowing," her friend answered, pouring her a cup of tea from the pot. "I thought you'd have guessed the reason why before you'd even sat down."

"I didn't. My . . ." She paused, laughing, confounded. "A baby. My congratulations. Does Trubridge know?"

"Yes. He's delighted, of course. Everyone is." Belinda handed Edie her tea, and once she'd taken it, her friend leaned closer, her eyes dancing with mischief. "I think even Landsdowne may be happy about it," she said, referring to her loathsome father-in-law, the Duke of Landsdowne, who'd been violently opposed to his son's marriage. Belinda, despite having been married once before to the Earl of Featherstone and despite having lived a decorous life as a widowed countess prior to her marriage to Trubridge, was still an American, and Landsdowne loathed Americans. The consolation in that, as Edie had wickedly pointed out, was that most Americans, herself included, loathed him back.

"Really?" She gave her friend a skeptical glance over the rim of her teacup. "Will he stay happy if it's a girl?"

"Probably not," Belinda said, laughing. "But as much as I detest that man, I can't blame him for wanting a boy. Every peer wants that."

"Yes." Edie took a gulp of tea, and her cup rattled a bit as she put it back in its saucer. "Every peer wants that."

Belinda, always quick to appreciate nuances, shot her a worried glance across the table, but she was too tactful to ask any questions with Joanna present. Edie was glad, for the last thing she wanted was to discuss her own marital situation, especially with Belinda. Her friend was a matchmaker, and though she knew now that Edie's marriage to Margrave wasn't the love match she'd originally thought when she'd endorsed it to Edie's father, Belinda was enough of a romantic to find notions of separation hard to accept.

"I can't believe we're both in town at the same time," Belinda said instead, tactfully changing the subject.

Edie jumped onto the new topic at once.

"I know! When I called at Berkeley Street earlier today, I fully expected your butler to tell me you'd already gone off to Kent."

"I'm sorry I wasn't in when you called. I was actually here, having luncheon with a client. Open less than a fortnight, and the Savoy is already a favorite with our fellow Americans. Still, you received my invitation to tea and were able to accept, so everything turned out well."

"You still have clients?" Edie asked, rather surprised by that. "Trubridge has allowed you to keep up your matchmaking business then?"

It was Belinda's turn to be surprised. "Why wouldn't he?"

Edie shrugged. "Oh, I don't know. Men don't usually allow their wives to engage in commerce, do they?"

"He knows better than to try and stop me," Belinda said, laughing. "And he can hardly disapprove. Since he's engaged in commerce himself, it would be hypocritical."

Not many husbands would care about the hypocrisy of it, but Edie refrained from pointing that out. Instead, she gave a polite smile, took another sip of tea, and reached for a tea cake from the tray.

"So," Belinda went on, "despite being

176

married, I still come to London quite often, even in August. Your arrival in town, though, is a shock."

It wasn't, really, considering the circumstances, but of course, she couldn't explain what had brought her here. "Is it?" she asked, and took a bite of cake.

"Of course it is! Darling, prying you away from Highclyffe in summer is like prying a barnacle off a rock."

The tea cake in her mouth suddenly tasted like sawdust. Edie took another swallow of tea, but that didn't help. It didn't stop the awful reality that no matter what happened with Stuart, her days at Highclyffe were numbered. Soon it would no longer be her home. She'd known that from the moment she'd seen her husband standing on the platform, yet, until this moment, she hadn't appreciated just how awful it would feel. She hadn't considered how it would be to say good-bye to the only place she'd ever lived that felt like home.

*You'd really let it all go? Turn your back on everything you've built?*

Stuart's words echoed back to her, and her spirits began sinking. She'd have to relinquish Highclyffe, for Stuart would never let her continue to have charge of it now that he was home. And why should he?

Highclyffe was his home. It could no longer be hers.

No more picnics at the Wash. No more digging for clams with Joanna on the shore, or exploring the tide pools, or bathing off the rocks. No more picking chestnuts in autumn and planning new spring gardens during the rainy wintertime. No more work with the village charities, work she'd always found so gratifying. No more purpose to her life.

"Heavens, Edie, what's the matter? You've gone quite pale."

Belinda's voice pulled her out of these dismal contemplations with a start, and she found both her friend and her sister staring at her with concern.

"Edie?" Joanna put a hand on her arm. "What's wrong?"

"Nothing, dearest," she lied, forcing a smile to her lips. "I must not have eaten enough lunch today. The sugar in the tea and cakes is going to my head a bit."

Joanna seemed satisfied by that, for the concern in her face diminished, and her hand slid away from Edie's arm. "You didn't eat much at lunch, that's true."

"Have a sandwich," Belinda suggested, but as Edie took one, more of her husband's words insisted on invading her mind.

*I wanted to ravish you over the cucumber sandwiches in the worst way.*

Damn it all, she thought as she took a bite of sandwich, she didn't want to be ravished. And if leaving Highclyffe behind was the price she had to pay to avoid it, then she'd pay that price.

There were other places to live. There were other houses that could be made into a home. She could go anywhere in the world she wanted. But as she thought of where she might go when the ten days were over, Edie feared no place on earth would ever seem like home again.

When it came to women, Stuart had never been the sort of man who needed to plan ahead. Not for him carefully written romantic letters, or bouquets of flowers chosen for their appropriate sentiment. Not for him long courtships with lingering glances and chaperoned walks and quick, furtive presses of hands. For him, winning a woman had never been a thought-out campaign or a chess match.

But during the cab ride from the Savoy to his club, he had cause to wonder if a little planning ahead in regard to Edie might not go amiss.

Granted, he'd improvised his way into

spending the coming ten days with her at Highclyffe, which was certainly preferable to chasing her hither and yon. At Highclyffe, there was privacy, and shared memories together — a few anyway. But he only had ten days, and he knew he would need to use every single minute to his best advantage. But as he stared out the carriage window and pondered what his strategy for those precious days ought to be, he found himself rather at a loss.

Looking back, he appreciated with some chagrin that his luck with the fair sex had made him quite cocky as a young man. That is, before one determined girl with cool green eyes and an even cooler heart had come along and shredded his rather high opinion of himself and his appeal. No, his experience with other women had never been of much use in dealing with Edie, and he doubted it would be enough to win her over now. If he was going to seduce her, he'd need far more than the shallow tactics he'd employed with women in his salad days.

The hansom cab jerked to a halt, and he came out of these speculations to find himself in front of White's. He exited the cab, grimacing as he did so, for thanks to all the time he'd been spending in hansom cabs and trains, his leg hurt like the devil, and he wished he'd walked the mile from the Savoy to White's. Still, it was nothing a second whisky and soda wouldn't alleviate.

He paid off the driver and went into the bar of the club, where he acquired a drink, hooked his walking stick over the arm of a comfortable leather chair, and sat down. Propping his right leg onto a footstool, he settled back to sip his whisky and contemplate what his next move ought to be.

Glancing around, he wondered what his fellow peers would think of his dilemma. Few, he suspected, would understand. Some would ask why he didn't just enter his wife's bedchamber, remind her of her duty, ignore her objections, and get on with producing the required heir. Others would regard it all as hard lines and advise him to find a mistress and let the dukedom fall to his brother. To his mind, the former had never been an option, and the latter was no option now.

This situation certainly wasn't turning out as he'd envisioned during the journey home. His imaginings about what making a real marriage with Edie would be like had been based on the idea that she'd be over that other chap by now, and though that had seemed to be an accurate assumption on his part, it had also made no difference whatsoever. He cut no ice with Edie, he never had. Perhaps he never would.

That thought had barely gone through his mind before he shoved it out again. Contemplating failure was pointless, and he refused to do it. Instead, he concentrated on the one task before him, the only one he needed to worry about right now. He had ten days to persuade her to kiss him. If he could do that, he'd have all the time he needed to win her over properly.

Ten days to a kiss. How easy such a game would have seemed to him before he met her. But with Edie, it seemed rather on par with his ability to climb Mount Kilimanjaro. She wasn't the sort to be paid a few compliments, plied with champagne, and carried upstairs, a fact for which he supposed he ought to be grateful since his days of carrying a woman anywhere were over. A bit of champagne wouldn't hurt, of course, and might enable her to let down her guard a bit, but he needed more than that. He needed to ignite her desire. But how?

"Stuart?"

He turned to find the Marquess of Trubridge at his elbow, along with another gentleman he'd never seen before. Stuart set aside his drink and reached for his stick.

"Don't stand up," Nicholas said, as Stuart moved to rise. "It's all right."

Stuart ignored that. "Nick," he greeted as he slid his leg off the footstool, grasped his stick, and rose to shake hands. "God, man, how long has it been?"

"Two years at least," Nicholas answered as he accepted the handshake and gestured with the glass of whisky in his other hand to the lanky, brown-haired man beside him. "Are you acquainted with Dr. Edmund Cahill?"

"I haven't had the pleasure."

"Then may I present him to you? Doctor, this is Stuart James Kendrick, the Duke of Margrave. He's an old friend of mine from Eton days."

"And from carousing around Paris together on occasion, so I've heard," the doctor put in, smiling.

"Is it my reputation that precedes me?" Stuart asked Nicholas. "Or yours?"

"Yours," his friend answered at once. "My carousing days are over."

Stuart lifted his walking stick. "As are mine, I'm afraid. Please join me," he added at once, before the usual awkward pause over his injured leg could occur.

The other two pulled chairs closer to his. Stuart shoved aside his footstool, ignoring

183

the protests of the other two, and insisted a table be moved to the center of the group.

"I've read about some of your adventures in Africa from the newspapers, Your Grace," Cahill told him once they were all comfortably settled and the drinks had been brought. "Quite a feat, navigating that stretch of the eastern Congo."

"Not to mention finding a new species of butterfly," Nicholas added. "God, I shall always envy you the scientific research you've done."

"Most people only care about the hunting exploits," Stuart told him wryly. "They want to hear about the elephants and the lions, not the butterflies."

"Well, you're among scientific-minded men at the moment," Cahill said. "We understand the importance of insect life to the natural order. On the other hand," he added, grinning beneath his thick brown mustache, "lions do seem much more exciting."

"And dangerous from what I understand," Nicholas murmured. "Sorry about the leg, old chap," he added, taking a sip from his glass.

Stuart frowned at those words, for it wasn't like Nick to thrust forward an awkward topic. "As I told you when I wrote, it wasn't that much of a surprise. Safari and exploration work can be hazardous, and I always went into the bush half-expecting something of the sort. And I came out of it rather lucky." He thought of Jones and took another swallow of whisky. It burned his throat. "At least I didn't die."

"Hear, hear," Nick approved, lifting his glass to confirm that sentiment before he also took a drink. "But what about your leg? Still painful?"

"A bit stiff, but I can manage."

"A muscular injury?" Cahill inquired in a voice so bland that Stuart was instantly suspicious.

"Forgive his curiosity," Nicholas put in. "It's professional. Dr. Cahill's got a practice in Harley Street, and his specialty is injuries to the muscles."

"Indeed?" Stuart muttered, glaring at his old friend. "What a coincidence that the pair of you happened to be here this after-noon at the same time as I."

"Not a coincidence at all, actually," Nicholas countered, grinning, oblivious to Stuart's accusing stare. "I heard you were in town and staying here at the club when I arrived, and I immediately dispatched a note to Cahill here, begging him to abandon his other patients for the rest of the afternoon and join me. We've been lounging here about half an hour or so, waiting for you to stroll in."

"Missed me that much have you, Nick? I wish I could say the same, but I never miss interfering, irritating friends who decide they know what's best for me."

"Cahill did wonders for my shoulder after Pongo shot me," Nicholas went on, impervious to insults. "The man's a marvel."

"You flatter me, my lord," Cahill murmured, shifting in his chair, looking a bit embarrassed by the marquess's praise and this clearly unwelcome interference in his friend's medical condition.

Nicholas, however, waved aside the doctor's embarrassment as easily as he had Stuart's irritation. "The thing is, Cahill, Margrave's in pain. He won't discuss it," he added, overriding Stuart's strenuous denial. "Can you do anything for him?"

"No, he can't," Stuart said before the doctor could answer. "I've consulted two doctors already. The scar tissue is extensive, the pain has to be lived with, and there's an end."

Cahill gave a cough. "That's not necessarily true. There are therapeutic techniques that can be employed to ease pain and increase your mobility."

"What techniques? Soaking myself in mineral waters? One of my doctors recommended that, and though I tried the spas at Evian on my way home, it accomplished little except to ease the pain for a few hours." He lifted his glass. "If that's all I'm to get for my trouble, I'd rather soak in whisky."

"Drinking is hardly an adequate remedy," Nicholas objected.

"Well, I did consider cocaine and laudanum." Stuart took another swallow, savoring the gratifying burn. "But whisky tastes better."

"For God's sake, man, if you're in pain, becoming a dipsomaniac is hardly a solution. Something else must be done."

"I'm not a dipsomaniac." He took another swallow from his glass and grimaced. "Not yet, anyway. And even if I were, it's not your business."

"I'm bloody well making it my business."

"Gentlemen, please," Cahill cut in. "If an actual doctor might be allowed a word? Mineral baths can help, but as His Grace already concluded, they are an inadequate remedy. As for cocaine and laudanum, I know many doctors dispense them without a thought, but to my mind, their addictive properties make them undesirable options.

And while I've nothing against a good whisky, I might be able to suggest a more effective course of treatment."

"Such as?" Nicholas asked, ignoring Stuart's groan of aggravation.

"That depends." He looked at Stuart. "Do you find walking provides relief, Your Grace?"

"Yes, actually," he was forced to admit. "Walking helps."

"Then exercises to stretch and elongate the muscles could offer significant improvement, particularly if combined with massage and warm mineral baths. But I should have to do a complete examination before I could recommend any specific treatments."

Stuart's attention was caught at last. "I believe you might be able to help me after all, Doctor," he said, straightening in his chair. "I should like you to conduct an examination, but I haven't much time. I'm off to Norfolk tomorrow, so our consultation would have to be this evening. Will that do?"

"Of course. We could adjourn to my surgery after we've finished here."

"Excellent." Stuart leaned back in his chair again, and although he could feel his optimism returning, he knew possible treatments for his leg had nothing to do with it.

# CHAPTER 9

That evening after dressing for dinner, Edie sat down with Joanna and impressed upon her the importance of discretion. At least, she tried. Her sister, however, failed to see why informing Stuart of their whereabouts while in London had been a breach of discretion.

"He's your husband, isn't he?" Joanna countered, seeming understandably bewildered. "Aren't husbands and wives supposed to know each other's whereabouts? What if something happens?"

"Stuart and I are not . . . we're not like other husbands and wives. We're separated, as you know."

"But he's home now, and he wants to make amends." Joanna looked down, plucking at the counterpane of Edie's bed where they were sitting. "And he's terribly nice. Handsome, too. Don't you like him?"

"Darling, it's not that simple," she said

with a sigh.

"He obviously still likes you. You must have liked him, too, when you married him. Can't you try to like him again?"

"Not in the way you mean," she said, the admission tasting strangely bitter on her tongue. She thought of the romantic girl she'd been before Saratoga, and as she had done that night in the maze with Stuart, she wondered what might have been. "When I was younger, perhaps, before —" She broke off, remembering who she was talking to.

"Before what? Before Frederick Van Hausen came along?"

"You know about that? But you were only eight."

Joanna seemed surprised. "Of course. I remember Daddy shouting the house down about how Van Hausen would have to marry you because he'd ruined your reputation."

If only that were all he'd ruined. Edie looked across the room at her dressing table, staring at her reflection in the mirror. Suddenly, a wave of longing swept over her that she hadn't felt for years, a longing for the things Frederick had stolen from her.

"Is that what you mean, Edie?" Joanna's voice broke in. "I remember Daddy's saying we'd have to come to England to find you a husband because your reputation was ruined. Oh!"

The exclamation was sudden, and Edie tensed as she saw understanding dawning in Joanna's eyes. "Is that why you married Stuart? To salvage your reputation?"

Edie relaxed. "Yes, partly," she answered. "It wasn't for love," she added, and though she saw the hint of disappointment in Joanna's face, she was glad that she was the only one who'd suffered from her shame and disgrace. She had that consolation, at least. "Not everyone marries for love, dearest," she said gently.

"I know."

"And love is no guarantee of a successful marriage anyway. Some marriages work out, and some don't. Ours . . . didn't."

"But you could try, couldn't you?"

Could she? Edie tried to set aside the panicky feeling that always came with such contemplations and pondered that question as objectively as she could, but as she considered what it would mean, she shook her head. "No, I don't think so. It's too late for that."

"But I don't understand this at all!" Joanna burst out. "Too late? You talk as if you're old, and you're not. You're only twenty-four."

"It's not a question of age." It was a ques-

191

tion of fear, shame, and pain. She knew that, and though she hated having those emotions hanging over her like a shadow, she had long ago accepted them. At least, as her life was now, they hid, lurking but bearable, in the shadows. If she and Stuart had a real marriage, he would want, expect, and perhaps even demand access to her body whenever he liked, and she would not be able to bear that. "I am content with my life as it is, and I don't want to change it. I'm happy, and I hope . . ." She paused and took her sister's hand. "I need to know that whatever happens, you'll stand by my decisions and respect them. Please tell me that no matter what, you're on my side."

"You're my sister!" Joanna said stoutly. "Of course I'm on your side!"

The next morning, however, even that contention was to be called into question.

When they arrived at Victoria Station, Stuart was already on the platform waiting for them, and the sight of his tall frame amid the swirling steam of the train reminded her forcibly of when she'd see him at Clyffeton Station two days ago and he'd turned her life upside down. With his tanned skin and carved walking stick, he still had that air of the exotic man from foreign places, but this time, he wasn't surrounded by stacks of steamer trunks and cases of crocodile leather. The only thing at his feet was an enormous picnic basket, and the letters stamped on the wicker proclaimed that basket to be every bit as British as plum pudding and Queen Victoria.

"Fortnum and Mason?" Joanna cried with delight, having also noted the inked F&M monogram on the side. "Ooh, Edie, look. Fortnum and Mason!"

"Yes, Joanna, I see it," she answered, looking at her husband. "Bribery, Stuart?"

"You call it bribery. I call it lunch." He doffed his hat and bowed. "Good morning, ladies," he said, and bent to give the dog a pat. "Hullo, old boy."

Snuffles, however, was living up to his name by an avid inspection of the picnic basket, and he gave Stuart's greeting nothing more than a halfhearted wag of his docked tail. When the dog nudged the lid with his nose to try to lift it, Stuart bent down, wrapped a hand around the terrier's middle, and lifted him up. "No," he said firmly. "That is definitely not for you."

"I'll take him, Your Grace." Reeves stepped forward and suited the action to the words. "Best if I board and settle him in his crate anyway."

"You'll need your ticket." Stuart tucked

his stick under his arm and rummaged in the breast pocket of his gray herringbone-tweed morning coat. He pulled out four tickets and handed the one for second class to the maid. "Your lunch is taken care of. I've arranged for that."

"Thank you, Your Grace." Reeves, that staunch, efficient grenadier of a lady's maid, tipped her lips upward in what looked suspiciously like a smile. Edie couldn't believe her eyes.

"What have you done to my maid?" she demanded in a fierce whisper the moment Reeves was far enough away not to hear it.

"Edie, really," he murmured, giving her a look of reproof. "As a gentleman, I couldn't possibly answer such an inappropriate question." With that, he donned his hat, brushed a speck of lint from his coat, and pulled his stick from under his arm, then turned his attention to the girl who was now following Snuffles's example and attempting to have a peek in the picnic hamper. "Joanna, no peeking."

She straightened at once. "But I love Fortnum and Mason! It's my favorite store in London. Edie's, too."

"Is it?" He glanced at Edie, a smile tipping the corners of his mouth. "Fancy that."

That smile was far too self-assured for her

peace of mind. "You seem quite pleased with yourself this morning," she remarked.

"And that bothers you?" His smile widened into a grin. "Starting to worry already, are you?"

"I'm not worried, I'm amused," she said with dignity, and nodded to the hamper at his feet. "Do you really think you can wheedle your way into my affections with that picnic basket?"

"No," he answered at once. "Which is why it's not for you. It's for Joanna."

The girl gave a cry of delight. "For me? Ooh, how lovely!"

Edie met the laughter in Stuart's eyes with a wry look. "I can't believe that you are bribing my sister to be your partner in crime."

He gave her a look of mock apology. "I have no shame, it seems."

"You must indeed be desperate to resort to such tactics," she said with perhaps more assurance in her voice than she actually felt. "But Joanna is still my sister. You can't buy her loyalty."

"Are there chocolates in there?" Joanna asked. The girl bent down again, but Stuart used the tip of his stick to shut the lid again before she could acquire an answer to her question.

"I said no peeking. You'll have to wait for lunch to find out what's inside. Be a darling," he added, cutting off her protest about waiting as he held out the remaining tickets. "Take charge of these for me."

When Joanna complied, he reached for the handle of the picnic basket and picked it up. "Shall we board?"

Without waiting for an answer, he turned away and started for the train, Joanna beside him. Edie followed in their wake, watching as he crossed the platform, and though he seemed to be managing the heavy basket rather well, she couldn't help noticing the stiffness of his right leg as he moved, and she wondered if she ought to call for a porter. When he stood aside at the entrance of their first-class carriage so that she and Joanna could board, she did not follow her sister up the steps and onto the train. Instead, she paused beside him, gesturing to the basket. "Perhaps I should carry it —"

"No, thank you. I can manage."

"If you won't let me take it, you should have a porter do so."

"I've never been much good at doing what I should."

His voice was light, but there was an unmistakable hint of steel underneath that told Edie arguing about it would be useless.

She boarded the train, but as she followed her sister along the aisle between the fat, high-backed armchairs that lined each side of the car, she glanced back over her shoulder to watch him. He was able to ascend the steps with the basket in one hand by leaning heavily on his walking stick with the other, but Edie could tell it hurt. She caught the grimace that crossed his face, and even though it would probably have done no good, she wished she had argued more strenuously about a porter.

"Edie?" Joanna's voice called to her from the other end of the coach, but Edie didn't turn around. Instead, she kept her gaze on the man now coming toward her along the aisle.

"Are you always so foolishly stubborn?" she asked him as he halted in front of her.

"I'm afraid so." He smiled. "Are you sure you don't want to just give in? I'll make it worth your while, I promise."

"Edie!" Joanna's voice came again, impatient and eager. "Do stop dawdling and come look!"

She took a deep breath, heartily grateful for the distraction. Turning away from those smoky eyes, she found her sister standing about a dozen feet ahead of her with a wide grin on her face.

"Heavens, Joanna, you look like the Cheshire cat. What is making you smile like that?"

"Look what's in your seat." With a dramatic flourish she gestured to her right, and Edie stepped forward to peer over the high back of her chair. There, in all its splendid English glory, was another Fortnum and Mason picnic hamper.

"That one's yours," Stuart's voice murmured behind her.

A cry of delighted surprise was out of her mouth before she could stop it, but she pressed her lips together at once, hoping he hadn't heard it. He might be playing to win this game, but so was she, and she didn't want to show him a shred of encouragement. But when she turned toward him and looked into his eyes, she knew it was too late.

"I'm glad you like my gift," he told her, laugh lines creasing the corners of his eyes. "It has all your favorites, too. Fresh bread and Irish butter, olives, pâté de foie gras, smoked salmon, cherries . . . there's even a tin of your American baked beans in there, though why you like them so much truly baffles my British palate."

"How do you know what my favorite Fortnum and Mason foodstuffs are?" But even as she asked the question, she was sure she already knew the answer. "Joanna, really!" she said, feeling hopelessly outmatched at the moment. "Did we not discuss the importance of discretion just last night?"

"I didn't tell him anything!" Joanna denied, laughing as she took the seat kitty-corner from Edie's, her back to the engine. "Not this time, I swear. Although I would have if he'd asked me," she added, and leaned around her sister to look at Stuart. "She likes champagne, too."

He leaned around Edie to offer his reply. "Thank you, petal, but I've always known that. Which is why," he added as he straightened and returned his attention to Edie, "the conductor has an excellent bottle of Laurent-Perrier chilling on ice for you at this moment."

"You brought me champagne, too?"

"Of course. What else would one drink with a Fortnum and Mason hamper? The real question is . . ." He paused a fraction of a second, and when he spoke again, his voice was a low murmur only she could hear. "How shall you thank me?"

Her stomach dipped, an odd, weightless sensation rather like riding the electric lift at the Savoy. She tried to ignore it. "With a simple thank-you?"

"How mundane."

She saw where this was going. "I suppose," she murmured back, "you'd like a
kiss instead?"

He leaned closer, and as she looked into
his eyes, she saw their silvery gray depths
darken, turning smoky. For no reason at all,
she blushed, even before he said, "God, yes."

Her toes curled in her shoes. The tips of
her fingers began to tingle.

"You could do it right here," he went on,
his voice still low enough that only she
could hear. "It would shock all the pas-
sengers in first class out of their snooty British sensibilities. Think how fun it would be."

"You have strange ideas of what's fun,"
she scoffed, striving to sound as derisive as
possible, but to her mortification, her voice
came out in a strangled whisper because
she couldn't seem to breathe properly.

"You only say that because you haven't
kissed me." His lashes lowered, his gaze
dropped to her mouth. "Yet."

The warmth in her fingers and toes
flooded through the rest of her body in an
instant. Her skin flushed, her throat went
dry, and her limbs felt inexplicably languid.
It was such an unexpected feeling, so unlike
anything she'd ever felt before, that she
didn't know what to do.

She wanted to move, but couldn't seem to find the will to do so. She wanted to look away from those smoky eyes and the promise in their depths, but she couldn't do that either.

It was just a picnic basket, champagne and a bit of flirtation, just the sort of thing any man bent on seduction might do, and she'd told herself only yesterday that such tactics would not work on her. The idea that she might be softening already forced Edie out of her flustered daze.

"We should sit down," she said primly. "People are starting to stare, and despite your blatant attempts to flirt with me, I have no intention of giving them a reason for such scrutiny."

"Really, Edie, where's your sense of adventure?" He sighed, shaking his head. "Have it your way, but if we are to sit down, you'll have to move back a bit first."

When he lifted the basket in his hands, she realized what he meant, and she took several steps back to be out of his way. He moved to set Joanna's lunch on the small table beneath the girl's window, then he removed Edie's from her seat and put it on her table so that she could sit down. He took the chair opposite her, and just in time, too, for he'd barely tucked his hat and stick beneath his seat before the final whistle blew and the train began moving out of the station.

"Where's your picnic hamper?" she asked, raising her voice a bit to be heard above the puffing steam engine as it worked to pick up speed.

He laughed, leaning back in his chair. "Even I, as fond of Fortnum's as I am, thought three hampers was a bit thick. I'm hoping to sponge off you."

"I haven't looked in my basket yet." She gave a sniff. "I don't know if I want to share."

"So you'll let me starve?"

"You won't starve. There's a dining car. Or Joanna will share with you. You've become her new best friend, it seems."

He leaned forward, moving closer to her. "Jealous?" he murmured. "Afraid you're being displaced?"

"No!" she denied, her reply far too vehement. She was a bit jealous, she realized. How ghastly.

"Don't worry," he said as if reading her mind. "You're still her favorite. I'm a very distant second."

"Third," she was happy to inform him. "Daddy is far ahead of you."

"I stand corrected. So, won't you share

your lunch with me? C'mon, Edie," he coaxed, "I brought you champagne and everything."

"You are the most absurd man!" she said, but her voice was not nearly as stern as she would have liked. "And unlike my sister, I can't be bribed."

"But it's an excellent vintage, the same one we were drinking that night in the garden."

She glanced at Joanna, then leaned closer to him. "Keep your voice down," she admonished. "You remember the vintage of the champagne we drank?"

"I remember everything about the night we met, Edie," he said, his voice low in compliance with her request. "How could I not? It changed my life. The last time you and I drank champagne together, wonderful things happened. I'm hoping history repeats itself."

"You mean if I drink it, you'll leave?" She smiled sweetly. "Fetch the bottle."

"You are quite determined to keep me at arm's length, aren't you?" He tilted his head, studying her. "I would dearly love to know why."

"No," she said with feeling, "you wouldn't. The champagne notwithstanding," she rushed on before he could pursue the point,

"I'm not sure you're playing fair. You are allying my sister on your side, which is two against one. Where is your British sense of sportsmanship?"

"I intend to employ all the weapons in my arsenal. And in her defense, Joanna isn't who told me about your love of Fortnum and Mason."

"Then how did you know?"

"Reeves, of course. I bought her a hamper, too. You see?" he added, as she gave a groan. "It's not two on one, but three. You'll be even more outnumbered once we reach home. I'll have the other servants on my side as well. Soon, all of us will be aligned in a vast conspiracy to impel you to kiss me."

Appalled, she straightened in her chair. "You can't do that!" she cried. "You can't!"

"What can't he do?" Joanna's voice called from across the aisle, intruding on their conversation and making Edie realize how loudly she'd spoken.

"It's nothing, dearest," she answered her sister, and leaned closer to Stuart once again. "You are not intending to tell the servants about our bet, surely?" she whispered.

"I already warned you, I will use whatever weapons I've got."

"The servants have been answering to me for five years," she said, rallying. "You think you can earn their loyalty in a matter of a few days?"

"I don't have to earn it. I was born with it. I am the duke. Besides," he added, leaning back in his seat with a grin, "Cecil's a useless twit who can't be dragged out of Scotland, and all the servants know it. So the hope of having an alternate heir to the dukedom will spur everyone at Highclyffe to the most shameless acts of matchmaking. You haven't a prayer."

Edie fell back in her seat, too horrified to reply. The ten days ahead suddenly seemed like a lifetime.

They arrived back at Highclyffe just before teatime, and Edie made for her room straightaway, fearing that soon it would be the only refuge she had. But even the privilege of privacy usually accorded to a married woman in her boudoir wasn't quite as private as she'd hoped.

She had barely changed into a pale pink dressing gown, dismissed Reeves — after offering yet another lecture on discretion where her husband was concerned — and lay down on her bed for a nap, before there was a rap on her door.

"May I come in?" Stuart's voice, though muffled by the heavy door, was unmistakable, but before she could answer with a most emphatic refusal, he opened the door. "Are you dressed?" he asked through the opening.

Edie was off the bed in an instant. "No, I am not dressed!" she lied, hoping to stop him from coming in. "And you have no right to push into my room."

"I'm not pushing in, I'm in the corridor. And since you're not dressed, I'm not looking. I'm exercising true gentlemanly fortitude and staring at the carpet."

His head was bent, and he did seem to be looking at the floor, and Edie sighed, giving it up. "For heaven's sake, you don't have to stare at the carpet, and I'm not naked, so stop imagining the possibility."

"I'm always imagining that particular possibility," he said, and opened the door wider, straightening to look at her. "I sat outside my tent in Kenya at night and imagined it quite often."

"Oh, you did not." He'd thought about her while he was in Africa? Naked? Her face grew hot, but at the same time, her heart gave a queer little leap in her chest that had nothing to do with embarrassment.

"Yes, Edie, I did." He came in, but when

he started to close the door, it was a step too far into her privacy for Edie to bear.

"Leave it open."

His dark eyebrows lifted a bit at the sharp edge to her voice, but he didn't quibble. "If you like," he said, and pulled the door wide again. "I just didn't think the corridor was an appropriate place to discuss my carnal imaginings about you while I was in the bush. And by the way," he went on, meeting her eyes across the bedroom, "I have no intention of stopping that particular activity now that I'm home."

The color in her cheeks deepened. She felt vulnerable, exposed, as if she really were naked. She wrapped the folds of pale pink silk more tightly around her and turned away, feeling the sudden, desperate need to do something. She walked to her dressing table, sat down, and began fiddling with the bottles as if selecting which hand cream to apply was suddenly the most important thing in the world.

"I'd ask what you thought about me while I was away," he went on as she opened a jar, "but I'm reasonably certain you never spared me a thought."

"That's not true." The words came out before she could stop them, and she wished she could take them back, for they made her feel even more vulnerable than before. "It would have been impossible," she said, striving to sound offhand about it as she lifted her gaze to look at his reflection. "Everybody talked about you all the time. Your navigation of the Congo was in all the papers. And that butterfly you discovered was in all the scientific journals."

He leaned a shoulder against the door-jamb, watching her face in the mirror, grinning in a way that made her wish even more that she'd held her tongue. "You read the scientific journals, do you?"

She opened the jar, scooped out a dollop of cream, and began rubbing it into her hands with wholly unnecessary vigor. "Was there something you wanted?" she asked, desperate to change the subject.

"Actually, yes. I came to ask if you would like to take tea with me on the terrace by the library?"

Her hands stilled at a memory of tea on the terrace. Something he'd said flashed through her mind.

*Shall we, Edie? We are married, after all.*

"Tea together?" she asked, striving to appear cool and indifferent as she looked at his reflection in the mirror. "Is this to be part of your two hours today?"

"I'm not intending to require it, if that's

what you mean. I simply thought having tea together would be a good opportunity for us to become better acquainted. And," he added softly, "I have fond memories of that terrace."

There was tenderness in his face. It hurt to see that, for it made her think of what she might have had if Saratoga had never happened.

"I don't think," she said after a moment, "that tea on the terrace with you is a good idea."

"It's only tea, Edie. Joanna and her governess will be there, too." He smiled a little. "So, you see? I'm foiled again in my desire to ravish you over the cucumber sandwiches."

Heavens, if she couldn't even sit down with him for something as innocuous as tea, the coming ten days would be unbearable. "You're right, of course," she said. "Give me a few moments, and I'll join you on the terrace."

He nodded and left, and Edie returned her attention to the mirror, noting her flushed face with some chagrin. The idea that he'd been imagining her naked body flustered her, flummoxed her, and made her afraid, but with a wholly different sort of fear than she was used to. It made her wonder what he would think if he saw the real thing, and she feared it would surely be a disappointment.

Which was a ridiculous fear indeed. Not only because he'd never have the chance to see her naked but also because she didn't care in the least what he thought of her. Edie picked up her brush and started to push some wayward curls back from her forehead, but then she realized what she was doing and stopped. If she didn't care what he thought, why was she primping?

Edie slapped down the brush, stood up, and tugged the bellpull for Reeves to help her change into a tea gown. As for ravishing her over the sandwiches, he could think it all he liked, but even without the presence of Joanna and Mrs. Simmons, he wouldn't have a chance of success.

# CHAPTER 10

When Stuart came out to the terrace, he found Joanna already there. With her was the same small, indomitable-looking, gray-haired lady he recognized from the Clyffeton train platform as Joanna's governess. The girl's introduction confirmed the fact.

"A pleasure to meet you at last, Mrs. Simmons. I see that you have returned from your aborted journey to Kent. I must offer you my apologies, for I fear I was the cause of your departure without your pupil."

Her faded blue eyes twinkled a bit, indicating that despite her firm mouth and unassailable aura of propriety, she had a sense of humor and was well acquainted with Joanna's willful streak. "It is a pleasure to meet you as well, Your Grace, and no apology is necessary, I assure you." She gestured to the table, where tea things had been laid out over a pristine white tablecloth. "Shall I pour you a cup of tea?" she asked.

"Thank you, yes. I'd love one."

"Did you see Edie?" Joanna asked. "Is she coming down to join us?"

"She'll be here in a moment. No sugar, Mrs. Simmons," he added as he watched the governess pick up the sugar tongs. "And no milk or lemon, either. I like my tea plain."

"Without even any sugar?" Joanna asked, looking at him askance.

"I grew accustomed to drinking it plain while I was in Africa," he explained. "We couldn't very well cart milk, sugar, and lemons into the bush. But mostly, I drank coffee, for it was far easier to obtain."

"Joanna and I read about your expedition in the Congo," the governess said, placing his filled cup in its saucer and handing it across the table. "Didn't we, Joanna?"

"We read all about it in the newspapers," the girl said as she slathered cream onto a scone. "It sounded terribly exciting."

"More disastrous than exciting, I fear," Stuart said, taking a sandwich from the tray. "It's amazing we were able to complete the expedition, for everything that could possibly go wrong did so. We lost a cartload of supplies, including medicine, powder, and shot, all my men were laid low with a bout of fever for three weeks, and we were attacked twice by marauders. And, if all that wasn't bad enough, we had both English and French cartographers. It was to be a cooperative expedition, but there was little cooperation about it. The rivalry was fierce, and because I was the guide, I was expected to keep the peace."

"The same sort of rivalry exists in matters of religion, it seems," Mrs. Simmons told him. "Our vicar, Mr. Ponsonby, is very committed to missionary work, as I'm sure you know. He mentioned once how terribly difficult it is for Anglican missionaries to operate in the French territories because the Catholic officials and guides are so unhelpful."

Stuart shifted in his chair, and he couldn't help rolling his eyes at the mention of the vicar. Ponsonby was a self-righteous windbag who knew nothing about Africa or its people. Fortunately, Mrs. Simmons was occupied with pouring herself a second cup of tea, and by the time she looked up, he'd managed to conceal his distaste for the man. "Yes, Mr. Ponsonby is quite committed to missionary work," he said, trying out of sheer politeness to keep his negative opinion out of his voice. "But the Congo is a bit savage, even for men of . . ." He paused and coughed. "Men of the cloth."

"Which, in his view, makes what you did all the more splendid. He said that cartography expedition provided maps and information that have proved invaluable to the missionary work."

"I'm delighted to hear it," he said, and he feared he had been unable to inject the proper amount of enthusiasm into his voice. "Still, after that trip, I decided to conduct future expeditions exclusively within the British territories. It's far easier to arrange, and I find Kenya and Tanzania much more pleasant than the Congo."

"We saw the butterfly you discovered," Joanna told him. "It's on display in the British Museum. We saw it last year."

"I didn't know they'd put it on display. Last I'd heard, they were only considering it." He glanced at Mrs. Simmons. "I'm glad to see you are taking your pupil on outings such as the British Museum. My sister's governess thought French and how to curtsy were enough for a girl."

"I don't agree with that sort of limited education, it's true," Mrs. Simmons said, "but I can take no credit for that particular outing. Her Grace took Joanna to see your butterfly."

A flash of white caught his eye, and he looked up to find Edie standing in the

French door to the library. "Did she, indeed?" he murmured. "How gratifying."

She had changed into a tea gown of white lawn and Battenberg lace, and the bright, white color made her seem radiantly lovely as she stepped out into the sunlight. The image of her naked amid white sheets flashed through his mind just as it had the last time they'd taken tea together, and his throat went dry.

"Actually, I didn't," she said as she came out onto the terrace. "I took her to see the paintings. There was a Monet exhibition, and Joanna loves art. The butterfly happened to be on exhibit at the same time."

"But you wanted to see it, too," Joanna said with an unmistakable, impish glee. "You told me so."

"Did I?" Her face was smooth and cool as marble, not even a blush to indicate what she might be thinking. "I don't remember."

Stuart stood up, and as he watched her cross the terrace, he fancied he could see the lithe, slim outline of her body beneath the loose layers of white fabric, and desire began flooding his body. He tried to stop it, telling himself that what he saw beneath the layers of white fabric was his imagination, but that didn't seem to help much, and he was relieved when she sat down, for he could then do the same and allow the table to conceal, at least partly, what he felt.

But he couldn't conceal the look on his face, apparently, for she paused in the act of reaching for the teapot, looking at him across the table. "Is something wrong?"

He shoved imaginings of her naked amid the sheets out of his mind and hastily invented an excuse. "I'm stunned, Edie. You went to see my butterfly?"

She didn't reply. Instead, she bent her head to pour her tea, and the hat she'd donned, a wide-brimmed straw affair trimmed with white ribbons, successfully shielded her expression. "Joanna and I both wanted to look at it," she said. "Everyone was talking of it at the time."

"It was a lovely thing," Joanna put in. "Bright, bright blue, with yellow dots. I did a watercolor of it."

"Did you, petal? I should like to see that."

Joanna paused, her scone halfway to her mouth. "Would you, truly?" She tossed aside her napkin, dropped her scone back onto her plate, and stood up. "Edie had it framed and put it in the drawing room. Come and I'll show it to you."

"Really, Joanna," Edie said without looking up, displaying a great fascination with the choice of cakes on the tea tray. "Allow

216

the man to at least drink his tea first."

"I'll look at it after dinner, petal," he promised, and settled back in his chair to enjoy the view he had right in front of him.

Pity about that hat, he thought, studying his wife across the table. He understood the protection a hat afforded her fair skin, but he still wished she'd take it off, for he'd have liked to see her bright, brilliant hair in the sunlight as he had that afternoon five years ago. Still, it was probably for the best that she kept it on since the added distraction would hardly be helpful to keeping his desire in check.

And it was important that he do so. For it to count, Edie had to kiss him, not — alas — the other way around. Thanks to his consultation with Dr. Cahill, he now had a strategy by which he might bring that about, but to implement it would require quite a measure of control and self-discipline. That wouldn't be easy if he was going to become aroused simply by watching her walk across a terrace.

Still, before he even worried about that particular problem, he had another to solve. He controlled two hours a day of her company, but he couldn't force her compliance with what he had in mind. To gain her willing cooperation would be a bit tricky, for she was bound to perceive his true intentions straightaway.

By the time she finished her second cup of tea, Stuart had managed to put his desire aside, at least enough that it would not be painfully obvious the moment he stood up. When she set down her cup and put aside her napkin, he spoke before she could rise from her chair. "Shall you be wanting any more tea, Edie, do you think?"

"I don't believe so. Why do you ask?"

"Because if you've finished, I think you and I should take the dog for a walk. He could do with a walk after being cooped up for hours on that train, don't you think?"

"I'm sure Snuffles would love a walk. Perhaps you and Joanna —"

"Joanna hasn't finished her tea," Stuart cut in before Joanna could speak. "No, Edie, I fear it's up to us."

He ate the last bite of his sandwich, grabbed his walking stick, and stood up. "Come on. You can spend the next two hours showing me what you've done to the gardens while I've been away."

The moment he mentioned the time frame, she understood. She gave a nod and rose to her feet, albeit a bit reluctantly, as he came around and unhooked the loop of the leather lead from the back of her chair.

"Come on, old boy," he said to the dog as they started across the terrace toward the steps down to the south lawn. "I refuse to call you Snuffles. Why your mistress would ever give a ripping terrier like you such a ridiculous name, I can't think."

"Don't blame me," Edie said, as they turned onto the gravel path that led across the lawn to the gardens. "Joanna named him."

"And you allowed her to give that name to a Norwich terrier with over a century of impeccable breeding behind him? Edie, really!"

"Well, she was only eleven at the time, and she had recently lost her cat. Under the circumstances, I just couldn't bear to say no. I spoil her, I know," she added with a sigh.

"Raising a child is never an easy thing, I imagine, especially when you seem to be doing it all yourself. What of your father?"

"I prefer having Joanna with me, and my father finds it convenient to oblige. It's a common enough thing for a widower to feel. Raising a daughter would rather impinge on the life he leads, you see."

He did see. He saw more than she probably realized. But then, his impression of her father had always been that of a man

219

who liked to arrange his life for his own convenience. Her next words rather confirmed it.

"Daddy comes every year to visit, assures himself that we're getting on all right, then happily goes back home to his mistress and his business deals. He adores his life — drinking at the Oak Room, playing cards at the House with the Bronze Door, yachting at Newport . . . all that sort of thing."

"He owns racehorses, too, doesn't he?"

"Yes."

Something in that curt, clipped answer startled Stuart. He cast a sideways glance at her, but he could see nothing amiss in her profile. She looked as coolly unflappable as usual, and he concluded he'd imagined the sharpness of her reply.

"And you don't mind?" he asked, curious. "It's a big responsibility, having full charge of Joanna, and not really yours to assume."

"I wouldn't have it any other way. I love Joanna, and I like having her with me, not only because she's my sister but also because she's quite good company. And —" She broke off, her steps slowed. And then she stopped.

"And?" he prompted, halting on the path beside her.

"I hate the idea of handing her care over

to anyone else," she said slowly. "I want to watch over her myself every minute. I want to be sure always that she's happy, well looked after, and safe."

"Of course. I should feel the same in your place. Although I'm not sure I would have been quite so torn over sending my sister off to school," he amended with a laugh. "We are talking about Nadine, after all. I fear I'd have had to send her to be finished well before her fifteenth birthday unless I wanted to go mad. My sister is a breathtakingly lovely, very sweet featherbrain, as you have no doubt observed for yourself."

Edie laughed, too. "A younger sister with intelligence isn't necessarily a good thing, you know. Joanna's too clever by half."

"Yes, so I've noticed," he answered. "Which is why you really shouldn't procrastinate about sending her to school."

She shot him a wry look. "Why do you say so? Because I might choose to use her as a chaperone?"

"No, Edie. I'm saying it because I genuinely think school would be good for her. And Willowbank is an excellent institution for both academics and the arts, and it would be challenging enough to keep her occupied. It would also prepare her to enter society. They call it a finishing school for that reason, after all."

"I know, and I am not procrastinating. I'm not," she insisted in response to his skeptical look. She resumed walking. "It's just that she won't be attending to Willowbank now, since we'll be going to New York."

He didn't debate the point. Instead, he tugged at the terrier's lead, and the dog, which had been burrowing amid a mound of the lady's mantle that lined the path, moved to join him as he resumed walking by Edie's side. "Let's go down to the Roman Temple," he said, nodding to a flagstone path nearly covered with creeping thyme and bordered by clumps of fennel and spires of mullein. "Flagstones are a bit easier for me to walk on than this gravel."

"Of course. You should have said something sooner," she admonished, as they veered onto the other path. "Are you certain you want to spend our two hours together walking?"

"At least part of it. Unless —" He broke off, glancing at her profile, liking the pretty, golden freckles scattered across her nose and cheek, noting with masculine appreciation the luminous quality of her skin and the delicate shape of her ear below the wide-brimmed hat. "Walking seemed the best thing, but if you've a more enticing suggestion to offer, I'm listening."

Soft pink bloomed in her cheeks, and he liked that, too. Her tendency to blush was one of the few things that enabled him to gauge what she was thinking, and he needed all the indicators he could find right now.

"I only meant that I shouldn't want you to be in pain," she said primly. "And I was under the impression that walking was painful for you."

"It is, but my leg always feels better afterward. I like walking with you, by the way," he added. "You don't rush me, and I appreciate it. Thank you."

"You're welcome, but I hardly think that's something for which you need to thank me. Anyone else would surely do the same."

"No, I'm afraid you're quite wrong, there. Most people tend to go too fast, then have to stop and wait for me, and it always makes me feel terribly self-conscious, so I usually walk alone. But you don't rush me or display any impatience, and I appreciate it."

They emerged into the Roman Garden. Designed to resemble a Pompeii courtyard, it had a central fountain, bordered on three sides by a strip of turf and a thick wall of trees and shrubbery. Along the fourth side stood the marble temple built by his great-great-grandfather, a wide limestone structure fronted by marble columns and topped with a slate roof. Beneath the pediment, a wrought-iron bench looked out over the fountain.

He decided now was as good a time as any to broach the subject he'd brought her out here to discuss. "Still, I wouldn't mind sitting for a bit," he added, pointing to the bench. "I've always liked this bit of the garden. It's one of my favorite places. I used to come here to read."

"You did?"

"You sound surprised."

"I am, rather, because I like to read here, too. I know it's called the Roman Garden, but I call it the Secret Garden because it's tucked back in this isolated corner. It's quiet here, peaceful. And I find the sound of the fountain soothing."

"I feel the same, so we have something in common, then." He smiled. "A good thing for husband and wife, don't you think?"

She didn't reply, but being an optimistic fellow, he decided to take that as a good sign. They walked up the limestone steps, where he looped the handle of the terrier's lead beneath one leg of the bench. Snuffles immediately began rooting around amid the lady's mantle and lamb's ears at the edge of the steps, while he spread his handkerchief across the seat for Edie.

They both sat down, and Stuart immediately grimaced as he leaned against the ornate back of the seat. "If we both intend to come here and read, I say we invest in a more comfortable bench. This one's a bit hard for sitting."

"True. I never thought about that, for I always lie in the grass when I read." She pointed to a patch of turf in the shade of a gnarled oak. "Just there."

"I used to do the same." He set aside his stick and stretched his leg out in front of him, relieved that the tightly cramped muscles had been loosened by their walk. "But nowadays, lying on the ground is a bit tricky."

"Your leg feels better now than it did when we started, though, I hope?"

"Yes, it does, thank you." He paused a moment, then added, "I consulted a doctor in London yesterday, by the way."

"Did you? You seemed dead set against it when I suggested it."

He met her surprised look with a rueful one. "It was Lord Trubridge's doing. While you were having tea with Lady Trubridge, her husband was dragging me off to Harley Street."

"And did the doctor prescribe a course of

treatment?"

"Yes." He turned toward her on the bench. "But to follow his prescription, I need your help."

"My help?"

"Yes. The doctor recommended daily walks, followed by exercises to stretch the muscles of my injured leg, and lastly, a massage with a special liniment. For that, I shall require an assistant."

Her eyes went wide as she appreciated what he was asking of her. "You want me to . . . to massage your leg?"

She made it sound as if he'd just asked her to jump off a cliff. "Yes. The stretching is also more effectively done with the aid of another person, so I shall need your help for that, too."

She was shaking her head before he'd even finished speaking. "No. I can't. I won't. You can't possibly expect me to —"

"I can, and I do," he interrupted, cutting off her flow of refusals. "I'm in pain, Edie. I didn't think there was anything to be done about it, but Dr. Cahill has convinced me otherwise. But his course of treatment impels me to ask for your help."

"I don't see why it has to be me. Surely, a valet —"

"I don't want a new valet."

"I've discerned that," she said, her voice softening a little. "But Stuart, you shall have to replace Jones at some point."

"I know. And I will, but I'm not ready, Edie. Not yet. And even if I were, it wouldn't matter. With this, I want your help and yours alone."

She looked away. Her fingers weaved together, pulled apart — an agitated gesture. "If alleviating the pain in your leg is the purpose, then I don't see why it matters who assists you."

"It matters to me." He reached up, entwining a curl of her hair around his finger. It looked like fire against his tanned skin, and it felt like silk. He tucked it back, and he heard her sharp, indrawn breath as his fingertips brushed her earlobe. "Skittish as a gazelle," he murmured, and cupped her cheek in his palm, turning her face toward him.

She went rigid beneath his touch. "I don't —" She broke off, frowning as she lowered her gaze to his shirtfront. "Please don't touch me."

Despite her words, she didn't pull back or turn her face away, and he took advantage of the fact, sliding his thumb across her mouth, savoring the velvety softness of it. Her lips trembled, but other than that, she stood utterly still beneath the light caress. "Why not? Is it really so awful to have me touch you?"

The moment he asked the question, he wanted to kick himself in the head, because if she answered in the affirmative, what the hell was he supposed to do then?

"It's not . . ." She paused, but she still didn't pull away. "It's not appropriate."

That wasn't at all the same thing, and Stuart felt a rush of relief. "Not appropriate? I know we're almost like strangers, but we are married. Why so reticent?" Even as he spoke, a possible explanation occurred to him, and he lowered his hand to his side in surprise. "Edie, are you still a virgin?"

Her face flooded with color. "That is a most improper question!" she cried, and jumped to her feet. "You have no right to ask me such a thing."

"Since I'm your husband, I rather think I do." He stood up. "Under ordinary circumstances, of course, a husband would never have to ask his wife that particular question, at least not after the wedding night. But we are not in ordinary circumstances, and it's important for me to know. Have you never made love?"

She looked away, pressing a palm to her forehead and giving a short laugh, as if unable to believe they were even having this conversation. "No," she said in a strangled voice, her face scarlet, "I have never made love. There," she added, lowering her hand and returning her gaze to his, her flushed face resentful and defensive. "Does that satisfy your curiosity?"

He drew a deep breath and let it out slowly, trying to think. This put what he was asking her to do in a different light. He'd always assumed Edie and that Van Hausen fellow had been lovers, but clearly, that had been an erroneous assumption on his part. And given the right circumstances, any incident, however innocent or trivial, could blacken a girl's good name.

That explained her reticence. Many young women were modest to the point of prudery; it was pounded into them as a virtue from the time they were born. Virginal fear was a common thing, particularly if a girl hadn't had many suitors and there was no mother to explain the facts of life to her. "Thank you, Edie," he said after a moment. "Thank you for telling me the truth."

She shifted her weight from one foot to the other, understandably uncomfortable. "Yes, well, now that you know, I'm sure you see why what you're expecting me to do is impossible."

"I don't see any such thing. To my mind, this makes what I'm expecting all the more necessary."

"You can't be serious! I have no intention of . . . of . . . massaging you or stretching you or whatever else you have in mind. I won't do it."

"So, you're saying you wish to renege on our bet? If so, then you'd best tear up that separation agreement, because you haven't a prayer of obtaining my signature nine days from now unless you live up to the terms we agreed upon."

"I shan't allow you to make advances upon my person!"

"I already warned you I would, but this isn't an advance on my part because I won't be touching you. You'll be touching me."

"I fail to see any difference."

"The difference is that you'll be in complete control of the situation. I thought you'd like that," he added as she shook her head in refusal, "since you're so bossy."

She bristled, seemed to take issue with that description. "That's a fine accusation, coming from you, since you seem to be the one issuing orders!"

"Only for two hours a day."

"You're doing this because you think it will make me desire you."

"I'm as transparent as glass, it seems."

"It won't, Stuart." There was a hint of desperation in her voice he hoped made her words a lie. She ducked her head, staring down at the ground. "It won't."

He refused to contemplate that possibility. "I'm in pain, Edie, and I'm tired of it, and I don't want to drink to excess or dose myself with laudanum, and I'd like to be able to take a walk without dragging along my leg as if it's made of wood. I was skeptical that anything further could be done, but Dr. Cahill assured me that his course of treatment will significantly reduce the pain and increase my mobility, if done daily. And since I am allowed to command two hours a day of your time, this is how I want us to spend it."

"Oh, for heaven's sake," she burst out, "this is the most ridiculous, absurd, futile —" She broke off, clearly having run out of adjectives. At last, she heaved an aggravated sigh. "Oh, very well," she muttered, and turned away to unhook Snuffles's lead. "Have it your way, then."

"You'll do it?" He blurted out the question, so startled by her unexpected capitulation that he forgot he hadn't allowed her a choice. "Thank you."

She straightened, and when she turned to

look at him, her cool green eyes were lit with those fiery gold sparks. "It's stupid to fight you. We both know if I refuse, I lose by default, and I have no intention of letting that happen. Besides, if your leg heals properly, you might decide to go back to Africa, and I can live here at Highclyffe without you just as I did before."

She jerked the lead. "Come on, Snuffles," she said, and turned to start back toward the house.

"We'll begin tomorrow after tea," he called to her retreating back as she stalked away. "And be sure to let me know what you would like us to do during your two hours."

"Oh, I have several things in mind," she shot back over her shoulder as she walked away. "Believe me."

Despite that vehement vow, Stuart couldn't help being relieved. At least she'd agreed to his plan. If she had continued to balk, he wouldn't have known what the hell to try next. As for what she had in mind for him, he could only hope her intent wasn't to shoot him with a pistol. Edie was a redhead, after all.

# CHAPTER 11

Shooting him with a pistol, Stuart found out the following afternoon, was not what Edie had in mind at all. Still, her plan for their time together proved to be almost as awful.

"And I can't tell you how much we of the Church appreciate your efforts, Your Grace," Mr. Ponsonby said for perhaps the fifth time since Edie and Stuart had arrived at the vicarage for tea. He beamed at Stuart with beatific pleasure. "You paved the way for our work quite splendidly."

Had he known how splendidly, he'd have avoided the expedition altogether, but he didn't say so. Wisely, he stuffed his mouth with a bite of seed cake instead.

"Your maps have enabled us to take the word of God into the deepest jungles of Africa," the vicar informed him. "The souls of many poor, brown babies have been saved by baptism since our missionaries have penetrated the African interior, and it's all due to your efforts."

Stuart pasted a polite smile on his face. "I'm delighted to hear it," he said, and managed to refrain from pointing out that medicines and food would be far more useful to the native peoples than dunkings in the Congo River.

"And so much valuable work is being done. Let me tell you all about it."

"No, no, really," he hastened to say, "it's not necessary to give me a full account."

"Oh, but I insist. You must know just what your brave and intrepid exploration has done for our missionary work. Even Her Majesty the Queen was most impressed. She is a cousin of mine, you know, and holds our work — and yours, too, of course — in the highest regard."

He thought he heard a choked sound from Edie, who sat beside him on the sofa, and as the vicar began a long, pompous, thoroughly aggravating dissertation on the churches that had been built, the barrels of clothing — stiff collars and corsets, he had no doubt — that had been shipped, and how many lost souls had been saved, Stuart ate many bites of seed cake and cast many furtive, longing glances at the clock, but after over an hour of the unceasing monologue, he couldn't help forcing a word in.

"You've been able to transport food into some of these places during times of famine, I trust?"

"Food?" The vicar blinked at him.

"Well, yes." Stuart offered an apologetic smile for interrupting the flow of missionary accomplishments. "Food is rather an important thing. They can't eat churches and clothes, you know," he added with forced jocularity.

"Food for the body is important, of course, but it's the food of the spirit, Your Grace, that is of greatest importance," Ponsonby said as he sat back and folded his hands over his substantial stomach.

"Quite." Stuart ran his finger around the inside of his collar and cast another desperate glance at the clock, but since he still had over thirty minutes to go before Edie's two hours were up, he felt impelled to turn the conversation to something a bit less nauseating. "I hope you feel we've been keeping up our part here in the parish while I've been away?"

"Yes, indeed. Oh, quite." The vicar paused to give Edie a beneficent nod. "Her Grace has been most generous as far as the parish is concerned. Most generous. Sales of Work, fetes, donations, and subscriptions. If I may say so, Her Grace tends to place a bit too much emphasis on our little hamlet — not that I'm criticizing, Your Grace," he added to Edie with a deprecating wave of his plump hand in Edie's direction. "But I do wish," he added, returning his attention to Stuart, "that the duchess possessed the more far-reaching, more worldly view that you and I hold, Your Grace."

Stuart jumped on those words, happy to take his revenge where he could. "I fear the duchess has a woman's view of these things, dear Vicar," he said gravely. "Somewhat narrow and confined."

Edie choked on her tea, something which, given the circumstances, he found quite gratifying.

"Yes, yes," the vicar replied. "We men have a far greater talent for appreciating the wider world. The ladies are more inclined to ponder the minor matters of life."

"Indeed," Stuart was happy to agree. "But we must allow the frail sex their little vagaries, mustn't we?"

That remark earned him a well-placed elbow in the ribs, and much to his relief, spurred Edie to bring tea with the vicar to an early end.

"Forgive us, but we really must be going," she said, and set aside her teacup. "The duke has only been home a day, you know," she added as she stood up. "And we've so many calls to make."

Stuart reached for his stick and was on his feet before the vicar had the chance to protest, and he was too relieved by their imminent departure from the vicarage to worry about what other ghastly visits Edie had in store for them. "Right," he added firmly. "Many calls."

"Of course, of course." The vicar, who obviously spent a great deal of time eating sandwiches while he pontificated about the spiritual state of the world, had a bit of a struggle getting out of his chair, but they were soon led out of the drawing room. "Shall I see you for early service on Sunday, or late service?" he asked, pausing with them in the foyer as his maid opened the door.

*Neither,* Stuart wanted to reply, but Edie spoke before he could think of saying the word out loud.

"Early, of course. Having been in heathen parts for so long," she added, smiling, "the duke is looking forward to attending church services with great anticipation."

"Naturally, naturally. We shall see you for early service, then. And I look forward to discussing our missionary work at greater length with you many times in future, Your Grace."

Stuart managed to hide his lack of enthusiasm for that prospect only until they were on the other side of the vicarage gate.

"He'll wait in vain for those conversations," Stuart assured her as they started walking down the lane that led back to the house. "I'd rather be thrust into a medieval Inquisition torture device than discuss anything about Africa with that man."

"What?" Edie glanced at him, her eyes wide with a pretense of astonishment and a definite smile lurking at the corners of her mouth. "But, Stuart, don't you want to hear more about the souls of the poor African babies?"

"Babies who don't need food, apparently," he muttered, jerking at his tie. "I'd forgotten just what a pompous nincompoop the man really is."

"He is, isn't he?" She started laughing. "Oh, you should have seen your face when he expressed his gratitude for your exploration because it furthered his missionary work! It was beyond description."

"I'm glad to know that you enjoyed yourself so thoroughly at my expense," he said, and he wondered in some chagrin if she intended to force him into tea with the vicar every day. But then, he turned his head to look at her, and any chagrin he might have felt vanished in an instant. She was looking at him, and her face was lit with laughter. Her smile, wide and lovely, made him catch his breath.

"On the other hand," he murmured, "if you intend to smile like that every time you enjoy yourself at my expense, I believe I shall be able to stand it quite happily."

Her smile faded, and she looked away at once, but when she lifted her hand to touch the side of her neck, the self-conscious little gesture told him she was more affected by the compliment than she let on. "Then you won't mind if we make one more call on our way back. You haven't met the new curate, Mr. Smithers."

He groaned. "Edie, no. First the vicar, and now the curate?"

She pointed to a narrow lane that branched off from the one they were walking. "His cottage is just there."

"But that's the gamekeeper's lodge."

"No, I built a new lodge for the gamekeeper a few years ago, one closer to the wood. This one, being so close to the church and the vicarage, is much better suited to the curate." She paused, then added in a diffident voice, "Perhaps you disagree?"

"No, actually, I think it was a fine idea. You did well." He was watching her as he spoke, and thought his words pleased her. But when she started down the lane to the curate's cottage, he stopped at the road. Pleasing her did not extend that far.

She paused a few steps ahead and turned to look at him over her shoulder. "Aren't you coming?"

"I am not calling on the curate. The vicar was enough for one day. Besides," he added, as she opened her mouth to debate the issue, "we don't have time."

She glanced at the enameled brooch watch pinned to the lapel of her green réséda walking suit. "But I have twenty minutes left."

"Which is hardly enough time for a call. You can deduct the twenty minutes from my time," he added, desperate to avoid another conversation with a member of the religious community.

"Oh, very well," she said, giving in, smiling like a cat with the cream. "If you insist upon being such a stickler about time."

"I shall be if you insist we call upon people as ghastly as Ponsonby."

"It doesn't matter anyway, I suppose. You'll meet the new curate when we attend Evensong."

"Evensong?" He looked at her, determined

240

to put his foot down about that. "I might have to go to Sunday service, but I will not attend evening prayers, too, not with that idiot Ponsonby. No, Edie. That is a step too far!"

"But I always attend Evensong. We conduct the committee for the Sale of Work afterward. You should come to that, too, because it's an ideal way for you to reacquaint yourself with several of the local gentry. My, you do seem quite adamant," she added, as he continued to shake his head in refusal. "So you prefer to just give in now, then, and sign our separation agreement?"

He eyed her askance. "You're serious about this?"

"Of course," she said, and resumed walking. "Mr. Ponsonby can tell you all about the missionary efforts in South America afterward." The words were barely out of her mouth before she was laughing again. "After all, you men appreciate the wider world so much more than we women do."

"Wider world, my eye," he muttered, falling in step beside her. "The fellow's never been beyond the cliffs of Dover in his life. I'd forgotten just what a fool he was. And so dull. How could I have forgotten those ghastly Sunday sermons when I was home from school for the holidays?"

"They are too terrible for words," she agreed. "Half the congregation falls asleep."

"It doesn't have to be that way, though. I'm the duke, after all. I can sack him and find a new vicar."

"I'm afraid you can't. He is a cousin of the Queen, you know," she added, adopting a hint of Ponsonby's lofty tone.

Stuart made a sound of derision. "The relation is so distant, it's hardly creditable. I'm more closely related to Her Majesty than he is."

"Still, there are some things that just aren't done, and sacking the vicar is one of them. You'll have to put up with him, I'm afraid. That's the way things are."

He grinned at that. "So you've learned some battles against tradition aren't worth fighting, have you?"

"Yes, I suppose I have. Fighting centuries of tradition all the time rather wears one out."

He chuckled. "Wellesley gave me the impression he's gone a few rounds with you."

"We've had our fair share," she said with a sigh. "He told you all about it, I suppose?"

"No. He's trained too well to be that indiscreet. But he mentioned that you have a rather — how did he put it? — American way of doing things."

"The ultimate insult!" she said, sounding amused. "Still, we're all right now, he and I. We've come to a sort of compromise about the way things are done. I tell him what I want, he advises me on how it's been done in the past, and I tell him thank you very much, now do it my way."

Stuart gave a shout of laughter. "That's your idea of compromise, is it?"

"Well, yes," she admitted, laughing with him. "I am the duchess, after all. It's not easy, though. Running a large estate like this is an exhausting business."

"It is tiring." He slid a sideways glance at her. "Which is why it's best to have a partner."

"Then I fear you shall be perpetually exhausted in future."

Stuart laughed at the tart reply. "You're so stubborn, Edie. But then, I've always known that. So tell me, what's your plan for us tomorrow?"

"I thought we'd go over the account books with Mr. Robson. It's necessary," she added, as he gave a groan.

"We shall meet with him if you insist, but I'd hardly call it necessary."

"You need to be ready to take things over

243

again after . . . after I'm gone."

He wondered if there was a hint of wistfulness in those last few words. He hoped so. "I refuse to contemplate the possibility of your leaving me. I'd much rather think about the two of us running things together as man and wife."

"And you call me stubborn?"

He made a face. "I fear ours is rather a situation of pot meeting kettle. Still, Edie, a meeting with the steward is what you want to do tomorrow? Really?"

"You did say I have my choice."

"Well, you could at least choose things that are fun," he grumbled.

"You didn't have fun today? What a shame." She looked away, but not before he caught the mischievous smile that curved the corners of her mouth. "I did."

Edie's enjoyment of the day, however, proved far too short-lived. Since yesterday, she'd willed herself to not think about their conversation in the garden and what he expected her to do, but as the house came into view, she could no longer avoid thinking about it. With each step closer to the house, her apprehension grew.

She tried to tell herself his request was hardly something to get worked up about.

He seemed to think her participation in these exercises would somehow inspire her to want him. That might work, she supposed, if she were a normal woman with a normal woman's desires. But she wasn't, and a few exercises and a bit of massage weren't going to change that.

Massage. She'd have to massage him. Touch him. Edie's uneasiness deepened, and though she tried to will it away by reminding herself of Stuart's assurance that she would be in complete control, that didn't help, for she knew how quickly and easily a woman's control could be taken away.

Stuart wasn't Frederick, she reminded herself. Nothing like him at all, and yet, that perfectly reasonable point didn't reassure her. But then, if fear could be assuaged with reason, she'd have been free of fear a long time ago.

By the time they reached the house, dread was like a stone in her stomach, and when they entered the library, she could no longer stand the suspense.

"All right then," she said and stopped, turning to face him. "Let's get on with this. Show me what it is you want me to do."

Her abruptness took him back a bit, she could tell. "Well, I can hardly show you in

245

here." He pointed to the French doors along the wall, all of which were wide open to let in as much air as possible on the sultry summer afternoon. "We've no privacy here."

*Oh, God.* He wanted privacy. She opened her mouth, but no words came out, for her throat seemed dry as dust. She gave a little cough. "I fail to see why privacy is needed," she managed at last.

"Because I prefer not to reveal my weaknesses where anyone could walk in and see them, particularly servants."

Edie bit her lip. She couldn't fault him for that. She knew all about wanting to hide pain and weakness. "I see."

"I'm glad you understand. So, do you prefer my bedroom or yours?"

Appalled, Edie cast aside any inclination to empathy. "I am not going to your bedroom!"

"Very well, yours it is, then. I shall see you there in fifteen minutes." He turned away, ignoring her spluttering protest, and started for the door to the corridor. "Wear comfortable clothes," he added over his shoulder.

She didn't move to follow. Instead, she glared at his retreating back. "The sooner these ten days are over, the better," she muttered.

"I agree." He paused in the doorway and

turned to give her a provoking grin. "The sooner you kiss me, the sooner we can move on to things that are even more fun."

"Fun" wasn't the word Edie would have used. At this moment, "agony" seemed a more appropriate description. She waited several minutes to be sure she wouldn't encounter him on the stairs, then went up to her own room and changed into a tea gown of blue silk with a high neck and a wrapper of ecru lace. She might have to help him stretch and exercise, but wearing a tea gown and a loosened corset were as comfortable as she intended to get.

Her maid had barely done up the buttons at her back when there was a rap on her door. Edie took a deep breath, then nodded to Reeves. When the maid opened the door, however, the sight of Stuart almost had her order Reeves to close the door again.

He had changed into a pair of loose-fitting gray flannel trousers, a plain linen shirt, and black smoking jacket. The shirt had no collar or stud, he wore no waistcoat, and the smoking jacket wasn't even properly tied, and the sight of him in this partial state of undress made her even more nervous than before.

She didn't know if she could do this. He'd promised he would not make advances, but even if he kept his word, just the idea of being in such intimate circumstances with him, of touching him and . . . and massaging him seemed impossible.

Her apprehension only increased when he came inside, pulled the door wide, and told her maid, "You may go down, Reeves, and have your tea. You shan't be needed for at least an hour."

Edie watched her maid go out and close the door behind her, and the soft sound of the latch clicking into place seemed as loud as a gunshot. In the silence that followed, she could hear her own shallow breathing, and when he cast a long glance over her, Edie had to fight the impulse to bolt for the dressing room and lock the door.

The air in the room seemed oppressive despite the open windows, and his first words did nothing to relieve the tension. "Are you wearing a corset?"

She colored up at once, and he sighed. "Edie, I told you to wear comfortable clothes."

"I am!" She grasped a handful of blue silk and ecru lace. "This is a tea gown."

"Even under a tea gown, I don't see how a corset could be considered comfortable, but I suppose it's up to you."

He kicked off his house slippers and

crossed the room toward where she stood near the foot of the bed, reaching into the pocket of his smoking jacket. "Here," he said, pulling out a pocket watch and small, green glass bottle. "Hold these."

"I appreciate the purpose of the liniment, of course," she said as she took the items from his hands, "but what is the watch for?"

"I'll explain in a moment," he said as he untied the sash of his smoking jacket and slid it off his shoulders.

"What are you doing?" she cried, a ridiculous question, since the answer was plain as day. "You can't undress in my room!"

He stilled, the garment caught behind him at the wrists. "I'm only taking off my jacket," he said, a frown of puzzlement creasing his brow at the violence of her reaction. "I can't really move about if I'm wearing it. I would have left it off altogether," he added as he took it up and draped it over the footboard, "but I didn't want to shock the servants. Wellesley would see me wandering the corridors in nothing but a shirt and trousers and keel over from the shock. To say nothing of the housemaids."

Edie got hold of herself with the reminder that this was no time to be missish. "Well, don't take off anything else," she muttered, and turned to put the liniment on her dressing table. "What do I have to do?"

"I'll show you." He cupped his hand over the side of his right leg. "When the lioness sprang, she caught me here and here," he said, demonstrating with the tips of his fingers where the animal's teeth had gone into the front and back of his thigh. "The injury tore my hamstring and quadriceps muscles."

"Ouch." Edie grimaced. "The pain must have been excruciating."

"The pain didn't last long — not then, at least. The wound was bleeding pretty badly, and it only took a few minutes before I passed out from loss of blood. Luckily —"

He broke off abruptly and his hand formed a fist at his side.

Edie looked up, and the frown on his face gave her a bit of a turn. "Stuart? Are you all right?"

"Sorry," he said and pressed his fist to his mouth with a cough. "It's just that this is harder to talk about than I thought it would be." His brow cleared and he lowered his hand. "Luckily, we'd driven the lions off by then, and my men managed to stop the bleeding. But that night, infection and fever set in."

"You told me you nearly died. So it was

the infection, rather than the wound itself, that almost killed you?"

"Yes. For three days, it was touch and go. On the third night, I was so far gone, my men were making preparations to bury me. I felt my life going, I knew I was dying, and I can't explain why I didn't. I just . . . refused to do it. Sheer stubbornness on my part, I suppose. The fever finally broke, and when I was strong enough to be moved, two of my men took me back to Nairobi. I thought I was all right, then, but in hospital, I got another infection. Odd when you think about it, for I'd never caught anything before. I don't even have malaria, and in Africa, that's saying something."

"Well, obviously, when you decided to get sick, you did it thoroughly."

"Yes, I suppose I did," he said with a bit of a laugh, and though it sounded a bit forced, Edie was glad to hear it. "But the fever broke again, and I made it through all right."

"Thank heaven you didn't develop gangrene. Or rabies. Or . . ." She stopped, pressing a hand to her chest at all the ghastly possibilities. "God, Stuart."

"The doctor was worried about both, but thankfully neither happened. I did have muscle damage, though. I was bedridden for three weeks, and even after I was on my feet, it was another two months before I could use my leg at all. And by then, atrophy had set in, and I was as wobbly as a newborn colt. Slowly, I got better, but the doctors said I'd probably never walk right again."

She nodded, striving to keep her face from showing any twinge of pity, for she could tell he hated that. "And did Dr. Cahill agree with their assessment?"

"Not completely, no. He's uncertain if my leg will ever be quite right, but he believes a regimen of walking and stretching the muscles of my leg will increase my mobility, break up the scar tissue, and help alleviate the pain. But I shall have to do this sort of regimen every day for the rest of my life."

"I see." Edie fell silent, studying his face for a moment. It was the same dark, handsome face she'd seen at the Hanford ball, and yet it was different. It wasn't, she realized, a reckless face anymore. "Stuart, what happened to Jones?"

He swallowed and looked away. "I'd rather not talk about that, Edie, if you don't mind."

She nodded, for if anyone knew what it meant to not want to discuss painful subjects, it was she. "Right," she said, forcing a brisk note into her voice. "So what would you like me to do?"

"Just stand there for a moment." Using the footboard, he lowered himself to the floor until he was in a prone position at her feet. It hurt, she could tell by his face, and she couldn't help thinking of the man she'd first met, a man who had moved through a crowded ballroom with the grace of a leopard. *He must hate this,* she thought. *After the life he's led.*

"Hand me the watch." His request interrupted her thoughts, and Edie complied, banishing any melancholy about the man he had been. At least he was alive. "Dr. Cahill gave me two stretches to start with," he went on. "I'm to do three of each."

"But what is the watch for?"

"I have to hold each stretch for thirty seconds, and gradually increase the time to a full minute." He lifted his injured leg until it was perpendicular to the floor. "Come closer, Edie, and wrap your arm around my leg. Closer," he added as she moved a step forward. "Your body should be flush against the back of my thigh."

Edie complied, feeling terribly awkward. She'd never done any nursing in her life, and what she knew of that particular skill could fit in a thimble. And she was fully aware of his leg pressed against her torso.

"Yes. Now, we're going to stretch my hamstring. Put your free hand on the ball of my foot and slowly press my toes toward my chest. I'll tell you when to stop."

She started to do as he asked, but the moment she did, he inhaled sharply, and she slacked her hold, stricken. "Did I hurt you?"

"No," he said. "It pulls, but it doesn't hurt. Do it again, only this time, don't stop until I tell you. There," he said, as she complied. "Now, don't let go for thirty seconds. And keep your arm tight around my leg so my knee stays locked."

Edie would never have thought a mere thirty seconds could seem so long. The room was warm, the air still, and their position shockingly intimate. She could feel the heat of Stuart's body all along hers — his heel beneath her breasts, his taut thigh against her abdomen, his hip against the side of her foot. This was beyond anything in her experience; with the exception of Frederick, she knew nothing of men, or intimacy either.

"All right," Stuart said at last, and the sound of his voice thankfully pushed thoughts of Frederick out of her mind. Edie let out her breath in a rush of relief and lowered her arms to her sides.

Stuart shook his leg a bit, then nodded.

"Do it again, and go a bit farther this time."

The second stretch was easier for her. The intimacy of it wasn't quite as shocking, and her apprehension eased. For him, though, it was harder. She discerned that by his breathing, for it was deeper, more forced than before. "Do you want me to ease back?" she asked.

He shook his head, and on the third stretch, he instructed her to take it even farther.

"Are you certain? I don't want to hurt you."

"You won't. I'm aware of how far I can push my body, believe me. Besides, even if it did hurt, I wouldn't mind." His gaze skimmed over her face, and his eyes seemed to darken to the color of smoke. "Not with the view I've got, anyway."

Edie could feel the heat of his gaze as if she were standing by a fire. She stirred, but that move only made her more acutely aware of his leg pressed against her body, so she stilled and looked away. She was afraid, suddenly, but it was an entirely different sort of fear than she was used to.

"Not susceptible to my blatant attempts at flirtation, I see." When she didn't answer, he moved against her, and she let go of his leg. "Oh, very well, if you won't flirt back, I suppose I shall have to show you the next exercise."

"That might be best. I don't flirt." She didn't say she had no talent for it. He probably already knew that.

He rolled onto his stomach. "Kneel down behind me," he said as he turned his head to the side and bent his injured leg. "You're going to stretch my front thigh muscle," he said as he held the watch beside his face to mark the time. "So you'll wrap your hand around my shin with your right hand and press my heel toward my bum."

It was a good thing he wasn't able to see her face, she thought as she complied with these instructions, for she knew she was blushing like mad. "How's this?"

"Yes, but harder. Use your weight. Rest your left forearm on my spine and brace your shoulder against the back of my foot. Good. Now lean in. More. A little more. Ssst," he hissed as she hit the tension point. "Hold it there."

This was a far more intimate exercise than the previous one. Even through a corset and three other layers of fabric, Edie was acutely aware of the tip of her breast touching his buttock and the side of her other breast pressed against his calf. Never had thirty seconds seemed so long.

When he finally called the time, she was so relieved that she couldn't help a heavy sigh.

He heard it. "Are you all right?"

"Of course," she assured him at once although she feared the breathless quality of her voice might not have made her reply very convincing.

But if he noticed, he didn't tease her about it. "Good," he said. "Do it again."

She did, and because she had to press harder this time, the thirty seconds seemed like a hundred. Everywhere his body touched hers, he felt scorching hot. Slowly, as the seconds ticked by, she became aware of other things: the slow, deep labor of his breathing, the hard muscle of his calf beneath her fingertips, the scent of sandalwood — his soap, perhaps? Inexplicably, her body began to tingle.

The third time, she was aware of all that and something more. She could feel tension rising within her own body, a thick, strange sort of tension she'd never felt in her life before. It unfolded inside her, warm and slow, but it also strengthened and deepened with each second that passed, until it felt almost . . . luscious.

*Shall we, Edie?*

She closed her eyes. She could feel the

rise and fall of his body beneath her with each breath he took. Everything else in the world seemed faint and far away.

"That's thirty seconds."

His voice pulled her out of the strange daze she'd fallen into. She sank back on her knees, and only when he rolled over and sat up, did she realize that her breathing was as hard and labored as his.

The room was hot, the air was still, her heart was thudding hard in her chest.

He smiled, and it hurt, piercing her like an arrow. "I think I like that one," he said softly.

She strove to catch her breath, but she didn't even know why she was breathing so hard. "Why are you doing this?" she whispered.

He tilted his head, studying her. "Why do I have the feeling we are not talking about my leg?"

"I understand why you want . . . what you want," Edie went on, not even knowing what impelled her to pursue the topic. "But why with me?"

He sat up straighter, drawing closer to her. "We've already discussed this. We're married, Edie."

She felt a curious sense of disappointment at that answer, and she didn't even know why. What on earth had she been expecting him to say? "You could probably gain an annulment if you petitioned for one. After all, I'm refusing to give you your . . . your . . ."

Her throat felt suddenly dry as dust, but she forced the words out. "Your conjugal rights. They might grant an annulment to you because of that."

"I don't care if they would." His gaze roamed over her face. "I don't want an annulment, Edie."

"And if it were granted," she went on as if he hadn't spoken, "you could remarry."

"I like the wife I have, thank you." He touched her, his fingertips gliding over her cheek so softly that she couldn't seem to find the will to pull back.

*You wouldn't,* she thought, squeezing her eyes shut. *Not if you knew.*

"You could find someone much better suited to you than I am," she said, hearing a note of desperation enter her voice, "someone much prettier —"

"Prettier?" he interrupted with a scoffing sound. "You think you're not pretty?"

She swallowed painfully and opened her eyes. "We both know I'm not."

His gaze roamed over her face for what seemed an eternity. "I don't know anything of the kind," he said at last.

She hated this, hated his open, appraising stare, hating more how raw and vulnerable it made her feel. "Now who's lying?" she whispered, and looked away.

"We both remember that afternoon on the terrace." His palm cupped her cheek, and he brought her gaze back to his. "And although I can't be completely certain why it sticks in your memory, I'll tell you why it sticks in mine. I said something that afternoon that made you smile, and that was the first time you had ever — and I mean ever — smiled at me."

"So?" The question was a tight, hard whisper, like the knot of fear inside her. She could hardly bear it, this light, tender caress, and yet . . . and yet, she was free to yank his hand away if she chose. *Stand up,* she thought, *walk away.* She didn't move. Her hands curled into fists at her sides. "What's your point?"

"My point is that you're right."

"About what?" She looked down, staring at his chin, trying to stare past him altogether, trying not to feel anything.

"About you not being pretty," he mused, his fingertips tracing featherlight explorations across her cheeks, down her temples, and along her jaw. "Because when you smiled at me that day, I didn't think you were pretty at all." He paused, his fingertips stilled. "I thought you were beautiful."

At those words, something fractured inside her. She caught back a sob. "I can't give you what you want, Stuart. You should find someone who can."

"But what about you, Edie? What about what you want?"

His thumb brushed back and forth across her lips, and it took all she had to force words out. "It doesn't seem to matter what I want."

"But it does matter." This light caress was almost unbearable. "Don't you want children?"

Fear pushed up higher, up against her heart, and it hurt. Like pushing a bruise. "No," she lied.

"Why not?" He stopped caressing her mouth. He leaned closer, and she tried to turn away, but his hand slid into her hair, holding her still.

"Oh, don't!" She jerked back, and the wrapper of her tea gown caught on his cuff link, tearing the delicate lace. The sound was like a match to powder, igniting her into action.

"I can't do this." She scrambled backward on her knees, trying to get to her feet and get away, but somehow, her skirts had become pinned beneath his hip. "Let go!" she cried, any shred of reason dissolving into sheer panic. She tugged desperately at her skirts. "Let go, let go, let go!"

He lifted his hips, freeing her, but by the time she managed to find her feet beneath the layers of lace, silk, and muslin and stand up, Stuart had also risen, levering himself up by use of the footboard. "Edie, wait!"

He grasped her wrist as she started to turn away, and when she pulled, he didn't let her go. Instead, his grip tightened, and she froze, gripped by fear, and shame, and a sudden, terrible sense of inevitability. Why run? What would be the point?

She stared down at the torn lace of her wrapper. It was a small tear, only an inch or two, and yet, she felt ripped apart, exposed, as if there were a scarlet *A* emblazoned on her chest. Her free hand lifted, and she watched it shake as she drew the edges of the wrapper together.

"My God." Stuart's voice seemed to come to her from a great distance away, but though his hoarse whisper was barely discernible over the roar in her ears, it was enough to tell her that he had realized the truth. His hand let go of her wrist as if she burned. "My God, of course. How dense

I've been."

His hand came up to touch her face. She flinched, and though his hand fell away, the fear inside her began forcing its way to the surface. She fought hard to hold it in, just as she had done so many times before, striving not to come apart.

Her chest began to hurt from the effort it took to breathe. The scent of eau de cologne seemed to fill her nostrils and wrench her stomach. Shame washed over her, burning her skin like the lye soap she'd used six years ago to scrub it all away.

"Edie, look at me."

She shook her head in refusal, but even as she did, she knew that unless she wanted to slip out in the middle of the night and run away, she'd have to look at him some time. And she could run to the ends of the earth, and it still wouldn't matter, for she could never outrun what had happened to her.

Steeling herself, she forced her gaze up, but the moment she saw his face, she felt her composure fracturing apart. She turned away, running for the door. She ran, not because of fear, but because the shocked, appalled look on Stuart's face was more than she could bear.

# CHAPTER 12

Stuart had felt many powerful emotions in his life. He'd been in the idiotic throes of first love and the dark depths of grief. He'd been awed by the breathtaking beauty of an African sunset and stopped in his tracks by the vibrancy of a girl's freckled face. He'd known lust, hunger, joy, and despair.

He thought he'd known rage. Until now.

Stuart stood in Edie's bedroom, and he knew all the angers he'd ever experienced before were nothing but petty irritations. Rage was different. Rage was this — his blood seething through his veins like lava, his head feeling as if it would split apart, blackness descending over his eyes and blotting out everything but Edie's shaking hand pulling her clothes together.

In that tiny action, the truth had come to him like a lightning flash, shocking him into utter paralysis as Edie had run out. He couldn't follow her, even now. He couldn't move, or even think, not with this rage erupting inside him. He could only feel.

Standing here, in a prim and pretty English bedroom of lavender silks and velvets, he felt more savage, more primordial than any beast he'd ever encountered in the African bush.

He wanted to kill the son of a bitch who'd done this to her. He wanted to hunt him, track him, bring him down and shred his flesh to his bones. He wanted to confront her father and demand why the hell he hadn't done something to avenge her. He wanted to flay himself for not seeing the truth before now. He wanted to get drunk, start a fight, put a hole through a wall — do anything but the one thing he knew he had to do.

Stuart took a deep breath and rubbed his hands over his face, working to govern the violence inside himself. Rage would be of no help right now.

He reached for his walking stick, took up his shoes, and returned to his own room. He dressed for dinner, and somehow, putting on a starched bib shirt, white waistcoat, black trousers, and black dinner jacket helped him tamp down the rage inside. As he tied his white silk tie into a proper bow, as he fastened shirt studs and cuff links, as he tucked a white pocket square into place, he was able to set aside the part of his soul that was raging beast and regain the part that was civilized man.

Then, and only then, he went in search of his wife.

He found her in the Roman Garden, or as she called it, the Secret Garden. She was sitting on the bench where they'd sat the day before, but as she caught sight of him emerging from between the tall clumps of fennel and spires of mullein, she jumped to her feet. "What do you want?"

He stopped, studying her across the courtyard, considering how to proceed without causing her more pain or making things worse. He'd come out here to comfort her, but looking at her now, he suspected she would welcome comfort about as much as she would welcome having a tooth drawn.

He took a deep breath. "It wasn't just your heart he broke, was it?"

Her face twisted, and it was like a knife going into his chest.

"He . . ." Stuart paused, working to force the words out. "He violated you."

She made no sound, she shed no tears. She didn't move or speak. She just looked at him, and no answer to his question was necessary. Her pain hung in the sultry sum-

266

mer air between them, and Stuart's rage drove even deeper, spread even wider.

From the beginning, he'd sensed her pain; he just hadn't seen the true reason for it. Or maybe he just hadn't wanted to see? This wasn't a broken heart or a virgin's fear; this wasn't something simple. Still, he knew the truth now, and as horrific as it was, there was no going back, so what was he supposed to do with the knowledge? God, in a situation like this, what was any man supposed to do?

"I want to kill him, Edie," he said, voicing his first impulse. "I want to board the next ship for New York, find that bastard, and kill him."

"You can't," she said dully. "I appreciate the gesture, but you can't. Here, a duke might perhaps get by with murder, but in New York, they've no such sentiment. They'd hang you. Besides, don't you think I thought of killing him? How many ways I plotted it? For a while, it was the only thing I lived for. But one . . . gets past that. There was Joanna to think of, you see. And her future."

"I know I can't murder him. But there are other possibilities."

"What? A duel over my honor?" She laughed, and it made him flinch. "I met him for a rendezvous. I never dreamed —" She stopped, and shook her head. "It doesn't matter. We were seen afterward, he refused to marry me, so by society's reckoning, I was a jumped-up slut, a slick little baggage who tried to trick a true gentleman into marriage and failed. There's no honor to fight over, especially not six years later."

"A duel is quite tempting, I confess, but it isn't what I'm thinking of."

She shook her head. "He's rich, he's powerful, he's quite untouchable."

No man was untouchable, but Stuart didn't say so. Instead, he drew another deep breath, reminded himself of what was important right now, and once again pushed his rage back down. He'd have time for that another day. "I can't begin to imagine what you endured, and I don't expect you to tell me about it, but —"

"Good." The word was like a rifle shot.

"But if you ever want to —"

"I shan't. Now please go away."

She was like a wounded animal, he thought, looking at her. Fear and pain were in every line of her — in the taut stillness of her form and in her watchful, wary stare. She wanted to be alone, to lick her wounds, and though she'd been that way all along, he couldn't let her stay that way.

More than ever, she reminded him of a gazelle, and he decided that was the only way to approach her. Slowly, moving with infinite care, he took a step closer, then stopped as she caught up the folds of her skirts. He took another step, and she glanced around as if trying to determine which way to run. But the lush shrubbery all around rather hemmed her in, and when he took another step, she must have decided not to go crashing through it. Instead, she lifted her chin and faced him down. "I would really like to be alone if you don't mind."

"I do mind," he answered, continuing around the fountain toward her with slow, measured steps. "By my estimation, I am still entitled to thirty minutes of your time today."

"You can't be serious." She stared at him, clearly aghast. "You can't expect to continue with this now!"

"I can, and I do." He watched her pale face go even whiter, but he could not withdraw, he could not leave her to this alone. She was his wife. "Nothing has changed, not for me. And I have eight days left. Unless you intend to renege?"

She shifted her weight and cast another furtive glance around.

"You could, of course," he went on as he began mounting the limestone steps. "But that would mean you'd have to run away from me."

He stopped in front of her. It was nearing dusk, the time of day when colors seemed most vivid and scents most potent. He could see the gold specks in her green eyes and the coppery glint in her red-blond hair. He could smell the fragrance of the garden, and he could smell her fear. "And running would be rather futile, don't you think?"

"You know nothing about it," she said through clenched teeth. "Nothing."

"But I do know about fear. I've faced it, more than once. That's what one has to do with fear, by the way. Face it and defeat it because you can't ever run far enough or fast enough to escape from it."

A sob tore from her throat, but she caught it back, biting down on her lip.

"I also know about pain," he went on. "I know about being wounded. But Edie, wounds do heal. There might be scar tissue left behind, but if you hold on long enough, even the deepest wound can heal."

Her head came up. Those gold specks in her eyes flashed like sparks. "So that's what you think?" There was derision in her voice. "You think you can heal me?"

"I was rather hoping we could heal each other."

"You don't need me to heal your wounds. We both know you could hire a valet to help you, or you could be treated by the local doctor. You don't really need me at all."

"Don't I?" It was his turn to look away, but as he stared past her shoulder to the intricate wrought-iron plaque that hung on the limestone wall behind her, his mind flashed back to the night he'd almost died. "That's where you're wrong, Edie. I need you more than you could possibly know."

"I don't see why."

"It doesn't matter, not right now." He forced himself to look at her again. "I came out here to comfort you, not the other way around."

She looked past him, staring at the fountain. "That was kind of you, but I'm beyond needing comfort."

"Are you?" He noted the blank impassivity of her face. "Are you, indeed?"

She stirred. "We should go in. It's almost time for dinner."

"Not yet," he said as she started to step around him. "There's one thing I want to say." He lifted his left hand to cup her face. She leaned back, evading his touch, a forcible reminder of what was at stake. So he moved back a step and opened his hand in front of her, offering it.

She looked at it but didn't move to take it.

"You don't have to take my hand," he said. "You don't have to kiss me, or bed me, or do anything else you don't want to do, Edie. There is only one thing I'm asking of you."

She kept her gaze on his palm. "What's that?" she whispered.

"Give me a chance." He paused, ducking his head a bit so that he could look into her face. "Give us a chance. I need that, and I think you need it, too."

He waited, and it seemed an eternity before she spoke.

"Tomorrow morning, we'll meet with Mr. Robson to go over the books. Ten o'clock." She stepped around him, but she didn't move to go down the steps. Instead, she stopped. "As to the other," she said over her shoulder without looking at him, "I'll try, Stuart. For the next eight days, I'll try. That's all I can promise you."

He watched her walk away, and he could only hope eight days was enough to buy him a lifetime. Just now, it didn't seem the least bit likely.

Of all the things Edie might have expected

to feel should Stuart ever discover the truth, relief had never been one of them. If she'd ever paused to contemplate the awful prospect that he'd uncover her secret, she would have predicted the result to be a deepening of the emotions that already haunted her. But to feel relief that he knew? No, Edie never would have predicted that.

And yet, in the wake of his discovery, she felt lighter, as if a weight had been lifted from her shoulders, and it was only then that she appreciated what a burden a secret could be when one carried it all alone.

But that didn't make anything easier. Despite a sense of relief, Edie felt even more vulnerable and exposed than before, and for her, dinner was awkward and embarrassing.

Joanna, however, saved the day by asking him about Africa, and throughout the meal, they were regaled with descriptions of that continent's breathtaking scenery and exotic animals, and tales of life in the bush. Joanna and Mrs. Simmons listened with rapt attention, and, though another time, Edie might have been equally fascinated, tonight she was too preoccupied to care much about stories of rhinos and elephants.

That he still wanted to continue astonished her. He knew the truth now. Didn't he see that what he wanted was hopeless?

And yet, even as she asked herself that question, she felt restive, uncertain. Was it hopeless?

She glanced up from her dessert to study him across the dining table. The dining room was the only one in the house still lit by candles, and in their mellow glow, glimmers of the African sun could be seen in his dark brown hair and bronzed skin. Laugh lines creased the edges of his eyes and mouth as he told Joanna some tale about taking a dandified Italian count on safari. He looked splendidly handsome in his dinner jacket, but then, he was a handsome man. She'd always known that.

*If I'd been five feet tall with bad teeth and a potbelly, I don't think the proposition you made to me would ever have occurred to you. I think you were at least a little bit attracted to me the moment you first saw me. I know damned sure I was attracted to you.*

His words in her room at the Savoy came echoing back to her, and for the first time, Edie wondered if there might be some truth in them. Would she have thought up the idea of marrying him if he hadn't been so terribly attractive?

As if he sensed her watching him, he looked across the table, and when she looked into those beautiful gray eyes, she felt the same strange, shivery feeling she'd felt the first time he'd ever looked at her.

She'd been desperate to find a way to avoid going back home, but until Stuart, she hadn't seen a way. And then he'd looked at her, with that quizzical frown on his brow and slight smile on his lips, and she'd felt his attraction like the pull of a magnet. Preoccupied with all the other emotions swirling around in her that night, she hadn't admitted it, or even realized it was there, and she'd always believed it was serendipity and nothing more. But now, looking at him across the dining table, she realized he was right. Amid her fear and panic, there had been attraction too, lurking beneath, suppressed and unacknowledged.

And like the girl in the garden at Hanford House had done, she looked at him now and wondered what her life might have been like if she'd met him first, before Saratoga, when she'd been innocent, unsullied, whole.

The room suddenly felt suffocating. Edie looked away and set down her fork. "Forgive me," she said, and stood up, bringing conversation to a halt and Stuart to his feet. "If you don't mind, I'm going to my room. I've a bit of a headache."

"Would you like a Beechum's Powder sent up?" he asked. "I have some."

"No, that's quite all right. I just want to go to bed. Good night, everyone."

She escaped the dining room and went upstairs, but even her bedroom wasn't much of a sanctuary. Not now, not since he'd been there. Edie leaned back against her closed bedroom door and stared at the floor where he'd touched her face and told her she was beautiful when she smiled, where he'd learned her secret and her shame.

*Nothing has changed, Edie, not for me.*

How could that be? How could he want her now? But he did. He wanted her because he thought she could be a normal woman, with a normal woman's desires.

She lifted her hand, her fingers touching her face as Stuart had touched her, and she wondered for a moment if it was possible. But then, she thought of what would come after he touched her face and called her beautiful, of the invasion of his body into hers, and hope vanished like a candle blown out.

Saratoga had happened. There was no going back.

The following morning, they met with Mr. Robson as planned. From Stuart's point of view, it was a wholly unnecessary meeting, for his steward had been forwarding quarterly reports for all the ducal properties to his club in Nairobi during his entire absence. But he didn't tell Edie that, for after the tumult of yesterday, she probably needed someone to be a buffer, and the dry, businesslike Scotsman was as good a buffer as any.

When she asked Robson to inform him of the current condition of the various estates, Stuart ignored the steward's slightly puzzled expression and gave the other man an encouraging nod. As Robson enumerated the various renovations made to the various ducal properties, he listened to everything he already knew with full attention.

It wasn't until the two hours were up that she ended the meeting. She then mumbled something about luncheon with the other members of the Sales-of-Work committee and a pressing need to pay calls on ladies of the county, and dashed off.

He appreciated that she felt the need to put some distance between them. And truth be told, he needed it, too.

He'd known from the first that Edie wasn't like any other woman he'd ever met. In coming home, he'd known she would not welcome the idea of a real marriage between them. And in making that wager, he'd known winning a kiss from her wouldn't be easy. He'd also thought he knew the reasons behind all that, but now he appreciated that he hadn't had a clue.

The truth, when it came, had shocked and enraged him. The initial shock had now passed, and his rage had been pushed down to a rolling simmer deep in his guts, but now he had to deal with something far more difficult, something all his vast but shallow experience with women had never taught him.

He would need to evoke pleasure in a woman whose only experience with love-making was brutality. He would need to bring her desire to life after another man had tried to kill it. As he pondered the question of how to go about it, he felt hopelessly at sea. It was probably the first time in his entire adult life that he was with a woman he had no clue how to seduce.

It scared the hell out of him.

And what if he failed? What if no matter what he did or tried to do, it wasn't enough? Every woman deserved the pleasures of lovemaking — not only the physical release, but also the tenderness, the intimacy, and the sheer fun of it, and it was a man's office to see that she received them. If he failed, Edie might never know those things.

Everything in him rebelled against that notion. She was his wife. She deserved those pleasures, by God, and it was up to him that she had them. But how?

All he had to do was win a kiss, but he knew if he pushed too hard or too fast, she'd flee, their wager be damned. And if he succeeded in winning their bet, there was no guarantee she'd keep to the terms afterward. Could he blame her if she didn't? Even if she stayed, could he make her happy? The horrific thing that had happened to her was like a wall between them. What if he couldn't breach it? What if she decided one day she couldn't stick it, and she left him?

Stuart forced his mind away from hypothetical scenarios and back to reality. He had to win a kiss. That was his only goal. As for the rest, he'd have to worry about that when he got there.

# CHAPTER 13

If Edie thought leaving Highclyffe for the afternoon would enable her to escape from Stuart, she was sadly mistaken.

Ladies of the county expressed great delight at the duke's return, commented about how happy she must be, and assured her that she need have no further worry about fulfilling her duty, for now that the duke had come home, there was sure to be a son and heir in the nursery before long.

Edie, feeling hemmed in on all sides, finally gave up making calls and returned to the house, where she found it vitally important to forgo tea and sort through the storage rooms in the attics with Mrs. Gates instead.

But she could not avoid being alone with him forever. At five o'clock, one of the housemaids came up and informed her that His Grace had finished his tea and was waiting for her on the terrace so that they might take their evening walk together.

She went down to join him with a feeling of dread, but much to her relief, he did not refer to the mortifying events of the day before. As they took Snuffles for a stroll through the gardens, she kept their conversation on safe, neutral ground: the fine, hot weather, the news in the village, and the condition of the herbaceous borders, and he seemed content with these mundane topics.

Afterward, she went to her room and changed into the same sort of loose-fitting tea gown she'd worn the day before, and just as she had the day before, she kept her corset on. Stuart might be right that it would be easier for her to assist him if she didn't wear one, but to her mind, the more barriers between them, the better.

Not that it seemed to make much difference, for by the time he tapped on her door a few minutes later, she was as jumpy as a cat on hot bricks.

When she opened the door, the sight of him in his smoking jacket was a forcible reminder of the intimacy the day before and the painful revelations that had followed. When he closed the door behind him, the turn of the key in the lock drove her to the other side of the room. When he slid off his shoes and shrugged out of his smoking jacket, she busied herself with straightening the bottles on her dressing table, but that only made things worse, for the green glass bottle of liniment was among them, and she could not for the life of her imagine ever being at ease enough in his company to apply it.

When he asked if she was ready to begin, she rose from the dressing table and crossed to where he stood, but she couldn't quite meet his gaze.

He noticed it at once. "Edie, you don't need to be nervous."

"I'm not nervous," she denied, and the moment she said it, she grimaced at how horribly unconvincing she sounded. "All right, yes," she admitted. "I am."

"So am I, if that makes you feel better." He laid down, rolled onto his back, and stretched his leg toward the ceiling. "After all," he added as she wrapped her arm around his thigh, "you have all the power here."

Since she never would have chosen to be in this position, with his leg pressed against her body and heat spreading through her own, she didn't feel like she had any power at all. "How so?"

He spread his arms wide. "I'm at your

282

mercy. If I misbehave, you can make me pay for it."

She didn't see how, since they both knew he could easily overpower her anytime he wished, but she didn't explore the point, and they completed all the stretches without any further conversation. The intimacy of assisting him was even more acute than the day before, however, and she was quite relieved when they were finished.

"Is it starting to help?" she asked as she stood up and moved a bit farther away. "The walking and the stretching?"

"I think it is." He wriggled his leg experimentally, then stood up, testing his weight on it a bit. "Yes, I really think it is," he said after a moment. "It's a bit sore, but I expect that liniment Cahill gave me will help. Where did you put it?"

She froze, and all her mortification of the day before came roaring back tenfold. "I can't, Stuart," she blurted out, rubbing her hands down the sides of her gown. "I can't do that part."

He didn't seem surprised. He nodded. "You don't have to, Edie, if you don't want to."

His quiet acceptance of her refusal impelled her to reiterate her point. "I want to help you," she said, and crossed to the

283

dressing table to retrieve the bottle. "I do. But after . . . after yesterday, you must see that there are some things I can't bear. Here," she added, shoving the bottle at him.

He took the bottle from her outstretched hand. "Edie —"

"I know you want me to do it," she said, her cheeks growing hot, "and of course, I know why. I mean, I'm not some young, green girl."

For some strange reason, that made him smile.

"But it's a step too far, Stuart. It's too . . . too . . ." She looked away, working to force the last word out. "Intimate."

"Edie, stop." He put the bottle in his pocket and took a step closer, putting his hands on her arms. "You don't have to justify anything to me." He ducked his head, so he could look into her averted face, and he said, "You know, I think this finally gives me the opportunity I've been waiting for."

"Opportunity?" she echoed, and the word sounded faint to her ears.

"Yes. There's something I feel I need to say, but I haven't known quite how to bring it up, and this only underscores the fact that I must. Before I leave you to change for dinner, might we sit and talk for a moment?"

She would have preferred to bring this

interlude to an end, but she gave a reluctant nod. She gestured to the two plum velvet chairs flanking the fireplace, but when she took one, he did not take the other. Instead, he crossed to her dressing table and pulled out the cushioned stool tucked beneath it. Carrying it by one of its wooden legs, he brought it across to where she sat and placed it directly before her.

His knee brushed hers as he sat down in front of her, but it would be silly to object since they had been in much closer proximity only a few minutes earlier.

With that thought, the room seemed even warmer than before, and she wished that the open windows offered some sort of breeze. She shifted a bit sideways and folded her hands primly in her lap. "What is it you wanted to discuss?"

"Anytime there are confidences between people, it's always awkward afterward." He stretched out his right leg beside her chair, set aside his stick, and leaned forward, crossing his forearms over his left knee. "Please believe that I don't want to make things harder for you, or cause you any further embarrassment or pain, but there is one thing about what was revealed yesterday that I need to address."

She glanced past him to the door, feeling

a bit desperate. "I'd rather you didn't."

"I'm sure. And I wouldn't if I didn't feel it was absolutely necessary. It's damned difficult though . . ." He fell silent, pressing a fist to his mouth, and he looked away for a long moment. She waited, hands clenching more tightly in her lap with each moment, wishing he would just say it, whatever it was.

At last, he stirred, lowered his hand, and looked at her again. "Edie, I have the feeling that you were wholly innocent when this happened to you, that you had no experience at all. Am I right?"

*Oh, God.* Edie's hands came apart to grip the arms of her chair. "Why are you asking me this?" she whispered harshly, turning her face aside.

"Because if that's so, then there's something you may not know, something you need to know. Among all animals, humans included, there are rules. Whether it's a pride of lions or a colony of monkeys or a man and a woman alone together, one of the most basic rules of any society is that the female always has the right to refuse the male's advances."

Edie wriggled in her chair, so uncomfortable that she could hardly breathe. "I really don't want to talk about this, please."

"I know you don't, and I'm sorry to cause

you distress, but it's important we get this quite clear. Edie, please look at me."

She forced herself to comply. His face was grave, and when she looked in his eyes, the tenderness she saw there was almost her undoing. But as difficult as it was to hold his gaze, she did.

"I daresay you don't believe that that particular rule exists," he went on. "Some men break it, obviously." He grimaced at that, and he paused long enough to draw a deep breath. "But I want you to know that between us, Edie, it is inviolable."

"That's an easy thing for a man to say, Stuart," she choked.

"I realize that," he said gently. "But we both know my intent is to seduce you, and despite what I learned yesterday, that hasn't changed. It's only fair to warn you that I will make advances. I might pick up your hand, for instance."

He leaned forward, reaching for her hand — slowly, giving her plenty of time to snatch it back if she chose. Edie didn't move.

He lifted her hand in his, holding her fingertips in a loose grip. "You can pull away if you want to." The pad of his thumb brushed back and forth across her knuckles. "Do you want to?"

The caress was featherlight, and yet it

made her tingle — with apprehension and something more. "You're only holding my hand," she said, trying to sound indifferent. "It seems harmless enough."

"True, but I might turn it over." Slowly, he did so, and his thumb brushed her palm. It tickled, and she gave a start of surprise. He stopped, and she knew he was waiting for her to make a choice. She didn't move.

"I might . . ." He paused. Cradling her hand in his, he lifted it. His eyes met hers as he pressed her hand to his cheek. "I might kiss it."

He turned his head, still holding her gaze, and pressed a kiss into her palm.

She felt it through her entire body, a sensation that was not fear at all. She gave a gasp of surprise and jerked her hand away, but even after she had pulled away, she could still feel the warmth of his lips against her palm.

Resisting the impulse to tuck her hands behind her, she forced herself to say something. "I don't suppose . . ." She paused, striving to put an acerbic note into her voice, "I don't suppose you could just resist the temptation to make these advances?"

The question, when it came out, was a breathless rush, not nearly as biting as she'd have wished.

"I'm afraid not," he answered, and though his voice was grave, there was a hint of a smile at the corners of his mouth.

"I knew that's what you'd say," she muttered.

"The stakes are high, Edie, and I'm playing this game to win." His smile vanished. "But if there's anything I ever do, or try to do, that you don't like, or don't want, you don't have to justify your objection. All you ever have to do is say no."

That was too much to bear. "I did say no!" she cried, her hands balling into fists, her control threatening to splinter apart. "I said it to him. I said it over and over and over."

Stuart's mouth tightened, and for a moment, she could see her pain in his face. Pain, and anger — anger, she realized that was on her behalf. "I'm sure you did. But I am not him." He reached out, fingers gliding along her cheek to push back a stray lock of her hair. "Always, Edie, always try to remember that. I am not him."

With that, he looked away, glancing at the clock on her mantel. "I see that I have used a quarter hour more than my entitled time today," he said, shoving back the stool and reaching for his walking stick. "You can dock me for it tomorrow, if you like," he said, his voice light. "Although I rather hope you don't, for I'm sure you have some very exciting plans for us tomorrow."

She drew a deep, steadying breath and stood up, grateful for his offhand teasing, for it helped her regain her composure. "I do, actually. Very exciting plans."

"A few rounds of whist with some of the county's elderly spinsters?" he guessed as he rose to his feet. "Or Evensong perhaps?"

"Neither of those. Not tomorrow, at least. We are going into the village to do some shopping. Joanna and I need to visit Miss May's."

"The milliner?" He groaned. "Tell me you're joking."

"My outing, my choice. You set these rules, remember?"

"There are limits, Edie," he grumbled. "The vicar, Mr. Robson, and now Miss May's?"

"We might stop by the draper's shop as well."

"Worse and worse! Still, these blatant attempts to bore me to death shan't succeed, for no matter what we do, I don't find you the least bit boring. I enjoy your company, even if it's only for a visit to the milliner's and the draper's. But," he added as he turned away and started toward the door, "just so you know, I might have to snatch a kiss from you along the way to liven things up."

Edie's heart gave a hard thud of alarm in her chest at that possibility, but she realized in horror that right alongside it, she also felt a tiny but unmistakable dash of anticipation. The idea that she might be looking forward to the possibility of being kissed by him was so startling and so muddleheaded that he had already crossed her room and opened the door before she managed to think of a suitable reply. "Even if you did kiss me," she said, mustering her dignity, "it wouldn't count."

"True." He paused in the doorway and grinned at her over his shoulder. "Unless you kiss me back."

"It still wouldn't count!"

He merely laughed, slipped out the door, and closed it behind him.

The following afternoon, they went to Miss May's millinery establishment, but Edie only forced Stuart to endure twenty minutes of hat shopping before she purchased the packet of feathers she needed, and they departed the shop. Joanna begged to be allowed to peruse the painting and sketching supplies available at Fraser's Emporium, and Edie agreed, sending Mrs. Simmons in to accompany her.

"So Joanna likes to muck about with paints, does she?" Stuart asked, as the girl and her governess disappeared into the shop.

"She adores it," Edie told him. "She's quite good, too, even with oils. Whenever we're in London, she wants to visit the museums and the art galleries. The Royal Exhibition is near her birthday, so I always take her to it. She loves painting."

"Does she, indeed?" He frowned, looking thoughtful as he glanced into the window of Fraser's. "That knowledge might prove useful," he murmured.

"Oh? How so?"

He returned his attention to her. "Oh, Christmas, you know. And her birthday." He pointed toward the door. "Don't you want to go inside?"

"No, no. I have another shop to visit. We'll call for her on the way back."

"Whitcomb's?" he guessed, as they continued on up the High Street. "I suppose that's where we're headed?"

She laughed. "The draper's? No, no, I won't subject you to that, not after you've been such a sport about going to Miss May's."

"That's a fortunate thing for both of us, then. Since you are not making me endure contemplation of buttons and pins, I won't continue conjuring plans for revenge."

"Have you been making such plans, then?"

"I have, but don't expect me to tell you what they are. I intend to hold them in reserve in case you decide to drag me along to one of your charity committee meetings."

"I would never do that." She made a face at him, thinking of the calls she'd made the day before and all the delight his return from Africa had evoked among the ladies of the county. "With you at our meeting, we'd never accomplish anything. The women would be far too occupied fluttering around you to do any work."

"If they did, would it make you jealous?"

"No," she countered at once. "I'm the only woman on the committee under sixty."

"Ah, but what if that weren't the case?" He slanted her a wicked look. "If all the women were young and beautiful, what then?"

The jolt of jealousy was so unexpected and so violent, it caught her completely by surprise, and she almost tripped on the sidewalk. It was suddenly incumbent upon her to pretend great interest in Haversham's Confectionery Shop, and she stopped, turning toward the window. She leaned close to the glass, cupping her hands on either side of her face as if to keep off the glare. But it was really to hide her expression, for she feared what she felt was written all over her face.

He leaned close to her ear, tilting his head to duck beneath the brim of her hat. "Keeping mum on that score, are you?"

"No need," she murmured, working to sound as prim and indifferent as possible. "I told you when we married . . ." She paused, swallowed, and said the rest. "You could bed any woman you wanted, and I wouldn't care."

"Edie," he said, his voice softly chiding. "C'mon, toss a chap a crumb of encouragement, will you?" He nuzzled her ear, right there on the High Street. "Just a crumb. Tell me that the idea of another woman makes you a tiny bit jealous."

Her face was hot, flushed, and she wanted to press her cheek against the glass. "Maybe," she whispered, admitting the wretched truth. "Just a tiny bit."

He laughed, a low, soft laugh against her ear, and seemingly satisfied, he pulled back. "Do you want something from Haversham's?" he asked.

"Um . . . I'm not sure," she lied, trying to

concentrate on the rows of petit fours and tea cakes lined up in display cases and not on the fact that though he was standing a full foot away, she could still feel the brush of his lips against her ear. "I'm deciding."

"Like sweets, do you?"

He made it sound so terribly naughty. "Some sweets, yes," she said, and straightened away from the window. "I think I will go in. I see they have chocolates, and Joanna loves those."

"Then I shall leave you for a few minutes. I need to go across to the telegraph office for a bit. I shan't be long."

"You wish to send a telegram?"

"Several, actually." He didn't explain. "If you'll forgive me?"

She watched him point across the street, and she shook her head. He didn't owe her explanations of his correspondence. "Of course."

She was glad for the separation. By the time he returned to fetch her, enough time had passed for her cheeks to cool and her poise to return.

"No chocolates?" he asked, noting her lack of a pastry box as she stepped out onto the sidewalk.

"Not today." She turned and resumed walking up the High Street. "I'm having them delivered."

"So, where are we going next?" he asked, falling in step beside her. "Or do you intend to keep me in suspense?"

"We're already there," she said, and stopped again, two shops down from Haversham's, pointing at the bright blue door beside her. "I want to visit Bell's Antique Shop."

"Antiques, my eye." Stuart made a disparaging sound as he moved around her to open the door. "Nothing in Bell's is older than the reign of George II."

Edie couldn't help a giggle at that, causing him to pause with his hand on the knob.

"What's so amusing?" he asked.

"Stuart, any object from the reign of George II is older than my *country.*"

He grinned back at her. "True enough," he said, and opened the door.

Inside the shop, Edie wandered over to the jewelry, thinking she might find a brooch or buckle to suit the hat she was making over, but she'd barely leaned over one of the glass cases before Stuart called to her from another part of the room.

"Edie, come look at this."

She glanced in the direction of his voice, but whatever he was looking at was obscured from her view by a lacquer red

Oriental cabinet. She circled around it, and as she moved to stand beside him, she saw that what had captivated his attention was a large music box made of walnut, with burled veneers, brass handles, and a mother-of-pearl inlay on the top. Displayed on a matching table, it was a beautiful piece.

Mr. Bell, always quick to discern an interested customer, came bustling over. "It's a Paillard music box, Your Grace. Swiss mechanism, of course, with a twenty-key organ and three cylinders."

"Given that level of sophistication, it must be of fairly recent manufacture."

"Oh, yes, it's quite new. It belonged to Mrs. Mullins, of Prior's Lodge. She had it delivered from Zurich only last year, but she died shortly afterward. Her daughter lives abroad and didn't want it, so her solicitors asked me to sell it for her."

"Mrs. Mullins died?" Stuart looked up, momentarily diverted. "I say, that's a shame."

"Yes, yes, but she was ninety, you know."

"Quite so." He ran his hands over the lid. "May I?"

"Certainly."

Stuart opened it, and as he did, Mr. Bell pointed to a small knob on the side. "One turns that to begin the music. Allow me to demonstrate." He did so, and at once, the melody of a waltz began to play.

Edie was watching Stuart, and she saw a smile curve his mouth. "Strauss," he murmured. "Too bad it's *Vienna Blood*. I prefer *Voices of Spring.*"

He looked at her, and Edie's mind flashed back to the ballroom doorway at Hanford House — his beautiful gray eyes looking at her, Strauss's *Voices of Spring* waltz playing, and destiny drawing her to him like a magnet. "You remember," she murmured.

Mr. Bell gave a tiny cough. "There is a cylinder for *Voices of Spring,*" he said, and opened the drawer of the table beneath the box. "Here."

Stuart didn't bother to look. Instead, he waved a hand in Mr. Bell's direction, and his eyes remained locked with hers as the shopkeeper tactfully disappeared. "I remember everything about that night, Edie."

"Me, too." She colored up at once, but she couldn't look away. Instead, she smiled a little. "Your tie was undone."

He smiled back. "Was it? I'm not surprised though I daresay I shocked everyone in the ballroom by appearing in such a state of undress." His smile faded. "You know, when I first saw you that night, I thought of asking you to dance with me, but I didn't know

298

you, or anyone standing near you, and I didn't see much point in obtaining an introduction anyway since I was intending to leave in a few days. But now, I wish I'd done it, Edie. By God, I wish I'd hauled you into my arms right then and there and pulled you out onto the ballroom floor, proprieties be damned." He looked down at his walking stick. "I wish I had known I'd never dance again. I'd have liked my last dance to be with you."

Edie's heart twisted in her breast. She felt his pain, and it hurt her, too. She studied his bent head for a moment, then she said, "I appreciate the romantic sentiment, but you'd have regretted it straightaway. I can't dance."

"What?" He looked up and made a sound of disbelief. "Stuff. Every girl can dance."

"I can't. I'm awful. Because I'm so tall, it makes it awkward for my partners. And," she added with an apologetic grimace, "I always want to lead."

He laughed, and, to her relief, that seemed to shatter his sudden melancholy. "Now that," he said, "I can believe."

"Whenever I danced, the results were always painfully embarrassing for the poor man in question — smashed toes, twisted ankles, wounded pride."

"If so, it serves him right. No man who dances well ever allows his partner to lead." He paused, and his lashes lowered. "Not on the ballroom floor anyway."

He glanced over her, and her body warmed with each place his heated gaze touched her. By the time he met her eyes again, she felt as if she must be melting into a puddle right there in front of him.

If he perceived how she felt, he didn't show it. Instead, he turned and put the lid down gently on the music box.

That surprised her. "Don't you want to buy it?" she asked.

"No." He didn't look at her, but his voice floated back to her as he walked away. "Some chances don't come twice."

# CHAPTER 14

They had tea on the terrace when they returned, and afterward, Stuart expressed the desire to tour some of the cottages, so they took Snuffles and headed in that direction for their evening walk.

They passed the rose garden on their way back to the house, and Stuart's steps slowed beside a pillar rose of deep lavender with a few late blossoms on it. "That's a pretty rose," he commented and stopped.

Caught by surprise, Edie stopped beside him, giving him a dubious look as he cupped one of the blooms and inhaled the scent.

He glanced at her, caught her expression, and laughed. "You look as if I just declared the sky a lovely shade of green," he said, and let go of the flower.

"I've never thought of you as the sort of man who would care much about roses."

"No? But then, you don't really know me well enough yet to judge, do you? What's this rose called, by the way?"

"I haven't decided what to call it yet."

"You grafted this?" The question was uttered in a tone of such innocence, Edie was instantly suspicious.

"I did." She studied him through narrowed eyes. "Why do I have the distinct impression you already knew that?"

He grinned. "You're too clever for me. Very well, I shall admit the truth. I had a long conversation with Blake after we met with Robson yesterday."

"Did you?"

"Yes. I told you I'd soon have the servants on my side," he added, his grin widening. "Blake, you'll be sorry to hear, told me all about your love of rose gardening and was eager to show me your latest creation. Perhaps another day you'll show me the other roses you've grafted?"

She gave a sniff and looked away. "As if you care two straws about my roses."

"But I do care. I'm interested because it's something you love, and I want to know more about the things you love."

"Most of the things I love would bore you, I suspect."

"Would they? What makes you say so?"

"Grafting roses?" she countered. "Would you ever find that interesting?"

"I don't know. I might."

She shook her head, not able to credit it. "You've traveled all over Africa, you've seen elephants, rhinos, lions —" She broke off, mindful of his injury. "The point is, rose gardening would be very small beer after that to a man like you."

"A man like me." He fell silent, looking down at Snuffles, who was burrowing between two boxwoods of the hedge that lined the path. "You mean the man I was, I think," he added after a moment.

"I'm sorry," Edie said, stricken, remembering their conversation in Mr. Bell's shop earlier. "I don't mean to remind you of painful things."

"Why shouldn't we talk of it?" He shrugged as if it didn't matter. "I'm not the same man I was, and no denying it. And I don't just mean because of this," he added, gesturing to his leg. "I was a restless sort of chap, that's true, and I took to safari work like a duck to water. I loved wondering what was over the next hill, and I loved finding out. But what I never understood until this happened to me was that if one's always going to new places, one never stops long enough to see the beauty in the old places." He glanced around. "Highclyffe, for instance. I took it for granted all my life, but never realized how much I loved it here. Now, I'm much more appreciative of it than when I went away."

Edie considered that. "I suppose," she said after a moment, "that if one has faced the possibility of death, one's perspective about everything is bound to be altered as a result."

"Yes, that, too. But there's an even simpler aspect to it than that. My injury slowed me down. I couldn't go dashing off anywhere I wanted at the drop of a hat. I was forced to bring my life down to a much slower pace."

"You must have hated that."

"I did at first. It was like hell. But, after a bit, I began to see things I'd never bothered noticing before. I used to be the sort who had to be hit over the head with something to truly notice it." He paused. "That's why I noticed you."

"Well, it's hard not to notice a girl who is six feet tall," she said, laughing, trying to make light of that particular flaw. "And, it becomes impossible not to notice her when she chases you out to the garden and proposes marriage to you."

"No, no," he said, shaking his head, "that's not what I mean at all." He moved closer, close enough that the ruffled jabot of her tea gown brushed his chest. "For one thing, you're not taller than I am," he murmured, and his finger brushed beneath her chin, lifting her face. "See?"

Edie went still beneath the light touch, but she couldn't pull back. She couldn't look away as his gray eyes darkened to that smoky color.

"As for the other, shall I tell you why I noticed you?" He didn't wait for an answer. "You were looking at me, staring really, and your gaze was so fierce, so intent, and I couldn't imagine why."

She forced herself to say something. "How terribly rude of me."

"It was riveting. I felt as if I'd just been pinned with an arrow." He laughed a little. "Cupid's arrow, possibly."

She frowned a little, uncertain. "Are you flirting with me?"

His gaze roamed over her face, an open, unnerving stare, and she wanted, suddenly, to look away. But she didn't. "No, Edie. I am a bit of a flirt, I know. I always have been. But in this case, I'm quite serious. When I first saw you, I felt as if I'd just run straight into something wholly outside my experience. You weren't like any girl I'd ever seen before. The way you looked at me wasn't coquettish — not a bit. But it wasn't uninterested either. I didn't know what it was. I'm still not completely certain how to define it, even now."

She had no intention of helping him on that score. There was no way she'd admit that her first sight of him had been equally shattering. Not Cupid's arrow, but riveting just the same.

"Anyway," he went on, "I loved Africa because it appealed to the man I was then. It's a continent of enormities — elephants, stretches of plain as far as the eye can see, sunsets that are so stunning, it's as if the sky's on fire. But I'm not that man anymore. Nowadays, I'm much more appreciative of things like a walk in the garden, and a pretty rose." He dropped his walking stick to the grass and plucked one of the roses off the pillar. Then, ignoring her protest, he untied her bonnet and pulled it off.

"Hold this," he ordered, shoving the bonnet into her hands. He ran a hand over the short stem to be sure there were no thorns on it, then he leaned sideways, tucked the stem into her hair behind her ear, and straightened to admire his handiwork. "There, now," he murmured. "That's a sight any man can appreciate."

"You'd say something like that to any woman you wanted to seduce."

"This is more than seduction. This is

courtship."

"I wouldn't know the difference," she said with a little laugh, looking down at her hat. "I've never had either."

He didn't reply, and when she looked up again, she found him watching her in a way that made her catch her breath.

"You deserve both, Edie," he said. "And I intend to see that you have them."

It was all very well to talk to Edie about courtship, but later, in her room with her arms wrapped around his leg, Stuart couldn't help thinking seduction much more appealing.

The first time she'd stretched his leg, the pain had been severe enough to hold his desire in check, and her subsequent revelation shocking enough to keep it at bay.

But now, even knowing the ghastly thing that had happened to her wasn't enough to stop arousal from stirring in him when she touched him. He kept reminding himself of what she'd been forced to endure at another man's hands, but his masculine imagination proved stubbornly resistant to such gentlemanlike considerations.

He'd been given a glimmer of hope yesterday in kissing her hand, and another earlier today by her admission that the idea of him with another woman made her jealous. Two indications she wasn't as indifferent to him as she might like to appear. But, nonetheless, reality had to proceed much more slowly than his imagination, and he tried to remember that he was only torturing himself with speculations about taking off her clothes or kissing her beautiful skin, for such things were probably a long way off. But that didn't help much either, and he could only conclude he was a glutton for self-punishment.

By the midst of the second exercise, with her body behind his and her weight pressing him to the floor, he was contemplating how delicious it would be if he could somehow reverse this position, and he knew this had to stop, or he'd go mad.

She certainly wasn't having any fantasies about taking off his clothes and kissing him, and that was really the crux of the problem. He just didn't know what to do about it. How did a man seduce a woman under these circumstances? How did he make her want what had only brought her pain?

"You're very quiet," she commented as she sat back.

"Am I?" He stretched out his leg, stirred it a bit to shake out the taut muscle, then bent it again so she could begin the third stretch to his quadriceps and reached for his watch.

"Yes."

She leaned in, her forearm pressing against his back, her hand around his calf, her breast against his . . . God, he really needed to stop thinking about these things.

"Is something wrong?" she asked. "Are you in very much pain today?"

"Not precisely." Blinking, he tried to focus his attention on the watch in his hand, but each second that ticked by seemed like an hour. "I'm just not in much of a mood for conversation," he said, and in those rueful words, he wondered if he'd just found a way forward.

When he'd taken her hand the other day and kissed it, he knew she'd felt pleasure in it. But she'd snatched her hand back at once, too hampered by apprehensions to allow the pleasure to continue. Words were far less threatening, and could be just as seductive. Not flattery or pretty compliments, no, but something else entirely.

"Thirty seconds," he told her, and when she sat back, he set his watch aside and rolled over. "I'm not talking much because the things I'm thinking right now are things I'm not sure I can discuss with you."

He paused, his gaze roaming over her, and

he watched her body tense and her hands flatten on the floor as if to push her up — the gazelle readying to flee. "For instance," he murmured, "I'm thinking about how much I like it when you wear white."

"Oh." It was a hushed sound of surprise, mingled perhaps with a hint of relief. Her hand lifted self-consciously to the high, ruffled collar of her tea gown, the same one she'd been wearing the other day on the terrace. "Dressmakers tell me it's a good color for me. They say it flatters my skin and my hair."

"I daresay it does, but that's not quite the reason I like it."

He sat up, and she tensed, rising on her knees as if to stand, but he merely leaned back to rest his weight on his arms, and she relaxed again, easing back on her heels. He waited, and after a moment, her curiosity got the better of her. "Is white your favorite color, then?" she asked.

"No, actually. Blue's always been my favorite color. But I like white now, too. I have done ever since that day five years ago when we sat on the terrace together."

She stirred, stirring his hopes. "You do like to bring up that day."

"It's a favorite memory of mine. You were wearing white, and I liked it because it evoked images in my mind, images of you naked in my bed. Sheets, as you know, are white."

Color bloomed in her cheeks. Her hand tightened at the ruffled collar of her gown, her thumb rubbed the blue cameo at her throat. "You shouldn't say these things," she whispered. "It's unseemly."

"It's honest."

"It embarrasses me."

"Yes, I know." He sat up, but he didn't touch her. "Nonetheless, I'm afraid that's not enough of a deterrent for me, Edie. Because when I say things like that, I'm hoping it arouses you, and I want you to be aroused."

The rosy tint in her cheeks deepened, giving him a hint it might be working. Her pale pink lips parted, but she didn't speak, and he took advantage of her silence.

"I was imagining you amid those white sheets, with your red-gold hair all around your shoulders and that gorgeous smile on your face, and it took my breath away. And I looked at these pretty, gold freckles . . ." He paused to brush his fingertip ever so lightly over her nose and cheek.

"Don't tease me about my freckles," she choked, and pushed his hand down.

"I'm not. I looked at them, and I wondered if you had them everywhere, and I started reckoning up how long it would take me to kiss them all. It was a topic I contemplated many times while I was away."

She went utterly still, but her breathing had quickened, and he knew he'd hit at last on something that might bring the gazelle close enough to catch.

"And the other day, when you came out on the terrace in this?" He fingered the soft folds of lawn spread out over the carpet around her. "The sun was out, and I fancied I saw the outline of your body underneath. Oh, just the faintest trace — the curve of your hip, your long, long legs. But it was more than enough to set my imagination to work." He paused, his own breathing none too steady as he looked back up and met her eyes. "So you see? That's why I like it when you wear white."

"Goodness." She looked away, a hand pressed to the base of her throat. "And I had on three petticoats."

He could discern that she was aroused by the things he'd said, but she was also hotly embarrassed, and he decided it was best to pull back. The dance of romance always had some push and pull.

"Yes, well, we men have vivid imaginations," he said in a joking sort of way. "Why do you think we like to watch ladies play tennis?"

She made a choked sound, smothered laughter. "Oh, dear, if the ladies learned this masculine secret, I fear none of us would dare to wear white outdoors again."

"Well, don't give it away, Edie, or I shall be resented by all of mankind. It wouldn't affect me, of course, for in my case, the damage is done. Those images of your long, lovely legs are engraved on my brain, and there's no getting rid of them now." With that, he glanced at the clock. "Ah, my two hours are up, I see. We'd best change or we'll be late down to dinner and Wellesley will cluck like a hen."

He grasped the footboard, stood up, and held out his hand to help her to her feet. When she rose, he kept her hand in his long enough to press a quick kiss to it, but he also let it go straightaway, deciding it was best not to push his luck. Anticipation was part of this game, and as he'd told her yesterday, he was playing to win.

# CHAPTER 15

With only Edie, Joanna, and Mrs. Simmons in residence, dinner at Highclyffe was usually a simple, five-course affair, unless Edie was entertaining guests. Since Stuart's arrival, however, Mrs. Bigelow and Wellesley had been pressing her for more elaborate menus. Preoccupied with other concerns about her husband's return, Edie hadn't had time to address the issue. That night, the cook and the butler apparently decided to take matters into their own hands.

Canapés, soup, fish, lamb cutlets, and a dish of baked mushrooms came and went, and when the butler brought in a joint of beef and a dish of potatoes dauphine, Edie felt impelled to inquire further on the subject. "Heavens, Mrs. Bigelow is quite ambitious tonight, Wellesley. How many courses has she prepared?"

"Ten, Your Grace."

"Ten? For four people?"

"Mrs. Bigelow felt — and I concurred, Your Grace — that the return of His Grace required a joint, game, a second vegetable, a more elaborate dessert, and fruit with a strong cheese, in addition to the usual fare."

"I see." She looked across the table at her husband, who merely grinned back at her. "Far be it from me to question what a duke needs in the way of sustenance," she murmured, but the minute Wellesley went to bring another wine, she looked at Stuart. "Did you ask for all that food?"

"And usurp your duty to select the menu, Duchess? Never. But I'm not complaining. There's something to be said for a ten-course meal after years of eating mainly out of tins and packets."

"Well, I hope Mrs. Bigelow finds good use for the leftover food. Ten courses, indeed."

"I don't think we've ever had ten courses before," Joanna said, sounding rather awed. "Not by ourselves. How lovely!"

Despite her enthusiasm, Joanna was yawning profusely by the time dessert arrived, the consequence of eating far too much rich food, and Edie decided enough was enough. The dessert plates had barely been cleared away before she stood up.

"I think we'll go through," she announced, "and leave Stuart to his port and cigar."

The other three rose as well, but Stuart refused the masculine custom of after-dinner port in the dining room with a laugh. "No, Edie. Being back in civilized society is all very well, but I shall go through with you and have my port in the drawing room. I don't smoke, and I have no desire to sit in here and drink in isolated, ducal splendor. Wellesley, would you have Mrs. Bigelow send fruit to the drawing room and take the port through with it?"

If she had given such unorthodox instructions to Wellesley, he'd have at least cocked an eyebrow and looked disapproving. But in Stuart's case, he simply bowed, murmured, "Very good, Your Grace," and glided from the room to follow instructions, the footmen in tow.

Edie made a sound of exasperation. "Really, that man is the end all," she muttered to Stuart, as they walked through to the drawing room. "He never questions anything you say," she added accusingly.

"Of course not, Edie. I'm the duke."

It occurred to her that if she ever did go off her trolley and decide to live with her husband forever, the question of Wellesley would become quite an exasperating state of affairs. "And I'm the duchess. But that never seems to cut any ice with Wellesley."

Stuart merely laughed. "You seem to get your way with him in the end."

"But it's always such a battle."

"That's only because you're American. Sadly, Wellesley is a snob of the highest degree."

"If we were in the States, I'd have sacked him ages ago."

"But we're not in the States, so you can't. Wellesley is as much a part of Highclyffe as the walls."

"A fact in which you seem to take great delight," she said, noting his gleeful expression.

"A bit like the vicar, darling," he countered wickedly, grinning back at her. "It's the way things are."

He paused outside the drawing room and turned to Joanna and Mrs. Simmons. "Whist, ladies? There are four of us."

Joanna shook her head with another enormous yawn. "I'm terribly tired. I think I'll just go up to bed. Good night, everyone."

"I believe I shall accompany you, Joanna," Mrs. Simmons said, and bowed to Stuart. "Good night, Your Grace."

Edie felt a stab of desperation. "You don't have to go up just because Joanna does, you know," she assured the governess. "You are more than welcome to stay. I'm sure His

Grace won't mind. We can play piquet with three people."

Mrs. Simmons showed no desire to co-operate with that plan. "Thank you, but I believe this would be an excellent time for me to write some letters. I am quite far behind on my correspondence of late, and my family, I fear, is feeling neglected as a result. If you don't mind?"

Edie plastered on a smile and refrained from a desperate impulse to point out that there was stationery right here in the drawing room. "Of course. Good night."

"Good night, Your Grace."

With the departure of her sister and the governess, she felt off balance, partly in light of his torrid confession earlier in her room. Even now, just thinking about it, she felt a blush creeping into her face. "Perhaps I'll go up, too. It's eleven o'clock."

"Why don't you stay down here with me for a bit? We could talk, or read." He gestured to the gaming table nearby. "Or we could play a game."

"That depends," she said wryly, "on what sort of game you had in mind. Did you arrange this? Joanna and Mrs. Simmons going off and leaving us alone?"

"Upon my honor, I didn't. And if you prefer to go to bed, I won't press you. But I would like you to stay."

She took a deep breath. "Do you intend to make advances?"

"Well, I'd like to," he admitted, flashing her a provoking grin. "But only if you give me an opening."

"I shan't."

"Then you don't have anything to worry about, do you?" He moved to the gaming table and pulled open a drawer. "Cards?" he asked, holding up a deck. "Or backgammon? Or chess?"

She considered which offered her the best chance of winning. "Chess."

His grimace seemed reassuring. "All right," he said as he dropped the cards back in the drawer and shut it. "But you already told me you play very well, so I may not prove enough of a challenge for you. I don't play chess often, myself."

"All the better for me, then," she said, and took the chair he pulled out for her.

He moved to sit opposite her at the small table, and they opened the drawers to pull out chess pieces and place them on the inlaid chessboard. But when she started arranging the white pieces in front of herself, he stopped her. "No, no, we have to pick colors," he said, took up a pawn of each and hid them behind his back.

"A gentleman usually lets a lady go first," she reminded.

"Usually." He held out his clenched fists. "But I didn't think you'd need that sort of advantage."

"I don't," she assured and pointed to one of his hands, but when he opened his fist to reveal a white pawn, she couldn't help grinning. "Still, it's nice to have it just the same."

"Hmm. Joanna warned me you were ruthless at games," he said, as they arranged their chess pieces. "She says you never let her win, even when she was a little girl."

"I shan't let you win either just because you're a man," she warned and made her first move, sliding her queen's pawn forward.

"I should hope not." He pushed out a pawn of his own. "Because I intend to claim a kiss when I win, but being a man of honor, I can't claim it if I haven't rightly earned it."

His words and the low intensity of his voice caused her to look up, and when she did, she knew he meant what he said. His lashes lowered to her mouth, and her lips began to tingle. Her insides quivered. She wanted to think of something clever to say in reply, but she couldn't think of a thing.

Wellesley, thank heaven, chose to enter

the room just then, and she was spared any need to reply.

"Your port, Your Grace," Wellesley announced, gliding into the room with a laden tray. "And the fruit."

"Excellent." He nodded to a table nearby. "Put it there, but move the table within reach, will you? And pour us both some port, unless the duchess prefers something else?"

"No, port is lovely, thank you, Wellesley."

The butler poured out two glasses, though Edie suspected he was itching to point out that port was usually reserved for the gentlemen, and that ladies were supposed to drink madeira or sherry. "Will there be anything else, Your Grace?"

"No, thank you, Wellesley," he said, and returned his attention to the board. "You may go. If we need anything, we'll ring."

"Yes, Your Grace." He bowed and moved to depart.

"And close the door behind you," Stuart called after him just as he reached the doorway.

"Was that necessary?" she asked, as the butler obeyed and the door clicked shut behind him.

"I thought it best to have privacy."

She moved her knight. "You mean you're

hoping privacy is needed."

He grinned back at her, unrepentant. "Well, yes, that, too. You could have objected."

That, she realized in chagrin, was an irrefutable point. She hastily invented a reason for her acquiescence. "I don't know what you'll take it into your head to say or do. You might take up my hand again, or . . . or something else. So it's best if the servants aren't here. They might be embarrassed by such displays."

"Oh, I see. It's the servants you're worried about." He moved another pawn. "I'm glad to know that I can ravish you in private with no fear of embarrassing you."

"No, you can't!" she cried, catching too late the smile lurking at the corners of his mouth. She gave a sigh of exasperation. "That isn't what I meant, and you know it. Stop teasing me."

"But Edie, this is important. I don't know which of my advances would be welcomed, and which would be spurned, so I am testing the waters at every opportunity."

"I don't know why, when I shall spurn them all."

"Ah, but will you? I know you're not indifferent to me, or you would have told Wellesley to leave the door open. And you admitted just this morning that the idea of another woman being with me made you jealous."

Oh, God, he would bring that up. She stared down at the chessboard, feeling hot and prickly all over again. It was too late to take back the humiliating admission now, but she couldn't help correcting him. "I said a little bit jealous."

"I stand corrected."

"And anyway, that seems like very flimsy evidence to me."

"Possibly, but I know what happened between us on that terrace five years ago, and I know what you felt then because I saw it in your face."

"You have a vivid imagination."

"Well, yes." His smile widened. "I believe I admitted as much this afternoon."

She stirred, her body growing hotter at his reminder of their conversation earlier in the day.

"But," he added, "I don't need imagination to know when a woman is truly indifferent to me and when she's not."

She wanted to present him with nothing but indifference because then maybe he would give up trying to win her over, but she couldn't seem to keep it up. He kept slipping past her defenses in ways he hadn't been able to do five years earlier, and she didn't know quite why. She wanted to be cold because then he might agree with her that separation was the only thing to do, but coldness was a hard thing to summon when he talked about what he imagined when she wore a white dress. "You know far too much about women, if you ask me," she muttered.

"My fair share," he admitted. "I was quite the ladies' man back in my salad days."

She didn't tell him her friend Leonie had mentioned all the hearts he'd broken when he went to Africa the first time, nor the fact that she'd had no trouble believing it. Gray eyes that glinted with humor, the lean symmetry of his face, his brilliant smile, his strong body, his quick wit, and most of all, his instinctive understanding of what appealed to women — all of those must have made women swoon in what he called his salad days. She returned her attention to the board and tried to concentrate on the game.

"Sadly," he went on, "that does me no good at all with you, since you ruthlessly cut me down to size at every opportunity."

She didn't reply. Instead, she moved her knight and took his bishop.

"That rather proves my point," he murmured. "Still, I can be ruthless, too," he added as he moved his rook and knocked down her bishop. "Check."

Edie gave a huff of vexation as he pulled her bishop off the board. "You said you don't play well."

"I said I don't play often. I didn't say I don't play well."

She made a face. "If you are so accomplished at the game, then why do you insist on trying to distract me?"

"Because it's a fundamental strategy of chess?" He propped his elbow on the table and his chin in his hand. "In all seriousness, I'm not trying to distract you because I want to win a chess game. I want to know more about you."

Edie didn't reply, and her silence caused him to give an aggrieved sigh. "Really, Edie, you are exasperatingly circumspect. I don't want to just sit and push chess pieces around with you. I want to know what interests you and what you like and what makes you laugh. I want . . ." He paused, waiting until her curiosity got the better of her, and she looked up. "Edie, I want to know what pleases you."

As she heard those words and looked into his eyes, she felt a faint answering thrill.

"What if we do this?" He leaned forward

and slowly eased his hand over hers. "What if I tell you what I like, and you tell me if you like it, too?"

His hand was warm over the back of hers. She thought of the day before, when he'd kissed her palm, and this afternoon, when he'd talked about how she looked in white, and a melting sensation that had become quite familiar to her during the past few days started coming over her again. But then she reminded herself of his deeper desires and what was at stake, and she snuffed out that answering thrill. "I think I already have a fair idea of what you would like," she said tartly, and withdrew her hand.

"And what's that?"

He waited, watching her, dark brows lifted in inquiry, as if he didn't know what she meant when they both know he did. As if he actually expected her to answer. As if she could articulate descriptions of masculine lust.

She flushed and looked away. "We shouldn't talk of these things."

"Why not? Any marriage worth its salt has to have honesty, so let's not dance around the point you're trying to make. Say it straight out. What do you think I would like?"

A flash of the summerhouse at Saratoga

ran through her mind, and instead of pushing it away as she usually did, she used it now, used it like a shield. "You would like," she said in a hard voice, "to fornicate with me."

There was a moment of silence before he replied. "When you say things about him," he said, his voice equally hard, "look at me. Look into my eyes. That way, you'll start to recognize the difference."

She straightened in her chair and turned her head to meet his gaze head-on. She saw anger there, glinting in the silvery depths of his eyes. "Am I wrong, then?"

"You are, actually. Quite wrong. I don't want to fornicate with you. I want to make love with you." He paused, and the anger in his eyes faded, melting away and becoming something else, something warm. "There's a world of difference between the two, Edie, and that's the quandary I face. How do I make you understand the difference?"

She looked back at him helplessly, her shield slipping. "I don't know, Stuart."

"I know you're afraid. I know you've had pain." He paused, making a fist and pressing it to his mouth as if striving for control. "I'd take it away if I could," he said after a moment, and lowered his hand. "But I can't. So all I can do is try to find ways to make you feel the other side of it, the side that is good and right and beautiful. That's what I want."

She felt hope stirring, a faint spark in a long, cold darkness. She reached for her port and took a hefty swallow. "You want what I can't give you."

"I don't think so, but I can see why you would believe otherwise. I admit," he added as she didn't reply, "that I want to kiss you and touch you and ravish you. Of course I do. I want to pleasure you. I know you don't believe there is pleasure in the act of love, but there is, Edie. Sweet, sweet pleasure. I want you to have that with me. I want it more than anything in the world."

His voice, low and resonant, beckoned to things inside her that she hadn't even known existed. Tongues of heat curled in her belly, and her fingers clenched around the pawn in her hand as she worked to extinguish it. "You're being very torrid today. First talking of how I look in white, and now this. Do you intend to make love to me with words, then?"

"Until I can make love to you with my body, yes. What other choice do I have?"

He seemed to have a special talent for asking questions she didn't know how to answer.

"Which brings us back," he said lightly, "to where we were, and talking about what I like and what you like, and where we might find some common ground." He plucked a peach from the bowl on the tea table beside them and reached for the fruit knife. "For example, I like peaches. Do you?"

It was such an innocuous question, and yet, she felt a strange reluctance to reply, for she sensed he was playing a game, and she didn't know the rules. "I think you already know I love peaches," she said at last, giving him a wry look. "You probably talked to Mrs. Bigelow in the kitchens, or asked Reeves, or Joanna. And that's why Wellesley brought us peaches tonight instead of raspberries or blackberries."

He grinned. "I already warned you that I'd involve them in my nefarious plans. But that doesn't alter the fact that I adore peaches, too." Propping his elbows on the gaming table, he sank the blade into the flesh of the fruit and carved out a wedge. "Would you like a bite?"

In any other context, she would take the words at face value, but there was mischief in his expression, and it made her cautious. But she was also curious. Curiosity won.

"All right," she said, holding out her hand. "Yes."

But he didn't pass it to her. Instead, he shifted the knife to join the peach in his left hand and lifted the wedge of fruit in his right, carrying it to her mouth.

She looked down at the peach slice in front of her face for a moment, then back up at him. "I'm not a child. No need to feed it to me." She tried to take the piece from his fingers, but he pulled it back.

"But I would like to feed it to you," he said. "How would that be?"

"Silly."

"You wouldn't like it?"

"Why would I?"

He chuckled, and she had no idea what he was laughing about. "So much you don't know, Edie. I look forward to a lifetime of bringing you up to snuff on erotic things."

She didn't bother to point out that she had no intention of giving him a lifetime of erotic things, or anything else. Still, arguing with him about that topic was a waste of breath, so she merely offered an unim-pressed sniff. "It's a piece of fruit. I don't see what's erotic about it."

"Only one way to find out." He once again held up the peach slice, and this time, she opened her mouth.

330

The fruit slid between her lips, slick, wet, and sweet. She chewed and swallowed as he lowered his hand and carved another piece. This time, he didn't feed it to her, but held it out to her instead. "Careful," he warned, as she reached to take it off the knife.

She heeded his advice, sliding the fruit off the blade, but when she moved to eat it, his next words stopped her. "Aren't you going to share?"

She paused, the peach slice halfway to her mouth, and as their eyes met across the table, she realized what he meant, and her stomach gave a nervous dip. Slowly, feeling terribly self-conscious, she held the fruit to his mouth.

He ate it off her fingers, then he fed another piece to her. Only this time, he allowed his fingertips to linger against her mouth. Her heart stopped, then started again as he pulled away.

He was watching her, smiling a little, and she felt compelled to say something, anything. "This reminds me a bit of when I was a girl, and I first learned to skate on ice," she blurted out.

His brows drew together, giving him that amused, quizzical expression he'd worn at the Hanford Ball. "I'm not sure I see the similarities," he said as he carved out another wedge of the peach and held it out to her.

She slid it off the knife. "It makes me feel the exact same way."

"Oh? How does it make you feel?"

"Nervous," she admitted. "Excited." She paused, grasping for adjectives. "Happy," she whispered.

That pleased him. His eyes creased at the edges with a faint smile. "Good."

"And," she added as she lifted the piece of fruit to his mouth, "it also makes me feel sure I'll fall, and it'll hurt."

"I won't let you fall." He took the fruit into his mouth, pulling her fingers with it, suckling her fingertips.

Pleasure flooded through her like a dark, hot wave. It was too much, and she cried out, shocked. Jerking back, she lurched to her feet, knocking over her chair in the process.

He stood up at once, setting aside the knife and the peach. "Edie —"

"It's late," she cut in, desperate to end this game he'd started, cursing herself for ever wanting to know what could possibly be erotic about fruit.

"My gazelle bounding away again," he murmured. He started around the table. "Edie, tell me what's wrong."

"Nothing," she lied, striving for calm when her senses were in tumult.

"Your hands are shaking."

"Are they?" She turned away, mortified, reaching for a napkin. "Heavens."

"I didn't mean to frighten you, or offend you."

"You didn't." She was panicky, not because of him but because of what he made her feel. It was crazy and wild and terrifying, and she didn't understand it. She'd never felt anything like it before. "Sorry to act like such a rabbit. It's just that I don't . . . I'm not accustomed to being . . . being touched or have my hand . . . kissed." Not that kissing her hand was what he'd done, precisely. "I don't like to be touched."

"I touched you yesterday," he reminded softly. "I kissed your hand then. Remember?"

How could she forget? That kiss was still pressed into her palm like a brand. Without looking at him, she dipped a corner of her napkin in her water bowl and dabbed at the sticky traces of peach juice on her chin and her fingers, but she feared it wasn't going to be as easy to remove the memory of his touch. "It startled me, that's all. I didn't expect —"

"What?" he prompted when she fell silent.

"You didn't expect to be aroused by it?"

She shifted her weight, hot and uncomfortable, her fingers tightening around the linen in her hands. "No, but I'll bet you knew I would be," she mumbled.

"There's nothing wrong with feeling desire, Edie."

Is that what this was? She set down her napkin and didn't ask that question. "I'm sorry," she said instead, "but I fear we shall have to finish our game another night. I'm going to bed."

"Of course." He reached for his stick. "I'll walk up with you."

"No, please, don't trouble yourself."

"It's no trouble," he said, moving with her toward the door. "After all, it's not as if we're at opposite ends of the house. Our rooms are side by side. And you're right. It is late. Probably best to seek our beds."

They stopped beside the closed door, and he reached out to open it for her, but he paused, hand on the knob. "Speaking of how late it is," he whispered, "what are the odds the hall boy's asleep on duty? Shall we see?"

Slowly, quietly, he opened the door and peeked through the opening, then looked over at her with a nod. "Really, Duchess, such laxity among the household staff is quite shocking," he whispered as if in disapproval. "Wellesley would be appalled if he knew."

This teasing side of him was something she was beginning to understand. When she was uncomfortable or embarrassed, he would often tease or joke with her. It was an effective technique, she had to admit, for she could feel her apprehension fading.

"Well, don't tell Wellesley," she whispered back. "The poor boy's probably exhausted. It's after midnight."

"Tattle to Wellesley? I wouldn't dream of it. He's got far too high an opinion of himself as it is. Still, we can't just tiptoe past the boy and have the housemaids find him in the morning." With that, he eased the door closed, then opened it again, making a great deal of noise in the process.

The hall boy jumped up from his chair at once, blinking sleepily and trying not to show it. "Your Graces."

Edie pressed her lips together, for she feared smiling at such a moment would embarrass the boy and give the show away. She ducked her head and stepped through the doorway without looking at him.

"We're off to bed, Jimmy," Stuart told him as he followed her toward the stairs. "Put out the lights down here, will you?"

"Yes, Your Grace."

"Familiarizing yourself with the names of the staff, I see," she commented, as they started up the stairs to the second floor. "I suppose even the hall boys and kitchen maids are on your side by now."

"Sally, the scullery maid, suggested I visit Mrs. McGillicuddy."

"The village witch? Whatever for?"

"A love potion, of course. To soften you toward me."

"Lovely." She groaned. "The entire staff thinks you're the poor spurned husband, and I'm the unforgiving wife?"

"No. I believe they think I've got my work cut out winning you over because I've been gone so long."

She thought he was probably sugarcoating things a bit, but she didn't pursue the point as they turned down the corridor toward their rooms. At her door, she turned to say good night, but he spoke before she did.

"So what exciting thing do you have planned for us tomorrow?"

"I'm glad you mentioned that. I would like to take Joanna to the Wash for a picnic. She likes to paint there, and she probably won't have any more chances before . . ." Edie paused, trying to ignore a forlorn little pang around her heart. "Before we leave."

"Edie, even if you do leave — which I'm not accepting for a moment, by the way — you and Joanna are always welcome to come back. Joanna can still go to Willowbank. It's a fine school. You could live . . ." He paused and took a deep breath. "You could live in London, bring her here for holidays."

The ache in her chest deepened. "I don't think that would be a good idea, Stuart. It would be hard on her and painful for me."

"Would it be painful? Then why go?"

"Tonight's rather proof of why, don't you think?"

"No. What I think tonight proved is that you are a vibrant woman, capable of deep passions despite what happened to you. You are also my wife, you will always be my wife, and even a legal separation won't undo that. No matter what happens between us, you are free to come and go from Highclyffe anytime you please. This is your home. As far as I'm concerned, it will always be your home."

She didn't point out how impossible it would be for her to come and go from a place she loved when she would no longer be part of it. "Yes, well," she said, desperate to change the subject, "going to the Wash is an all-day excursion, so we'll miss our usual walk in the grounds, I'm afraid. By the time we finish dinner, it will be dark, and there's only a new moon tonight, making it too dim to see our way. But we can still do your exercises after dinner. Would that be all right?"

"That depends. Am I invited on this picnic?"

"Of course. I thought to make my two-hour session part of it."

"Yes, but those two hours are compulsory. What I want to know is if you want me to come. Is that something you would like?"

She shrugged, trying to seem offhand about it. "It might be nice. Joanna likes you. And you do have excellent taste in picnic baskets."

"I accept your invitation, then. And since you have such faith in my talents with picnic luncheons, I shall arrange the menu with Mrs. Bigelow." He smiled, his gaze roaming over her face. He lifted his left hand as if to touch her, but then let it fall.

She took a deep breath. "Right, then. I shall see you tomorrow. We'll start at nine o'clock."

"Don't go in yet. Stay a moment longer." When she hesitated, he spoke again. "Hands behind my back, I promise."

He set aside his stick, and clasped his hands behind him, but the move only brought his upper body closer to her. "Since we've been talking tonight of what we like, there's one more thing I'd like before we part."

Edie's heart thumped hard against her ribs. Her fingers clenched around the door-knob beside her hip, so tightly they ached, but she didn't open the door to duck inside. "And what is that?"

"I should like to kiss you good night."

Her heart thumped again, harder and more painful this time, anticipation added to apprehension and alarm and everything else she'd been feeling today. "We didn't finish our chess game. You can't claim a kiss for it."

He chuckled. "Perhaps not. But I'd like to kiss you anyway." He paused, then said softly, "Would that be all right?"

"N—" She stopped in the midst of her automatic refusal, then reconsidered for no reason at all, and amended her answer. "I don't know."

"Shall we find out?" He bent his head, moving in infinitesimal increments, giving her plenty of time to turn her face away or refuse him. She didn't move. She didn't say no.

"If you kiss me," she whispered instead, "it doesn't count."

"I know," he said, and pressed his lips to hers.

Edie froze at the contact, her back against the door, the knot of fear inside her hot and tight, pressing her chest. Her eyes wide open, she watched his close, saw his lashes come down, opulent, coffee brown lashes against bronzed skin. With his mouth on hers, she inhaled through her nose and caught the scent of sandalwood soap.

*Stuart,* she thought, and the hard, tight knot inside her opened a little, like a fist unclenching. Her hand lost its death grip on the doorknob and fell to her side. Panic eased back far enough for a new and different awareness to take its place.

The kiss was strangely light. No force in it, no pushing, no demands, just a warm caress against her lips. She closed her eyes, and her other senses came at once to the fore. Only their mouths were touching, but she could feel the warmth of his body like an imprint, almost as if he were pressed fully against her. Beneath the sandalwood, she detected other scents — earthier, deeper scents that were uniquely him. She heard the rustle of her silk dress and the hard thud of her own heartbeat as she stirred against the door.

His tongue touched the closed crease of

her mouth. At once, she brought her hands up between them, an instinctive reflex, her palms flattening against his chest to push him away. He stilled and drew back a little. The heavy satin of his waistcoat was smooth against her palms. Beneath it, she could feel the rise and fall of his breathing, and the strength in his hard muscles.

"I'd like to kiss you again, Edie," he said, his lips brushing hers as he spoke. "Would you like it?"

She felt suspended, caught between forces of equal power and impossibility. She hung there for what seemed an eternity while he waited, unmoving, his breath warm against her face. She didn't know if she would like it, but she knew she did not want to be afraid of it. She nodded, a stiff, quick little jerk of her head.

He smiled against her mouth, tilted his head and kissed her again. Pleasure rippled through her limbs, bringing heat.

His tongue touched her lips again, and she realized what he wanted. She opened her mouth. He tasted lush, like peaches and port, and when his tongue touched hers, she heard a moan come from her own throat, a moan that was not a protest of any kind. It wasn't like any sound she'd ever made.

He stirred in response, and for a brief moment, he pressed closer, but when she stiffened, he eased back, pulling her lower lip between both of his. He sucked gently, as if her lower lip were a piece of candy, and as he did, it evoked what she'd felt when he sucked her fingertips — as if he were pulling sensation from every part of her body — up her legs, along her spine, across her belly. She moaned again, and overwhelmed by sensation, she arched up closer to him. But then, her hips brushed against his hard arousal, and she was jolted back to reality. She tore her mouth from his and shook her head violently, flattening back against the door, pushing him. "Stop," she gasped. "Oh, stop."

He pulled back at once, straightening away from her. His breathing was hot and quick, but so was hers, mingling together in the quiet corridor. His eyes were smoky in the dim light, and when they looked into hers, she saw the desire in their depths.

She stared back at him, wordless, all her senses in tumult. Her lips tingled. She felt giddy and terrified and glad and miserable all at once. She couldn't seem to catch her breath.

"Good night, Edie," he said. He leaned forward, pressed a kiss to her forehead, and turned away. Taking up his stick, he started down the corridor to his own rooms.

She didn't turn to watch him go. She pressed her fingers to her tingling mouth and closed her eyes, listening to his footsteps and the tap of his stick as he walked away. She heard his door open, but by the time she turned her head to look at him, he was already gone. The door clicked softly behind him.

Edie didn't go into her own room. Instead, she stood there for a while, her fingers pressed to her lips, and she wondered if all a man's kisses were supposed to feel like that.

# CHAPTER 16

Had anyone ever asked Stuart to name all the girls he'd kissed in his lifetime, he could have offered a reckoning of some sort, but he'd kissed a great many, so the accuracy of such a list would probably be open to question. And had he been asked to provide details of any of those kisses, he'd have described each one the same way: a lovely prelude to better things.

Kissing Edie, however, was something he knew he was going to remember for the rest of his life. The first brush of her lips, so seemingly chaste, and yet, it had sent arousal pulsing through him in an instant. His hands behind his back, so damnably frustrating, and yet, so erotic it had made him dizzy. The taste of her, so sweet, making him fear that without her kisses in accompaniment, peaches and port would never be quite the same again.

He'd known he wasn't kissing a virgin in

the literal sense, but he knew it was his kiss that had awakened carnality inside her for the very first time. She, who had experienced only the sordid side, was now coming to know the blissful side, because of him. That had been his first goal all along, and an obsession from the moment he'd learned of the brutality committed on her. But now that that goal had been achieved, he was a bit awestruck in consequence, rather as he'd felt the first time he'd ever seen an African sunset or watched a gazelle run across the plain.

As he lay in his bed afterward and stared up at the ceiling, each breath he took recalled the scent of her hair and skin. Each time he licked his lips, he tasted peaches and port. Each time he closed his eyes, he saw her face, lips puffy from his kisses and her eyes wide with astonishment, and each time he formed the picture, it caught him up and held him tight, and he knew: *This* was what Fate had been trying to show him five years ago.

He hadn't expected anything like this. He'd come back thinking simply to make a life with the woman he'd married, and during the voyage home, he'd harbored hope that it would be a happy union, with sweet lovemaking and the children that usually came along with that, but that was as far as he'd allowed his expectations to go. Oh, he'd been wildly attracted to her from the first, no doubt about that, but his attraction hadn't been allowed to deepen, and he'd been away half a decade without any real knowledge of what he'd been missing. Now he knew, and it was so shattering that he didn't sleep a wink.

By morning, his mind had carved every exquisite detail of that kiss into his memory, his body ached with unsated lust, and he began to fear that even his heart might be in jeopardy.

He wasn't quite sure if the next six days would drive him to the brink of heaven or the brink of hell, but he had the feeling he might come to both before it was all said and done.

They went to the Wash the following day as Edie had arranged, and Stuart was glad Joanna and Mrs. Simmons were with them, for he badly needed their presence to regain his equilibrium.

An irony, that. Both he and Edie had assumed Joanna would be her shield against him, not the other way around. But he knew a kiss wasn't enough to make Edie fall into his arms, not by a long way, and even if that blessed event did happen in the next five days, his desire for her might remain unsated for much longer than that. Stuart knew he would need all the control he could muster. Nothing like the added presence of a fifteen-year-old girl and her elderly governess for making a man remember his propers.

They set out blankets and a canopy on a nice stretch of grass along the cliffs above the shore, and Stuart was grateful for that, too. Being out in the open like this, there was little privacy for stealing kisses. Although they could not be observed by anyone on the beach below, the grassy knolls around them offered little protection from the eyes of anyone coming down to the shore from the fields or the village. These were Margrave lands, but the locals were free to come anytime for fishing, bathing, or boating, and though Stuart didn't care much if people saw him kissing his wife on his own lands, he suspected Edie would never relax enough in such a situation to give him the chance to try.

Still, if he thought he could get through an entire day with her without having his resolve tested, he was mistaken. They had just finished lunch, and Joanna, who had spent most of the morning painting, decided she wanted to spend her afternoon in a different way.

"I want to go down to the shore and look for shells," she announced. "Can we go?"

"May we go," Edie and Mrs. Simmons corrected her in unison, causing Joanna to heave a long-suffering sigh.

"May we go, then?" she asked, and when Edie nodded, Joanna jumped to her feet and turned to him. "Stuart, you'll come, too, won't you?"

But he shook his head. "I'm afraid not, petal. Walking on sand's rather a rough go for me."

"Oh, sorry." She flashed him an apologetic smile. "I forgot about that. Well, if you can't come, then Edie should definitely stay and keep you company."

Stuart almost smiled at the conspiratorial wink she flashed in his direction, but he wasn't sure he appreciated the matchmaking assistance. He was trying to resist temptation, after all. Still, Edie was bound to go off with her sister anyway, so he supposed what tempted him wouldn't matter.

His wife, however, surprised him there. "You're right, Joanna. I believe I will stay behind with Stuart. Mrs. Simmons, you'll go with her? And take Snuffles, too," she added.

"Of course," the governess said, and moved to rise from the blanket.

Stuart set his wine on the tray beside him and stood up, offering the governess his hand to help her up. He waited until she and her charge had taken the dog, wandered down the hill, and disappeared over one of the sandy knolls that lined the shore before he settled back down on the blanket opposite his wife.

"So, here we are." He leaned back, resting his weight on his arms, and he made a great show of looking around. "All alone."

She took a sip of wine. From beneath the brim of her wide straw hat, she glanced toward Edward, who stood white-gloved and at attention nearby, then past him to where Roberts was lounging by the landau. "But we're not alone."

In that moment, Stuart proved his utter lack of willpower when it came to his wife. "Edward?" he called, without taking his eyes from her face.

The footman stepped forward at once. "Your Grace?"

"Why don't you and Roberts go for a walk?" he suggested, smiling as he watched a hint of pink come into Edie's cheeks. "Take an hour — no, two — and see a bit of the countryside. It's a fine day, and you don't have many chances for an afternoon off."

"Yes, Your Grace. Thank you, Your Grace."

Edie stirred, looking a bit uneasy as the footman and driver wandered down toward the beach and vanished from sight. "You didn't need to send them away. In staying behind with you, I didn't mean to imply anything by it. I simply thought we might talk a bit, that's all."

"Yes, well, I'm rather an optimistic fellow." He moved a couple inches closer to her, his left leg sliding along hers. The move pushed her willow green skirt up along her ankle, and even though it revealed nothing to his gaze but a bit more of her shoe, that didn't stop him from conjuring a picture of slim, pretty ankles beneath beige leather. "I'm hoping for more than conversation."

She looked down at the glass of wine in her hand. "You presume a great deal."

"I said I'm hoping for more, Edie," he said gently. "I don't presume that I shall obtain it."

"Still, you are very sure of yourself when it comes to women."

That made him laugh. He couldn't help it.

She blinked, seemingly taken aback. "What's so amusing?"

"I'm never sure of myself with you," he confessed. "Oh, I put on a good show, I daresay. A man has his pride, after all. But I haven't ever been sure of myself with you, not after you shredded me to bits at Hanford House and declared you didn't find me the least bit attractive. There," he added, making a wry face as he reached for his glass and took a swallow of wine. "Does that make you feel better?"

"Not really, no. For even if I believed you, which I don't, it would still put you miles ahead of me. I've no experience of men at all — at least," she added with a grimace, "no good experience."

He swallowed hard at the reminder, but she spoke again before he could reply.

"I didn't mean to bring that up." She gave a sigh. "My point is that I never feel as if we're on equal footing."

"That's because we're not." He sat up, set aside his glass, and spread his arms wide. "I'm completely at your mercy."

"You see, that's just what I mean," she murmured. "You always say such charming things."

"I only say them if they are true, Edie."

She looked away, shaking her head. "That's absurd. I don't see how you're at my mercy at all."

He would have been happy to explain how, and in precise detail, but she looked at him and spoke again before he had the chance. "Stuart, may I ask you something?"

The sudden intensity in her voice surprised him. "Of course," he answered, unable to imagine what she was going to ask. With Edie, it could be anything.

"Did you . . ." She paused and took a swallow of wine, as if she needed it. "Did you have many women when you were in Africa?"

Her jealous streak peeking through again made him smile. As he'd told her last night, if she was jealous, she wasn't indifferent, and that made all the difference in the world.

She perceived the reason for his smile at once, and she jerked her chin and looked away again. "Never mind," she said. "It's not my business."

"But it is your business. You're my wife."

"Still, we had an agreement about other women." She took another gulp of wine, then set it aside and began brushing grains of sand off of her skirt instead. "So I don't really have the right to ask about it."

He studied her bent head, and his amusement faded as he considered her question and realized what needed to be said. "You

352

have the right to ask me anything you like," he told her, "anytime you like, on any subject, and I'll answer you. You may not always like the answer, but it will always be the truth. If you really want me to answer that question, I will."

He waited, and after a moment, her curiosity impelled her to look at him again. "Did you?" she whispered.

"No, Edie, I didn't have any women in Africa. That's not to say I was celibate," he added at once to make things clear. "I wasn't. I had women, yes. But not in Africa. That's because —" He broke off, suddenly feeling deuced awkward, but he'd promised her the truth. "Syphilis is very common in Africa. I didn't want to catch it."

Pink washed into her cheeks. "Oh."

"It was usually easier to avoid feminine company altogether, but when things got desperate, I'd go to Paris."

"So you had a lover in Paris, then?" She gave a diffident little shrug, as if it didn't matter when he knew it did.

"No, Edie, no. No lovers, no mistresses, nothing of that kind. Only courtesans, and none of them meant anything to me. It was just basic need, physical release —" He stopped, grimacing. This conversation was becoming more awkward by the moment.

She bit her lip and was silent for several seconds, and he had no idea what she was thinking. "It seems an awfully long way to go for a courtesan," she said at last.

He took a deep breath and told her why. "If a man wants that sort of thing, Paris is the best place to go. It's easier to obtain condoms and find women who are —" He stopped again, and this time, it was his turn to look away. "God," he muttered and rubbed his hands over his face, forcing a laugh. "This isn't the sort of thing a man usually discusses with his wife."

"No, I suppose not."

He decided to steer the conversation to aspects of Paris's appeal that were easier to talk about. "But it wasn't just about women. I also had friends there. Trubridge was living in Paris then, sharing a house with Jack Featherstone. They've both been great friends of mine since Eton days. We'd carouse around, gamble, drink, and yes, chase skirts." He paused, then added, "You may not believe this, but whenever I was in Paris, I thought about coming all the way home. But I could never see the point of it. Not as things stood."

"No," she agreed. "There wouldn't have been any point. And thank you for being honest with me about the other women. I appreciate that it's a difficult subject."

He felt impelled to lighten the mood. "Yes, well, next thing I know, you'll be asking me what a condom is, and I shall really be in the suds."

"Oh, heavens, no." She waved that aside with one hand. "I already know what a condom is."

"You do?" That took him back. "Dash it, Edie, you didn't even know what a lesbian was until I told you. How in hell do you know what a condom is?"

"I'm a married woman, Stuart. Married women talk about these things."

"I see."

"My friends told me all about condoms ages ago. One or two even suggested I might need some and offered to obtain them for me. With you away and all that, they thought I might want male companionship."

"Indeed?" He began to feel a bit nettled. "Who are these friends? I'm not sure you should associate with them, Edie, really. Did they have any specific males in mind for this companionship?"

He could hear the testy note in his own voice. She heard it, too, and she pounced on it at once. "Now you're the one who's jealous."

"I'm not," he denied at once.

"You are!" She laughed as if astonished. "You really are."

"All right, yes. A bit. There," he added, as she laughed again. "Satisfied? Feel you've gotten a bit of your own back now? That we're on more equal footing?"

"Yes," she confessed, her smile the radiant one he liked so much. "I do, rather."

"Good. Now that I've answered your questions, there's something I want to know." He eased closer to her on the blanket, and her smile faded away, but he decided that the sacrifice was worth it when he was close enough that his knee brushed her hip, and his body was beginning to burn. "I want to know if these friends of yours told you the truly important things. Such as how luscious lovemaking can be if it's done properly."

The pink in her cheeks deepened. She looked down, apparently still too shy about this subject to hold his gaze. To his surprise, however, she answered his question. "From the way they talked, I could tell they all thought it was nice."

"Nice?" he echoed in disbelief. "That's all they said?"

"Most of them seemed to think it a very pleasant thing."

"Rather like a hot water bottle, in fact,"

he murmured.

She didn't seem to perceive the hint of sarcasm. "Some of them said it was deuced good fun. I didn't see how any of that could be so, but I never said anything."

"And now? After last night, do you think you might be starting to appreciate their point of view?"

"Last night?" she murmured, clearly trying to pretend she didn't know what he meant, but she still did not look at him. Instead, she pretended a vast interest in brushing bits of grass off her skirt. "Did something happen last night?"

"And you say you don't flirt? Edie, you are flirting with me right now." He bent his knee, deliberately rubbing it against her hip, savoring his own awakening lust, playing with fire. "Tell me more of what your friends told you about lovemaking, for I refuse to believe nice, pleasant, and fun were their only descriptions." He leaned in until his forehead touched the wide brim of her hat. "Did they tell you what bliss it is to be kissed and caressed?"

Only the lower half of her face was visible, so he couldn't look into her eyes, but he saw her lips part, quivering just a little, and that was encouragement enough. He pressed on, teasing her as he tortured himself. "Did they tell you that you can lift a man to ecstasy or drive him down to despair? That you can transform him to a beggar? Or make him feel like a king?" He ducked his head beneath her hat to look in her eyes. "You could do all of that to me, Edie. If you wanted to. That's why I'm at your mercy."

He heard her catch her breath. In her face was all the wariness he was used to, but along with it there was something else, something he'd never seen in her face before. A dawning awareness, perhaps, of her own power.

"Now I've done it." He eased across her body, his wrist brushing her hip, his fingers weaving into the grass at the edge of the blanket. "I shall be putty in your hands from now on, I fear."

The lust he'd been trying to keep in check all day was overtaking him now, thick and hot, but he no longer cared about stopping it. He knew he had to kiss her again. Right here, right now. He leaned closer.

"Edie!" The voice calling her name had both of them turning their heads as Joanna came over the nearby knoll of grass and sand, an enormous piece of gnarled driftwood in her hands. "Look what I found! Won't this be smashing for a still life?"

Stuart groaned and sat back. "School, Edie," he muttered. "The girl needs to go to school."

The sun was setting by the time they packed up the picnic things and drove back to Highclyffe. Joanna talked nineteen to the dozen during the ride, which to Edie was a blessing, for she was in no frame of mind to make ordinary conversation. All sorts of emotions were tumbling around inside her — bewildering, contradictory emotions.

There was fear, of course. That was always with her, something she'd accepted and learned to live with a long time ago. But, right beside it, other emotions were pushing up, fighting for space and light and air. Things like excitement and desire, longing and hope. Agony and uncertainty. Things that made fear seem almost comfortable, like a broken-in pair of leather shoes or a perfectly fitted glove. Fear, at least, was familiar.

She could feel Stuart watching her, taking occasional sideways glances at her profile, but thankfully, he didn't ask her any questions about her pensive mood. He didn't speak to her at all, except in polite inquiries about whether or not she was comfortable and if she'd prefer the top of the landau up instead of down. Beyond that, he talked mainly with Joanna, chaffing her about the huge chunk of driftwood taking up all the floor space in the landau and shamelessly praising the two watercolor landscapes she'd done of the coastline that morning.

It was nearly dark by the time they reached the house. Snuffles was sent below stairs for a bath, and everyone went to their rooms to change for dinner. But if Edie thought her bedroom would prove any kind of haven, she was mistaken. As she stood in front of the long cheval mirror watching Reeves lace her into a corset, Stuart's words of earlier in the day echoed back to her.

*You can transform him to a beggar . . . or make him feel like a king.*

She didn't see it. She tried, studying her reflection in the glass, but she knew hers was not the face to launch a thousand ships or topple a kingdom. She could only conclude that Stuart was either flattering her to turn her sweet, or he was blind. Because all she saw when she looked in the mirror was a plain woman with a mop of curly red-blond hair, a stubborn jaw, and a pale face sprinkled with freckles.

*I wondered if you had them everywhere, and I started reckoning up how long it would take me to kiss them all.*

She touched her fingertips to her breast-bone, tracing the faint gold dots. *It would take lots of time, Stuart,* she thought, *and lots of kisses.* Just like that, and heat began spreading through her body.

Her body. Well, that was a whole other issue, wasn't it? Edie sighed, and the flush of desire died away in the wake of cold realities. In the woman in the mirror, she saw the girl who had towered over her dance partners, been mercilessly teased about her freckles and her overbite, and who had possessed one of the most unimpressive bosoms in New York.

*. . . the curve of your hip, your long, long legs . . .*

Perhaps, she thought wistfully, she did have rather nice legs. But that was hardly enough to lift a man to ecstasy or drive him down to despair. What, she wondered, could Stuart possibly see in her that she did not?

She wasn't sure she wanted to know.

It was, she thought painfully, rather similar to the question she'd asked herself after Saratoga. What was it in her that had transformed Frederick Van Hausen from gentleman to animal? What had driven him to shove her down onto a splintered wooden table, rip her drawers apart, cover her body with his own, so heavy on top of her she couldn't breathe, and . . .

Her sharp intake of breath caused Reeves to stop lacing. "Too tight, Your Grace?"

She pasted a smile on her face. "Perhaps a bit," she lied.

"I'm sorry, Your Grace. It's just an evening gown does have to be tighter." She finished off the lacing at Edie's tailbone, tied and tucked the laces, then helped her into her corset cover and evening petticoat and turned toward the bed where she had laid out Edie's pale pink tea gown earlier in the day. "I'll go fetch an evening gown, then. If you're sure?" she added, pausing, pale pink silk draped over one arm. "You don't often wear an evening gown at home."

"I prefer one tonight." She didn't explain her reasons. The duchess didn't have to explain anything, ever. Except perhaps to the duke.

Reeves nodded, seeming pleased. "Which one shall I bring? The one in royal blue silk is ever so nice. Or perhaps the Nile green? Or the purple?"

"No." Edie shook her head at these choices. "Bring the brown one."

"Oh, no, Your Grace, no!" Reeves groaned. "Not the brown."

Edie turned in surprise, for her maid was staunchly proper, and had never once had the impertinence to contradict her. "Reeves, what on earth?"

The maid flushed at once, looking contrite. "Begging your pardon, Your Grace. It's just that the brown is . . ." She paused, sighed, and gave a gulp. "A bit dull. Matronly."

"Yes, exactly." Edie nodded, for dull and matronly made her feel much safer. "Perhaps some might even describe it as dowdy."

"Wouldn't you prefer something prettier? The royal blue is ever so nice with your hair. And it's got a lower bit of neckline to it."

Edie made a rueful face, studying her reflection. "As if that even matters on me."

"We could add a bit of padding." Reeves glanced at the clock. "We have plenty of time."

Edie looked past her own reflection to that of the maid. "And why," she asked, her voice suddenly brittle to her own ears, "would we want to do that?"

"Well . . ." Reeves paused. "It's just that the duke is home now," she said after a moment. "And I'm sure he would be wanting a fetching sight across the table after being in the wilds so long . . . and . . . and . . ." She studied Edie's reflected face, sighed, and gave up. "I'll fetch the brown."

Reeves vanished into the dressing room,

and Edie returned her attention to the mirror. "Padding, indeed," she muttered under her breath, smoothing down her corset cover over her small bosom. "I haven't worn padding since I was eighteen."

The girl before Saratoga had willingly worn padding and bust improvers under her clothes. She'd rubbed cherry juice on her pale cheeks and mouth, too, and dared to dream that a certain gentleman from the other end of Madison Avenue might fall in love with her. But then, Saratoga had happened, killing all of those girlish dreams and romantic ideas, snuffing out passion before she'd even had the chance to discover what it was.

It was too late now. Wasn't it?

Edie bit her lip, staring at her reflection, seeing Stuart's face in her mind, his eyes daring her to discover the bliss of being kissed and caressed.

*What did she want?*

That would have been an easy question to answer a week ago. She would have answered that she wanted what she had, that her life was perfect. She'd never dared to ask if there was anything missing.

She could hear his voice, assuring her she was a passionate woman. Was she?

She certainly felt stirred up since his

return. If passion was to be in a constant state of agonizing uncertainty, to be caught between fear and excitement, then Stuart was right. If passion was muddled wits, exhilaration, and stark terror, then yes, she supposed she was passionate. If he could create this much havoc in her in a week, what would happen if she gave him a lifetime?

She thought of his face, graver now than when she'd first seen it across a ballroom, a bit older, a bit battered and careworn perhaps, but still so devastatingly handsome, with eyes like silver smoke. A man who, by his own admission, had had many women, who knew just why peaches were erotic and what words to say to make a plain girl's heart twist in her breast. How many other feminine hearts had twisted just like hers? Probably too many to count.

Granted they were married, but what did that mean? Could a man like Stuart really stick with a woman like her? Could he really want her, love her, be faithful?

Heavens, she thought, appalled. She was piling up romantic expectations faster than an eighteen-year-old girl.

Was that what she wanted? To feel as she had then? To be the girl before Saratoga? To wipe it out as if it had never happened? Was that even possible?

Edie pressed her hands to her flushed cheeks, dismayed. Where was the self-assured duchess who ran five households on her own, raised a young sister, managed twelve immense charities, and gave some of the most popular Afternoon-At-Homes of the London season? She thought she'd become a confident, independent woman, but she now realized that all she'd done was place herself inside a safe cocoon where nothing could question her assurance, test her confidence, or threaten her independence.

No man to hold her down, degrade her, force her. That was true.

But also no man to kiss her mouth so tenderly it made her heart sing.

Edie pressed her fingers to her lips and stared at her reflection. She didn't need to make up her mind about a lifetime. As long as she didn't kiss him, she had five days before that decision had to be made. In the meantime, perhaps all she had do was . . . enjoy being a woman. And let him do all the kissing.

The maid came out of the dressing room, and Edie turned. "I've changed my mind. Bring the blue."

Reeves — that sober-faced, middle-aged

model of the perfect lady's maid — gave a delighted jump and grinned like a girl. "I'll do your hair up with the tongs, too, shall I? That would take the frizz from the sea air out of it."

"Oh, all right," she called, as the maid disappeared into the dressing room. "But I'm still not wearing any padding in my bosom!"

Edie returned her attention to the mirror and pushed a few frizzy curls off her forehead. "No need to take things that far."

# CHAPTER 17

When Edie came down, Stuart was the only one in the drawing room. He was sipping a glass of sherry and studying the watercolors Joanna had done earlier in the day, which were laid out on a table by the piano.

He looked up as she came in and smiled at once. "How pretty you look."

She stopped by the door and ducked her head, suddenly self-conscious. "It was Reeves's doing," she said, and fiddled with the shimmery blue skirt. "She seemed to think a duke home from the wilds of Africa deserved a wife in a pretty dress to look at across the table."

He laughed. "I wholeheartedly concur. We ought to give that woman a raise."

A thought struck her, and she looked up again, suspicious. "You didn't put her up to it, did you?"

"To what? You in a pretty dress with a delightfully low neckline?" He grinned.

"No, but deuce take it, I wish I had. On second thought," he added, tilting his head to study her as she crossed the room toward him, "perhaps not. I fear that neckline shall prove far too distracting for my peace of mind."

"If Reeves had gotten her way, I might believe you about that." She gave him a wry look as she paused beside him. "She suggested I should put padding in it."

"Did she?" He took a sip of sherry and turned toward her. "Whatever for?"

"To entice you, of course."

His gaze slid downward, then back up. "You don't need any padding to do that, Edie."

"Well, I told her no, anyway, so there we are." She gestured to the table and veered the conversation onto ground far safer than her bosom. "You're looking at Joanna's pictures, I see."

"If you want to entice me, Edie," he murmured, "I can tell you far more effective ways than padding your bosom."

A tingle of excitement ran through her — up her legs, along her spine, and up to the back of her neck, a heady sensation. She quivered inside, but not with fear. Instead, she felt as if there were a hundred butterflies fluttering inside her stomach. Desperate, she forced herself so say something. "I shouldn't wish to be a tease. To . . . to lead you on."

He smiled. "That's my lookout, not yours."

She considered that, doubtful. "There are some men who would disagree."

His smile vanished. "Then they are worthless curs, not men."

She looked into his eyes, saw the tenderness there, and a sudden sob of gladness pushed up against her chest. She caught it back. *How absurd,* she thought wildly, *to want to cry at such a moment.* "Yes," she managed. "They are."

He drew a breath and gestured to the glass in his hand. "I'm having sherry. Would you care for one?"

She grasped at the change of subject and the offer of a drink at once, feeling in need of both right now. "Yes, thank you."

She returned her attention to the paintings as he poured a sherry for her. "Your sister has great talent," he said as he brought it to her.

"She does." Edie took the glass he offered and gestured to the wall. "You've seen her painting of your butterfly."

"Yes, of course. I think she's shown me every one of her paintings by now. It will be interesting to see how she'll paint that piece of driftwood we hauled home today."

"It will be something brilliant. I speak as her very proud sister, of course."

"No, I think you speak as a very discerning critic of art."

They both laughed as they turned to study the watercolors. "Willowbank is a fine school for arts, Edie," he said after a moment. "No doubt, that's why you chose it. She ought to go."

Edie stared at one of the paintings, noting the exquisite lines of sand and grass, and a skewed angle of the sky that made it uniquely Joanna. "She doesn't want to go."

"But she needs to go. You know that as well as I do. You were ready to send her off, and I realize I'm the reason you haven't done so."

"No, you were just the excuse." She sighed. "The truth is I just haven't wanted to send her away. I've put it off far too long, I know, but we've never been separated, except for that month after you and I were married and Daddy took her to Paris. And I hate the idea of having her out of my sight. If anything were to happen —"

"They will chaperone her every minute, Edie."

"I know, I know. And you're right. The

day you arrived home from Africa, I'd finally worked up the nerve to send her, but then, when she jumped off the train and came home, it was such a relief to put the whole thing off again and keep her with me a bit longer."

"You'll miss her terribly, no doubt. But that's what school holidays are for."

As he spoke, Edie realized that it wasn't just about missing Joanna or her need to watch over her sister that lay at the heart of her reluctance to send her away. It was also the idea of being alone here at Highclyffe that had always made it so hard. Joanna's absence would have brought home to her the loneliness of her life. The loneliness of being an independent woman who ran charities and built gardens to keep herself busy, who knew that unless she constantly entertained guests, she would have to eat her meals in the ducal dining room alone and picnic at the Wash by herself.

Everything was different now, of course. Regardless of what happened in the next five days, she would never live alone at Highclyffe. She might be living alone elsewhere, but not here. "I don't know if I want her to go to Willowbank. I don't . . . I don't know where I'll be living, and I want to be near her. Until things are settled with us, I don't think I should commit her to a particular school."

He was silent for a moment, then he nodded and gave a little cough. "Yes, of course. Still, Willowbank's in Kent, so . . . it's easy to reach from . . . from London. Europe, too, if you . . . chose to live there." He spoke slowly, his frequent pauses making it seem as if he had difficulty with getting the words out. He looked away. "If you were to go back to New York," he said, his voice a tight whisper, "that might be different. It's so far away."

He would miss her, she thought. He wanted a real wife, children, all that, of course. He wanted her, too, she knew that. But the idea that he might desire her company, that he would miss her if she was gone, was a sudden and startling realization. "I was never going back to New York," she blurted out. "That was just a bluff to throw you off if I decided to run away."

"What?" He turned his head to stare at her, clearly astonished. "Quite a convincing bluff," he murmured after a moment, studying her face. "You bought passage, if I recall."

She shrugged. "Yes, well, a bluff ought to be convincing. And I could afford it."

"You are the most surprising woman,

Edie. Every time I think I know what you're about, you confound me again."

"I was panicked. I didn't know what you intended, if you were going to . . . to force me, or drag me home, or . . ." Now she seemed to be the one who had difficulty saying things. She drew a deep breath. "But I would never go back to New York. Never. I couldn't. I would see . . . him . . . see that smirk on his face —"

She broke off abruptly, watching his mouth tighten to a thin, grim line.

"He will pay, Edie. I promise you, he will pay."

She smiled a little. "Again, it's very gallant of you to offer vengeance on my behalf, but it doesn't matter. The damage is done. It's over."

"Is it? There might be —" He stopped abruptly and shook his head. "Never mind. How did we move onto this ghastly topic? We were discussing Joanna and her art." He took a deep breath. "As I was saying, Willowbank is very conveniently located, and just the right school for her talents. If you are not intending to return to New York, then it is still the best school for her, at least in England. And no matter what happens between us, there is no reason why you can't remain in England. You don't have to go running off to France or Italy to escape me."

"I know that now. And I would prefer to stay in England. It's home to me now. As for Joanna . . ." She paused and took a deep breath. "You're right, of course. I'll . . . I'll break it to her after dinner."

She started to turn away, but his voice stopped her. "Don't do it yet. Rather than order her to go, it might be best if she wants to go, don't you think?" He grinned. "That way, she won't leap off the train at the last minute, or refuse to write you, or smoke cigarettes, cause trouble, and get herself sent down."

Edie laughed. "That's right, you overheard our conversation about it all on the train platform. I'd forgotten about that."

"Do you agree?"

"Of course, but she's adamantly opposed to going. How on earth shall you persuade her?"

"Leave that to me. My campaign begins over dinner."

If Edie had any doubts about Stuart's ability to change Joanna's mind about school, by the end of dinner, those doubts were gone. Females, she ought to know by now, were wax in his hands.

He started his campaign by mentioning to

Mrs. Simmons his tour of Italy when he was twenty-one. Mrs. Simmons, a great lover of art, had also been to Italy, and through the first six courses of the meal, the two of them discussed the exquisite paintings within the Vatican's Sistine Chapel, Venice's picturesque canals, Florence's Ponte Vecchio and Pitti Palace, and the breathtaking beauty of the Tuscan countryside. Joanna listened with avid interest and asked dozens of questions, but since Willowbank was in Kent, not Italy, Edie saw no point to this Italian tour.

Until dessert.

"Oh, I would love to go to Italy." Joanna fell back in her chair with a dreamy sigh.

"Indeed?" Stuart turned to the girl in surprise. "I never would have thought you'd want to go there, Joanna."

"Are you joking?" The girl stared at him as if he were the most hopelessly dim-witted person in the world. "It would be like a dream come true. Think of the landscapes I could paint there! How could you ever think I wouldn't want to go to Italy?"

"Because you don't want to go to Willowbank, of course." Stuart paused, frowning as if confounded. "Therefore, I assumed you had no interest in going to Italy either."

Joanna wasn't the only one who looked at

him in bewilderment. Mrs. Simmons looked equally confused, and even Edie, who knew his intentions, was baffled as well.

"What does Willowbank have to do with Italy?" Joanna asked.

"It hardly matters, since you're not going." He paused for a sip of wine. "But Mrs. Calloway is intending to take a group of her most talented second-year pupils to Italy next autumn."

"What?" Joanna was aghast. She was not the only one.

"I didn't know of any such tour," Edie said, and looked at Mrs. Simmons. "Did you?"

"No, indeed," the governess answered. "Mrs. Calloway is a great admirer of the Masters, of course, and all the girls at Willowbank learn to study their techniques, but I know nothing of this Italian business."

"She's wanted to do it for several years, apparently," Stuart told them. "But they've been in need of a sponsor. She heard I was home, and she wrote to me, asking if I'd do it. Apparently, she feels that a duke would lend a certain cachet to the whole thing, and since Joanna was going there, she thought I might be amenable to the idea. I shall be happy to sponsor their trip, of course."

"But you can't!" Joanna cried, her fork clattering to her plate. "You can't sponsor other girls going to Italy and not me."

"Joanna!" Edie reproved. "There is no need to rattle the silver and be impertinent."

"It's all right, Edie," Stuart said. "It's bound to be a bit shattering to know other girls will be taking her place on a trip to Italy." He turned to Joanna. "Petal, I'm sorry you won't be going, but I see no reason to deprive other talented young ladies of their chance to paint the Tuscan countryside and study the works of Michelangelo because you don't want to do so."

He took another sip of wine and resumed eating his blackberry tart and cream.

"But — but — but —" Joanna's voice stuttered into silence, and Edie almost felt sorry for her. Not since she was a little girl had Joanna looked so much like she wanted to cry.

Edie continued eating dessert, but she watched Joanna out of the corner of her eye, and when she saw the girl bite down on her lip, just the same way she did when she was in a state of agonizing indecision, she knew Joanna was wavering, and she wasn't surprised when the girl turned to her.

"Edie, is it too late for me to go to Willowbank?"

"No." Edie looked across at Stuart, who leaned back with his wine, giving her a wink over his glass. "Of course it's not too late."

The August lilies were blooming. Edie knew that because the luscious scent of the flowers wafted through the open French doors as she and the others walked down the corridor toward the music room after dinner, and she almost regretted that their day at the Wash had prevented her from taking the usual evening walk with Stuart. The gardens smelled lovely.

Stuart seemed to read her thoughts. "Lovely night," he commented. "Perfect for a stroll."

"Yes," she agreed, smiling at him over her shoulder as she walked through the doorway of the music room. "Such a pity it's not a full moon."

But the moment she entered the music room, Edie realized that if they wanted to go for a walk in the grounds, no moonlight would be necessary. Through the French doors, she could see lanterns, dozens of them, their lights flickering in a line along the terrace and forming a serpentine trail through the gardens beyond. She stopped just inside the door with a cry of amazement. "Stuart!"

He stopped behind her. "Who needs a full moon?" he murmured. "I instructed Welles-ley to arrange it all before we left this morn-ing. Do you like it?"

"Like it?" She laughed, delighted, and once again looked at him over her shoulder. "It's wonderful!"

He didn't smile, but he didn't have to for her to know she'd pleased him. She saw it in his eyes.

"What's wonderful?" Joanna asked behind them. "And why are you two blocking the doorway?"

Edie moved into the room, allowing Jo-anna and Mrs. Simmons to also see what he'd done, then she started out to the ter-race, with Stuart beside her.

"Oooh," Joanna breathed, following them outside. "It looks magical, doesn't it? Like something out of a fairy story."

"Yes, it does." Edie laughed again and looked at Stuart. "Now we can go for our walk after all."

He gestured to the stone steps nearby. "Shall we, Edie?" he asked, and the soft question and the look in his eyes as he asked it made her catch her breath.

"Yes," she said, and moved toward him. "Let's go."

"Can I come, too?" Joanna asked.

"No," she and Stuart answered at the same time, and she knew both of them had the same reason for refusing Joanna's request. Leaving the girl staring wistfully after them, they started down the lanternlit path.

"We forgot Snuffles," Stuart commented, as they entered the rose garden. "He's still below stairs somewhere."

"He can miss his walk this once." She looked around. "Joanna's right. The lanterns do make everything look magical."

"Poor girl," he said, laughing. "Did you see her face when we said she couldn't come with us? She looked like a wounded puppy."

"The other was worse," Edie reminded. "When she learned she wouldn't be going to Italy because she wasn't going to Willowbank. Really, Stuart," she added, trying to sound severe and failing completely, "Mrs. Calloway taking pupils to Italy, indeed! And don't tell me she wrote to you, for I shan't believe it."

"She didn't." He gave her a sideways smile. "But don't you dare give me away."

"I won't, but what do you intend to do about Italy?"

"It's obvious, isn't it? They'll have to go."

"All that to persuade my sister that she wants to go away to school! You are so outlandish."

"But you like it, Edie. Admit it, you like it."

"I suppose I do. Perhaps it's because I never do anything outlandish that I like it when you do."

They entered the Secret Garden, and she found her accusation of his outlandishness proved yet again, for lanterns had been placed all around the fountain, giving the white marble statue of three sisters and the water that poured over them a magical glow. "You see?" she said, laughing. "That is just what I mean. I suppose you told Wellesley to have the footmen place the lights just where they would illuminate the fountain perfectly."

"I did." He stopped beside the fountain. When she stopped beside him, he turned toward her and reached out to touch a fold of her skirt, rubbing shimmery blue silk between his fingers. "I like this dress," he said. "Or, rather, I like you in this dress."

"Indeed?"

"Yes, indeed. Did you wear blue because it's my favorite color? Say yes," he added when she hesitated, smiling a little. "Throw me a crumb."

She laughed. "All right, yes," she admitted. "I did."

His smile faded and he let go of the silk.

He lifted his hand to the exposed skin above the low neckline of her dress but he didn't touch her. Instead, he paused, fingertips a hairsbreadth from her skin. He looked into her eyes.

"I'm thinking right now how much I want to touch you." He paused. "If I do, would that be all right?"

She considered, nodded. "Yes."

The pad of his index finger touched the side of her neck. She drew in her breath sharply and let it out slowly as his fingertip glided down the column of her throat. She strove to stay perfectly still, but her heart began to race before he'd even reached her collarbone.

His fingertip nestled there, in the indent at the center of her collarbone, and he began tracing tiny circles in that spot, around and around, at the base of her throat.

"I . . ." She stopped, forgetting entirely what she'd meant to say, for the gentle, musing caress of his finger was spreading heat throughout her body and robbing her of her wits. She felt her knees going weak, and when his free arm slid around her waist, she welcomed it, for he kept her on her feet.

"I'm going to kiss you." He didn't ask if it would be all right, he didn't wait for an answer, he just did it, capturing her lips with his in a lush, openmouthed kiss. Tender, yes, but deeper, fuller, with something new in it — an urgency that took her by surprise.

But she didn't stop him, and when his arm tightened, pulling her closer, she came without resistance. He felt her yield, and she knew it excited him; his body stirred against hers.

Her hand lifted, curled at the back of his neck, raked through his hair. Her tongue met his, willing and hot, and for a brief, shining moment, it was glorious.

He made a stifled sound, and with no warning, he grabbed her arms and pushed her back, away from him. His hands fell to his sides.

Breathing hard, they stared at each other. "I didn't tell you to stop," she panted, working to clear her dazed senses. "Why did you?"

"I did it out of self-preservation," he said between ragged breaths and rubbed his hands over his face. "Much more of that, and it would have been absolute torture for me to stop." He paused and looked into her eyes. "But even then, I would have stopped, Edie. I would have."

She nodded. "I believe you, Stuart."

"Best if we go back," he said, and bent to

reach for his walking stick. She realized she hadn't even noticed when he dropped it.

Neither of them spoke as they walked back to the house. Edie couldn't, for she was too dazed, too overwhelmed by his kiss and her own response to it to make conversation. She could only think he felt the same.

She also knew he was in a state of arousal, she'd felt it when his body pressed against hers. She wasn't afraid of it, exactly. But she couldn't imagine what would happen when they were in her bedroom, and she was helping him with his leg. Would he kiss her again? she wondered wildly. How could he not? Would he try to make love to her? What would she do if he did?

When they reached her room, she opened the door, but when she stepped across the threshold, he didn't follow her. Surprised, she stopped and turned in the doorway. "Stuart?"

"I think it might be best if we forgo the exercises tonight."

She felt a hint of relief, and yet, right alongside it, she also felt a stab of disappointment that their evening was coming to such an abrupt end. She worked not to let either emotion show on her face. "Of course. If you're sure?"

"I am. It's late, and I have to leave first

385

thing in the morning."

"Leave?" she echoed in dismay.

"Yes. I think I'll take the milk train. It departs quite early."

She shook her head in bewilderment. "But where are you going?"

He seemed surprised by the question. "Kent, of course. Now that I've managed to convince Joanna to go to Willowbank, I have to go rushing down ahead of her and see Mrs. Calloway. Somehow, I have to persuade that good lady, whom I have never met in my life, to take a group of schoolgirls to Italy at our expense, and to lead all the girls to believe it was her idea."

Edie lifted a hand to her throat where he'd touched her earlier, and she felt sure he'd have no trouble with the task of cajoling Mrs. Calloway. Even the redoubtable, no-nonsense headmistress of a girls' school wouldn't be immune to his charm. She certainly wasn't. "I'm sure you'll find a way to talk her into it," she said faintly.

"I hope so, or I shall really be in the suds with Joanna."

"When will you be back?"

"Day after tomorrow, I expect. I shall stop in London on the way down. I want to see Dr. Cahill and hear his opinion of how my leg is getting on. And I have some other business to conduct. So I'll stay at my club that night and go on to Kent early in the morning to see Mrs. Calloway. I'll be back here by about teatime, I should think."

"So you want me to wait to send Joanna off until after you've returned?"

"Yes. I would like to say good-bye to her before she goes, if that's all right."

"Of course." She paused, cleared her throat. "Well, good night, then."

He smiled a little and leaned closer to her, his lashes lowering. She knew what that meant, and this time, she met him halfway.

The moment his lips touched hers, all the heady feelings he'd aroused earlier in the garden came rushing back, but she barely had time to savor them before he was pulling away.

"Good night, Edie."

It took her a moment to open her eyes, and when she did, he was already turning away.

She almost reached out to touch him, hoping it might make him linger. Though she managed to check the impulse, it still left her standing in the doorway of her room in dazed astonishment, and as she watched him walk down the corridor to his own room, she wondered suddenly if she might be in danger of losing the bet they'd made.

After all, had anyone told her a week ago that she'd be standing here in a state of arousal, dejected because her husband had not come into her bedroom, frustrated because his good-night kiss had been far too short, and unutterably depressed because he was leaving her for two whole days, she'd have called that person crazy.

Stuart knew that sometimes, in the game of love, strategic retreat was in order. Usually, that meant a deliberate act designed to make the other person more eager. In his case, however, it was more a matter of distance enabling him to regain his equilibrium.

It meant giving up two of his precious ten days, but he had no choice. He needed distance and time away because he needed to regain his control. He'd almost lost his head in the garden, not to mention outside her room with her bedroom door wide open, and he didn't want to risk temptations of that sort. He couldn't, not with Edie. He had to keep his head.

To stand there in the garden with her, her mouth beneath his, open and willing, had been so sweet, and she'd come into his arms without resistance, but every instinct he had told him she wasn't ready. Not for what he wanted.

He ached with lust. He burned with it. He'd wanted to pull up the skirts of that glistening blue gown and take her down into the grass last night, right there in the garden, and it had been like ripping himself in half to push her away.

And then, standing at her bedroom door with her invitation to come inside hanging in the air had been like an invitation straight into hell. To have her hands on him in any way at that point would have been akin to torture and possibly damnation as well, for even he wasn't completely sure what he'd have done after that.

No, best all around that he'd managed to resist, even if it was the hardest thing he'd ever done, and he'd seized on the excuse to go to Kent like a lifeline, and London, too. As he'd told her, he had business to do there, business that would help him to remember his priorities. His needs were not a priority. And with his body in such a hopeless state, he needed something useful to occupy his mind.

Because he'd taken the milk train, he arrived in London by midmorning. He stopped at his club, and as he'd expected, he found letters waiting for him there —

from Trubridge, Featherstone, and his other two closest friends, Viscount Somerton and the Earl of Hayward. They had all received the telegrams he'd sent off the day he went shopping with Edie in the High Street, and they all agreed to his request for a reunion in town to welcome him home. All he needed to do was name the day, and all four promised to be there. A fifth letter was also waiting for him in response to another of his telegrams, a letter he hadn't expected quite yet and one that made him think perhaps Pinkerton's deserved their reputation as the finest detective agency in the world. They were certainly efficient.

In reply, he sent a boy across town at once with a request for an immediate appointment, then he went upstairs for a bathe and a shave and to have the laundry at White's press the morning suit he'd brought with him. Suitably attired for town, he went down to the dining room to have lunch while he waited for a response to his inquiry.

It came by half past one, and by two, a hansom cab was depositing him outside Pinkerton's London offices. He was ushered at once into the luxuriously appointed office of Mr. Duncan Ashe, leading detective of the agency.

"Your Grace." Ashe, a tall fellow of about

his own age with russet brown hair and an agreeable, clean-shaven face, gestured to the comfortable leather chair opposite his desk. "Please sit down."

"Thank you." He availed himself of the invitation. "And thank you for making time for me today. I'm sure you are quite a busy man."

"Not at all. We are honored to have Your Grace as a client, and we are happy to assist you at any time."

He smiled. Rank did have its privileges. "You indicated in your letter to me that you have some of the information I requested?"

"Yes. Some. It's only been two days, so anything I have from our New York offices had to be conveyed by telegram." He paused. "The expense for cables back and forth shall be quite high, I fear."

Stuart waved that trifle aside. "It doesn't matter. Money is no object."

"I took the liberty of assuming that from the urgent wording of your telegram. I've supplemented what we've been given by our New York agency with information we've been able to gather from newspapers archived here in London. Scandal sheets, mostly, both British and American. It's not much, as I said, but I expect to have a complete dossier for you by next week. In the meantime, I thought you would wish to hear what we have thus far?"

"I am all ears."

Ashe opened a file on the desk in front of him. "Frederick Van Hausen. Born in New York City, thirty-one years of age, the only son — only child, actually — of Albert and Lydia Van Hausen. Educated at Harvard. There was some scandal involving him there, something illegal, but he wasn't prosecuted. Father got it hushed up, apparently. I don't have details, but I can probably obtain them, if you like."

"I do like. Find out all you can. Go on."

"He is unmarried. He was engaged for a brief period last year to Miss Susan Avermore, also from a prominent New York family, but the marriage didn't come off. Some say it's because he expected Miss Avermore to bring an income from her father with her when they married, and her father refused flat out. But we haven't had time to verify that. His parents have a home on Madison Avenue, but he no longer lives with them. He has a brownstone of his own just off Central Park. He also owns a summer home in Newport. Van Hausen is quite the sportsman, plays tennis and golf, sails yachts, owns racehorses —"

"Racehorses?" Stuart frowned, thinking

back to the other day, and Edie's short, clipped answer about her father's race-horses.

"Your Grace?"

He shook his head. "Sorry, I was wool-gathering."

"The Van Hausen family is one of the wealthiest and oldest families in America. Knickerbockers, Your Grace, if you are familiar with the term."

"I am. So," he murmured, "Van Hausen fancies himself an aristocrat, does he?"

"They all do. That's how other Americans regard them. Rather the same way men of my class here in England regard a man such as you. Not that a Knickerbocker is anything to a duke, of course," he rushed on, looking a little abashed.

Stuart smiled in reassurance. "I take no offense, Ashe. Go on."

The detective turned a page. "The father owns a shipping company and is very successful, very wealthy. Van Hausen had an enormous sum settled on him by his father when he came of age, but American men are also expected to take up a profession and earn their living. In fact, there's enormous pressure to do so."

"Ah, so he's had to cut his own jib, has he?" Stuart murmured. "How's that working out for him?"

"Not so well. He tried for the bar, and failed. He turned his hand to business investment and speculated with his money, but lost a lot of it. The racehorses, for example, have cost him dear. He leans toward riskier investments that promise higher profits."

"So he's a gambler." Stuart considered. "And intemperate. Eager to make his mark in the world and do it quickly. A man who cares what people think of him."

"He seems so, certainly."

That boded well. Stuart leaned back, one knuckle pressed to his lips as he stared past the detective toward the wall, past the painting of the Thames that hung there, trying to see all the way to New York and into the mind of the man he intended to destroy. "He's the sort of man who wants power. He doesn't have it, but he thinks he's entitled to it by birthright. He's incapable of earning what he wants, so he wants what he hasn't earned. The sort of man who, if he wants something, thinks it's all right just to take it."

"Possibly. As yet, I can't say."

"I can." Stuart met the other man's eyes across the desk. "I can."

He considered a moment. "Any other

scandals, Ashe? Anything involving women?"

The detective hesitated, toying with a pencil on his desk. "Other than your wife, you mean?"

"You may include my wife, and you've no need to worry about sparing my feelings on the subject."

"If you're asking for this information about her former lover because you think they might still be lovers, and you want to find grounds for divorce, I can't help you. Pinkerton's doesn't do that sort of thing. We have certain ethical lines we do not cross."

"I can assure you, I have no intention of ever divorcing my wife. And I already know the truth of the . . . incident with Van Hausen that ruined her reputation, but I wish to hear the gossip as well, for reasons of my own. You won't be violating your code of ethics."

Satisfied, Ashe nodded. "The duchess excepted, we don't have anything on other women, yet. The incident involving her — Miss Edith Ann Jewell, as she was then — occurred at Saratoga."

"Saratoga Springs, New York?"

"Yes, they hold race meetings there. It was six years ago, during the week of the Travers

Stakes. The Travers' is a bit like our Epsom Derby."

"I know what it is. Go on."

"Your father-in-law and Van Hausen both had horses running in the Travers Stakes that year. The gossip is that Miss Jewell cornered Van Hausen in an abandoned summerhouse near the course. Both of them were seen going in, him first, and then her a bit later. He came out about fifteen minutes after she arrived."

Fifteen minutes? Was that all? God, the bastard must have jumped her practically the moment she walked in the door. Stuart rubbed a hand over his face. He would destroy this man. Reduce him to tattered bits of flotsam. "Go on."

"She came out a bit later. Her —" Ashe paused.

"Go on," Stuart repeated in a hard voice.

"Her clothes were quite rumpled, her hat was askew, making it seem . . ." His voice trailed off, and he gave a delicate cough. "Word got round straightaway, of course, and it became a huge scandal. Her father demanded honor be satisfied, but Van Hausen flatly refused to marry her. She was very New Money, not of his class, and his claim was that he was an innocent party and that she was trying to compromise him and jump into his class by trapping him into marriage. His story was the one believed. It doesn't matter now, of course."

"Only because she's married to me." Stuart straightened in his chair. "So what have we got? A man who is greedy, overindulged, eager for power, thoughtless, unscrupulous, a bit of a gambler, and clearly a cad."

"That would seem an accurate summary, based on what we know."

Stuart smiled, pleased with the many possibilities such a profile afforded him, but then, he'd known there would be possibilities. A man who'd violate a woman against her will was bound to give his enemies ammunition to work with, and though Van Hausen might not know it, Stuart was definitely his enemy. "Excellent work, Ashe. I am impressed."

"Thank you, Your Grace."

"But I need more. Much, much more. We'll meet again when you have that dossier you're working up, but I'm certain even that won't be enough. I want to know everything there is to know about this man, about his parents, his friends, his business associates, his mistresses, everything. Keep digging until you've turned his entire life inside out from the time of his birth to this very moment." He stood up, bringing the other man to his feet as well. "Employ as many men as you need. Spare no expense. I want every detail you can find, down to what material he prefers for his underclothes and what he eats for breakfast."

"Yes, Your Grace."

With that, Stuart departed to return to his club, stopping along the way only long enough to send another telegram, this one to Edie's father. When he arrived back at White's, he walked straight into the bar and ordered a drink. He needed it.

# CHAPTER 18

Stuart was gone two days. He arrived home around teatime, just as he'd told her he would. Though she was engaged in a battle of croquet with Joanna, she kept watching for him, hoping he'd come out to greet them upon his return.

He did, and when she spied him coming across the lawn toward her, gladness rose in her like a bird soaring skyward.

Snuffles spied him at the same time and bounded across the grass to greet him. It took everything Edie had to move at a slower pace, and when they met halfway across the grass, she gripped her mallet hard, fighting the urge to toss it aside, fling her arms around his neck, and kiss his mouth.

"You're back," she said.

He straightened from petting the terrier and smiled at her. "Miss me?"

*Like mad.*

She didn't say it. Instead, she shrugged. "A little."

"Only a little?" He shook his head and sighed. "Heartless Edie. Still, you are wearing white today, so I can't complain."

She reached up one hand, fingering her high collar. "Just my shirtwaist," she felt impelled to point out. "My skirt isn't white."

His gaze lowered, then lifted. "That's a pity."

As always when he said things like that, her heart gave a hard thump in her breast, and she grabbed for a neutral subject. "It's very hot."

"Yes," he agreed. "It is."

A perfectly ordinary thing to say, and yet, the way he said it sent a warmth in her spreading through her body that had nothing to do with the weather.

"Stuart!" Joanna's joyful greeting saved her from having to think of a reply. Her sister stopped beside her, breathing hard from having run across the lawn. Joanna had none of her painful shyness with him. "You're back!"

"Hullo, petal." He grinned at her as he glanced at Edie. "I hope *you* missed me?"

She grinned back at him. "That depends. Do you know how to play croquet?"

"I do."

"But are you any good?"

"I was, actually. But I haven't played in years."

"Either way, you'll surely be better than me, so you must come and help me. Edie's beaten me three times already, and I'm about to lose again because I've got a tricky shot to make, and I don't think I can do it. You can take my shot for me."

"No, he can't!" Edie protested, indignant. "That would be cheating."

"Edie, Edie," Stuart chided, laughing. "You are so ruthless at games."

"She is," Joanna put in before she could answer. "I don't know why I even play with her. And she's very good. Please, help me, Stuart."

"I will, but it shall have to be another time. I'm going up to change while you and your sister finish your game, then I want tea on the terrace. I've been in a hot, crowded train all afternoon."

"After that, will you play?"

"Not today. After tea, I want to spend some time with your sister." He glanced at Edie. "Alone."

"Oh, very well," Joanna grumbled. "Perfect chance to win for a change," she added under her breath as she turned away, "and it doesn't come off. I'll never beat her."

"Really, Edie," he whispered as Joanna stalked off to make her shot. "Four games in a row? Be a sport and let her win one."

She looked at him, saw his cajoling smile, and gave in. "Oh, all right. You must be softening me up," she added, making it sound like an accusation.

"God, I hope so." He ducked his head beneath her straw hat, and planted a quick kiss on her lips. "I certainly hope so."

After tea, they went for their usual walk. Instead of going through the gardens, however, Stuart expressed the desire to tour the home farm, so they went that way, across the lawn and down the lane.

She couldn't help noting as they walked that his pace was slower today. "Does your leg hurt?" she asked.

"A bit," he admitted. "Trains are so cramped, it's difficult. And I didn't have you to stretch me out these two days."

"We can do that before dinner."

"Love to," he said at once, and again she felt an absurd burst of joy.

"How was London?" she asked. "Did you see the doctor?"

"I did. He's glad I seem to be improving, and he's given me some additional stretching exercises to add to my regimen. I also saw Mrs. Calloway, and she is delighted by the idea of a trip to Italy next year."

Edie's joy dimmed a little at the reminder of Joanna's impending departure.

"I'll miss her, too, Edie," he said, correctly interpreting her sudden silence.

That didn't make her feel better, but she nodded. "I know, Stuart."

Suddenly, he stopped walking. "I say, look where we are."

Edie came to a halt as well, looking around. "We're by the henhouses."

"Yes, exactly." He glanced around and grabbed her hand. "Come on."

She laughed, allowing him to pull her and Snuffles along. "You want to see the chickens? The dog will love that."

He gave her a look as if she were hopelessly dense. "Not the chickens, darling. The feathers."

"The feathers? What on earth for?"

He didn't explain. As he led her and Snuffles past the henhouses, the dog barked and growled, causing the hens in the fenced pen to flutter in alarm and vanish into the coop.

"We're frightening the hens," she told him. "If there are no eggs tomorrow, I'm telling Mrs. Bigelow that it's your fault."

Stuart was not dissuaded by that. He led

her around the corner of the henhouses to the feather house several dozen yards beyond, where he took Snuffles's lead from her fingers and tied the dog firmly to a nearby fence post. Then, he opened the door of the feather house, pulled her inside, and closed the door behind them. She blinked, for though the building had windows, the interior was dim after the bright sunshine outside, and it took several minutes for her eyes to adjust.

"So why are we in here?" she asked, glancing around at the wood-slatted pens where feathers were stored after being cleaned and dried.

He didn't answer. Instead, he tossed his walking stick into one of the pens, turned around, and leaned back against the wooden slats behind him. Resting his hands on either side of the top slat, he lifted himself to perch on the edge. He grinned at her. "You're looking at me as if I've lost my wits."

"Well . . ." she began.

His grin widened. "Oh, come on, don't tell me you've never wanted to."

She frowned, bewildered. "Never wanted to what?"

Instead of answering, he leaned back and fell straight into the feathers behind him.

She laughed as tiny feathers and bits of down floated up toward the ceiling and she leaned forward to look into his grinning face. "That's why you wanted to come in here?"

"Of course. My friends and I used to play here. Old Treves would grumble about it, with us mussing about in his feathers, but he never told on us. Not once." He laughed, looking up into her dubious face. "I can tell you did not grow up in the country, Edie."

"No. I grew up in a very large house in the middle of Manhattan with all the conveniences of modern life. Our feather beds and pillows came from a store."

"So you've never played in the feathers? You were deprived of one of childhood's greatest joys."

She glanced at the sides of the three-foot-high enclosure. "Will you be able to get back out?"

"Hell's bells, I didn't even think of that." He laughed. "Ah, well, I'll worry about that later." He slid backward, so that his entire body was in the pen. "Well, come on," he urged, "what are you waiting for?"

She pulled off her hat and tossed it aside, then she turned around, lifted herself onto the edge, and with a glance over her shoulder to make sure he was out of her way, she fell backward. She was laughing even before she landed next to him in a pouf of white.

"Fun, isn't it?" he asked.

She nodded, staring up at the wood ceiling, the floor of the loft above. "So you weren't allowed to play in here?"

"God, no. These feathers are for pillows and mattresses for the house, not for play. My father would have taken a crop to me if he'd known."

"A crop?" She turned her head and looked at him. "How awful! Your father must have been a tyrant."

"He was, rather. But —" Stuart paused and shrugged. "He bothered so little about us, it didn't matter. We almost never saw him."

His cavalier attitude about it rather startled her. She thought of his mother, and her cold haughtiness, and she didn't know what to say. "That's a shame," she said at last. "My parents were very attentive to me and my sister. Until my mother died, anyway. That changed my father, I think. Without my mother, he didn't know what to do with two daughters. He was a bit lost."

Stuart turned on his side, rubbing his head to dislodge any bits of down from his short hair, then he propped his weight on his elbow and rested his cheek on his hand, looking at her. "So you had to be both mother and sister for Joanna?"

"Yes, exactly. I was seventeen when my mother died. Joanna was only eight. I felt I had to take over."

"I understand. Nadine and I have exactly the same age difference. When my father died, though, my sister was already sixteen. But if she'd been a little girl, I would have been like father to her as well as brother. I almost wish that had been the case. I might have been able to save her from being completely scatterbrained."

"I doubt it. I hate to say mean things about your family, Stuart, but your sister isn't the brightest candle in the chandelier."

"No," he agreed, laughing. "She isn't, is she?"

"So you and your friends played in here?" She snuggled deeper, liking the feel of the feathers beneath her. "What did you do?"

"Oh, feather fights, of course. Didn't you have pillow fights with your girlfriends?"

"Well, yes, but we never had loose feathers like this."

"Then it doesn't count."

"What? Why not?" she demanded, feeling a bit indignant.

"Really, Edie, if you don't hit your opponent hard enough to break the pillow open and have the feathers flying everywhere, it is not a true pillow fight."

She watched as he picked up a handful of down.

"Stuart," she warned, but he didn't throw them at her. Instead, he plucked out one small feather, and tossed the others aside. Reaching over, he touched the feather beneath her chin.

She shook her head, laughing.

"You're ticklish," he accused, sounding far too delighted by the fact.

"No, I'm not." But even as she denied it, she laughed harder, squeezing her eyes shut, wriggling as he brushed the feather along her jaw.

"Edie, I never knew this about you," he teased. "I think things between us just got a bit more equal."

She felt his hand curve around her waist. "No, don't," she shrieked, still laughing. "Don't tickle me."

He didn't. For no reason at all, he stilled, and when she opened her eyes, he was staring at her, his face grave, his eyes dark and smoky.

She swallowed hard. "What are you thinking?" she whispered, but even as she asked the question, she already knew the answer.

"I'm thinking it's not in the sheets," he

murmured as he pulled a bit of white fluff from her hair. "But it'll do."

He bent his head and kissed her. It was more like the kiss he'd given her the other night in the garden rather than the sweet kisses outside her bedroom door. Familiar with his kisses now, her body responded almost at once, relaxing, easing, warming to him.

He explored her mouth, his tongue caressing hers, then pulling back, coaxing her to reciprocate. He finally broke the kiss, but she had time for just one gasp for air before he kissed her again. The kiss deepened, and the warmth in her deepened, too, growing hotter, centering in her breasts, low in her abdomen, between her legs. She groaned against his mouth.

He broke the kiss again, and she felt him easing back as if to withdraw. This time, instead of letting him go, she curled her fingers around the armholes of his waistcoat to keep him there. She did not want these kisses to end, not yet.

"Edie?"

She knew the question he was asking and she opened her eyes. "You told me it was bliss to be kissed and caressed, didn't you?" she whispered. "Here's your chance to prove it."

He smiled a little. He looked down at his hand where it rested lightly on her waist. Slowly, his palm slid upward over her ribs and across her breast. She inhaled sharply, and he stilled, then he looked into her eyes. A question.

She nodded.

His palm seemed to burn through the four layers of clothing she wore, straight to her bare skin, and yet she shivered. His gaze still locked with hers, he cupped his hand, then flattened it and cupped it again, shaping her small breast even within the stiff confines of her corset, and her body responded, her hips stirring against the feathers, her leg bending, then straightening, her back arching to press her breast closer to his hand. She felt strange, restless, as if every part of her body needed to move.

He didn't linger, though. His hand moved on, gliding up to the collar of her shirtwaist. His fingers stirred between the frills and found a button. She felt it come undone.

Slowly, he moved down, undoing buttons. By the time he reached her waist, she was quivering inside. She watched his hand as he pulled back the placket, his tanned skin so dark against her white shirtwaist and pale pink corset, so blatantly masculine against silk and lace. His hand slid away, and she watched as he bent his head, pressing a kiss to the top of her breast just above her corset cover.

She gasped, her body arching again. Her hands lifted from the feathers to cradle his head and touch his dark hair as he pressed kisses to her breast, her collarbone, and her bared shoulder.

Her breath was coming faster now, bringing to her senses the scent of sandalwood as his tongue touched her and tasted her. Once again his palm shaped her breast, and she couldn't stop her body from arching into the caress. She wanted more of this.

His fingertips curled over the edge of her corset, shoving beneath all her undergarments, the back of his hand scorching her bare skin. He worked his hand down within the tight confines of the garment over her breast far enough for his fingertips to touch her nipple.

It was electric, sending sharp sensation throughout her body. It was too much to bear, and she cried out, her hips jerking.

He eased back, his hand sliding out and away. He kissed her lips, her cheeks, her jaw, her ear. His hand glided down her hip, then he began pulling her skirt up.

She felt a jolt of panic. "Stuart?"

He stilled. "Do you want me to stop?" he

asked. His breathing was quick, ragged, but gently, he kissed her ear. So gently.

She swallowed, shoving panic down. This was Stuart, she reminded herself. Stuart. As long as she could see him, it would be all right. Looking into his eyes, she would remember the difference. "No, don't stop," she managed. "But look at me. Look at me when . . . when you touch me."

He lifted his head as his hand worked beneath layers of skirt and petticoat to her drawers. But even though she could see his face, even looking into his beautiful eyes, when he moved to slide his hand between her thighs, she seized up, that knot of fear pressing her chest. She went rigid and squeezed her legs together.

He stopped, waiting.

She felt again that suspension between fear and desire, that impossible conundrum. Her courage started slipping.

"Say my name," he told her.

"Stuart."

Her legs opened a little as she said it; his hand eased between.

"Stuart." A soft moan this time, making him smile, and her legs relaxed a bit more.

He shaped her inner thigh, the calluses on his palm catching on delicate nainsook as he slid his hand higher. He reached the apex of her legs, found the opening in her drawers. And then, he turned his hand, his fingertips touched her most intimate place, and she cried out. "Stuart!"

Fear transmuted into something else, something that made her cry out again, something that was not fear at all but pleasure. He moved his finger, sliding it over her, caressing her in tiny circles, an exquisite tease that made her shiver and moan and close her eyes. This was what he meant about the bliss, she thought. It was this.

He deepened the caress, sliding his finger between the folds of her feminine opening, easing inside her. She cried out against remembered invasion pulled up onto her elbows, and opened her eyes, fearing pain, instinct preparing her to fight. But there was no pain.

She looked into Stuart's face, so close to hers. His eyes were closed now, but she could still look into his face as he caressed her.

With each slide of his finger, her body jerked in response. Every breath became a pant. The pleasure became hunger, then raw need. It built in her, rolling in her body, deeper, heavier, stronger, and then, without warning, it broke apart inside of her, a wash of sensation so lovely that it made her sob his name. He kissed her hard, taking her sobbing cry into his mouth. His fingers continued to caress her, and each quick, luscious stroke renewed the pleasure, until she felt that exquisite explosion come again. She'd been wrong, she realized as she fell back, panting, into the feathers. It was this, this that was the bliss. Her eyes closed again. "Stuart."

It was a sigh. All she could say. There were no other words.

He heard her sigh his name, barely, over the thudding of his heart, but he knew it would whisper to him in dreams for the rest of his days. And nothing would ever be the same for him now. "I know, darling," he said, and kissed her again. "I know."

He wished he could do it all again, bring her to the peak, watch her climax, hear that soft, whispered sigh, but he knew he did not have time for it now. His control was slipping irretrievably away, his body was on fire, and need was clawing at him.

He wanted her so badly his hand was shaking as he unfastened the buttons of his trousers. He said her name and kissed her mouth as he worked his trousers down, and by the time they were around his knees, he felt as randy and desperate as a fourteen-year-old boy.

But he knew he couldn't take her like that, and he pulled her toward him onto her side, watching her eyes open. Their gazes locked, he pressed his hips closer to hers, and when the tip of his penis touched her, she sucked in her breath.

"It'll be all right," he promised her. "It won't hurt."

He slid his penis between her thighs, easing through the opening in her drawers, and watched her eyes widen in alarm. Her nostrils flared in fear. Her lips parted, quivering. "Say my name," he said.

"Stuart."

He nudged forward, entering her. "Oh, God," he groaned, and closed his eyes, pleasure shuddering through his body. He knew he ought to ask if he should stop, but he didn't. All the primal needs he'd been fighting so hard to contain surged up within him. He slid his hand to her buttock for leverage, and eased a little more into her.

She sucked in her breath, a shuddering gasp, and he prayed like hell she didn't decide to say stop. He waited, rigid, but she didn't say it. Instead, she wriggled her hips as if trying to draw him deeper.

He sucked in his breath. "Oh, God, Edie. Oh, God."

That was all he could manage, and then,

he just couldn't wait anymore. He rolled her on her back, moving with her, gathering her to him as he pressed kisses to her face, her hair, her cheek, anywhere he could. Though his blood was roaring in his ears, he heard her say his name. She did not say stop. She did not say no.

He thrust into her, entering her fully. She cried out, and so did he, an exchange of names. He thrust again. He was in her to the hilt, they were as close as two people could be, and yet, he wanted her closer. His arms tightened beneath her back, he buried his face against the side of her neck, and he moved in her, each thrust quicker, harder, taking him higher and higher until he reached the peak. He came in a wave of pure sensation, a climax so strong, that it flooded every cell in his body with pleasure. It was so luscious and so sweet, he tried to hang on to it, thrusting into her again, then again, but at last, he collapsed on top of her, panting against her neck.

"Edie." Her name seemed to echo in the hush of afternoon. And then, he frowned, with a sudden, keen awareness that something was terribly wrong.

A feeling he hadn't had in six months shimmered through him, making the hairs on the back of his neck stand up. With dread in his guts, he lifted his head to look into her face, and what he saw confirmed his worst fear. Her eyes were tight shut, her face pinched and wet with tears. He watched another slide between her closed lids and down her cheek, and it burned his chest, like acid thrown on his heart.

"Is it over?" she whispered without opening her eyes.

The question shredded him to ribbons, and he felt an utter dog. "Edie," he said, and kissed her tear.

She flinched, not much, but enough that it made him flinch, too. Her hands were on his shoulders, and she pushed to dislodge him.

He didn't move. "Edie, open your eyes, look at me."

She complied, but there was a blankness in her tear-streaked face that was more wrenching than her tears. She was looking straight at him, and she didn't see him. "Please, get off me," she whispered, pushing at him again. "Please, please. I can't breathe."

There was panic in her voice, he heard it, and helpless, sick with dismay, he rolled away from her and onto his back, staring up at the wooden ceiling of the feather house. Only a short while ago, they'd been laughing together, and now . . . oh, God. He rubbed his hands over his face, fearing ruin.

He wondered if she'd said no, and he hadn't heard it. He wondered if she'd cried out, "Stop," and he'd imagined it was his name.

Stuart buttoned his trousers. Guilt pressed him down, down, into the feathers, and he wanted to keep going, all the way down into the pit of hell, to burn. He'd made her cry. He wanted to cut his heart out.

Anguished, he closed his eyes, listening in agony to the rustle of fabric as she adjusted her linen and pulled down her skirts. Then she was crawling away, moving toward the side of the pen, and he knew they couldn't leave it like this. "Edie, wait," he said and sat up. "Don't go."

The anguish he felt must have been in his voice, because she paused by the side of the pen. "It's not your fault, Stuart," she said over her shoulder, but she didn't look at him as she said it. "It's not your fault. I . . ." She paused and drew a deep, shaky breath. "I never told you to stop."

That seemed no consolation, not when he could see the mark of tears on her cheek. She turned and climbed out of the pen, moving awkwardly in her skirts as she slid down the other side. She picked up her hat, but he spoke before she could depart.

"Edie, wait. Please, look at me."

She squared her shoulders as if it would be difficult, lifted her face, and turned, looking into his eyes. "I'm all right, Stuart," she said. "I'll be all right."

It was the qualification, the subtle change of wording in her second reassurance that hurt him the most, piercing straight through him like an arrow, and he could only watch helplessly as the woman he wanted more than life itself turned her back and walked away.

# CHAPTER 19

Stuart lingered in the feathers long after she was gone, wishing he could go back, do it all again a different way, but he couldn't. At last, he climbed out of the pen, brushed down from his clothes, and left the feather house.

Edie was long gone, of course, and she'd taken Snuffles with her, so he walked back to the house alone. His pace was slow, not because of the pain in his leg but because of the dread in his guts and the ache in his heart and the guilt that lay heavy on his soul.

He entered the house, but he paused by the stairs, looking up the curved, wrought-iron-and-marble staircase, knowing he had to go up, see Edie, talk to her. This had to be faced, discussed, dealt with, though what that meant, he didn't quite know. Hold her, though he doubted she'd let him. Comfort her, though he had no idea how. At this moment, navigating the Congo or facing a snarling lioness seemed far less daunting. If he made her cry again, he feared it would annihilate him.

"Your Grace?"

He turned, almost relieved by the postponement, however brief, of going upstairs. He turned to find the first footman standing there.

"Yes, Edward? What is it?"

"This came for you." The footman held out a tray on which reposed a folded slip of paper. "Telegram."

Stuart took it and unfolded it as the footman stepped back, waiting to see if he might need anything in response. *Good man, Edward,* he thought absently, and turned his attention to the message in his hands.

EAGER TO HELP STOP HAVE IDEAS STOP LETTER TO COME WITH MORE DETAILS STOP WILL SEND ANY FURTHER CORRESPONDENCE TO WHITE'S AS REQUESTED STOP GLAD YOU GOT SENSE AND CAME HOME TO MY GIRL STOP ARTHUR JEWELL

Stuart stared at the telegram, feeling slightly relieved by the fact that he had an additional ally, but not enough to take away the dread of going up to Edie. He'd come home to Arthur's daughter, true enough, but didn't seem to be doing too well at making her happy. He shoved the telegram in his pocket and turned to the footman.

"Edward?"

The servant once again stepped forward. "Yes, Your Grace?"

Stuart tilted his head, looking the fellow over. Edward was a bit younger than himself but far more tidy than he was. The footman's livery was smoothly in place, his shoes were polished to a high shine, his hair was neatly combed, and his tie was a perfect bow. "Edward . . . Brown, is it?"

"Brownley, Your Grace."

"Of course. Brownley. Forgive me." He paused, considered a moment longer, and made his decision. "How would you like to become a valet, Mr. Brownley?"

The footman stared at him in astonishment. "Your Grace?"

"I presume you've been the one starching my shirts and pressing my suits since I've been home?" When the footman nodded, he went on, "And I believe you've valeted before, when occasion warranted it?"

"Yes, Your Grace. When male guests stay at Highclyffe who've brought no valet along, I have sometimes had the honor of serving them."

"Excellent. I warn you, I won't be easy to

manage. I hate high collars, I'm forever undoing my ties and losing collar studs, and my leg gives me no end of trouble. Also, I've only ever had one valet. He died."

"Mr. Jones. Yes, Your Grace. He was a good man, I hear."

"Yes. He was." Stuart paused. "You'll travel in my service," he went on after a moment. "London in the season. Trips to Italy or France when my wife and I take a holiday — that sort of thing. But I won't ever cart you away from England for long. Would you like the job?"

"Yes, Your Grace. Thank you."

"Well, that's settled then. You may start by determining what I need in the way of clothes, for I'm quite sure my wardrobe is hopelessly outdated. And tell Wellesley he'll have to find a new first footman. You may go."

The servant bowed and departed for the servants' hall, and Stuart knew he couldn't stay down here, postponing the inevitable any longer. He turned and went up the stairs.

At his wife's door, he knocked. "Edie? May I come in?"

There was no answer. He waited a moment, then lifted his hand to knock again, but then the door opened, and he found

Reeves standing there. She didn't open it wider for him to enter. Instead, with a quick glance over her shoulder, she slipped out into the corridor and closed the door behind her.

"Is she . . ." He paused, took a deep breath. "How is she?"

"Well enough." She looked up into his face, and she must have seen something of what he felt, for her usual stiff, respectful rectitude softened. "She'll be all right, Your Grace. She's a bit upset, is all."

"May I see her?"

The maid hesitated. "Begging your pardon, sir, but I don't think that would be wise. She's . . . having a bath at the moment, you see."

The sort of thing anyone might do after intercourse. With any other woman, it wouldn't mean a thing. But with Edie, he had the feeling she was washing away far more than the traces of lovemaking. She was washing away the memory. Of the other man, or of him?

He stepped back, leaning against the wall opposite the door.

"You mustn't blame yourself." The maid's voice was gentle with understanding. "It's not your fault what happened to her."

He looked up, staring at the servant in

astonishment. "You know."

She didn't have to ask what he meant. "Yes."

"Did she . . . did she tell you?"

Reeves gave him a pitying look. "I've been her maid since she first put up her hair. I've always known." She paused. "Did she tell you, Your Grace?"

There was a hint of surprise in her voice as she asked. Stuart shook his head. "I . . . guessed. But she confirmed it." He lifted a hand helplessly. "What can I do?" he asked, and despair hit him squarely in the chest. "Reeves, what can I do?"

"Give her time, sir. She's distraught, but she'll be all right. She just needs a bit of time alone, and she'll get past it."

"Will she?" It didn't seem likely. He shook his head, looking away. "Will she?"

"You've only been home a little over a week. She just needs a bit of breathing room, so to speak."

"Of course." He considered. "I'll go back to London for a bit," he said after a moment. "I have business to finish there, but it will take about a week to complete. Is that long enough?"

"I think so." She smiled a little. "Just don't stay away five years this time."

He attempted a smile in return. "I shall

425

be lucky if I manage to stay away from her for five days."

The maid nodded, seeming pleased. "Good. Because she needs you." Reeves paused, hesitating as if she wanted to say more, then apparently decided she did. "She's always needed you."

Oddly, he was not surprised to hear it. An image of the girl in the ballroom at Hanford House came into his mind. "I've always sensed that," he said slowly. "I suppose I just wasn't ready to be needed. Until now."

He drew a deep breath and straightened away from the wall. "I'll be at my club. Take care of her, Reeves, until I return."

"I will, Your Grace. I always do."

He turned to start down the corridor to his own rooms, but he stopped again before he'd taken a step. "And Reeves?"

The maid paused, her hand on the doorknob. "Yes, Your Grace?"

He bent his head, staring at the floor. The ten days would be over before he came back. She hadn't kissed him. He'd only kissed her, and as she'd rightly pointed out, that didn't count. His right hand clenched tight around his walking stick, the fist of his left hand pressed to his mouth as he worked to say one more thing. Finally, he lowered his hand, looked at the maid over his shoulder, and spoke. "Don't let her leave me. No matter what you have to do, don't let her run off and leave me. That's an order."

It was an impossible order to fulfill. He knew that. If Edie wanted to leave him, her maid could hardly do anything about it, but he was desperate.

"I'll do my best to convince her otherwise, Your Grace, if she does want to go. But . . ." She paused a moment. "But I don't think she'll run away."

"I hope not, Reeves. I need her, too, you see." Stuart walked away, knowing he'd have to leave it at that, at least for now.

It was just on ten o'clock that evening when he and his new valet arrived in town and settled into rooms at his club. The next morning, he dispatched a new slew of letters to his friends, suggesting an evening at White's five days hence for a reunion, judging that Pinkerton's would have a fairly comprehensive dossier on Van Hausen ready for him by then.

In the meantime, Stuart knew he had to keep busy. Dragging Edward along, he visited various tailors, bootmakers, and haberdashers. Having been responsible for Stuart's laundry since his return, his new valet proved knowledgeable enough about his present wardrobe to know what he needed. He also possessed excellent taste in clothing and good judgment about fabrics. He wasn't Jones, but Stuart decided he'd do.

Stuart also went to Park Lane and inspected Margrave House, but it proved a completely unnecessary task. Though closed up at the moment, with everything swathed in dustcovers, he was able to determine that his London residence was shipshape and Bristol fashion. Not for the first time, he appreciated the fact that Edie had done quite well with his estates while he'd been away. But as he walked through the rooms, he hoped and prayed that he wouldn't ever have to live in them without her.

He attended a meeting of the London Geographical Society, where the members in attendance promptly gave him a standing ovation for his explorations in the Congo, which he found painfully embarrassing.

He visited the British Museum and saw his butterfly. While there, he introduced himself to the curator for scientific exhibits, and it rather tickled him that the fellow seemed to think he'd done something important. Somehow, compared to making things right for Edie, a new species of butterfly seemed terribly insignificant.

The tenth day of their bet came and went, and he wondered what she intended to do. He wondered if perhaps he'd made a mistake by leaving without using every moment of the precious time he'd had left. He tried to tell himself two days didn't matter, and it was just a silly bet anyway. He tried to convince himself that even though she hadn't kissed him, even though he'd pushed her too hard too fast, she'd stay. He tried to believe that.

He strove not to think about her too much, but that proved a futile effort. Having tea at the Savoy reminded him. A girl in Hyde Park with red-gold hair reminded him. And anything white, anywhere . . . well . . . he was doomed there, too. Lying in bed was the worst, enfolded in white sheets, feather pillows, and memories of the first time he kissed her and how he'd lain awake all night reliving that kiss over and over.

He wanted to write to her, ask if there was anything she needed, but of course, he didn't. If room to breathe was what she needed, if time and distance would help him keep her, he had to give them to her. He hoped she'd write, ask him to come home, but though he checked for his letters twice a day, none appeared with the Duchess of Margrave's coronet.

The letters he did receive lifted his spirits a bit. His friends confirmed the engagement for Friday night at the club. Pinkerton's informed him they had a dossier. And Arthur Jewell sent him a detailed outline of the various ways Frederick Van Hausen might be vulnerable. His father-in-law suggested they decide on a suitable plan when he came to England for his usual Christmas visit. Stuart wrote back his agreement with that plan, and he could only hope Edie was still with him at Christmas.

He engaged a private dining room at White's for Friday night, and when his friends began arriving, there was a fine single-malt whisky on the table, a menu ordered for dinner, and all the information he had on Van Hausen in a dispatch case beside his chair.

The Marquess of Trubridge was the first to appear. "How's the leg?" he asked, accepting a drink from his friend and taking the chair opposite Stuart's at the round dining table.

"You were right," Stuart admitted. "Your Dr. Cahill is a marvel."

Nick grinned. "Told you he was. Denys is right behind me, by the way. We came up from Kent together. He's paying off the hansom."

Denys, Viscount Somerton, walked in at just that moment, proving the truth of Nick's words, but he had barely greeted Stuart with a handshake and a slap on the back and accepted a drink before the door opened again, and the Earl of Hayward came in.

"Pongo!" the other three men said at once, a greeting that made the earl grimace. Lord Hayward, son of the Marquess of Wetherford, had been christened as James, but he was called Pongo by his close friends for some childhood reason none of them could actually remember, and it was a nickname he hated. "Call me by my name, you bastards, or damn this reunion and damn all of you." He glanced up and down Stuart as he accepted a drink. "How's the leg, old son?"

"Oh, sure," Nick grumbled. "Ask him about his leg, but not my shoulder."

James waved Nick's past shoulder injury aside as he sat down beside him. "I shot you. So what?"

"While I was saving his life!" Nick said, pointing at Denys with his whisky glass. "You were trying to shoot him, and I jumped in and took the damn bullet. Stupidest thing I ever did."

"I don't know about that, Nick," Stuart

objected. "You've done many stupid things."

"And he deserved it," Denys added as he took the chair on Nick's other side, next to Stuart. "Don't feel any guilt, Pongo."

James grinned. "I don't. But I fully remember that I was actually taking a potshot at you, Somerton, for making off with my girl."

"She flung herself at me in the most shameless way," Denys said. "I couldn't help myself."

"I was there," Stuart interjected, "and that is not how it was. She was actually chasing after me —"

This claim was immediately doused by a round of hearty derision, and a debate on the subject ensued, a debate interrupted without being resolved by the arrival of the last member of the party, Lord Featherstone.

"Sorry I'm late, gentlemen," Jack said as he came in and closed the door behind him.

"Forgive us if we're not surprised," Denys said over his shoulder. "You're always late."

"Cut my line a bit of slack, would you? I had to come all the way from Paris, after all. I just got off the train from Dover twenty minutes ago."

Jack circled the table as Stuart stood up to greet him. "Mauled by a lion were you?"

he asked, and stuck out his hand. "You'll do anything for a lark."

"Damn straight. Want a drink?"

"Of course. You don't think I came here for you, do you?"

Stuart poured him a whisky from the bottle on the table, and Jack took it. He then pulled out the empty chair to Stuart's right and sat down.

"So, gentlemen," Jack said as he sat down, "now that we've all welcomed the lion slayer home, what shall we do tonight? Dinner first, I assume? Then cards? Possibly a bit of slumming in the East End pubs? Or shall we find the prettiest dancing girls of London's music halls and cart them off the stage?"

"None of those for me," Nicholas said, and held up both hands, palms out. "I'm a happily married man." He lowered his hands, then reached for his glass and lifted it. "With a baby on the way."

This news was greeted with hearty congratulations and a toast.

"Nick may be out of it," Jack said as he refilled his glass and passed the bottle, "but what about the rest of you?"

Caught by Jack's inquiring eye, Stuart shook his head. "My wife and I have reconciled." He could only hope it was true.

There was a momentary silence as all his friends stared at him in uncertainty. It was Jack who asked the question in all their minds. "And are you happy about it?"

"I am, actually, yes." Whether he'd be able to make Edie happy or not was a whole different question. "And I'm happy to be home."

"Well, all right, then." Jack lifted his glass. "Here's to the hunter, home from the hill."

Glasses clinked together, were subsequently emptied, and the bottle went around again so they could be refilled.

"Still," Jack went on, "what are the rest of us supposed to do? Happily married fellows are such tedious company." He glanced at James and Denys. "Don't tell me either of you have become ensnared?"

"Not I." Denys lifted his drink. "Still quite the carefree bachelor."

"As am I," James added.

"Well, that relieves my mind. Later, we shall leave these two —" He paused, gesturing to Stuart and Nicholas. "And go off for a bit of fun, shall we?"

"You three can invade the brothels, taverns, and gaming clubs of London all you please some other time," Stuart said. "But not tonight. I didn't bring all of you here so you could carouse about town. Besides,

London in August is deadly dull, so you shan't be missing much."

"So why are we here?" Jack gave him an impudent grin. "Other than to see your scars, hear all about the mauling, and be suitably impressed by how bravely you fought off the lions?"

Stuart took a drink. "I don't want to talk about that."

"Stuff," Jack said in disbelief. "It's the perfect chance to brag, and you don't want to talk about it? Why not?" He took a peek under the table. "Lions didn't eat anything important, did they?"

Stuart took a swallow of whisky, and broke the news. "Jones is dead."

"What?" Jack's question was a harsh whisper amid the dumbfounded silence of the others. Slowly, he straightened in his chair. "Your valet is dead? What happened? Was that the lions, too?"

"Yes."

Jack sighed, raking a hand through his black hair. "Hell," he muttered. "And here I am being flippant about it. Sorry, Stuart."

The others added similar sentiments, but he waved aside sympathy. He found it impossible to bear. "Let's talk of something else, shall we?" Before any of them could choose a topic, he veered the conversation to what he wanted to discuss.

"Gentlemen, as wonderful as it is to see all of you, a reunion isn't why I've asked you here." He paused to be sure he had their full attention before he went on, "I have something to discuss with you, and I want to do it before the bottle goes around again, for it's quite a serious business."

Glasses were set down, the bottle pushed aside at once. Stuart reached into the leather dispatch case, and retrieved the dossier on Van Hausen. He stood up, dropping the sheaf of papers in the center of the table, then he glanced one by one at the faces turned toward him.

"I want to ruin a man," he said at last. "I want to humiliate him and destroy him. Thoroughly, completely, and without mercy."

Again there was a moment of silence. Again, it was Jack who broke it.

"Lawd," he drawled, tilting his chair back on two legs and grinning at Stuart, "this sounds just my sort of lark."

Denys cleared his throat. "It goes without saying that the man in question deserves it, but can you tell us why?"

"The gist, yes, but not the details. And I assure you it is a matter of honor. And justice."

James sat back, looking up at him. "The courts can't touch him, I assume?"

"No. He's American, a Knickerbocker, with a very rich, very powerful father."

"Pfft." Jack's sound of derision waved aside such trifles.

"Gentlemen," Stuart said, flattening his palms on the table, looking down at the sheaf of papers, "I would do this alone, but I can't. I need your help." He looked up, his gaze moving around the table to the faces of his closest friends, friends he'd had since boyhood. "We are all Eton men."

The other four nodded with understanding, but this time it was Nicholas who spoke first. "There's no more to be said. What do you want us to do?"

# CHAPTER 20

"Are you sure?" Joanna turned away from the entrance to the train car and looked at Edie. Beneath her straw boater, her beautiful face showed a twinge of uncertainty. Her brown eyes darted sideways, rather as an animal might look about, seeking escape. "I think I should wait until Stuart comes back."

"You can't," Edie told her for perhaps the tenth time. "The first day of term at Willowbank is Monday. That leaves you only two days to settle in. And I don't know exactly when Stuart is coming home."

"A week, you told me Reeves said. It's been ten days since he left. I'm sure he'll be back soon, maybe even today. I should wait. I didn't have the chance to say good-bye to him before he left."

The train whistle blew, indicating departure was imminent, and Edie caught her sister's shoulders. "I'm sure Stuart will understand why you didn't say good-bye. Now, you simply must board, dearest. You'll see us both in three weeks."

"How do I know that? You might leave him. You said you might, when he first came home."

She thought of how she'd been when she said that, and she couldn't help being a bit amazed at how a fortnight could change a person's whole perspective about life. "I'm not leaving him."

"Do you promise?"

"I promise." She planted a kiss on each of her sister's cheeks and started to turn the girl around, but when Joanna still resisted, she sighed and dropped her hands, planting them on her hips. "Joanna Arlene Jewell, have I ever broken a promise to you before?"

Joanna shrugged her shoulders, looked around the train platform, and shifted her feet. "No."

"Well, there you are, then. Your first day out is in three weeks, and Stuart and I will both be there to visit you."

"You'll bring Snuffles, too?"

"Him, too," she promised.

Joanna still looked doubtful. "Will you be all right? You'll have no one for company until Stuart comes back."

"I'll manage." Edie caught sight of the

steam issuing from the engines, and thankfully, when she put her arms on Joanna's shoulders this time, the girl actually allowed herself to be turned around.

But as Joanna stepped up onto the train car, she had to add over her shoulder, "Are you sure? It's an awfully big house."

"I'm sure, darling. Now, go aboard. Mrs. Simmons is waiting for you."

Joanna boarded the train at last. But just like last time, she opened the first window she could and kept talking. "I'm going to school if I have to, but if you leave Stuart and run away, I'm telling him where you are. I don't usually tattle, and I know I told you I'm on your side, and I am, honestly! But I promised him before he left that if you ran away, I would tell him where you went."

"What? When was this?"

"At dinner, when you ate in your room. He told me he was going away for a while."

Edie pounced on that. "Oh, so you did have the chance to say good-bye?"

"Never mind that now," Joanna said impatiently, waving one white-gloved hand in the air. "He told me he was going back to London straightaway, and when I asked him why, he said it was business. But he also said the two of you had quarreled, and that you might seem unhappy and that I shouldn't talk about it or ask you any questions, but that I should try to cheer you up and look after you. And he wanted to be back before I left for school, but he didn't know for certain if he would, and that's when he made me promise to tell him where you went if you did go running off. He said he wasn't about to let you leave him just because he did something stupid."

"He said that?" Edie groaned, for it confirmed exactly what she'd feared ever since his departure.

"Yes, so —"

The whistle blew again, the train jerked, and Joanna reached up to curve her hands over the edge of the open window sash to stay upright. Holding on to it, she stuck her head out the window. "So don't you run away, Edie, or I'll tell him where you are." Joanna started to cry. "I swear I will."

Edie was close to crying, too, but she held it back for Joanna's sake. "I'm not going anywhere," she shouted, hoping her sister could hear over the huffing steam engines. "I promise."

She waited until her sister's head vanished from view before she started to cry, but she didn't turn away as she had last time. Instead, she stayed on the platform until the train was completely out of sight. After all, with Joanna, one could never be too sure.

"No, I want Stuart's portrait to the right of mine, Henry," she said to the footman up high on the ladder in the portrait gallery. "To the right."

Beside her, Wellesley gave a little cough. "The Dowager Duchess always had the duke's portrait to the left of hers, Your Grace."

*Here we go again,* Edie thought. Why did even rear-ranging a few pictures in the portrait gallery have to be a battle?

"I'm sure the Eighth Duke looked splendid on the left," she said. "But I want the Ninth Duke's portrait to the right of mine."

He sighed, the sigh of the long-suffering British butler forced to deal with an American duchess who didn't know the way things were supposed to be. "Yes, Your Grace. It's just that on the right is not the way we're accustomed to having it at Highclyffe."

"Quite so," she said, just as she always said it, pleasantly firm. "But —"

"Your Grace!"

The interruption had Edie turning as Reeves came bounding through the open

442

doors at the end of the long gallery and halted. "He's back," she said, gasping for breath. "The duke has returned. He came to your room straightaway, looking for you. I suggested he wait there, and I came in search."

Edie started across the gallery at a walk, but by the time she reached her maid's side, she was running. "My room?"

Reeves nodded, and Edie started to run out, but then, she stopped. "Wellesley, His Grace's gift?"

The butler looked over at her, his face impassive. "I followed your instructions exactly, Your Grace."

She nodded and turned toward the door. "I'll believe that when I see it," she murmured, walked out of the gallery, then stopped and leaned back in the doorway. "On the right, Wellesley," she reminded, and departed as his heavy sigh echoed along the gallery.

She ran down the corridor to the stairs, took the steps up two at a time, and turned down the corridor to the family bedrooms, but before she reached her own, she knew she had to stop, take a moment, prepare.

This was important, and she had to get it right, for she'd gotten it so wrong last time they were together. She felt a sudden jolt of panic, but it wasn't the sort of panic she'd always felt in the past. This wasn't fear, this was just being nervous as hell.

Edie stood there in the corridor for several minutes, breathing deeply, striving to remember composure. She had to stay calm, explain fully, and most of all, she had to keep back tears, or she'd never get the words out at all. Finally, she took the last few steps and entered her room.

He was standing in front of her writing desk, looking out the window.

"You're home. Reeves said a week, but it's been longer than that —" She broke off, for he hadn't turned around as she'd spoken, and something in the rigid stillness of his body sent a shimmer of worry through her. "Stuart?"

His fingers tapped the surface of her desk. "Keating sent you the separation agreement, I see."

Edie glanced at her desk, where the document lay in plain view. Heavens, she'd forgotten all about it. "Yes, it came in the post while you were gone. But —"

His head moved, bringing his face into profile, but he didn't turn around. "Forgive me for invading your privacy. I came up to look for you when I arrived, and Reeves suggested I wait here while she went to find you. I didn't mean to pry. I just walked to the window, and here it was. It wasn't that I meant to read your correspondence."

"Of course not. I haven't even —"

"Do you want me to sign it, Edie?" He turned toward her, but with his back to the window, the bright glare behind him made it difficult for her to read his expression. "Because I will, if that's what you want. It's been more than the ten days we agreed on," he said before she could answer. "You haven't kissed me, so you've won the bet. And I know that trying to hold on to you by force would only cause you more pain, and I would die before I would do that."

"But Stuart, I don't want —"

"Remember when you asked me what happened to Jones, and I didn't tell you? I think perhaps I ought to tell you now."

She frowned, taken aback, not only by the change of subject but also by his reflective voice and somber mood. She shivered a little. "All right."

"We got a spot of work moving cattle from the train yard in Nairobi to a farm south of the Ngong Hills," he said after a moment. "In terms of distance, it's not that far, but it's a three-day journey. Five hundred head of cattle aren't exactly easy to move, not through lion country. It was our second night out. The men had made the fires as usual, and I checked them myself, as I always do. But at least one of them must have gone out. Who knows why? That's Africa for you. One minute everything's right as rain, and the next . . ." He paused and bent his head. "The next, your valet is dead, and you're watching men dig your grave."

"What happened?"

"Lions attacked the herd. One of them attacked Jones, and killed him." He looked up, but he didn't look at her. "I saw it. I saw her spring, I saw him go down, but I was out of shot and there was no time to reload. I used my whip to force her off, but —" His voice broke, and he stopped.

She couldn't stand not being able to look into his eyes. She started across the room. "But?" she prompted as she approached.

"But it was too late. He was already dead. He valeted me from the time I was sixteen, Edie. He followed me anywhere I wanted to go. He —"

His voice broke again, and again he stopped.

She halted in front of him, her heart aching for him, for she knew all about self-condemnation. "It was not your fault. That is the sort of thing that might happen to anyone in the bush, surely."

"Charming, you once called me," he said, once again veering to a different topic. "Shall I tell you why I seem that way? I figured out before I was ten years old that I'd never be loved by my own family, so I was damned well going to be loved by everybody else. By the time I was twenty, there wasn't a girl I wanted that I couldn't win, or a man I couldn't befriend, or a game I didn't know how to play. There wasn't a problem I wouldn't find a way to solve. I've always had the devil's own luck, and it made me such a cocky bastard. Hell, look at us. When I met you, my family was stone-broke, creditors were about to take everything, and then you came along and tossed all your money right into my lap. Pure luck, that." He made a wry face. "Is it any wonder Cecil hates my guts?"

"Cecil is an idiot."

That made him laugh, a little. "He is, rather."

His smile faded. "I talked Jones into going with me to Africa. He didn't want to go, but I talked him into it. All part of that charm of mine. And being the sort of chap who won't take no for an answer, I managed it."

"You must not blame yourself, Stuart. You

mustn't. Jones loved Africa. He wrote to the other servants, and sometimes Reeves would tell me what he said. He may not have wanted to go at first, but he had the time of his life there, in your service."

"I know that, but I just —" His eyes glittered, and he dabbed savagely at them with his fingers and thumb. "I miss him."

She reached out, touched his hair, his cheek. "Of course you miss him."

He leaned back against the desk, hands propped on the edge. "Do you know why I wanted to go to Africa in the first place? As I said, I was so damnably cocky. Even a continent wasn't big enough to conquer me, by God." He stretched his leg out sideways beside her feet, staring at it. "I never got malaria, or blackwater fever, or dysentery, or even a snakebite, but in the end, Africa still managed to put me in my place."

She didn't know what to say to that. "I'm sorry, Stuart. So terribly sorry. About Jones, about your leg, about —"

"I'm sorry about Jones, Edie, but I'm not sorry about my leg. I may limp for the rest of my life, but I'm not one bit sorry about that, and I'll tell you why." He straightened away from the desk, rising in front of her. "If that hadn't happened to me, I might never have come home, except in a box, and

I would never have known that the best thing I ever had in my life was right here. It's true that I never met a woman I couldn't win, but I also never met a woman who really mattered to me. Until I met you."

She made a choked sound, and she was terribly afraid she was going to cry now, and any of her hard-won composure would go utterly out the window. "Stuart —"

"The night we met, when I first looked at you, I felt as if Fate were forcing me to stop and pay attention. I felt as if Fate were saying, "Look, really look, at this girl, because she's important. She's going to change your life." Later, when you followed me out to the maze, I thought the impression I'd gotten was because of the money, but I was wrong. You asked me once what I could possibly want from you. What I want, Edie, is to know my life hasn't been an utter waste of food, water, and air. That everything I took for granted means something even if I almost threw it all away. That I can do good in the world rather than just have a good time. But most of all, I need to know that there is one person in the world who needs me, whose life is better because I am in it. I want that one person to be you. I love you."

Joy rose up inside her, joy, relief, and a poignant, sweet tenderness. "Stuart —"

"I'll sign the separation agreement, if that's what you want. But I'm asking you not to give up on us, Edie. And I won't care if it takes ten more days, or ten years, or the rest of my life, but I promise you that before I die, I'll make you know that you are safe, always, with me. Even when I want you so badly I can't sleep, I'll wait until you want me. I promise."

He stopped, and she waited, but when he said nothing more, she finally spoke. "Is that all?"

A gleam of defiance came into those beautiful gray eyes. "Yes."

"Good." She cupped his face in her hands, rose on her toes, and kissed his mouth. "That's my answer."

He frowned, and shook his head, telling her she'd just confounded him again. He opened his mouth, but she forestalled him, for she simply couldn't bear letting him do all the talking.

"I'm staying," she said. "I'm not leaving, not ever. And if you'd have let me get a word in, I'd have told you that the moment I walked through the door."

"But what about this?" He turned to pick up the separation agreement.

She snatched it out of his hand. "Keating sent it to me because I'd asked for it when I saw him in London, but I haven't even read it, and I'm certainly not signing it."

With that, she tore the blasted document in half and tossed the pieces in the air.

He swallowed hard, his eyes looking steadily into hers as half-sheets of paper floated down around them. "Are you sure you want to stay? Even after what happened in the feathers?"

"That wasn't your fault. I had a bout of panic. It happens. It will probably happen again." She knew she had to talk about this, so that he would understand and not blame himself. This moment was what she'd been preparing for ever since he left.

She took a deep breath, clasped her hands together, knuckles to her lips, hoping for the words that she'd been striving to find for days, the words that would explain what had happened to her that day in the feather house. "Remember when we played chess, and you said that if I talked of him, I should look into your eyes so that I would recognize the difference?"

"I remember. In hindsight, I realize I could hardly have expected you to see me as any different from him, but at the time, I was very angry with you for thinking he and I were in any way alike."

"I know you were angry. But it was right

of you to say what you did, because after that, whenever we were together, and I looked into your eyes, I would remember what you said, and it helped me to not be afraid. That afternoon, in the feather house, everything was —"

Her voice broke, and she had to stop for a second before going on. "It was wonderful, Stuart, all of it, until I couldn't look into your eyes or see your face. When you . . . when you came on top of me, it . . . it reminded me of before, with him. Because I couldn't see you."

Pain shimmered across Stuart's face, and it felt as if her heart were tearing in half because she hated causing him pain, but she could not stop now, or she wouldn't have the courage to say it all. And it all had to be said, so he would understand. And afterward, they would never have to talk about it again.

"He shoved me down on a table, he pushed up my skirt, he ripped down my drawers." She spoke quickly, forcing words out. "I told him to stop. He didn't. He came on top of me and . . . and did it. It happened so fast, and I was so shocked. I kept saying stop, but . . ." She shook her head and lifted her hand to the side of her face. "His face was buried against my neck, so I couldn't see him, and he never looked at me, not until afterward when he got up. And then, when he did look at me, he just smirked. He defiled me, rolled off me, buttoned his trousers, and smirked. He said we'd have to do that again one day. He didn't even pull my dress back down before he left."

She watched Stuart press his fist to his mouth, and she knew he did that only when he was in the throes of great emotion and trying to hold it back. She knew what he felt was pain, pain on her behalf, and she rushed on, "None of that matters anymore. It's just that —"

"It matters, Edie," he said, lowering his fist. "By God, it matters. He will pay."

"My point is that when you and I were in the feather house, when you . . . you . . . moved on top of me, I started to panic, but I could still look into your face, so . . . so it was all right. But then, you buried your face against my neck." She paused, blinking hard, striving to hold back tears. "I couldn't look at you. I couldn't look into your eyes. I couldn't . . . remember the difference."

"I see." He drew a deep breath and nodded. "Yes, I see."

"I wanted to tell you all this straightaway, tell you what happened, why I was crying. I wanted to try and explain, but I couldn't, Stuart. I just couldn't tell you." A sob erupted from deep inside her, and with that sob, the composure she'd worked so hard to maintain dissolved, the hard, tight knot of fear and anger and shame inside her cracked completely open, and she started to cry. "I've never told anyone."

His arms wrapped around her at once, and he held her tight as her tears came out, tears she'd tried to suppress for six years, tears that had come squeezing out of her that afternoon in the feather house, tears that she knew hurt him, too. But she couldn't stop them. They poured from her, soaking into his white linen shirt and pique waistcoat as his hand smoothed her hair and his voice said her name over and over, and the pieces of that hard, tight knot inside her floated slowly away into space and disappeared.

At last she was able to lift her head and pull back. She sniffed, and when he handed her his handkerchief, she took it.

"I swore I wasn't going to cry," she said as she dabbed at her face. "I know you were off in London flaying yourself for what happened between us, but I needed time to . . . to compose myself. I knew I had to explain, but I didn't want to cry while I did it because that would make it even harder for you, and I didn't want to make you feel even worse —"

He cupped her face. "Don't ever worry about me," he said savagely. "Ever. If you need to tell me about it, or about him, then tell me. I'll endure it. If you need to be alone, tell me so. Cry your eyes out anytime you like, pummel me with your fists and curse his name, throw plates against the wall or — hell — throw them at my head. But no matter what, don't ever worry about whether or not any of it will hurt me. Do you understand? And if what happened in the feather house ever happens again, if you ever feel that panic while we are making love, grab me by the hair, yank my head back, and shout, 'Look at me, Stuart, damn you!' "

A sound that was half laugh, half sob, came from her throat. That speech was so absurd and his ferocity so touching, she couldn't help it. "I'll try, I promise."

"Is there anything else that makes you afraid, or reminds you of him? Whenever you think of anything, you must tell me."

She thought for a moment. "Don't ever, ever wear eau du cologne."

"Ugh." He made a face. "I shan't, so you've no need to worry."

"Thank heaven for that." She dabbed at her face a few more times with his handkerchief. "Goodness, ten whole days to regain my composure, and it was no help at all in the end, was it?"

"But what do you feel, darling?" His fingers reached up to glide across her cheek, brushing her freckles. "What do you feel?"

She considered. "Relief," she said at last, pressing a hand to her chest. "My God, such relief."

That pleased him, for the corners of his eyes creased a bit in a hint of a smile. "Good."

"Still, I must look a fright now, and it's such a shame, because I had a surprise all planned for your return."

"A surprise?"

"Yes. And I have been looking forward to it for days, so you have to go now and let me fix my face." She folded his handkerchief and set it on her writing desk. "Let's both change for dinner, shall we? And then I want you to meet me at the bottom of the stairs."

"But what sort of surprise is it?"

"I'm not telling." She turned him and began pushing him toward the door. "You'll have to wait."

An hour later, after a few compresses of

cold tea leaves prepared by Reeves, Edie's face looked almost back to normal. The puffiness was gone, her eyes were no longer red, and a dusting of powder covered any remaining hints that she'd sobbed her eyes out. Laced into a blue silk evening gown, her curly hair piled up in a pretty way, with a few tendrils around her face, Edie thought she might even look rather pretty.

"Reeves, you're a wonder." Edie stared into the cheval mirror, amazed. "Thank you."

The maid smiled, meeting her eyes in the glass. "The wonder is your finally letting me put a dab of powder on your face and a bit of rouge on your lips."

"No padding in my bosom though. I don't need it." She paused, smoothing silk. "So I've been told."

She laughed, and her maid laughed with her, the two of them almost like girls giggling together before a ball.

Reeves adjusted the fluff of lace at her shoulder. "It's good to see you happy, Your Grace," she said.

"I am happy." Edie nodded, realizing just how true it was as she said it. "Though one would hardly have guessed it an hour ago." She smiled. "I confess, Reeves, I do like being the fetching thing he looks at across the table."

The maid smiled, remembering their conversation about that. "He's a good man, Your Grace."

"Yes," she agreed with all her heart. "A very good man. Speaking of him, I'd best go down, or I won't have time to give him his gift before dinner." She turned away from the mirror and started out of the room, but she paused by the door. "And Reeves?"

"Yes, Your Grace?"

"Take the evening off. I shan't need you until morning. And keep Snuffles in your room with you tonight."

With that, she left her bedroom and went down to meet Stuart, and when she saw him standing at the bottom of the stairs waiting for her, when he turned and saw her in a pretty blue dress, his expression made her glad that her life had turned out just this way.

"I bought you something while you were away," she said when she reached the bottom of the stairs. "I've been dying to show it to you." She grabbed his hand. "Come with me."

She led him down the corridor, past the library. He didn't say anything, but when they passed the music room and the billiard room, he knew there was only one possible destination.

"The ballroom? Edie, why are we going in here?"

"You'll see," she said as she pushed back the doors. "Come on."

He followed her into the glittering, gold-and-white ducal ballroom, but he barely stepped through the doors before he stopped in astonishment, staring at her gift to him. "Mrs. Mullins's music box?" he said. "You bought it?"

"I did. Now, you stay right there." She walked over to the instrument, which was sitting on its matching table against the wall, and pushed the knob. A moment later, the strains of Strauss's *Voices of Spring* floated through the room.

She turned and walked back toward him, stopping at what she judged was nearly the same distance they had been apart when they'd first seen each other at Hanford House, and when he smiled a little, tilting his head and giving her that quizzical look, her breath caught in her throat.

"There *are* second chances, Stuart," she said. "And this is one of them." She paused, waiting. "I'm here. The orchestra is playing Strauss. Come and dance with me."

"What? Here? Now?" A hint of what might have been panic crossed his face. "Edie, I told you, I can't dance anymore."

"You can't waltz now, I know. But since I can't waltz either, not to save my life, I don't mind. You needn't spin me all around the room. But you can sway with the music and hold me in your arms, can't you?"

He opened his mouth, shut it again. His eyes glittered, he blinked once or twice, and it was a moment before he could speak. "I think I can do that," he said at last.

He came to her, not the athletic, graceful leopard of the ballroom at Hanford House but her very own wounded animal. Her husband. Her lover. Her best friend.

He stopped in front of her and held out his hand. "May I have this dance?"

"You may," she said, equally grave, and together, they walked to the center of the floor. When he took her right hand in his and put his left hand on her waist, she lifted her own free hand to his shoulder, just as she remembered from all her previous dancing experiences.

But that was where the similarity ended. Her partner was taller than she was, he didn't push her or propel her or try to control her movements. It was he, not she, who moved slowly, awkwardly, trying not to step on her feet. It was hard for him, she knew, and painful — physically, and probably emotionally, too, and she stopped after only a few steps, for it was enough to illustrate the point she wanted to make.

"I think this is going to take a bit of practice," she said.

"Yes," he muttered, still staring down at their feet, looking terribly self-conscious.

"But that doesn't matter, Stuart, because we have our whole lives to get it right. Don't we?"

He looked up, those beautiful gray eyes piercing her heart, looking straight to her soul. "Yes, we do."

"I love you," she said and kissed his mouth. "I think I've loved you from the very beginning. But I was too afraid to let myself feel it."

"I think I felt the same." His hand came up from her waist to curve at the back of her neck, and he pulled her close.

She kept her eyes open just so she could watch his close, just so she could see those thick, dark lashes come down. Then she closed her own eyes, inhaling the scents of sandalwood soap and him. And then, his lips touched hers, and she savored the taste of his mouth.

*Stuart,* she thought. *My love.*

She pressed closer, and when she felt him, hard and aroused against her, she relished that, too. She loved him, the man that he was and everything that meant.

At last, she pulled back. "Stuart?"

He lifted his hand to smooth her hair. "Yes?"

"About this lovemaking business."

His hand stilled against her hair. "Yes?"

She bit her lip, considering how best to say what she wanted to say. "Since we've been talking of practice, I just want to warn you that as far as lovemaking goes, I fear it's going to be a bit like dancing for me, or . . . or skating on ice."

He laughed a little, his breath soft on her face.

"I shall need practice, Stuart. Lots of practice."

"Is that what you want?" he asked, and in his eyes was that tender, smoky look she loved.

"Yes." She paused a few seconds. "Stuart?"

"Yes, Edie?"

"I should like to practice now."

His face, handsome enough to break any girl's heart, twisted a bit, broke up — looking glad, so very glad that it made her heart sing. "If you're sure."

"I'm sure." Their fingers still entwined, she turned toward the door.

"Intend to lead, do you?" he asked, as she pulled him across the room.

"As often as possible," she said, making him laugh.

They paused by the door so he could retrieve his walking stick, then together they went upstairs and into her room. Once they were both inside, she turned the key in the lock.

"I've given Reeves the whole night off," she said, her voice shaking a little, but she looked at him steadily. "I'm counting on the fact that you've had enough practice at this to undo me."

He shook his head, laughing a little as she came toward him. "And here I'm almost wishing I'd come to this moment a virgin."

That surprised her. "Why would you wish that?"

"I was once so proud of myself for all the women I'd had, so vainly proud. And yet, now I'm rather ashamed of the fact, because none of those women have ever been to me what you are." He looked up. "I love you, Edie. I love you with every part of my soul."

Joy pierced her heart, a sting of joy so sweet that it was several moments before she could reply. "But if you were a virgin," she said at last, "I fear we'd never have gotten this far. I need you to be just the man you are, Stuart. I need to be reminded every day that I am a pretty, passionate woman, with golden freckles and lovely legs. I need you to touch me and caress me and make it like bliss. I need you to make love to me, and give me that sweet, sweet pleasure."

He laughed again, so merrily this time that she felt a bit nettled. "What are you laughing at?"

"Now who's being torrid?" he teased, but he sobered almost at once. "I can do all that," he promised and put his hands on her shoulders. "Turn around."

When she did, he began undoing the buttons along the back of her gown. It was a slow process, for the buttons were cloth-covered, and it seemed to take forever before he reached her waist. But at last, he was able to remove her evening gown, sliding it off her shoulders, down her waist, and over her hips. It sank to the floor in a pool of blue silk, and when she stepped out of it, he used his foot to push it out of the way.

He then removed her corset cover, tossed it aside, and began working to undo the laces of her corset. Not once did he hesitate over her intricate clothing, making her appreciate just how many other women he had undressed, but as she'd told him, she did not resent his past experience. Though the past few weeks had unearthed in her a jealous streak she hadn't known she possessed, now as he undressed her, she felt only desire. It deepened with every garment he so skillfully removed, and by the time she was down to her last layer of underclothes, she was so aroused she could hardly breathe.

He turned her around and sank down in front of her. He removed her evening shoes, then his warm palms were gliding up her calves to her knees. As his hands slid inside her drawers to remove the garters that held up her stockings, his fingertips tickled the backs of her knees, making her wriggle in protest.

He laughed under his breath, untying the ribbons of her garters and sliding her stockings down her legs. "My ticklish darling," he said. "I'm glad I have some bargaining chips with you."

"But —" She broke off, trying not to squeal as his fingertips slid beneath the hem of her drawers and began gliding upward, caressing the backs of her thighs. "But what do you intend to bargain for?"

"Hmm . . . there are so many possibilities." He paused, considering, his fingers gliding back and forth against the bare skin just beneath her bottom.

The sensation was so exquisite, her knees wobbled, she sucked in a sharp gasp, and had to rest her hands on his shoulders to prevent herself from sinking to the floor.

His fingers stilled. "Do you like that?" he asked.

"Yes." It was a soft, breathless admission.

He pulled his hands from beneath her drawers and lifted them to the garment's waistband. He slipped the hooks free, and slid the garment off her hips. "What about this?" he asked, ducking his head beneath the hem of her chemise to press a kiss to her bare stomach.

She cried out, her hands tightening on his shoulders. "Stuart," she wailed softly, shifting against his mouth as his tongue flicked lightly over her navel. "Oh, oh. That's too much."

He emerged from beneath her chemise and stood up. "Someday," he said as he bent his head closer to hers, "I shall have to show you just how pleasurable tickling can be."

He kissed her before she could inform him there was nothing pleasurable about being tickled. The kiss was one of those lush, deep kisses full of desire that she was coming to love so much, but when his hands reached for the hem of her chemise and he began pulling the garment up to remove it, she was seized by a sudden paroxysm of shyness. The notion of revealing to him one of the most disappointing features of her body caused her desire to falter, and she tore her mouth from his. "Wait."

He stilled. "What is it?"

She didn't want to explain. She wanted to regain the desire of before. She reached up to slide his black dinner jacket from his wide shoulders. "I think it's my turn to undress you."

That made him smile. "Taking the lead again, I see."

"Yes," she said, and pulled off his jacket. "I like being in charge."

"I like that, too, actually." His smile widened into a grin. "As long as you don't make me go to tea with the vicar."

She laughed, remembering that day. "I won't," she promised as she pulled the ends of his white silk bowtie. "I'm far too fond of you now to subject you to that sort of torture."

"Thank God for that," he muttered, as she reached for his collar stud. When she fumbled with it a bit, he showed her how to remove it, as well as his shirt studs and cuff links. He pulled off his shoes and socks, and as she turned to drop his studs and links into a dish on her dressing table, he removed his shirt and tossed it aside. She turned to face him again as he pulled off his undershirt, and the sight of his naked torso made her breath catch.

His bare skin, tanned by the African sun, gleamed like golden bronze. His chest was a wall of sculpted muscle and sinew, the sheer strength of it plainly obvious, and her heart slammed against her ribs. But the hard pounding of her heart was not from panic. Instead, she felt only desire as her gaze traveled downward, across the brown disks of his nipples, the washboard ribbing of his stomach, and the indentation of his navel.

She fanned her hands across his chest, appreciating rather than fearing the strength and power of his body. As she reached for the waistband of his trousers, the feel of his hard arousal beneath her hands evoked no fear, only a deepening hunger and a need for completion. But before she could slide his trousers off his hips, he stopped her.

"My turn." Again he reached for the hem of her chemise, but again, she resisted.

"What's wrong, Edie?"

"Nothing. It's just —" She broke off and looked away, her cheeks growing hot, even though she knew it made no sense to feel embarrassed now. "I'm feeling a bit shy, I suppose."

"Still? But why?" When she didn't answer, he kissed her. "Tell me."

She turned her face away. "My breasts are too small."

"What?" He made a sound of disbelief. "I don't believe it. Show me. Let me see them."

"They're too small to see," she mumbled, even as he began drawing up her chemise. "Even I can't see them."

He laughed, which only made her feel worse. But she stretched her arms toward the ceiling and allowed him to pull her chemise over her head. He dropped it to the floor and reached for her wrists, spreading her arms wide before she could cover herself. She squeezed her eyes shut, desire faltering in the wake of a dreadful sense of inadequacy. It seemed an eternity before he spoke.

"Edie, I fear there's something wrong with your eyesight," he said at last, causing her to open her eyes and look into his. "I can see your breasts perfectly, darling."

He let her wrists go. "Shall I tell you what they look like?" He smiled so tenderly that she feared she might cry all over again. "Since you apparently can't see them for yourself, I think I should."

His hands lifted to touch her. "They are

small, yes, and round, and perfectly shaped." His fingertips grazed lightly over the tops of her breasts, then beneath. "They're very pretty, too, creamy white, with golden freckles scattered over them, and these gorgeous, rosy pink nipples."

Edie watched his face as he caressed her breasts and described how they seemed to him, and she felt a sense of wonder. Never before had she ever truly felt beautiful, but she did now. Joy rose up inside, joy so powerful and so bright, bursting through her chest as if she'd swallowed a box of fireworks.

"Your breasts are perfect, Edie." He rolled her nipples gently in his fingers, spreading heat through her body. "Luscious and perfect, and I long to kiss them and suckle them and play with them for hours." An unsteady note began creeping into his voice as he spoke. "But I fear we're running out of time. I'm not sure how much longer I can hold out before I come utterly undone."

His hand slid away from her breast. He took her by the hand and led her to the bed where he guided her to lie down.

He started to unbutton his trousers, but she stopped him. "Wait," she said and sat up. "I'm supposed to do this part."

"Are you?" He resumed undoing buttons,

and her hands closed over his wrists.

"Yes." She felt his resistance, and it surprised her. "Now I think it's my turn to ask what's wrong," she murmured. "Wouldn't you like it if I undress you?"

"I'd adore it, but —" He broke off, shifting his weight. "It's just that I should warn you first . . ." Again, he paused, and this time, he cleared his throat before he tried again. "It's just that my leg's not in the best of shape, you know. Don't be too shocked when you see it."

In that moment, Edie knew that if she ever felt shy with him in future, all she had to do was remember this moment, for she had never loved him more than she did right now. "I let you look," she whispered. "Remember?"

"All right," he said, allowing her to slide his trousers linen off his hips. "But don't say I didn't warn you."

Edie looked down. He was fully aroused, but as she stared at his shaft, she felt only a deep, passionate tenderness. Her gaze moved lower, to the scars that crisscrossed his right thigh, and as she stared at the stark white lines, as she thought of the pain he had endured, it hurt her, too.

She reached out to touch his leg, running her fingers lightly over the scars, and she felt a tremor run through his body at the light caress. "I love you," she said, and heard his release of breath, a sigh of relief. She pressed her lips to one of the jagged white lines. "I love you."

He groaned in response, his hand tangled in her hair, and he gently pulled her head back. "God, Edie, don't. I'm not sure how long I can hold out as it is."

"Why should you have to?" she asked, easing backward onto the bed, pulling him with her.

He stretched out beside her, lying on his side with his weight on his elbow. "Because I have important things to do first," he said, and reached out his free hand to touch her. His fingertips grazed her breast, then slid lower, down over her ribs, then her stomach, then lower still.

When his fingertip reached the curls at the apex of her thighs, he stopped and looked up, meeting her gaze as he slid his finger between her folds. Their gazes locked, he stroked her over and over, tender and relentless, until her every breath was a pant, and her body was moving frantically against him, and she was sobbing his name. And then, she reached the peak, her head fell back, and she cried out his name over and over as the pleasure flooded through her in wave after wave, and she collapsed, panting, against the pillows.

He leaned over her to kiss her mouth. "I want to be inside you," he said, still caressing her. "Do you want that, too? God, please say yes."

"Yes." She nodded, emphasizing the point. "Yes."

"Then come on top of me." He showed her how, guiding her as she spread her legs apart over his hips and took his hard shaft into her body.

He felt thick and full inside her, and scorching hot. The sensation of being on top of him was glorious, and she moaned, her hips flexing.

He groaned, his own hips pressing up in response, urging her on. Sensing what he wanted, she began to move, rising up and coming down on top of his body, tightening her inner muscles again and again, using her body to stroke him.

"Yes, Edie," he groaned, his body jerking against hers again and again. "Oh, God, yes."

She moved with his rhythm, reveling in the power of pleasuring him, watching his face. When he came, she gloried in his climax, and when it was over, when he thrust up hard against her one last time, she followed him there, to the peak and over the edge of bliss. And afterward, when she settled beside him in the white, white sheets, his name on her lips was a soft sigh that contained everything she felt, all her love for him.

"Now I've done it," he said, as they lay side by side on her bed, holding hands, staring up at the ceiling. "I'll never lead again."

"Yes, you will." She rolled onto her side to look at him, and she smiled. "Sometimes."

# EPILOGUE

*Highclyffe, eleven months later . . .*

"Why is it that you always sponge off my plate?" Edie grumbled, as Stuart snatched another piece of bacon off her breakfast tray.

"Because I'm always in your bed when Reeves brings your breakfast, that's why." He grinned, not the least bit repentant, and popped the slice of bacon into his mouth.

She sniffed. "You could just have them send up a separate tray for you," she pointed out as she picked up the copy of the *Daily Sketch* that had been placed, as usual, beside her plate.

"I could, but it's much more fun this way." Stuart leaned over and started to kiss her, but she wasn't fooled by that, and even as she allowed him a kiss, she slapped his hand, preventing him from stealing any more of her bacon.

"I suppose I shall have to have a tray sent up, then," he said, as she opened her newspaper, "since you're so stingy." He turned and stretched out his arm to ring for Reeves, but her voice stopped him before he could tug the bellpull.

"Oh, my God."

Stuart's hand fell at the startled sharpness of her voice, and he turned to look at her. "What is it?"

Edie lifted her gaze from the newspaper and turned her head to look at him, her pretty green eyes wide with shock. "Frederick Van Hausen is dead."

He raised an eyebrow. That was an unexpected development. "Indeed?"

She nodded and returned her attention to the paper. "He shot himself four days ago."

"Suicide?" Stuart considered. He'd known things were about to break, of course. Jack's last telegram from New York had been short but clear.

FISH CAUGHT STOP EXPOSURE IMMINENT

But suicide? He hadn't anticipated that. Humiliation, yes. Ruin, yes. Prison, quite likely. But suicide? No, he hadn't anticipated that at all.

"He got caught in some sort of investment swindle," Edie said after a moment.

"Really?" Stuart tried to inject a convincing amount of surprise into his voice at that additional piece of news. "How shocking."

"Yes. He persuaded his friends and business associates as well as some British investors to put money into a company he started," she went on, her gaze still scanning the page as she spoke. "But it turned out to be a swindle on his part. And the scandal was about to come out and ruin him. He'd have gone to prison."

"So he shot himself rather than face it." Stuart smiled. What a nice bit of icing on the cake.

"Evidently. He'd heard about some gold mines and formed an investment company to mine them, but it turned out the mines didn't have any gold. He knew that all along, supposedly, but —" She broke off and looked up, awareness dawning in her adorable, freckled face. "The gold mines were in *Tanzania*. Stuart, did you have something to do with this?"

"Well . . ." He paused, considering how to answer. "Let's say that I put the appropriate people in place to take him right where I wanted him to go, shall we?"

She shook her head, clearly bewildered. "What do you mean, what people?"

"My friends, Lord Trubridge, Lord Featherstone, Lord Somerton, and Lord Hayward were the British investors he swindled. Your father provided us with invaluable assistance on the New York side —"

"My father? You pulled Daddy into this?"

"Of course. He doesn't know what Van Hausen did to you," Stuart added at once. "But when I asked him eleven months ago if he wanted revenge because the bastard ruined your reputation, he happily agreed."

"You arranged all this eleven months ago?"

"I started it then, yes. It's taken this long for the pieces to fall into place." He met her gaze steadily over the top of the paper. "I told you, Edie, he would pay for what he did to you. And now he has. More thoroughly than even I could have dreamed."

She lowered the paper, staring at him as if unable to quite take the whole thing in. "I wonder if Daddy knows that Frederick is dead?"

"Since your father is sailing a yacht around the Greek islands right now with his mistress, I very much doubt it."

"But Daddy helped you do this?"

"He jumped at the chance. He'd always wanted to do something of the kind. In fact, the whole investment scheme was his idea, for he knew Van Hausen was a crooked sort of chap, but he couldn't implement this sort

478

of plan himself because despite having a daughter who's a duchess, he just couldn't muster the level of influence in Knickerbocker society required to bring it all about. Enter my titled British friends. Lady Astor and her set were practically drooling when they visited New York. Jack flattered her shamelessly, I understand."

"Something Lady Astor no doubt appreciated," Edie said. "That woman likes nothing better than being buttered up."

"She introduced my friends to Van Hausen, as well as to many of his other acquaintances, and the rest is history."

"But Frederick would have investigated your friends. Once he discovered they were acquainted with you, why didn't he suspect something was up?"

"I believe it was implied that we'd had a falling-out. Bad enough that I married an inappropriate girl for her money. But then, I came home from Africa and wanted to breed children with her. Van Hausen believed all that rubbish without a qualm and didn't bother to delve any deeper. And when he heard that my supposedly former friends knew I'd discovered some gold mines in Africa, and how they wanted to get the jump on me, so to speak, Van Hausen practically stumbled over himself to form the company." Stuart paused, then went on, "I think the idea of scoring off me added to the appeal of the whole thing for him."

"Why? Because it renewed his pleasure at grinding jumped-up trash like me under his boot?"

"Something like that," he said gently.

"So you ruined him."

"We gave him the chance to evade the trap. An engineer's report showed the mines to have no gold in them, and once he discovered that, if he'd had a shred of decency, he'd have withdrawn, made good on the money to the investors, and walked away. But he didn't withdraw. He went ahead, he kept their money, he invested it elsewhere — with delicate hints conveyed through my friends to his friends, of course — and he lost that money, too. He committed fraud, and that's when we knew we had him dead to rights."

She paused, considering. "But surely you couldn't have known he'd kill himself rather than go to prison?"

Stuart shook his head. "No, although I suppose it's not surprising. He was a coward. He was also a greedy, selfish, insignificant man who wanted to be important. He felt he was entitled to things that didn't belong to him. Money, success." He looked into his wife's eyes. "Women."

She nodded in agreement, looking thoughtful. "And your friends did all this for you?"

"Yes. I didn't tell them what actually happened to you." He didn't say his friends had probably guessed that part, but went on, "They didn't need to know the details in order to help. They knew your reputation had been ruined and your honor besmirched, and that was all they needed to hear. We are Eton men. Honor means a great deal."

"But what happened to me was a year before you married me, and yet, they still helped you avenge me?"

He smiled. "They are damned fine friends."

"Do you suppose Frederick ever realized you were the one who brought it all about?"

"I doubt it, but it doesn't matter."

Edie seemed surprised by that. "Wouldn't you have wanted him to know it was you, at the end?"

He shrugged. "Why? I don't need the bug to look up and see me before my boot comes down and flattens him."

She made a choked sound, half laugh, half sob. "And you did it for me. Oh, Stuart."

"Darling." He pulled away the tray on her

lap, setting it aside. Then he opened his arms.

She came to him at once, tossing aside the paper, and buried her face against his chest. He felt her body trembling with reaction. "I can't quite believe it," she mumbled. "He's dead. He's dead."

"Yes." He caressed her back and kissed her hair. "It's all right, Edie. It's over. He can't ever hurt you, and he can't hurt any other women. Not now."

She lifted her head, stricken. "There were others, besides me? Tell me," she demanded when he didn't answer.

"There were two that I am fairly certain he assaulted. Both were before you. Similar circumstances, but his father managed to have it hushed up, for the girls were both servants. His father paid them off and sent them away. But . . ." Stuart hesitated, for he didn't want to tell her the truth, but he'd always promised her the truth when she asked. "But a man like that isn't likely to stop," he said as gently as he could.

"I never thought there might be others. I always thought it was me. I thought it was something I did, something about me that . . . that set him off. That I'd been a tease, or . . . that by agreeing to meet him,

482

I'd given him an expectation, or led him on, or —"

"No, my darling," he interrupted. "No. His actions had nothing to do with you. None of it was your fault."

"But there are probably other women who have been hurt by him after what he did to me? Oh, no, no," she moaned, looking stricken. "I should have known. I should have done something."

"Don't, Edie. Don't." He cupped her face, catching tears with his thumbs as they fell, brushing them away. "There was nothing you could have done."

"I could have told the world what he'd done, so other women would know and be warned against him."

"What makes you think anyone would have believed you? Given his position and yours, would anyone have listened to you? No. You had no proof to offer. Had you come forward, claiming he forced you, you'd have faced even more degradation and blame than you'd already suffered. Society always views these things as the woman's fault, especially since he got you to arrive at that summerhouse after him. I've no doubt he arranged it that way with you deliberately."

"He did, yes." She nodded. "It was his

idea. He claimed afterward that I tried to trap him."

"Well, there you are. And had you told the world what really happened, society would have condemned you for your lack of discretion more than him for his action. As to a plot of revenge, such as what I did, you could not have put together a group of investors to take Van Hausen down. Even your father didn't have the necessary influence to do that on his own."

"But —"

He pressed a thumb to her lips. "Edie, listen to me. You must not blame yourself. You judged, and rightly so, that there was nothing you could do other than kill him, and if you'd been caught, you'd have been hanged or sent to prison, and again, Joanna had to be considered. And even if you hadn't been caught, to suffer having murder on your soul? No." He shook his head. "Avenging you was my office. I knew that the moment I knew what he'd done to you. I only wish I could have wiped it out altogether, made it so that it never have happened at all, but I couldn't do that, so —"

"But I don't wish that," she interrupted, sitting up.

He frowned. "Of course you do."

"But I don't, Stuart." She shook her head.

"I don't regret that it happened. In fact," she added slowly, as if considering it, "if I could go back and change it, I wouldn't."

"What?" Shocked, he stared at her. Almost a year together, and she still said things that absolutely confounded him. "You can't mean that."

"But I do mean it. As awful as it was, if it hadn't happened, I never would have come to England. I never would have met you."

He shook his head. "Perhaps, but still —"

"Remember what you said that day in this very room how you didn't care if you limped for the rest of your life, because if that lion hadn't mauled you, you might never have come home?" She smiled, caressing his face. "Well, I feel the same way. Even out of bad things, good things can happen. Even things that are sordid or painful can lead to things that are beautiful."

Stuart's chest felt tight, his body pinned in place, Fate holding on to him and making him see the beautiful thing right in front of his eyes. "God, how I love you."

"And I love you." She kissed him, then sank back amid the pillows. "All that said, however, I can't pretend I'm not glad Frederick Van Hausen is dead."

"Agreed." He settled back beside her and closed his eyes. At once, an image of Van

Hausen putting a gun muzzle in his mouth came into Stuart's mind, and he took a moment to savor the sweet satisfaction of such a picture. But only one moment. Then he put the whole business aside. It was done, finished, settled right at last. It was time now to let it go.

"Stuart?" Edie touched him, her hand fanning over his bare chest, causing him to open his eyes. "What are you thinking?"

He turned and looked at his wife, in her white nightdress, surrounded by sheets and feather pillows, with her red-gold hair shining like fire in the morning light. "I'm thinking of what I'm glad about," he said. "I'm glad I went to the Hanford Ball. I'm glad you tore out after me and proposed. I'm not so glad you shredded my pride, but —"

"Oh, you needed it," she interrupted. "You were so damnably conceited."

He picked up her hand. "I'm glad you like it when I kiss your hand." He paused to press a kiss into her palm, feeling the way she quivered in response. "And I'm glad you made that silly bet with me about ten days and gave me the chance to win you."

"It's long past ten days now," she said, and shoved back the sheets that covered the lower half of his body. Pulling at her nightdress, she eased over him, straddling his legs with hers. "It's three hundred and thirty-some days now."

"Yes, and you're still trying to lead, I see." He leaned forward to kiss her, but she stopped him.

"Would you like to?" she asked, hand on his chest. "Lead, I mean?"

"That depends." He toyed with one of the pearl buttons on her nightdress. "Would you like it?"

"Yes, Stuart," she said. "I think I would."

He smiled, slipping pearl buttons free as he eased her off him and onto her back. With the buttons undone, he pulled the nightdress apart and slowly moved on top of her. "As long as you always remember the difference, my darling."

"I don't need to remember it, Stuart, because I know it." She smiled as she closed her eyes and turned her head so he could kiss her neck. "I know it in my soul."

The employees of Thorndike Press hope you have enjoyed this Large Print book. All our Thorndike, Wheeler, and Kennebec Large Print titles are designed for easy reading, and all our books are made to last. Other Thorndike Press Large Print books are available at your library, through selected bookstores, or directly from us.

For information about titles, please call:
(800) 223-1244

or visit our Web site at:
http://gale.cengage.com/thorndike

To share your comments, please write:
Publisher
Thorndike Press
10 Water St., Suite 310
Waterville, ME 04901